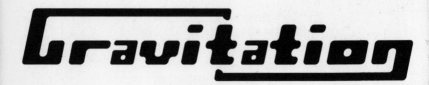

Gravitation

Volume 5

By
Maki Murakami

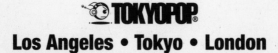

Los Angeles • Tokyo • London

Translator - Ray Yoshimoto
English Adaptation - Jamie S. Rich
Copy Editor - Aaron Sparrow
Retouch and Lettering - Jennifer Nunn-Iwai and Abelardo Bigting
Cover Layout - Raymond Makowski

Editor - Paul Morrissey
Digital Imaging Manager - Chris Buford
Pre-Press Manager - Antonio DePietro
Production Managers - Jennifer Miller, Mutsumi Miyazaki
Art Director - Matt Alford
Managing Editor - Jill Freshney
VP of Production - Ron Klamert
President & C.O.O. - John Parker
Publisher & C.E.O. - Stuart Levy

Email: info@TOKYOPOP.com
Come visit us online at www.TOKYOPOP.com

A 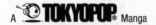 Manga

TOKYOPOP Inc.
5900 Wilshire Blvd. Suite 2000
Los Angeles, CA 90036

Gravitation Vol. 5

ISBN: 1-59182-337-4

First TOKYOPOP printing: April 2004

10 9 8 7 6

Printed in the USA

THE MEMBERS OF THE GRAVITATION BAND

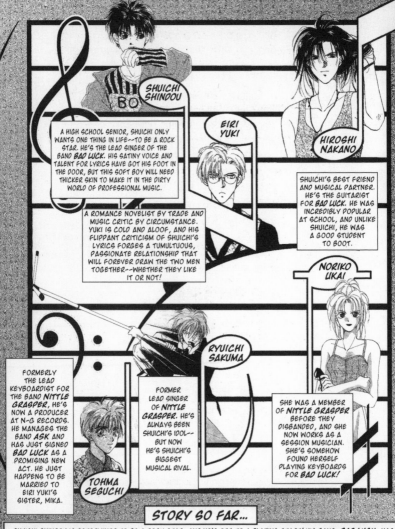

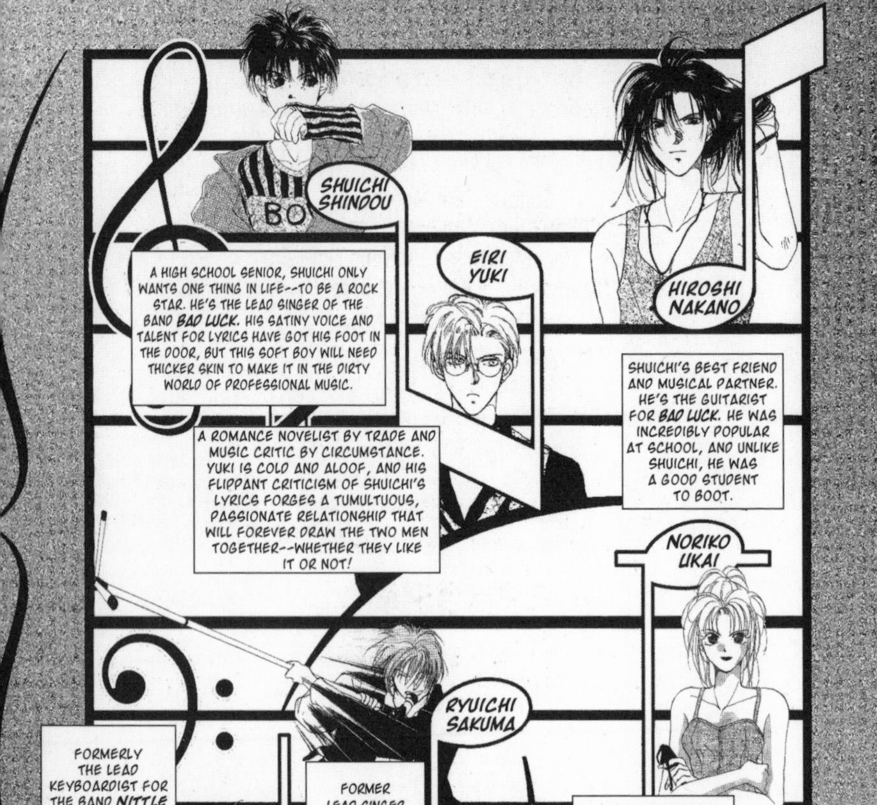
SHUICHI SHINDOU
A HIGH SCHOOL SENIOR, SHUICHI ONLY WANTS ONE THING IN LIFE--TO BE A ROCK STAR. HE'S THE LEAD SINGER OF THE BAND **BAD LUCK**. HIS SATINY VOICE AND TALENT FOR LYRICS HAVE GOT HIS FOOT IN THE DOOR, BUT THIS SOFT BOY WILL NEED THICKER SKIN TO MAKE IT IN THE DIRTY WORLD OF PROFESSIONAL MUSIC.
EIRI YUKI
A ROMANCE NOVELIST BY TRADE AND MUSIC CRITIC BY CIRCUMSTANCE. YUKI IS COLD AND ALOOF, AND HIS FLIPPANT CRITICISM OF SHUICHI'S LYRICS FORGES A TUMULTUOUS, PASSIONATE RELATIONSHIP THAT WILL FOREVER DRAW THE TWO MEN TOGETHER--WHETHER THEY LIKE IT OR NOT!
HIROSHI NAKANO
SHUICHI'S BEST FRIEND AND MUSICAL PARTNER. HE'S THE GUITARIST FOR **BAD LUCK**. HE WAS INCREDIBLY POPULAR AT SCHOOL, AND UNLIKE SHUICHI, HE WAS A GOOD STUDENT TO BOOT.
NORIKO UKAI
SHE WAS A MEMBER OF **NITTLE GRASPER** BEFORE THEY DISBANDED, AND SHE NOW WORKS AS A SESSION MUSICIAN. SHE'S SOMEHOW FOUND HERSELF PLAYING KEYBOARDS FOR **BAD LUCK!**
RYUICHI SAKUMA
FORMER LEAD SINGER OF **NITTLE GRASPER**. HE'S ALWAYS BEEN SHUICHI'S IDOL--BUT NOW HE'S SHUICHI'S BIGGEST MUSICAL RIVAL.
TOHMA SEGUCHI
FORMERLY THE LEAD KEYBOARDIST FOR THE BAND **NITTLE GRASPER**, HE'S NOW A PRODUCER AT N-G RECORDS. HE MANAGES THE BAND **ASK** AND HAS JUST SIGNED **BAD LUCK** AS A PROMISING NEW ACT. HE JUST HAPPENS TO BE MARRIED TO EIRI YUKI'S SISTER, MIKA.

STORY SO FAR...

SHUICHI SHINDOU IS DETERMINED TO BE A ROCK STAR...AND HE'S OFF TO A BLAZING START! HIS BAND, **BAD LUCK**, HAS JUST BEEN SIGNED TO THE N-G RECORD LABEL, AND THEIR FIRST SINGLE IS BURNING UP THE CHARTS! THEY EVEN DID A GIG ON A TV GAME SHOW! ALL THE WHILE, SHUICHI IS DESPERATE TO KEEP HIS ROLLER-COASTER RELATIONSHIP WITH THE MYSTERIOUS WRITER EIRI YUKI RED-HOT. BUT LOVE IS NEVER EASY. AYAKA USAMI WANTS TO COOL SHUICHI'S JETS, ESPECIALLY SINCE SHE'S EIRI YUKI'S FIANCÉE! AND TAKI AIZAWA, THE LEADER OF THE RIVAL BAND **ASK**, WANTS TO EXPOSE SHUICHI'S HOMOEROTIC AFFAIR IN THE HOPES OF STOPPING BAD LUCK'S CAREER COLD. TAKI ENTRAPS SHUICHI AND TAKES PICTURES OF HIM BEING RAPED BY SEVERAL GUYS, HOPING TO TRULY DESTROY HIM. EIRI RESPONDS BY BEATING TAKI'S BAND MEMBERS TO A PULP, AND RETRIEVING THE INCRIMINATING PHOTOS. LATER, EIRI REVEALS A SHOCKING TRUTH TO SHUICHI--HE ONCE KILLED SOMEONE WHILE LIVING OVERSEAS. ARE SHUICHI AND YUKI DESTINED TO DRIFT APART, OR WILL THEY REMAIN INEXORABLY INTERTWINED, HELD TOGETHER BY A FORCE AS STRONG AS GRAVITY?

CONTENTS

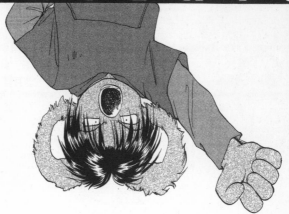

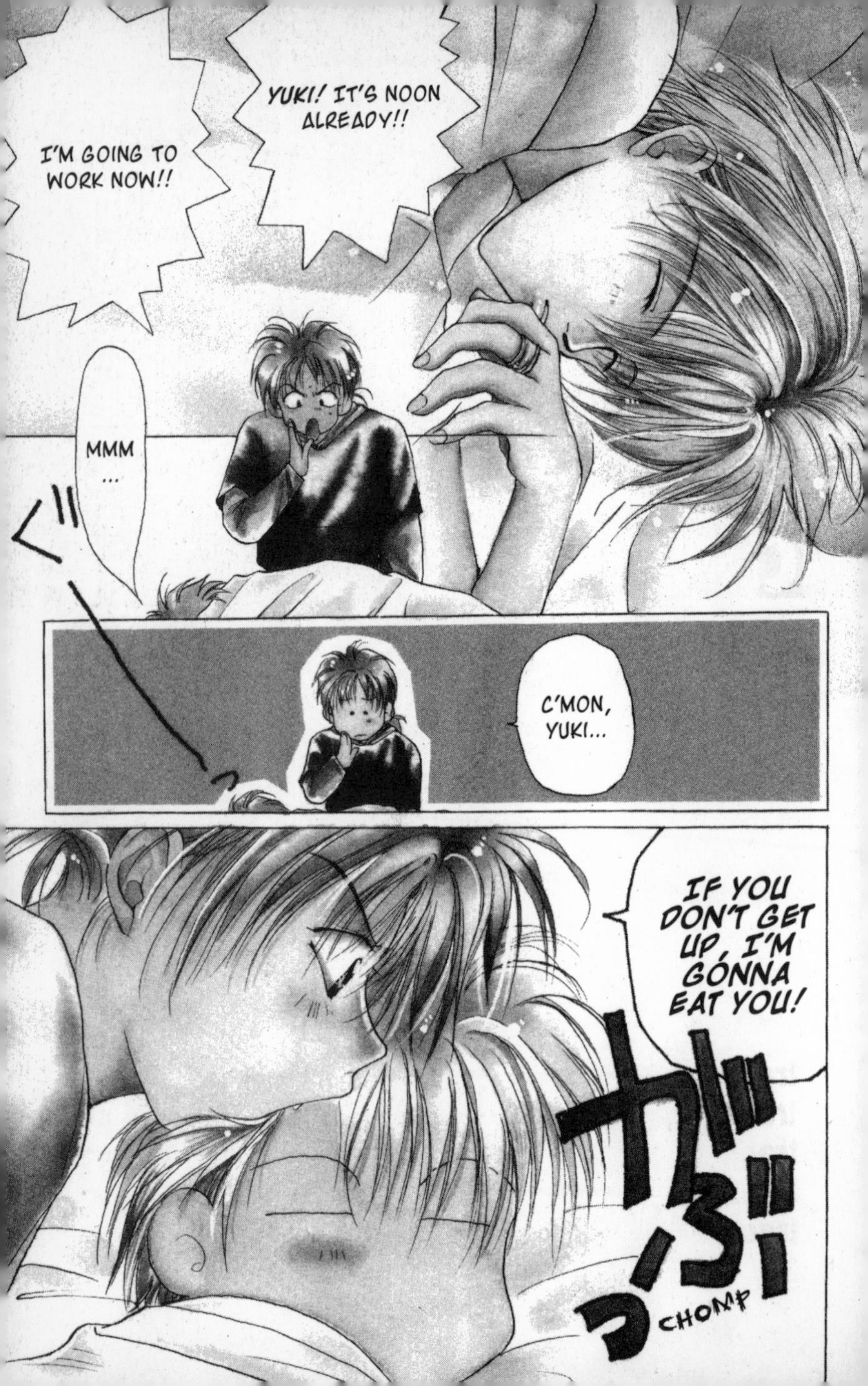
YUKI! IT'S NOON ALREADY!!
I'M GOING TO WORK NOW!!
MMM ...
C'MON, YUKI...
IF YOU DON'T GET UP, I'M GONNA EAT YOU!
CHOMP

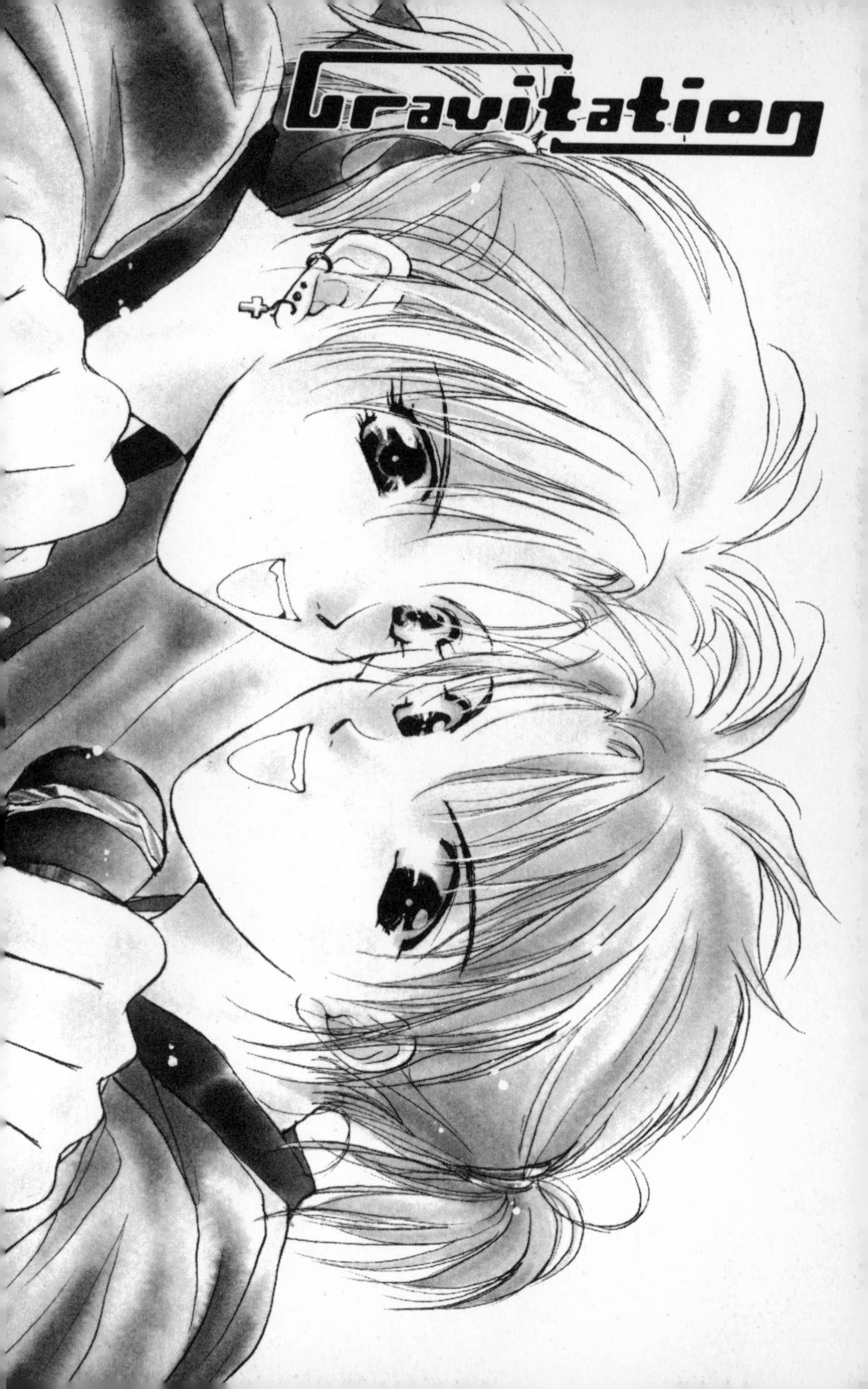
Gravitation

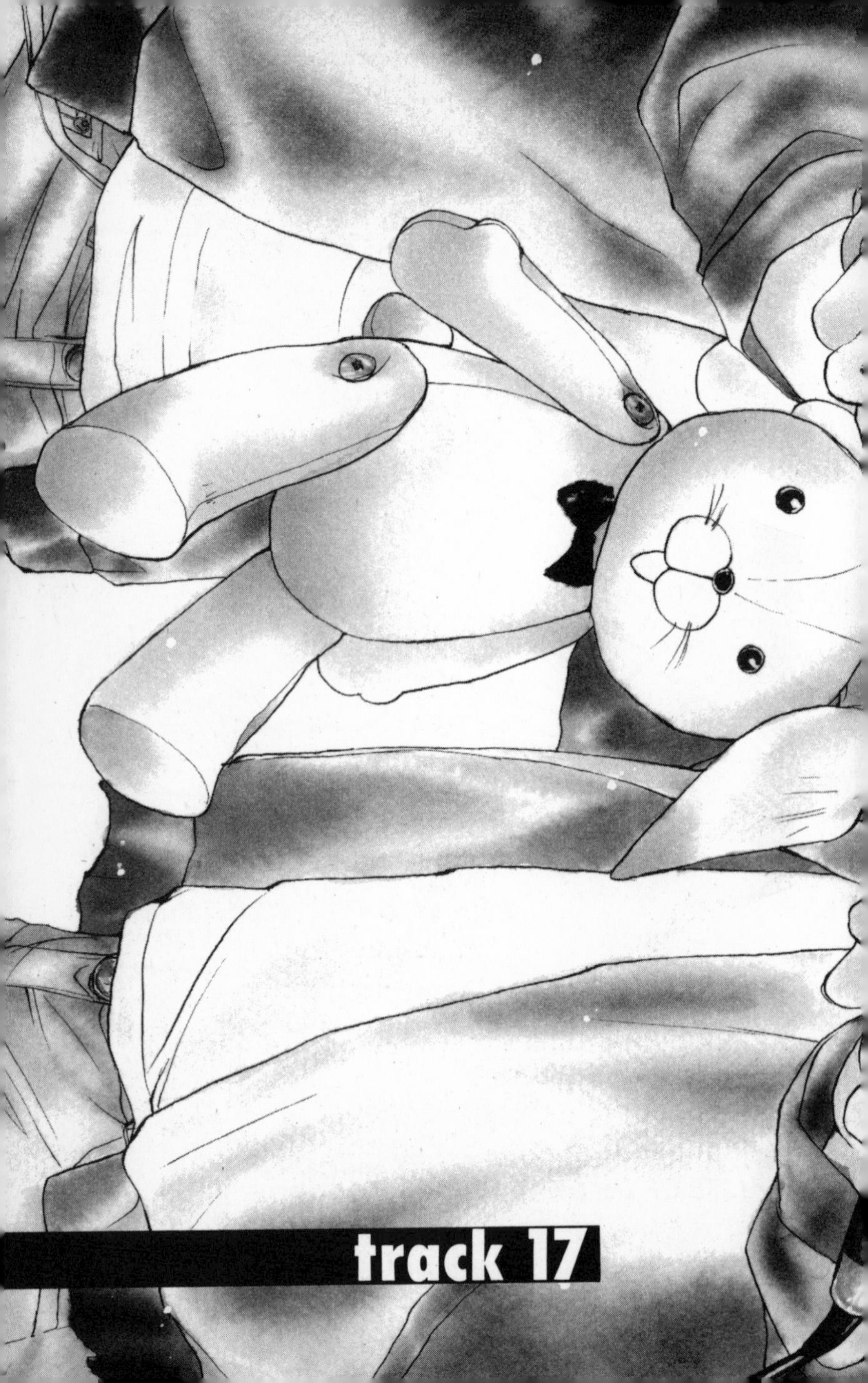
track 17

YAYYYYY!

WE MADE IT TO
BOOK 5!

HOW AMAZING AND
COOL!

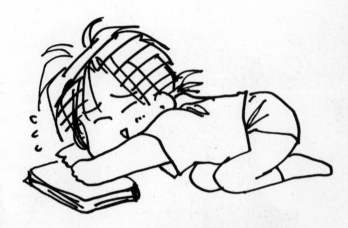

WHILE I WAS WORKING ON
BOOK 1, I COULDN'T SEE TAKING
THIS STORY PAST BOOK 3.
I THOUGHT THAT WOULD SURELY
FINISH IT, AND IF I'D KEPT MY
MOUTH SHUT, YOU PROBABLY
WOULD HAVE NEVER EVEN
KNOWN THAT!

IT'S A TRIP TO SEE THE STORY TAKE ON A
LIFE OF ITS OWN AND GO THIS FAR!

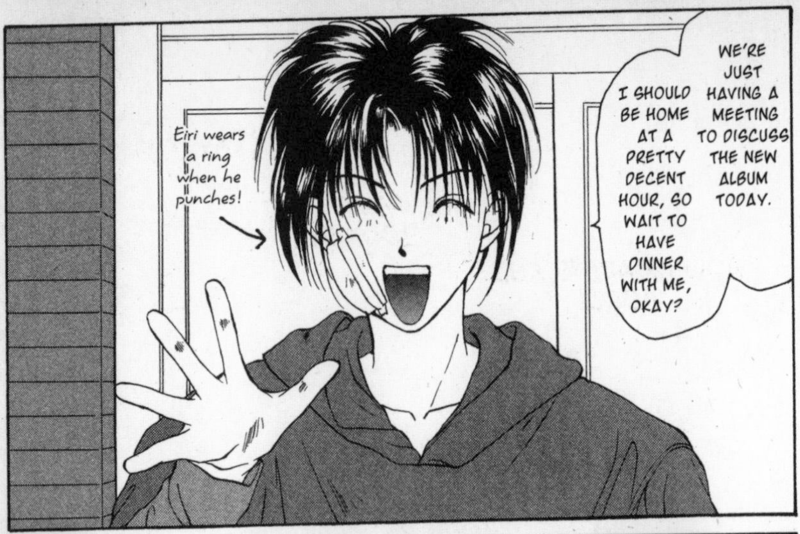
WE'RE JUST HAVING A MEETING TO DISCUSS THE NEW ALBUM TODAY.
I SHOULD BE HOME AT A PRETTY DECENT HOUR, SO WAIT TO HAVE DINNER WITH ME, OKAY?
Eiri wears a ring when he punches!

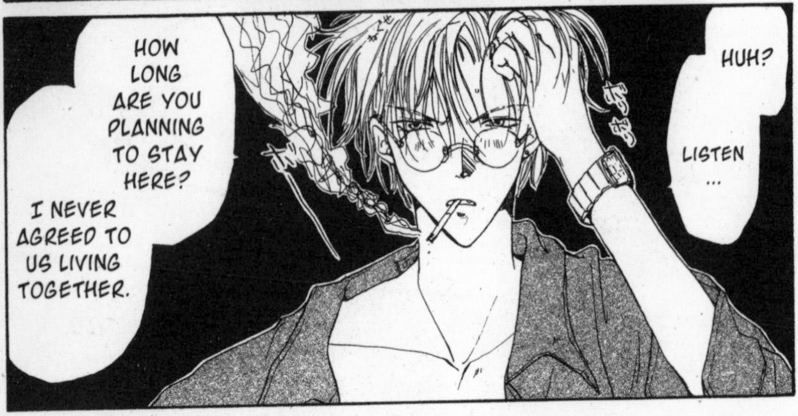
HUH?
LISTEN ...
HOW LONG ARE YOU PLANNING TO STAY HERE?
I NEVER AGREED TO US LIVING TOGETHER.

ABOUT GRAVITATION TRACK 17

I'll bet you're thinking, why are all the panels so big this time? Only three panels a page? C'mon, quit being so stingy! Are they too big? Am I being lazy? Is it easier to read? Just tell me what you think. Anything else? Like: "Shindou's hairstyle is impossible, I can't get into his character" or "I can see that you're too lazy to use reference photos for backgrounds, and so I can't get into the story." Or "You're mixing too much silly stuff with the serious stuff." Well, if you keep looking for things to complain about, you'll never stop. Aaaaaghhhhh! I would like for you readers to point those things out, but it sucks when you hear stuff like that all the time. Then again, I guess that's just the kind of person I am!

Maki Murakami.

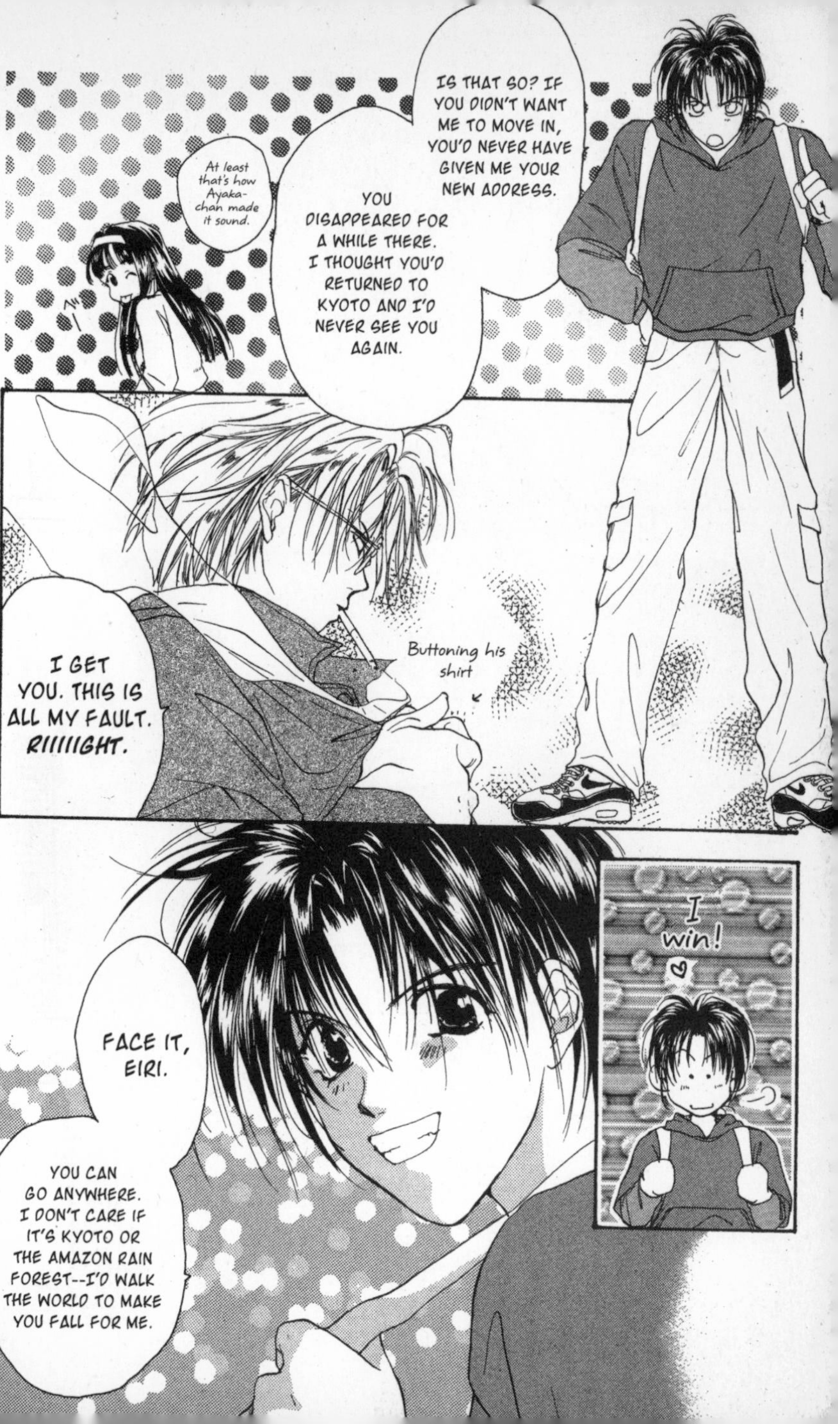
IS THAT SO? IF YOU DIDN'T WANT ME TO MOVE IN, YOU'D NEVER HAVE GIVEN ME YOUR NEW ADDRESS.
YOU DISAPPEARED FOR A WHILE THERE. I THOUGHT YOU'D RETURNED TO KYOTO AND I'D NEVER SEE YOU AGAIN.
At least that's how Ayaka-chan made it sound.
Buttoning his shirt
I GET YOU. THIS IS ALL MY FAULT. RIIIIIGHT.
I win!
FACE IT, EIRI.
YOU CAN GO ANYWHERE. I DON'T CARE IF IT'S KYOTO OR THE AMAZON RAIN FOREST--I'D WALK THE WORLD TO MAKE YOU FALL FOR ME.

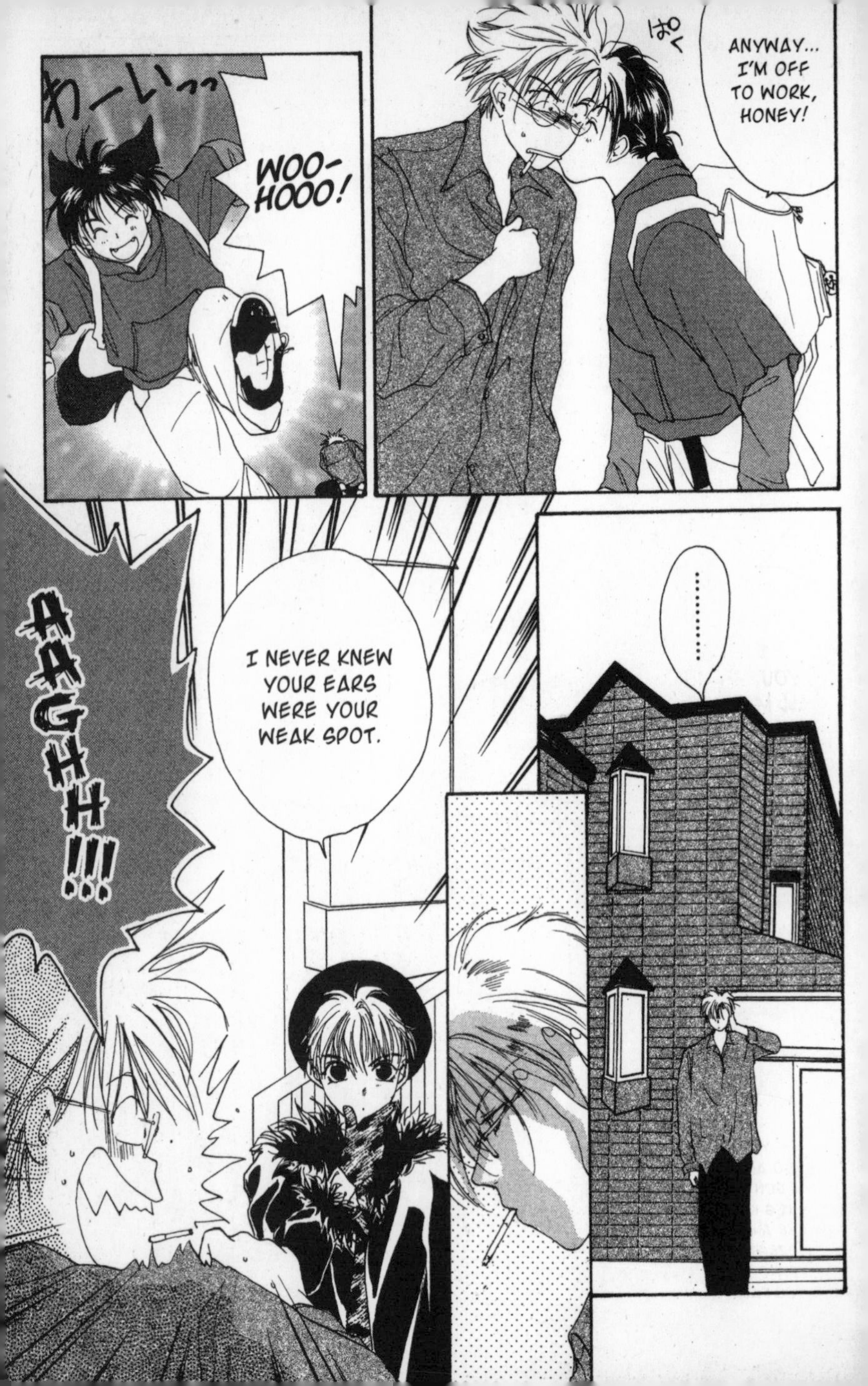
ぱく
ANYWAY... I'M OFF TO WORK, HONEY!
わーいっっ
WOO-HOOO!
......
I NEVER KNEW YOUR EARS WERE YOUR WEAK SPOT.
AAGHH!!!

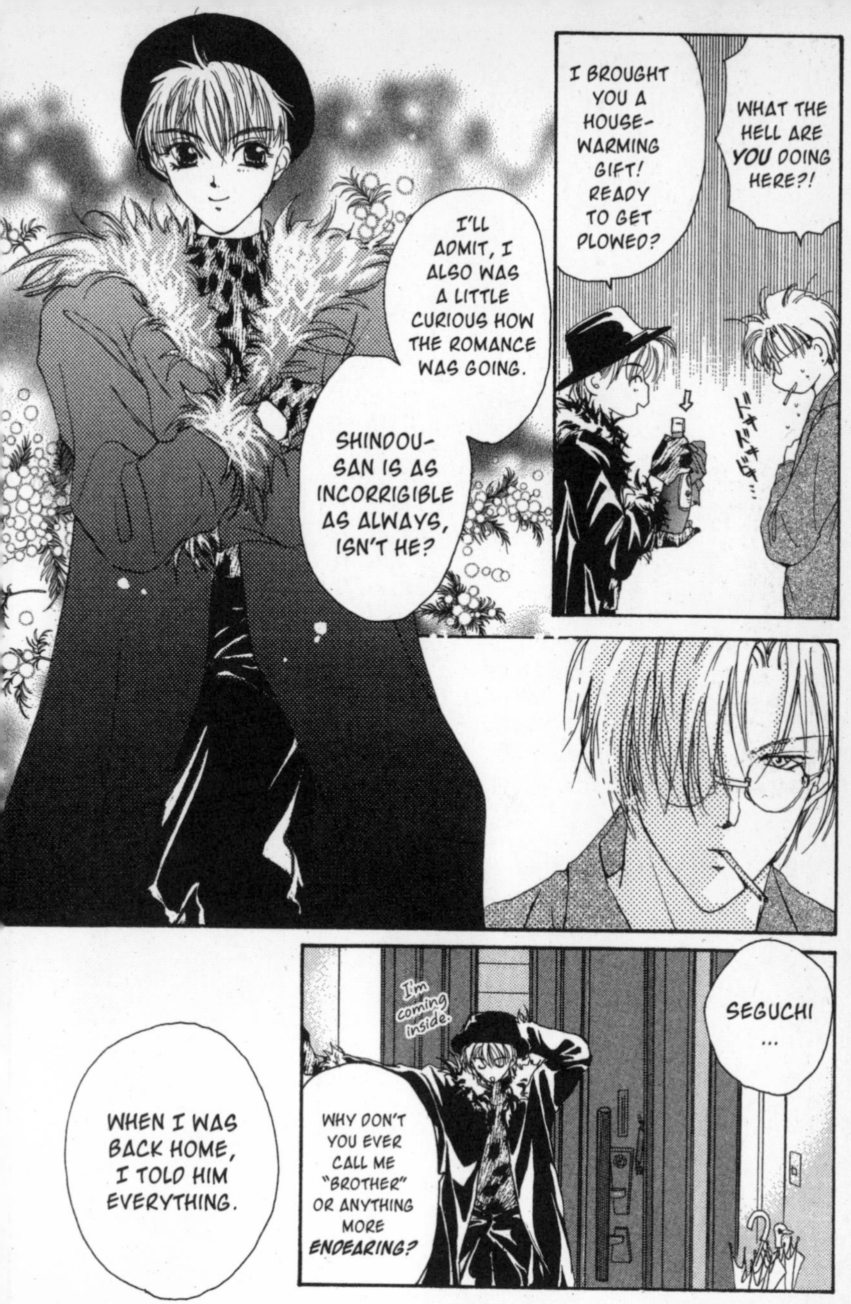
WHAT THE HELL ARE YOU DOING HERE?!
I BROUGHT YOU A HOUSE-WARMING GIFT! READY TO GET PLOWED?
ドキドキ…
I'LL ADMIT, I ALSO WAS A LITTLE CURIOUS HOW THE ROMANCE WAS GOING.
SHINDOU-SAN IS AS INCORRIGIBLE AS ALWAYS, ISN'T HE?
SEGUCHI ...
I'm coming inside.
WHY DON'T YOU EVER CALL ME "BROTHER" OR ANYTHING MORE ENDEARING?
WHEN I WAS BACK HOME, I TOLD HIM EVERYTHING.

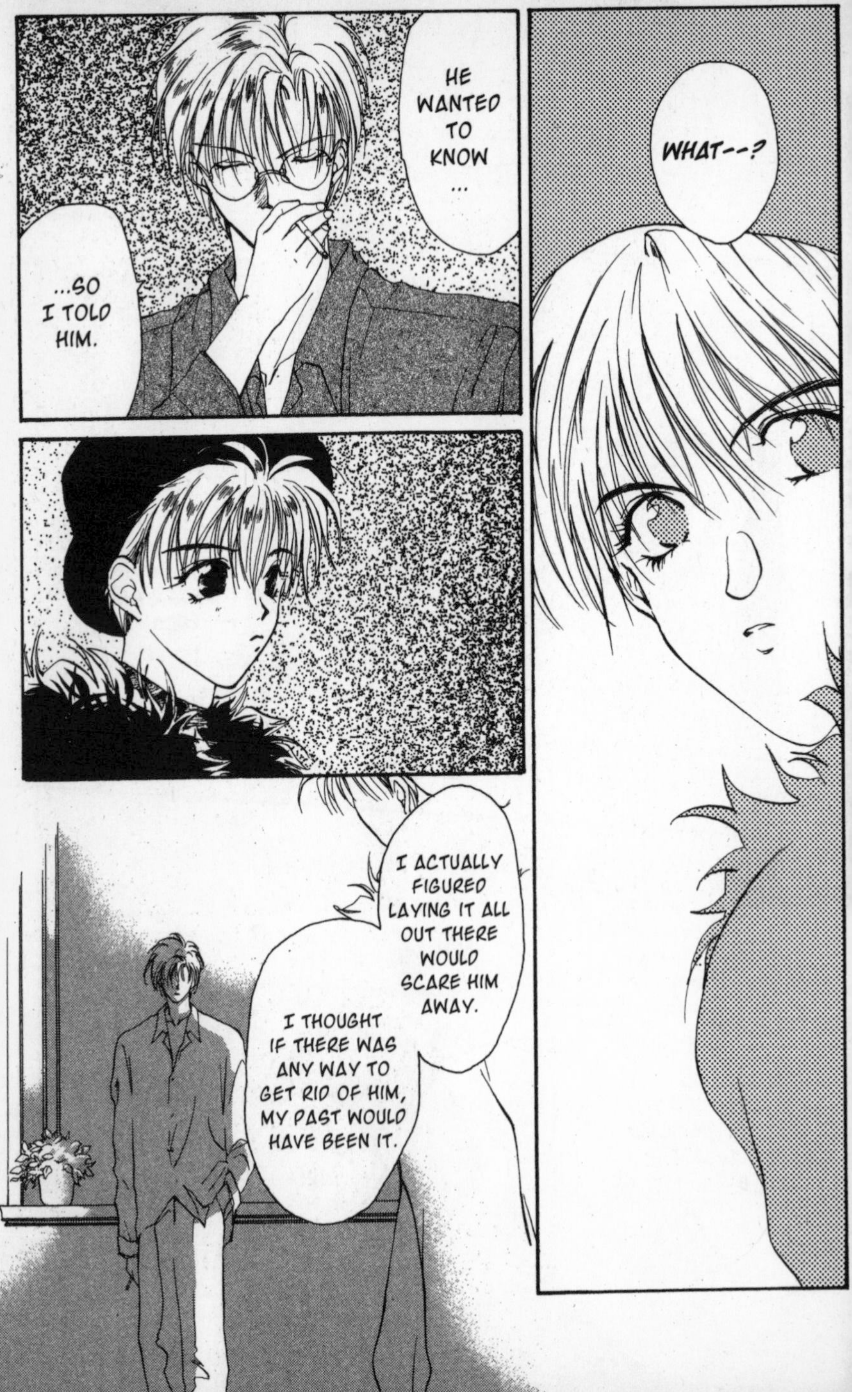
WHAT--?
HE WANTED TO KNOW ...
...SO I TOLD HIM.
I ACTUALLY FIGURED LAYING IT ALL OUT THERE WOULD SCARE HIM AWAY.
I THOUGHT IF THERE WAS ANY WAY TO GET RID OF HIM, MY PAST WOULD HAVE BEEN IT.

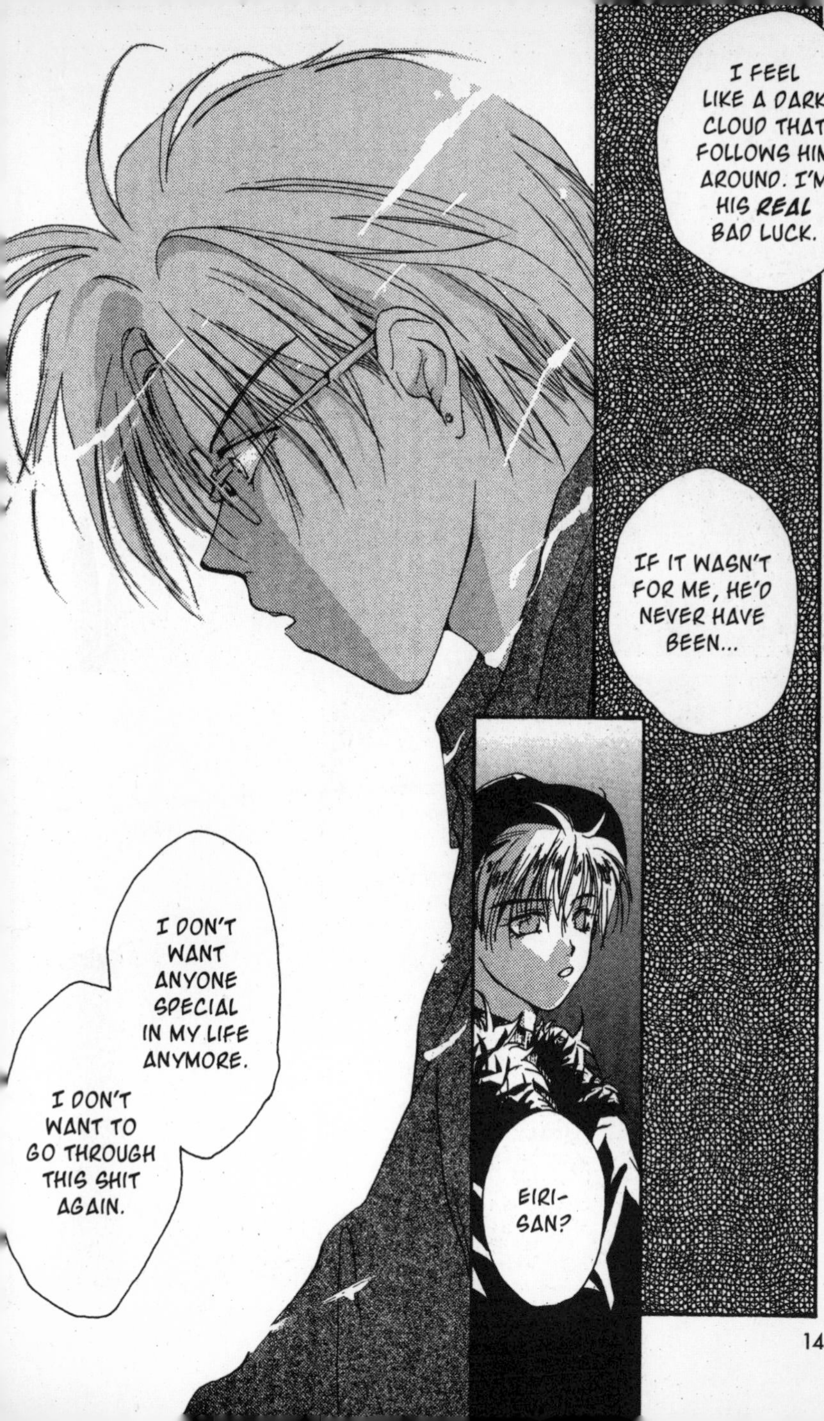
I FEEL LIKE A DARK CLOUD THAT FOLLOWS HIM AROUND. I'M HIS REAL BAD LUCK.
IF IT WASN'T FOR ME, HE'D NEVER HAVE BEEN...
EIRI-SAN?
I DON'T WANT ANYONE SPECIAL IN MY LIFE ANYMORE.
I DON'T WANT TO GO THROUGH THIS SHIT AGAIN.

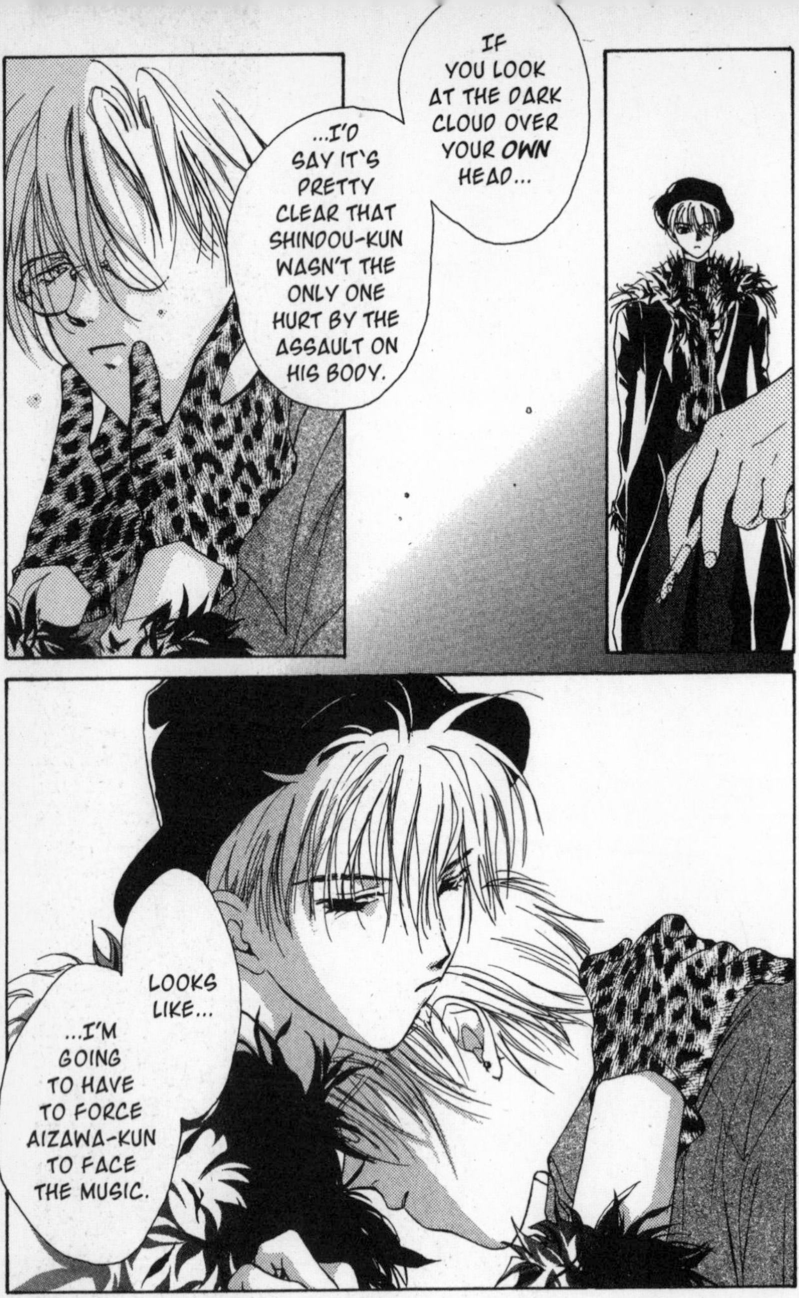
IF YOU LOOK AT THE DARK CLOUD OVER YOUR **OWN** HEAD...
...I'D SAY IT'S PRETTY CLEAR THAT SHINDOU-KUN WASN'T THE ONLY ONE HURT BY THE ASSAULT ON HIS BODY.
LOOKS LIKE...
...I'M GOING TO HAVE TO FORCE AIZAWA-KUN TO FACE THE MUSIC.

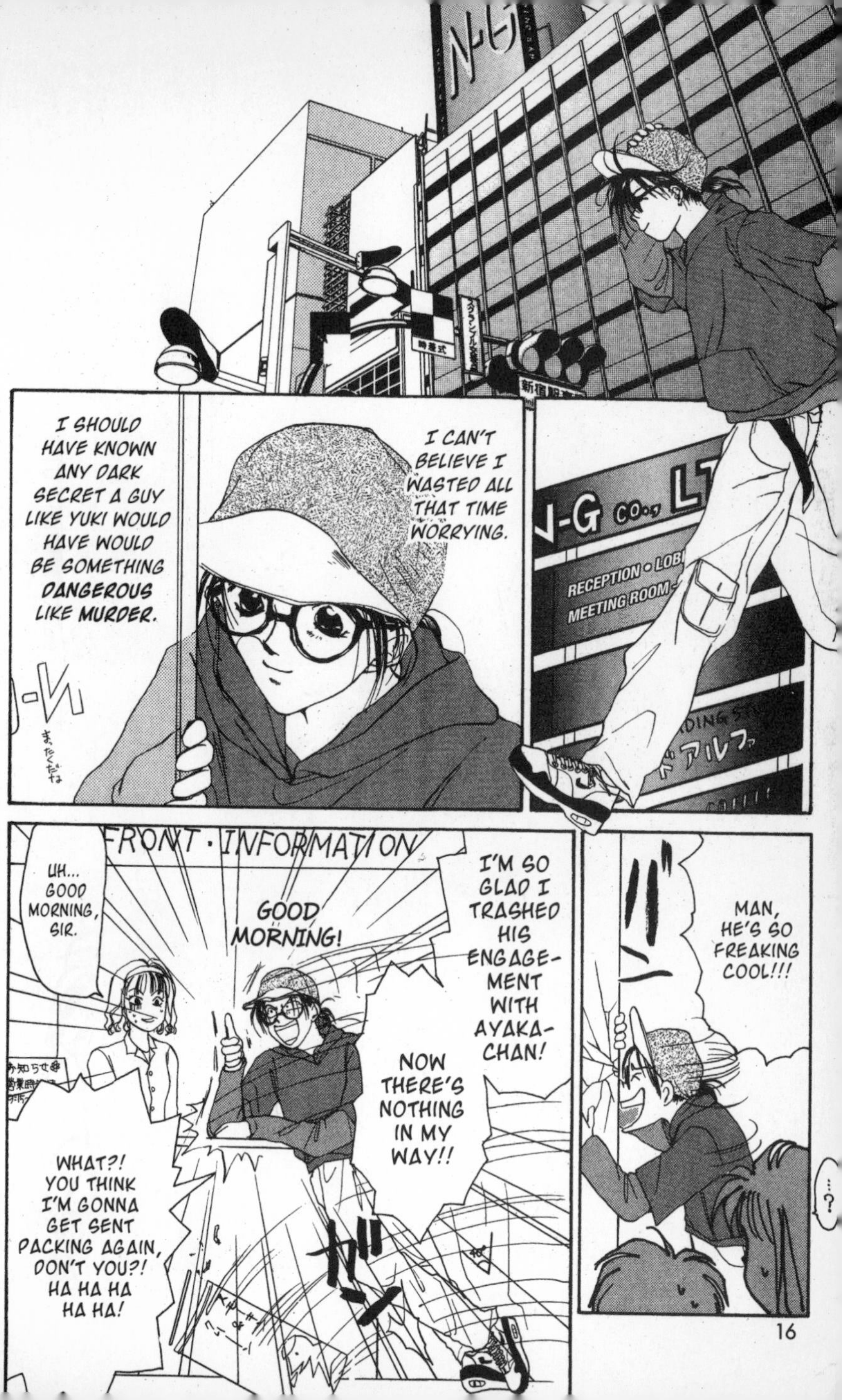
J-G CO., LT
RECEPTION • LOB
MEETING ROOM
I CAN'T BELIEVE I WASTED ALL THAT TIME WORRYING.
I SHOULD HAVE KNOWN ANY DARK SECRET A GUY LIKE YUKI WOULD HAVE WOULD BE SOMETHING DANGEROUS LIKE MURDER.
MAN, HE'S SO FREAKING COOL!!!
...?
FRONT · INFORMATION
GOOD MORNING!
UH... GOOD MORNING, SIR.
I'M SO GLAD I TRASHED HIS ENGAGEMENT WITH AYAKA-CHAN!
NOW THERE'S NOTHING IN MY WAY!!
WHAT?! YOU THINK I'M GONNA GET SENT PACKING AGAIN, DON'T YOU?! HA HA HA HA HA!

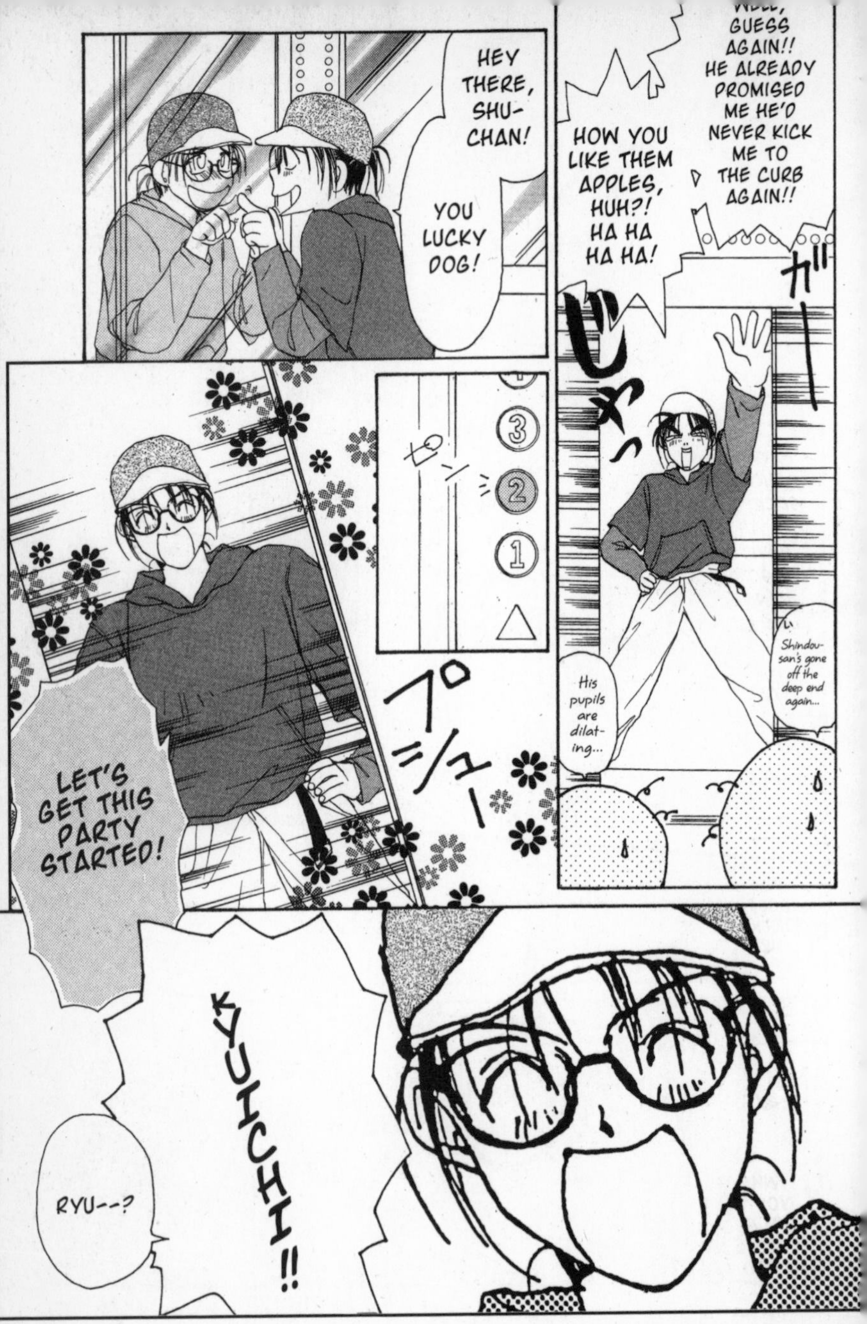

WELL, GUESS AGAIN!! HE ALREADY PROMISED ME HE'D NEVER KICK ME TO THE CURB AGAIN!!
HOW YOU LIKE THEM APPLES, HUH?! HA HA HA HA!
ガー
じゃっ
Shindou-san's gone off the deep end again...
His pupils are dilating...
HEY THERE, SHU-CHAN!
YOU LUCKY DOG!
ピン
プシュー
LET'S GET THIS PARTY STARTED!
RYUICHI!!
RYU--?

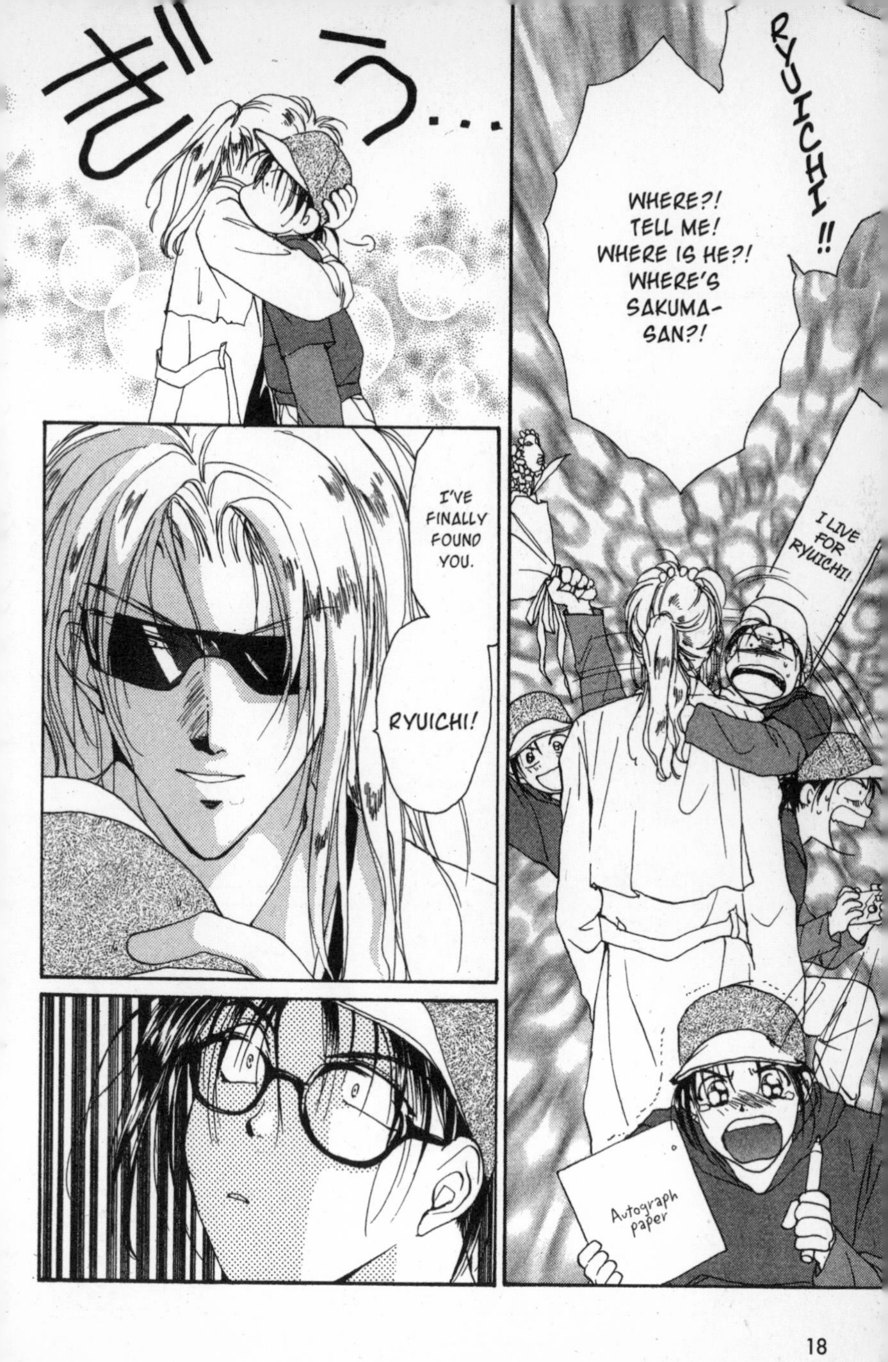
RYUICHI!!
WHERE?! TELL ME! WHERE IS HE?! WHERE'S SAKUMA-SAN?!
I LIVE FOR RYUICHI!
Autograph paper
ぎう...
I'VE FINALLY FOUND YOU.
RYUICHI!

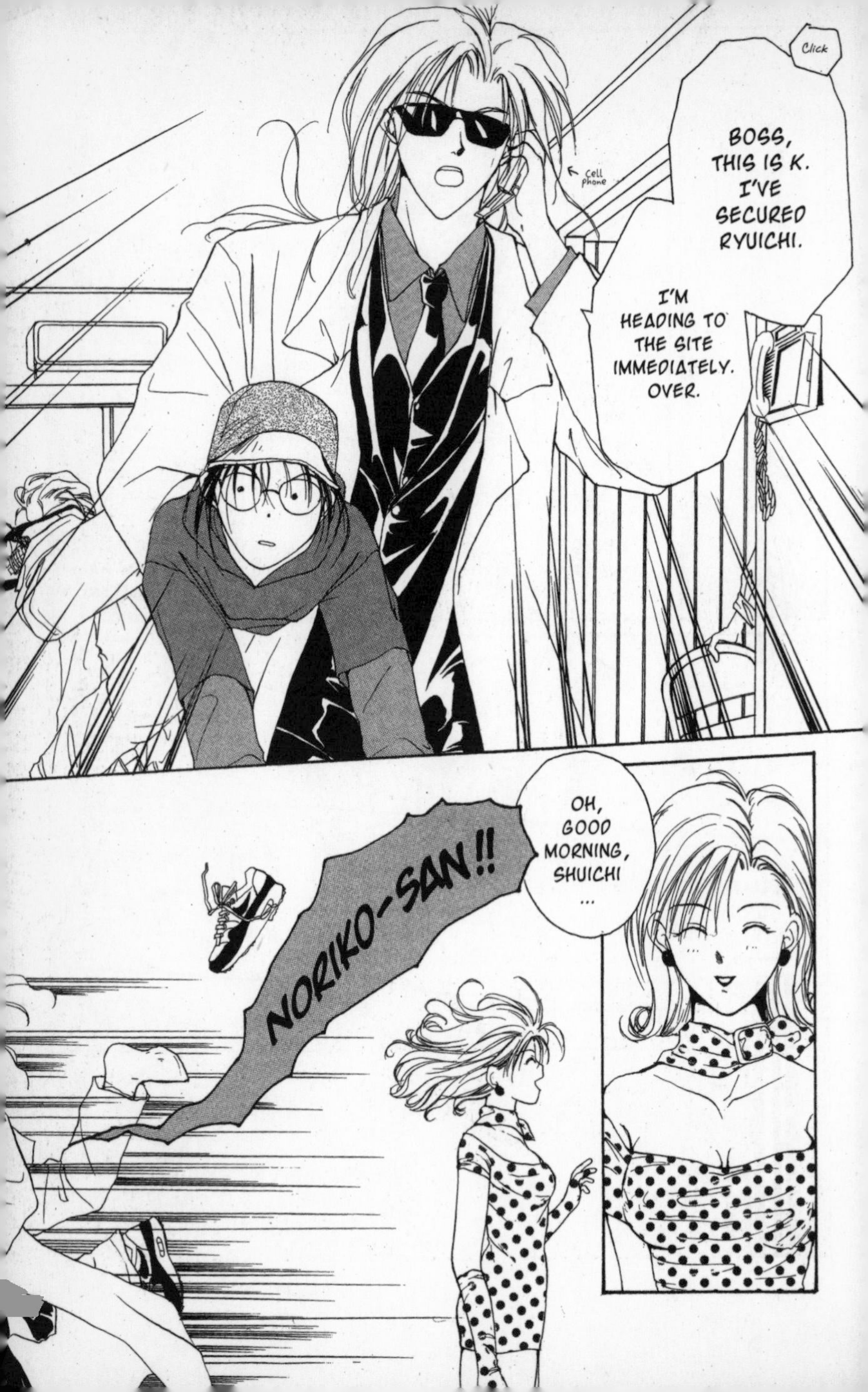
Click
BOSS, THIS IS K. I'VE SECURED RYUICHI.
I'M HEADING TO THE SITE IMMEDIATELY. OVER.
Cell phone
OH, GOOD MORNING, SHUICHI ...
NORIKO-SAN!!

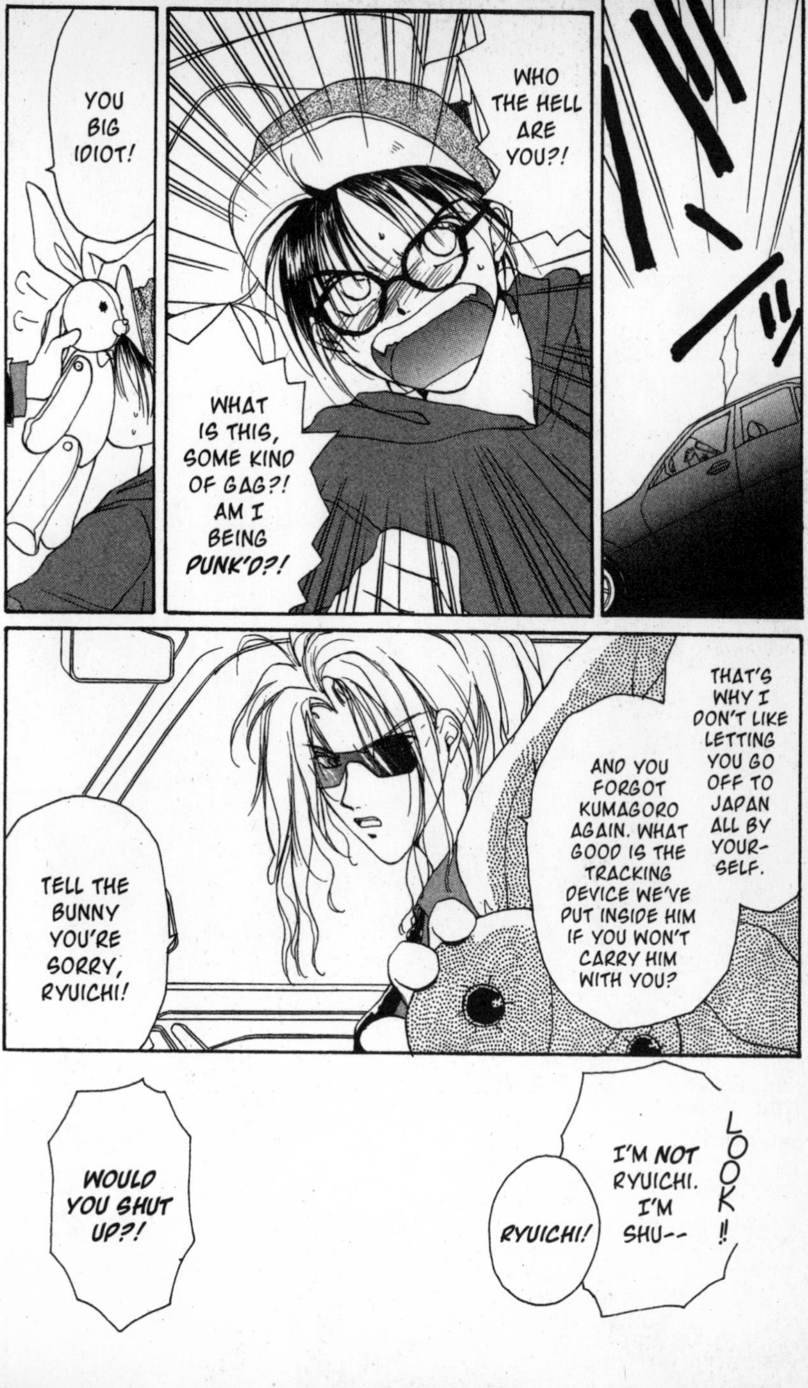
WHO THE HELL ARE YOU?!
WHAT IS THIS, SOME KIND OF GAG?! AM I BEING *PUNK'D*?!
YOU BIG IDIOT!
THAT'S WHY I DON'T LIKE LETTING YOU GO OFF TO JAPAN ALL BY YOURSELF.
AND YOU FORGOT KUMAGORO AGAIN. WHAT GOOD IS THE TRACKING DEVICE WE'VE PUT INSIDE HIM IF YOU WON'T CARRY HIM WITH YOU?
TELL THE BUNNY YOU'RE SORRY, RYUICHI!
LOOK!!
I'M *NOT* RYUICHI. I'M SHU--
RYUICHI!
WOULD YOU SHUT UP?!

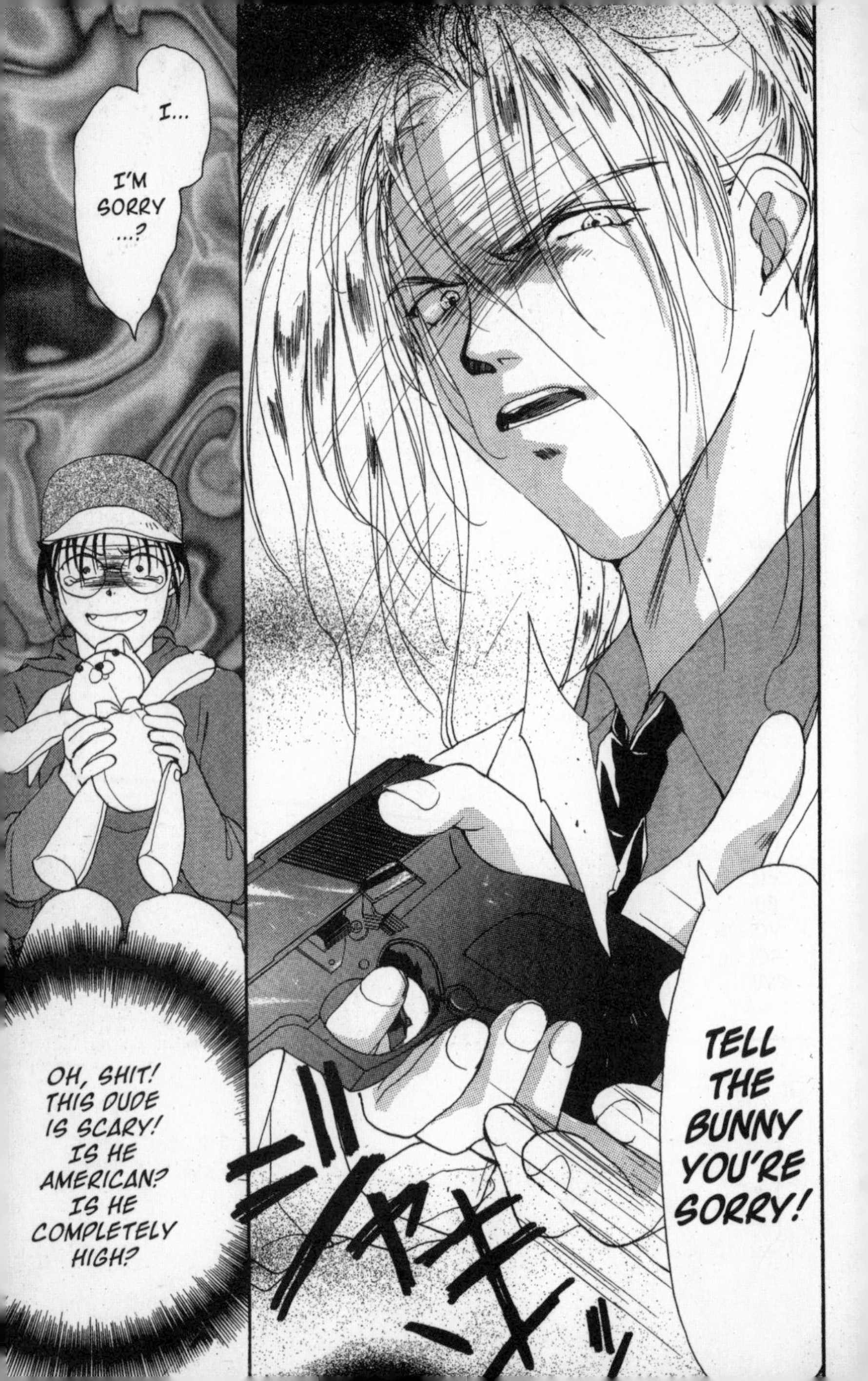
TELL THE BUNNY YOU'RE SORRY!
ジャキッ
I... I'M SORRY ...?
OH, SHIT! THIS DUDE IS SCARY! IS HE AMERICAN? IS HE COMPLETELY HIGH?

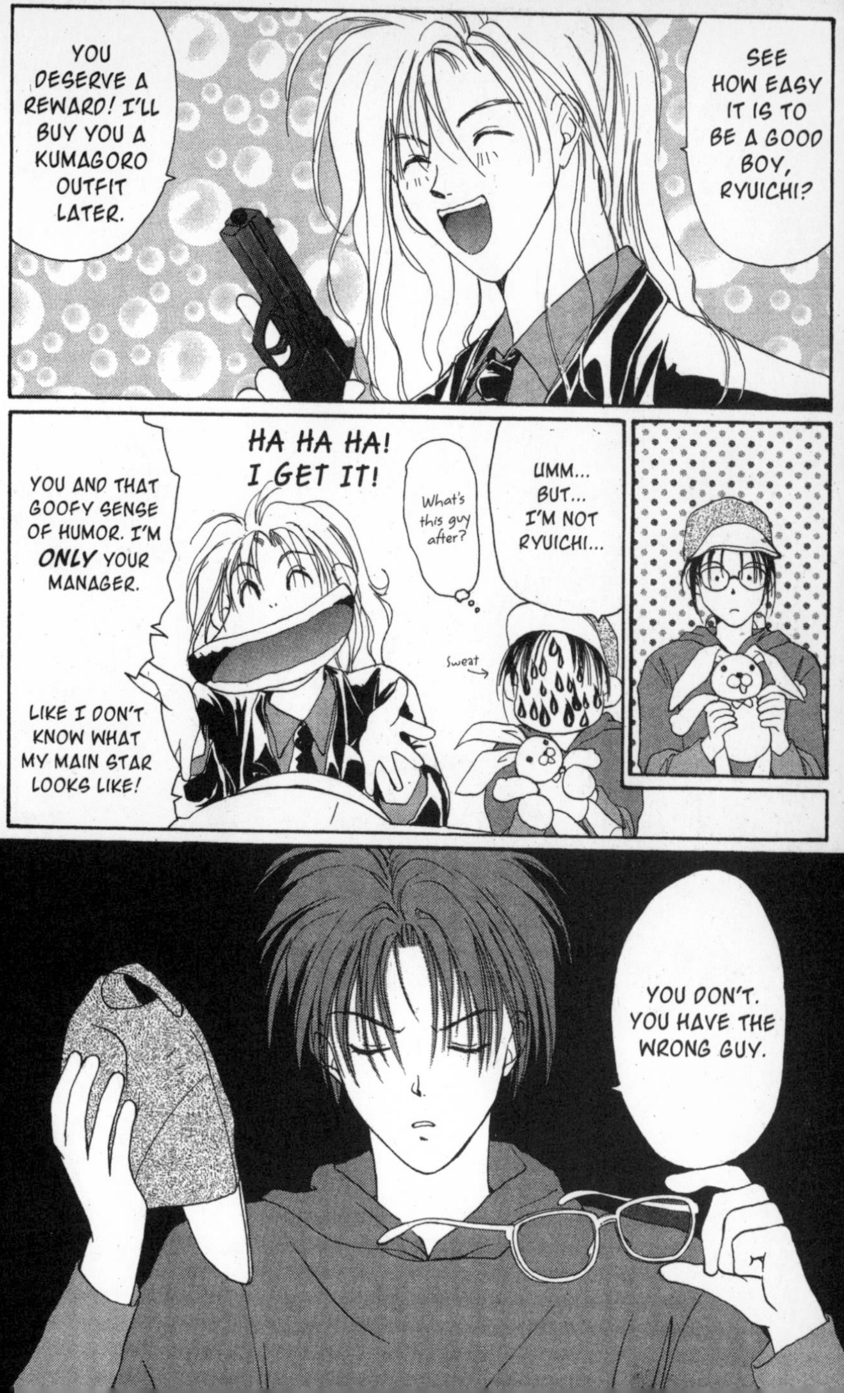
SEE HOW EASY IT IS TO BE A GOOD BOY, RYUICHI?
YOU DESERVE A REWARD! I'LL BUY YOU A KUMAGORO OUTFIT LATER.
UMM... BUT... I'M NOT RYUICHI...
What's this guy after?
HA HA HA! I GET IT!
YOU AND THAT GOOFY SENSE OF HUMOR. I'M ONLY YOUR MANAGER.
Sweat
LIKE I DON'T KNOW WHAT MY MAIN STAR LOOKS LIKE!
YOU DON'T. YOU HAVE THE WRONG GUY.

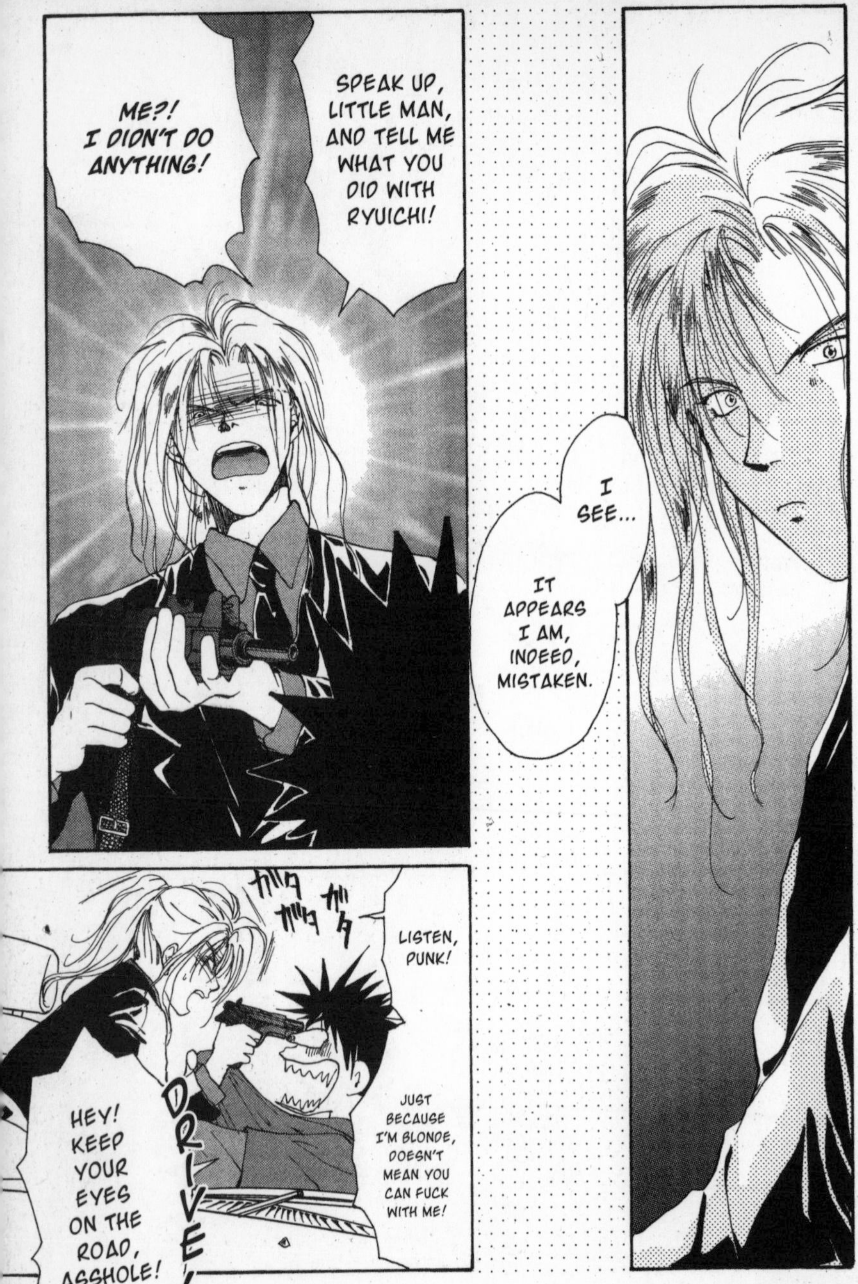
I SEE...
IT APPEARS I AM, INDEED, MISTAKEN.
SPEAK UP, LITTLE MAN, AND TELL ME WHAT YOU DID WITH RYUICHI!
ME?! I DIDN'T DO ANYTHING!
ガタ ガタ ガタ
LISTEN, PUNK!
JUST BECAUSE I'M BLONDE, DOESN'T MEAN YOU CAN FUCK WITH ME!
DRIVE!
HEY! KEEP YOUR EYES ON THE ROAD, ASSHOLE!

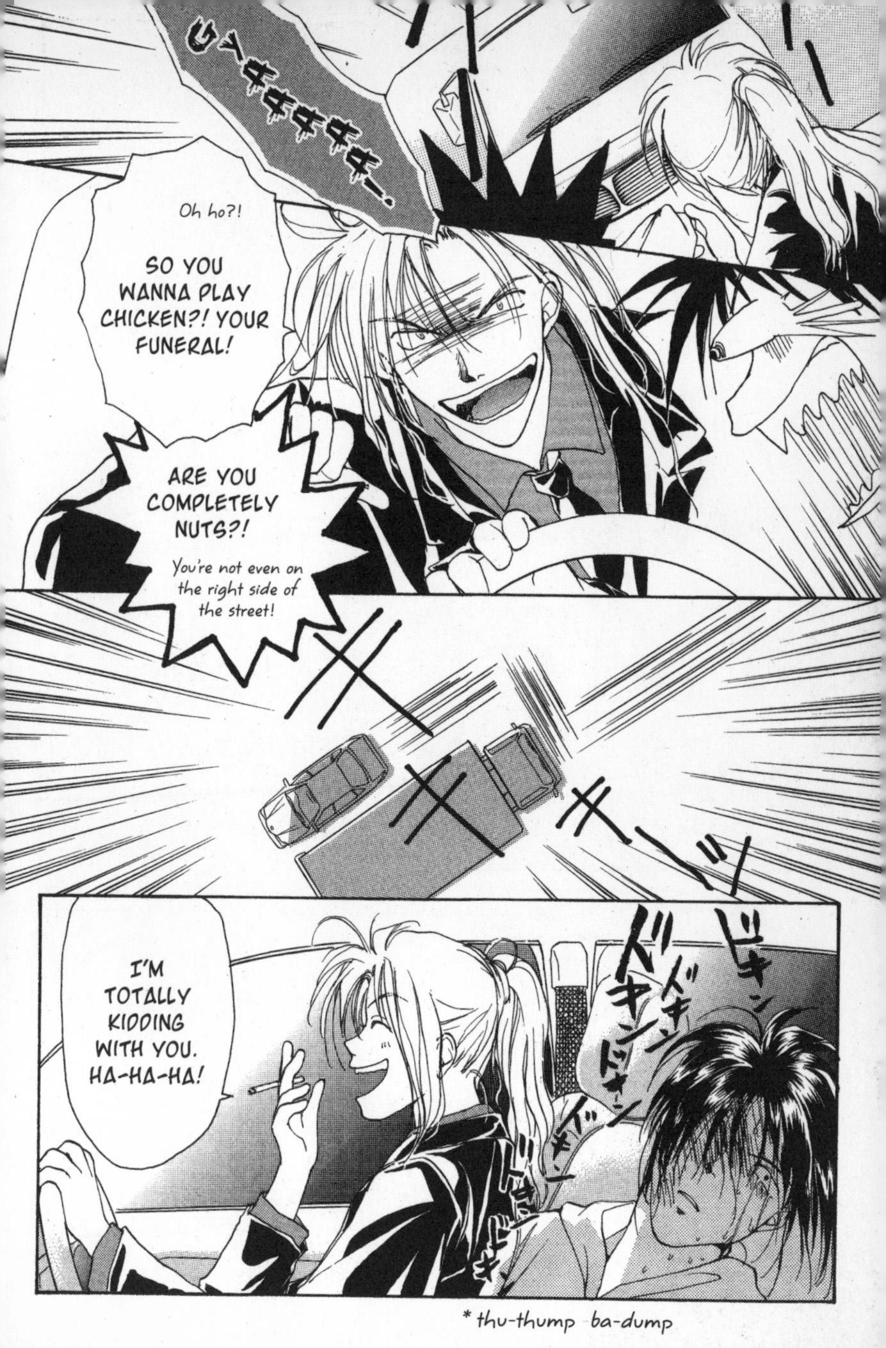
Oh ho?!
SO YOU WANNA PLAY CHICKEN?! YOUR FUNERAL!
ARE YOU COMPLETELY NUTS?!
You're not even on the right side of the street!
I'M TOTALLY KIDDING WITH YOU. HA-HA-HA!

* thu-thump ba-dump

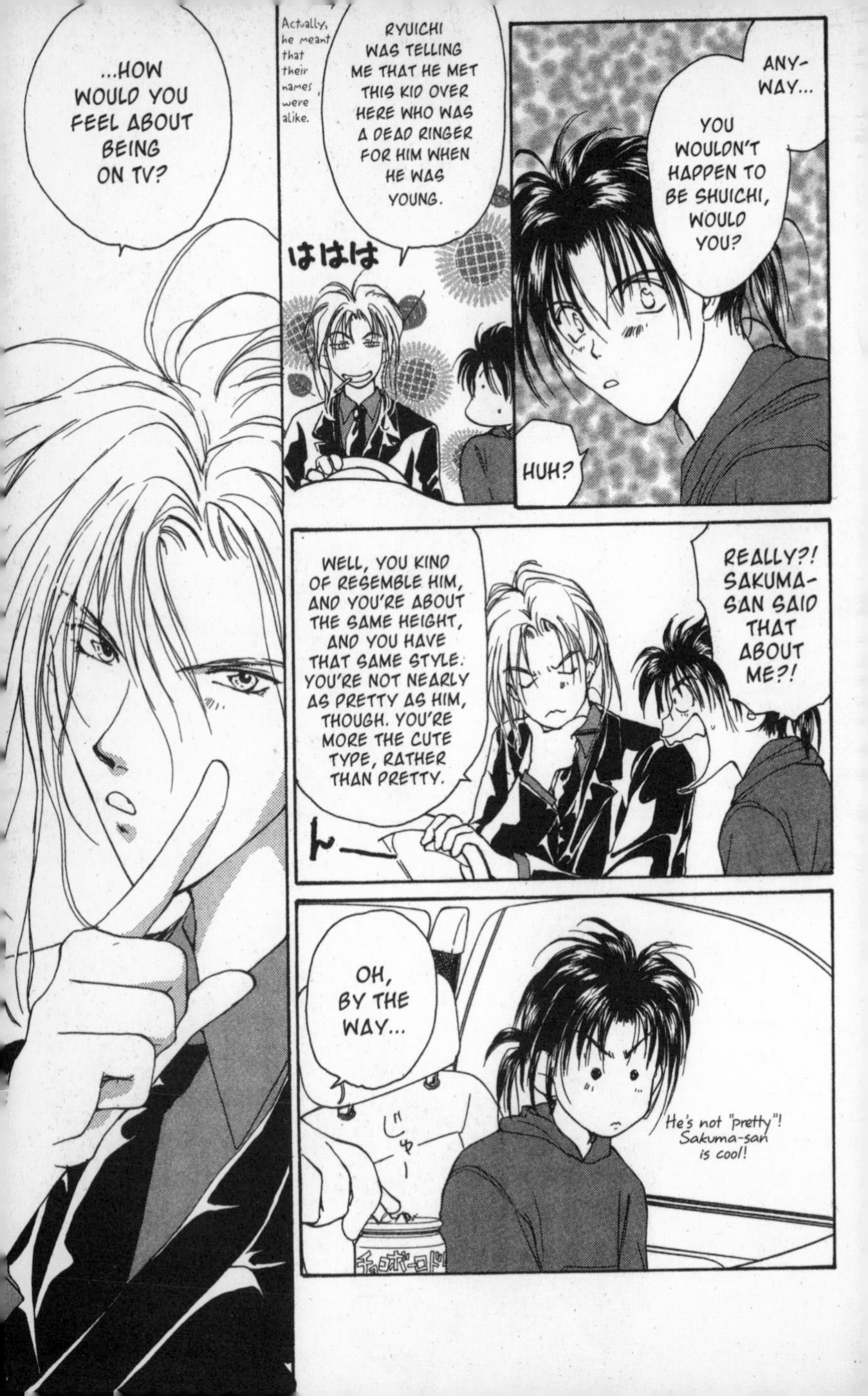
ANY-WAY...
YOU WOULDN'T HAPPEN TO BE SHUICHI, WOULD YOU?
HUH?
RYUICHI WAS TELLING ME THAT HE MET THIS KID OVER HERE WHO WAS A DEAD RINGER FOR HIM WHEN HE WAS YOUNG.
Actually, he meant that their names were alike.
ははは
REALLY?! SAKUMA-SAN SAID THAT ABOUT ME?!
WELL, YOU KIND OF RESEMBLE HIM, AND YOU'RE ABOUT THE SAME HEIGHT, AND YOU HAVE THAT SAME STYLE. YOU'RE NOT NEARLY AS PRETTY AS HIM, THOUGH. YOU'RE MORE THE CUTE TYPE, RATHER THAN PRETTY.
He's not "pretty"! Sakuma-san is cool!
OH, BY THE WAY...
...HOW WOULD YOU FEEL ABOUT BEING ON TV?

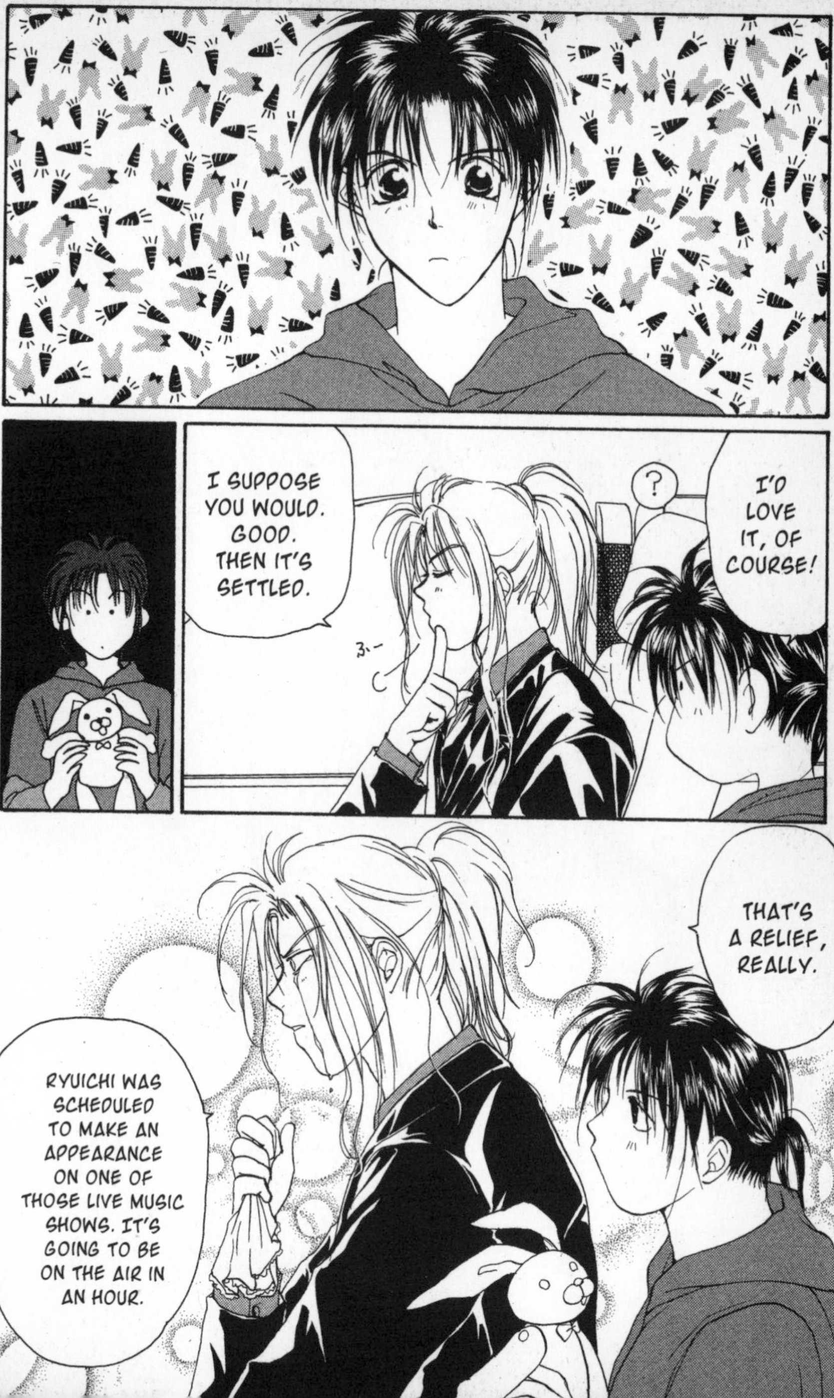
I'D LOVE IT, OF COURSE!
?
I SUPPOSE YOU WOULD. GOOD. THEN IT'S SETTLED.
ふー
THAT'S A RELIEF, REALLY.
RYUICHI WAS SCHEDULED TO MAKE AN APPEARANCE ON ONE OF THOSE LIVE MUSIC SHOWS. IT'S GOING TO BE ON THE AIR IN AN HOUR.

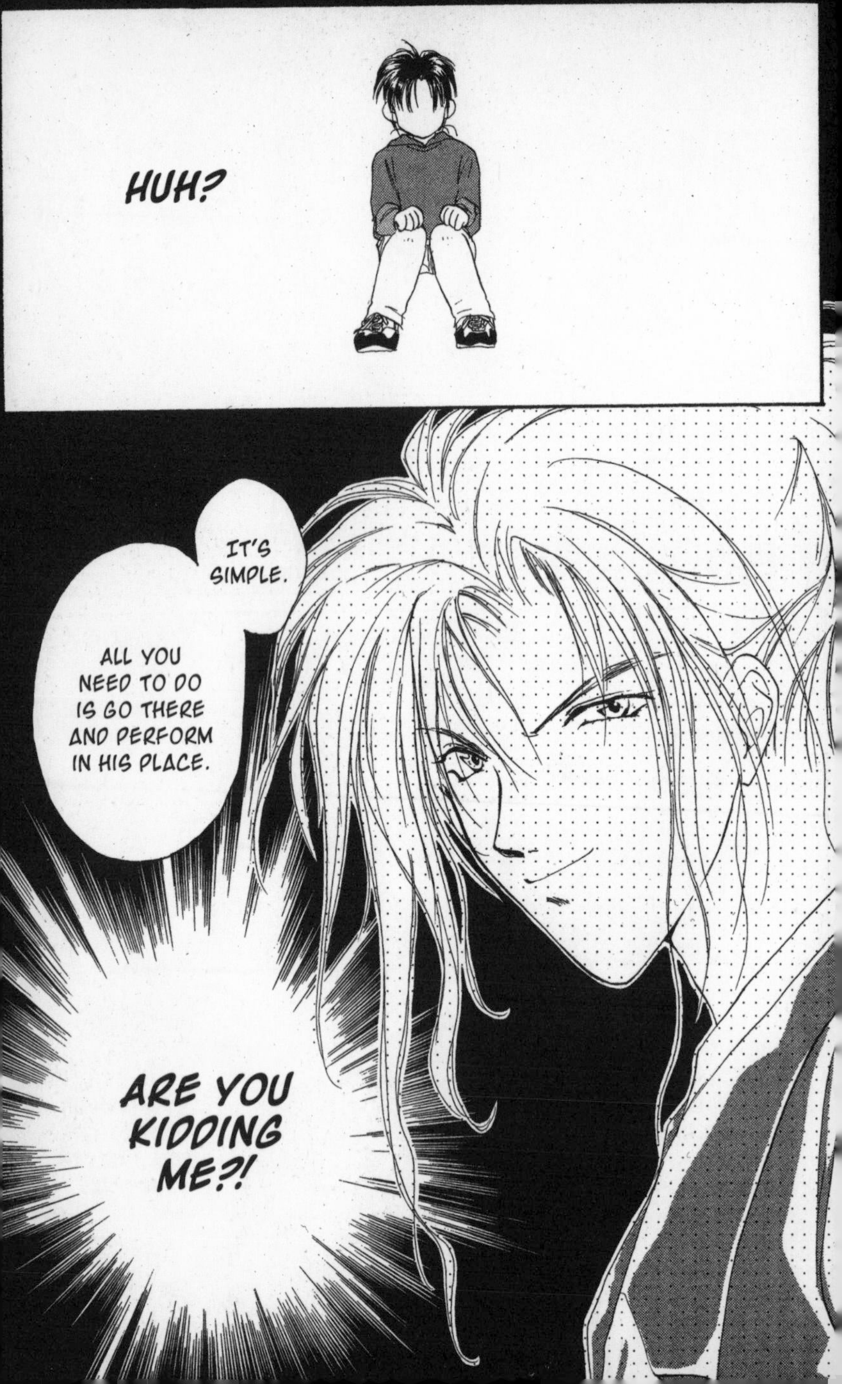
HUH?
IT'S SIMPLE.
ALL YOU NEED TO DO IS GO THERE AND PERFORM IN HIS PLACE.
ARE YOU KIDDING ME?!

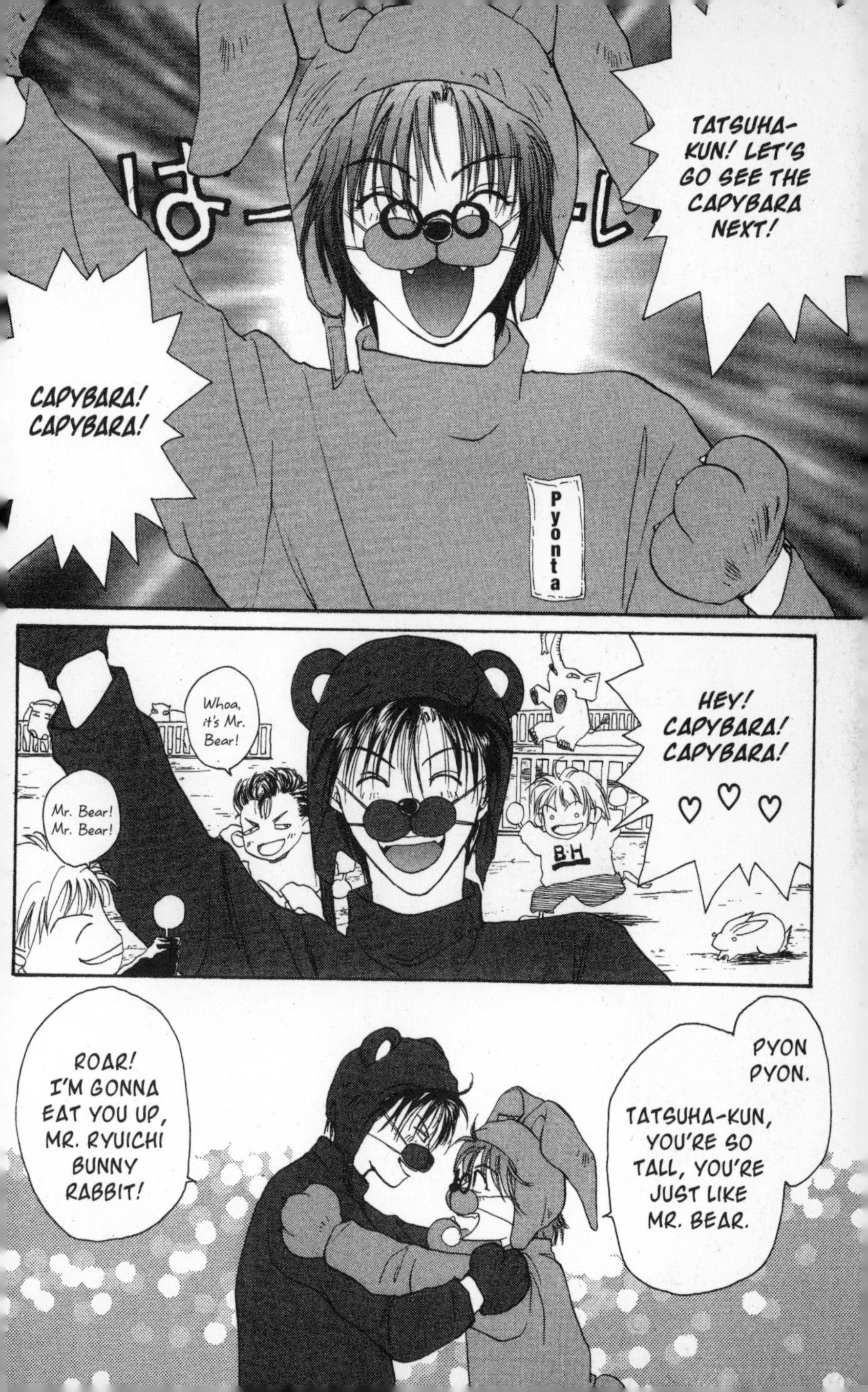
TATSUHA-KUN! LET'S GO SEE THE CAPYBARA NEXT!
CAPYBARA! CAPYBARA!
Pyonta
HEY! CAPYBARA! CAPYBARA!
Whoa, it's Mr. Bear!
Mr. Bear! Mr. Bear!
B·H
PYON PYON.
TATSUHA-KUN, YOU'RE SO TALL, YOU'RE JUST LIKE MR. BEAR.
ROAR! I'M GONNA EAT YOU UP, MR. RYUICHI BUNNY RABBIT!

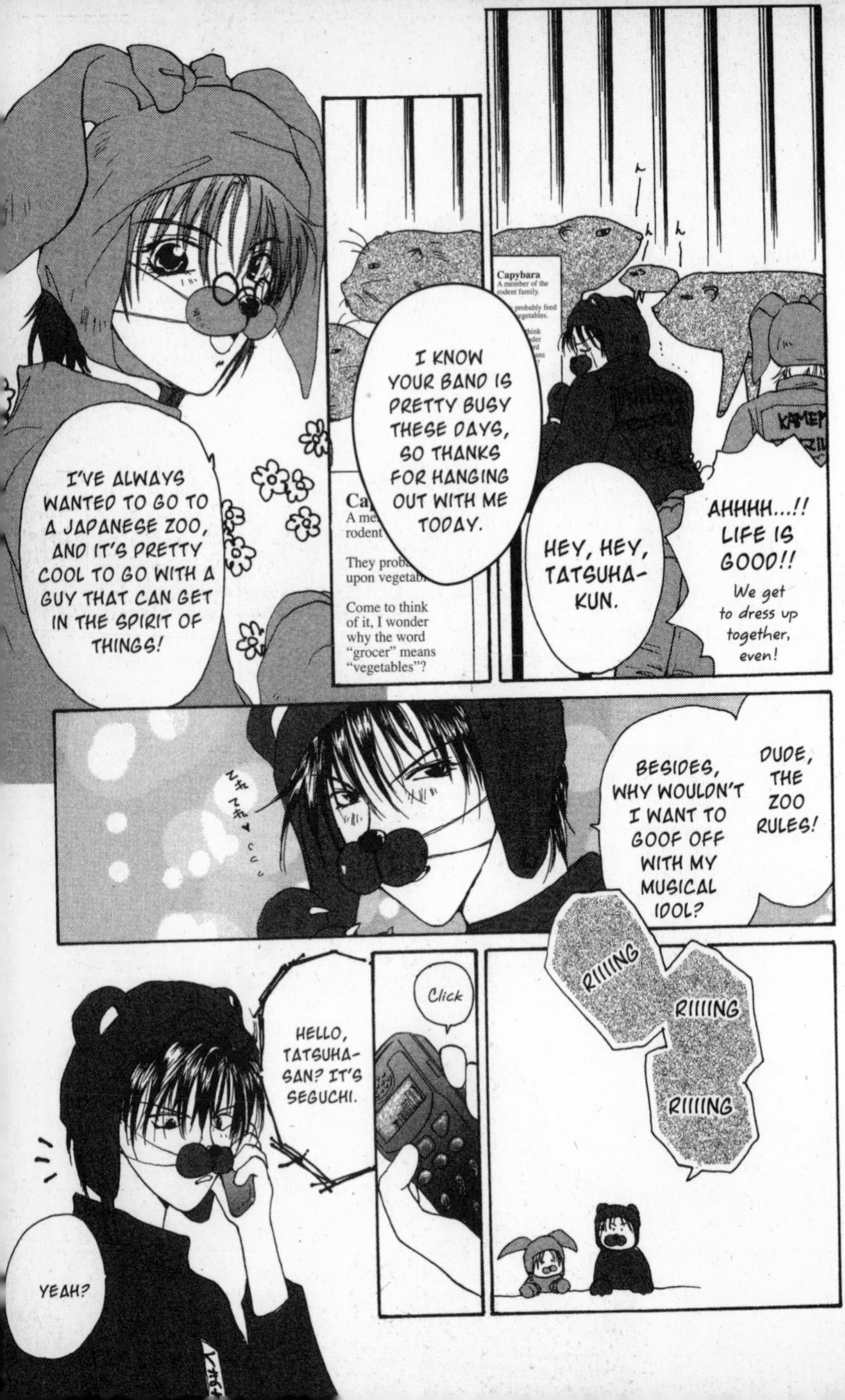
AHHHH...!! LIFE IS GOOD!!
We get to dress up together, even!
HEY, HEY, TATSUHA-KUN.
Capybara
A member of the rodent family.
They probably feed upon vegetables.
Come to think of it, I wonder why the word "grocer" means "vegetables"?
I KNOW YOUR BAND IS PRETTY BUSY THESE DAYS, SO THANKS FOR HANGING OUT WITH ME TODAY.
I'VE ALWAYS WANTED TO GO TO A JAPANESE ZOO, AND IT'S PRETTY COOL TO GO WITH A GUY THAT CAN GET IN THE SPIRIT OF THINGS!
DUDE, THE ZOO RULES!
BESIDES, WHY WOULDN'T I WANT TO GOOF OFF WITH MY MUSICAL IDOL?
RIIIING
RIIIING
RIIIING
Click
HELLO, TATSUHA-SAN? IT'S SEGUCHI.
YEAH?

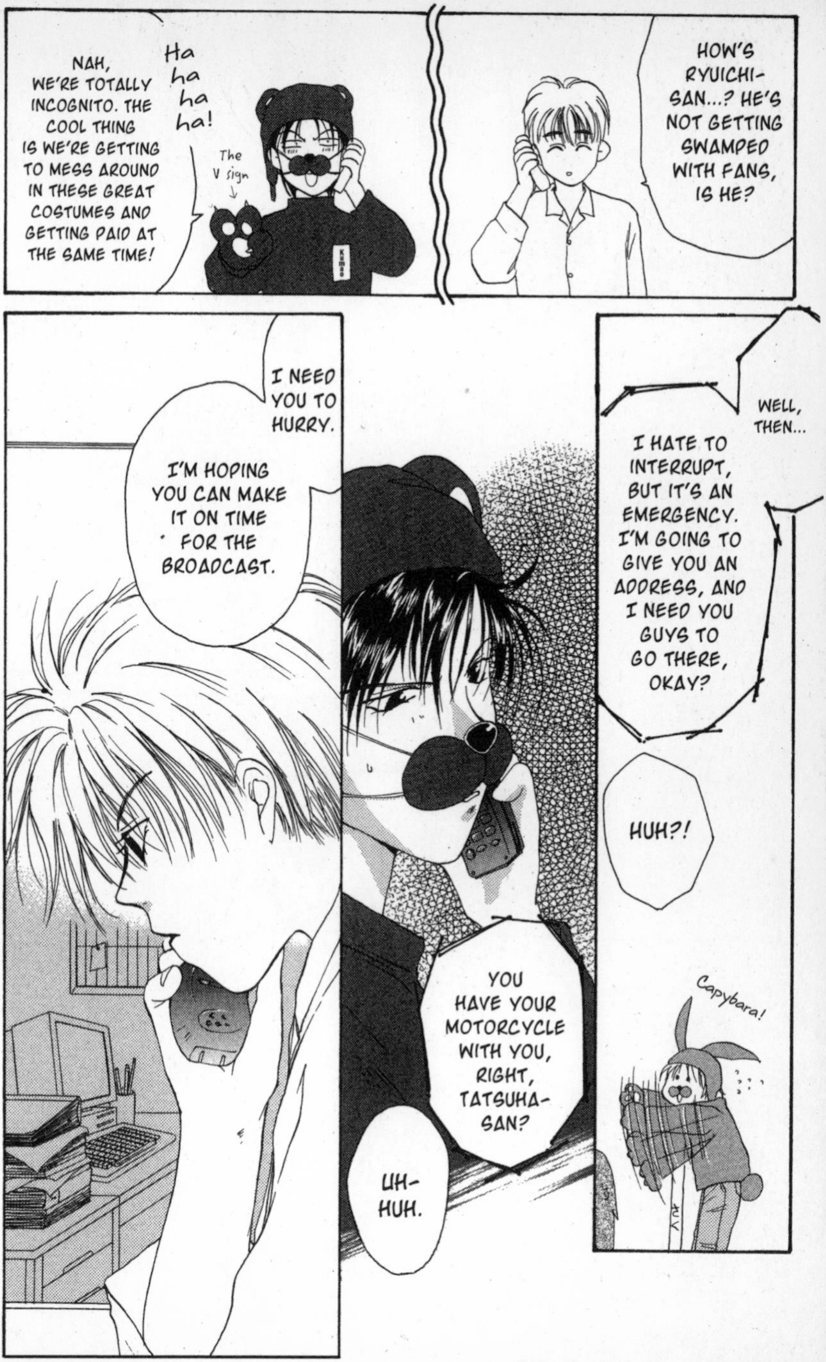
HOW'S RYUICHI-SAN...? HE'S NOT GETTING SWAMPED WITH FANS, IS HE?
Ha ha ha ha!
NAH, WE'RE TOTALLY INCOGNITO. THE COOL THING IS WE'RE GETTING TO MESS AROUND IN THESE GREAT COSTUMES AND GETTING PAID AT THE SAME TIME!
The V sign
WELL, THEN...
I HATE TO INTERRUPT, BUT IT'S AN EMERGENCY. I'M GOING TO GIVE YOU AN ADDRESS, AND I NEED YOU GUYS TO GO THERE, OKAY?
HUH?!
Capybara!
YOU HAVE YOUR MOTORCYCLE WITH YOU, RIGHT, TATSUHA-SAN?
UH-HUH.
I NEED YOU TO HURRY.
I'M HOPING YOU CAN MAKE IT ON TIME FOR THE BROADCAST.

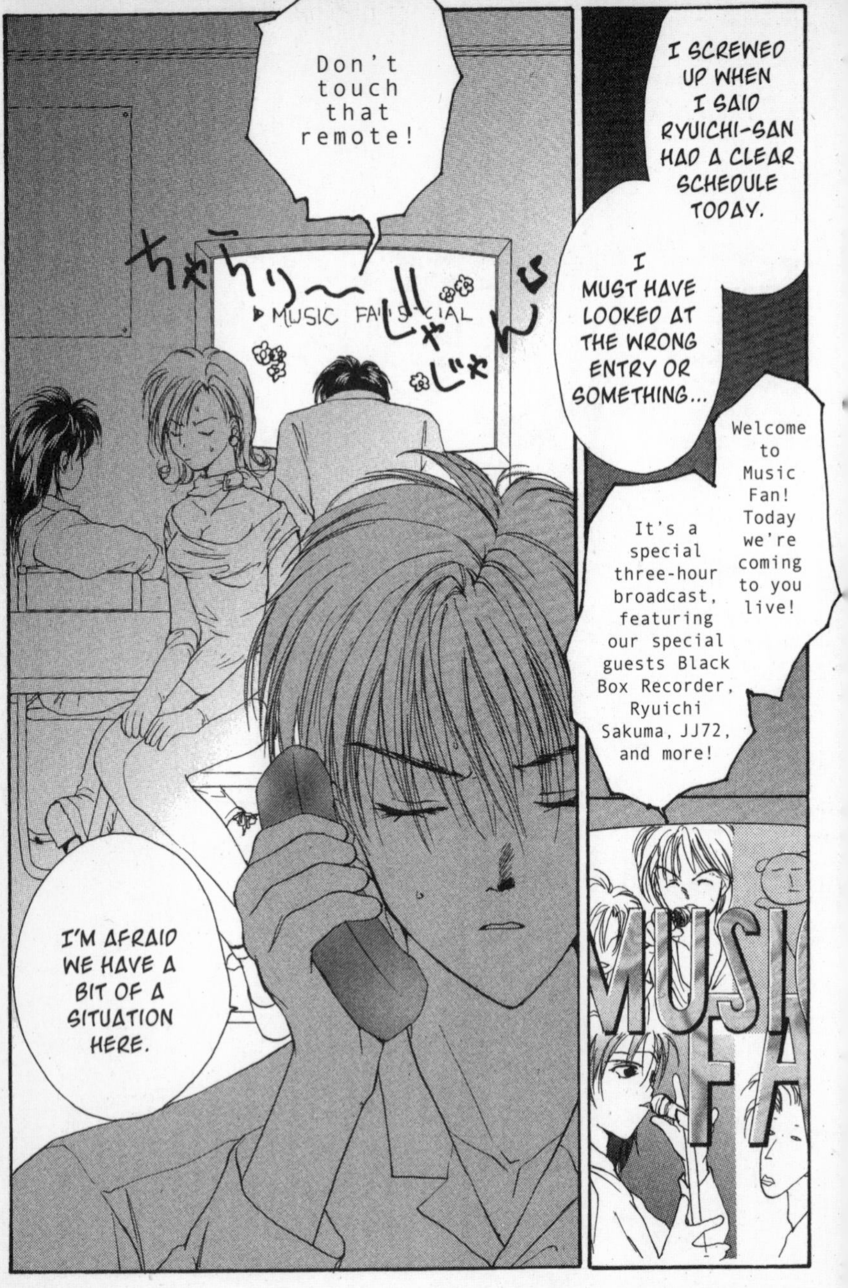
I SCREWED UP WHEN I SAID RYUICHI-SAN HAD A CLEAR SCHEDULE TODAY.
I MUST HAVE LOOKED AT THE WRONG ENTRY OR SOMETHING...
Welcome to Music Fan! Today we're coming to you live!
It's a special three-hour broadcast, featuring our special guests Black Box Recorder, Ryuichi Sakuma, JJ72, and more!
Don't touch that remote!
I'M AFRAID WE HAVE A BIT OF A SITUATION HERE.

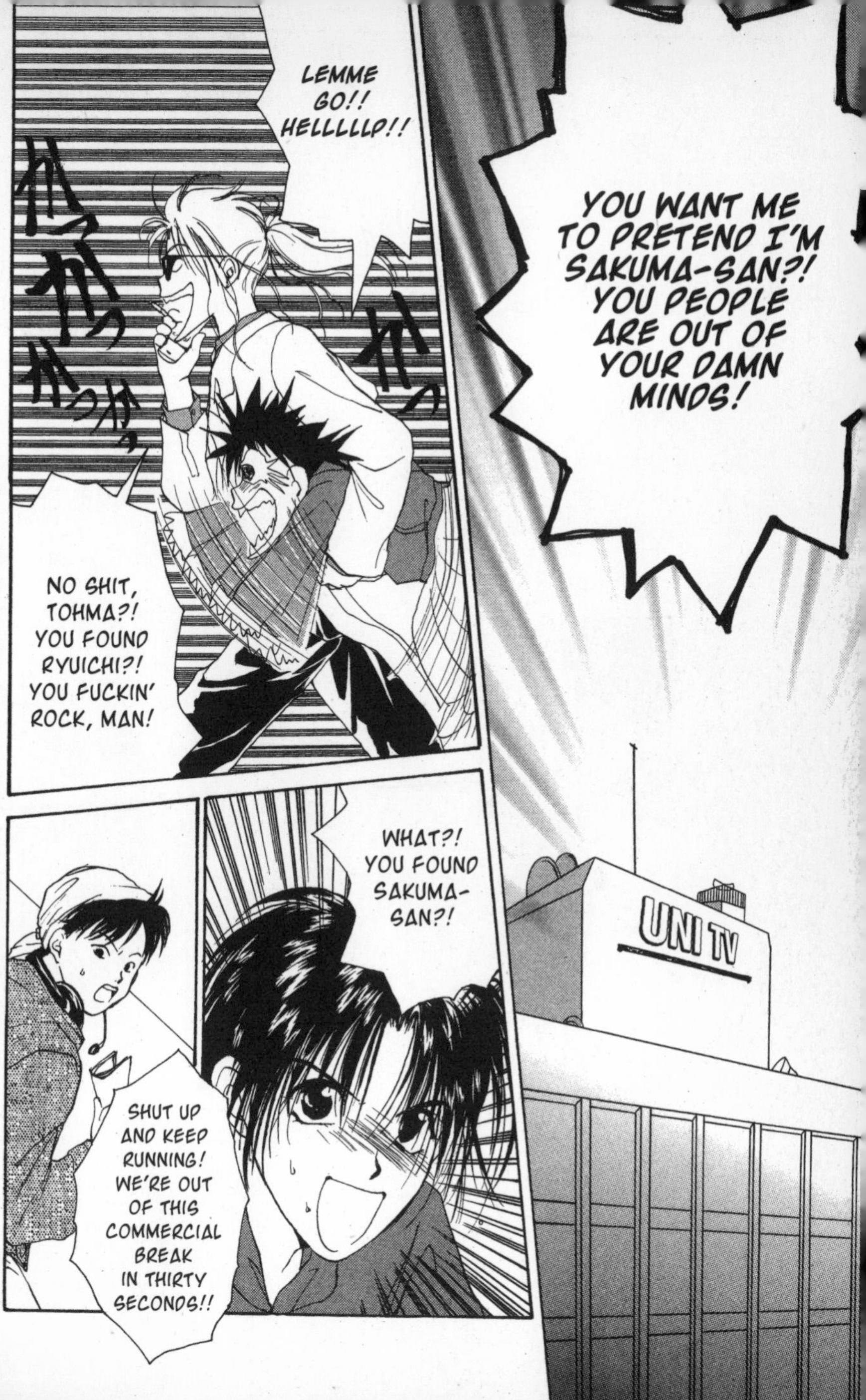
YOU WANT ME TO PRETEND I'M SAKUMA-SAN?! YOU PEOPLE ARE OUT OF YOUR DAMN MINDS!
UNI TV
LEMME GO!! HELLLLLP!!
NO SHIT, TOHMA?! YOU FOUND RYUICHI?! YOU FUCKIN' ROCK, MAN!
WHAT?! YOU FOUND SAKUMA-SAN?!
SHUT UP AND KEEP RUNNING! WE'RE OUT OF THIS COMMERCIAL BREAK IN THIRTY SECONDS!!

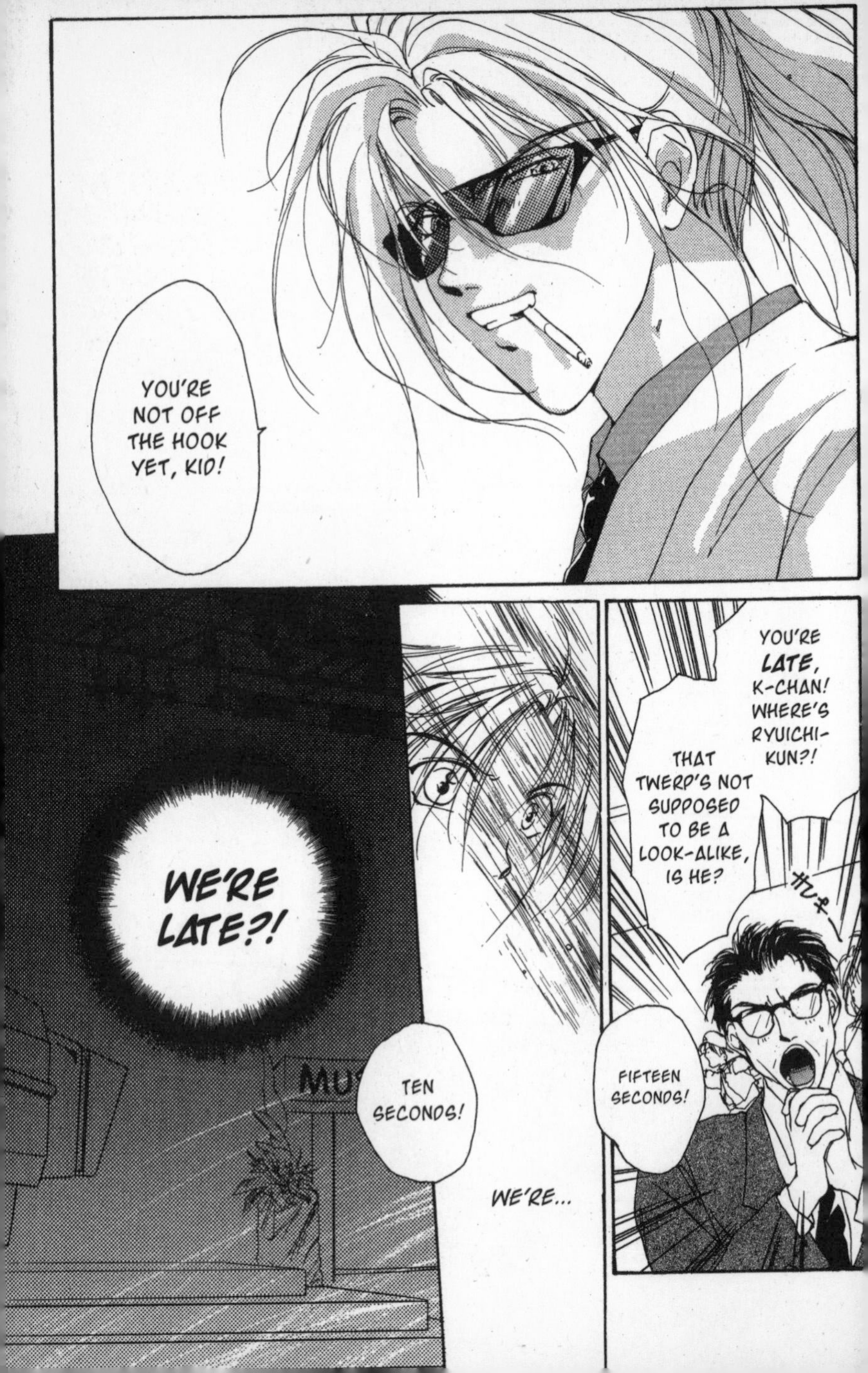
YOU'RE NOT OFF THE HOOK YET, KID!
YOU'RE LATE, K-CHAN! WHERE'S RYUICHI-KUN?!
THAT TWERP'S NOT SUPPOSED TO BE A LOOK-ALIKE, IS HE?
FIFTEEN SECONDS!
TEN SECONDS!
WE'RE...
WE'RE LATE?!

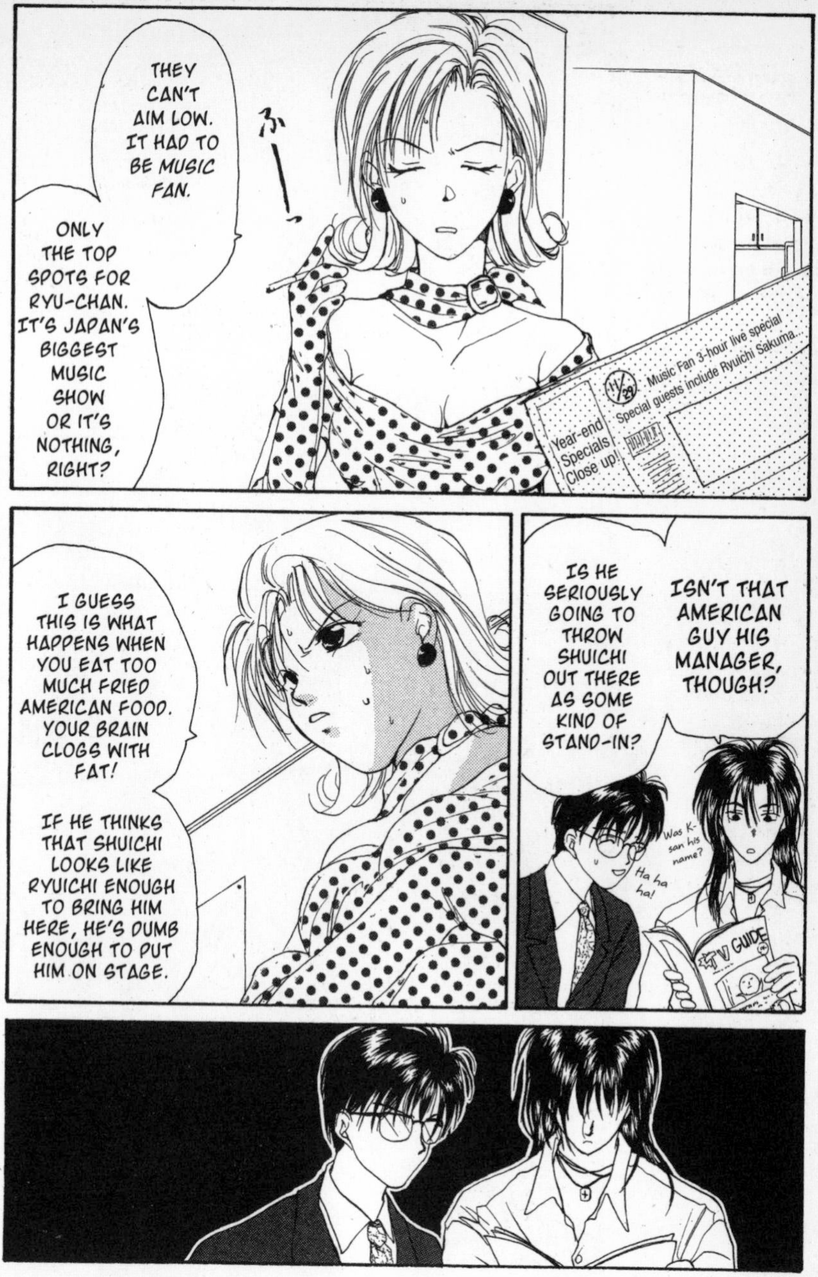
ふー
THEY CAN'T AIM LOW. IT HAD TO BE MUSIC FAN.
ONLY THE TOP SPOTS FOR RYU-CHAN. IT'S JAPAN'S BIGGEST MUSIC SHOW OR IT'S NOTHING, RIGHT?
11/29
Music Fan 3-hour live special
Special guests include Ryuichi Sakuma...
Year-end Specials Close up!
ISN'T THAT AMERICAN GUY HIS MANAGER, THOUGH?
IS HE SERIOUSLY GOING TO THROW SHUICHI OUT THERE AS SOME KIND OF STAND-IN?
Was K-san his name?
Ha ha ha!
TV GUIDE
I GUESS THIS IS WHAT HAPPENS WHEN YOU EAT TOO MUCH FRIED AMERICAN FOOD. YOUR BRAIN CLOGS WITH FAT!
IF HE THINKS THAT SHUICHI LOOKS LIKE RYUICHI ENOUGH TO BRING HIM HERE, HE'S DUMB ENOUGH TO PUT HIM ON STAGE.

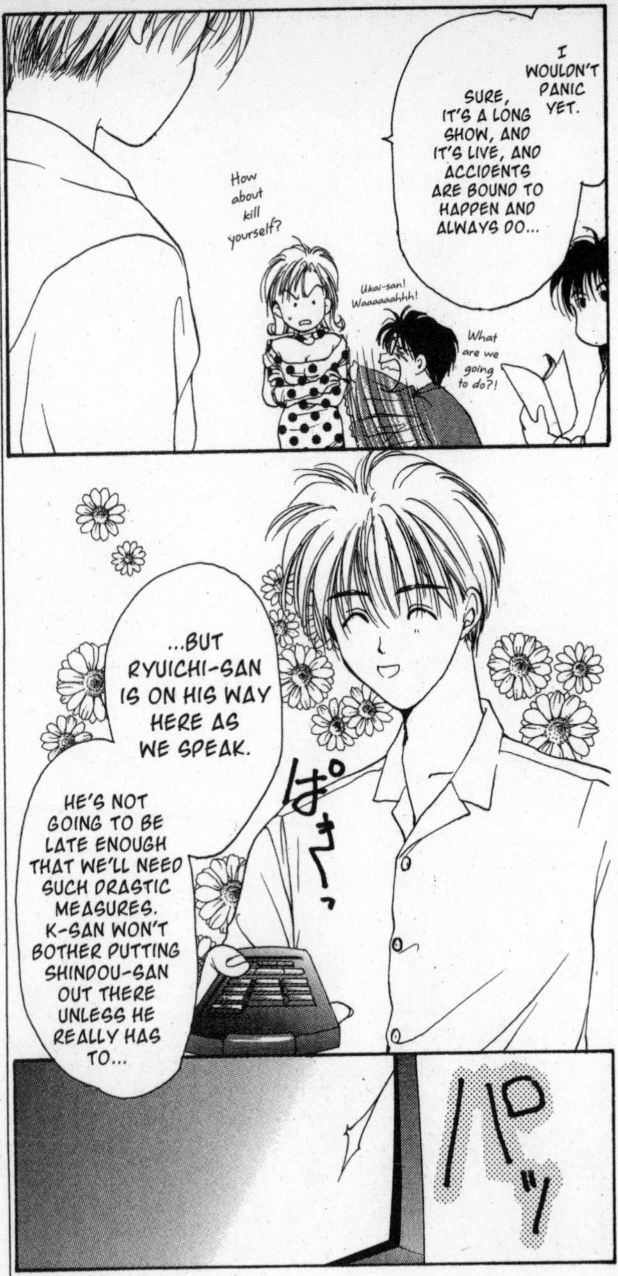
I WOULDN'T PANIC YET.
SURE, IT'S A LONG SHOW, AND IT'S LIVE, AND ACCIDENTS ARE BOUND TO HAPPEN AND ALWAYS DO...
What are we going to do?!
Ukai-san! Waaaaaahhh!
How about kill yourself?
...BUT RYUICHI-SAN IS ON HIS WAY HERE AS WE SPEAK.
ぱきっ
HE'S NOT GOING TO BE LATE ENOUGH THAT WE'LL NEED SUCH DRASTIC MEASURES. K-SAN WON'T BOTHER PUTTING SHINDOU-SAN OUT THERE UNLESS HE REALLY HAS TO...
パッ

CONTINUED

So this foreigner guy, K... He's a pretty new character, and though he's kind of out there, he was just going to be a bit player. How did his role get so big? At first, his long, naturally wavy hair was down to the middle of his back. Then, within a month, it was down to his waist! It's like mutant hair! It straightened out and doubled in length! Did anyone consider if he's wearing a wig? Or is he using hair extensions? Nah, I don't think he would ever resort to methods like that. I think you're just seeing things. When you're tired, nothing really seems to matter. That's the way he works. Who cares how long his hair is?

So I hope you understand... Do you...?

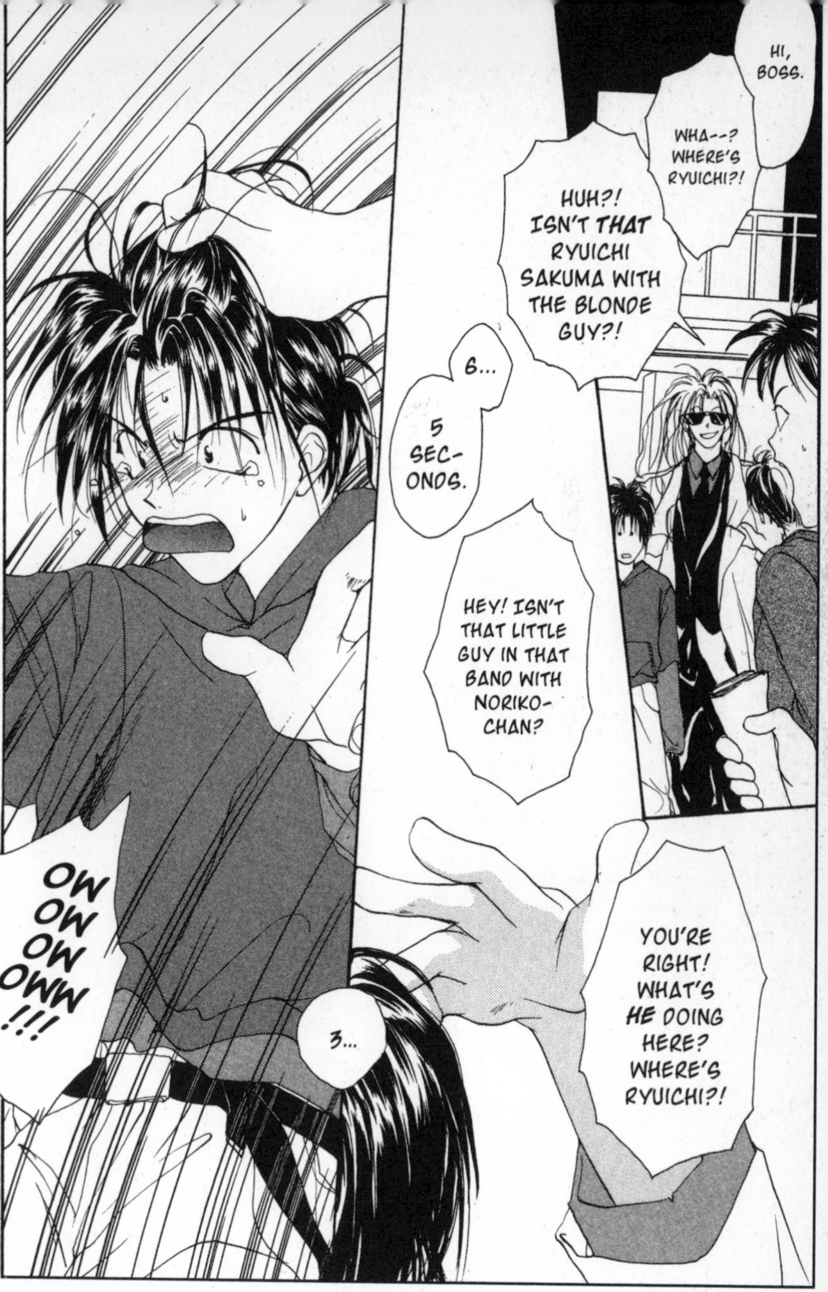
HI, BOSS.
WHA--? WHERE'S RYUICHI?!
HUH?! ISN'T THAT RYUICHI SAKUMA WITH THE BLONDE GUY?!
6...
5 SECONDS.
HEY! ISN'T THAT LITTLE GUY IN THAT BAND WITH NORIKO-CHAN?
YOU'RE RIGHT! WHAT'S HE DOING HERE? WHERE'S RYUICHI?!
3...
OW OW OW OWW!!!

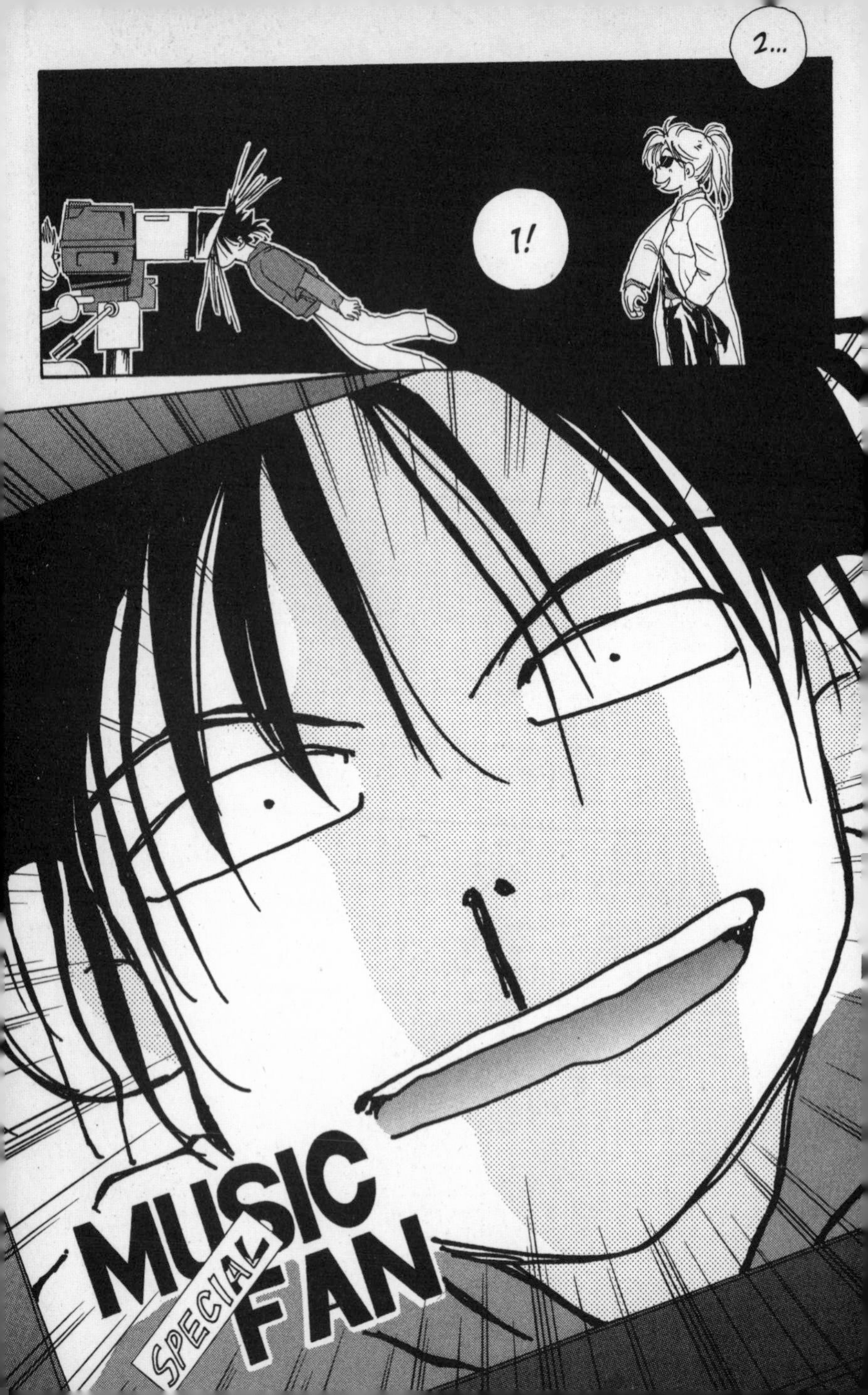

2...
1!
MUSIC
SPECIAL
FAN

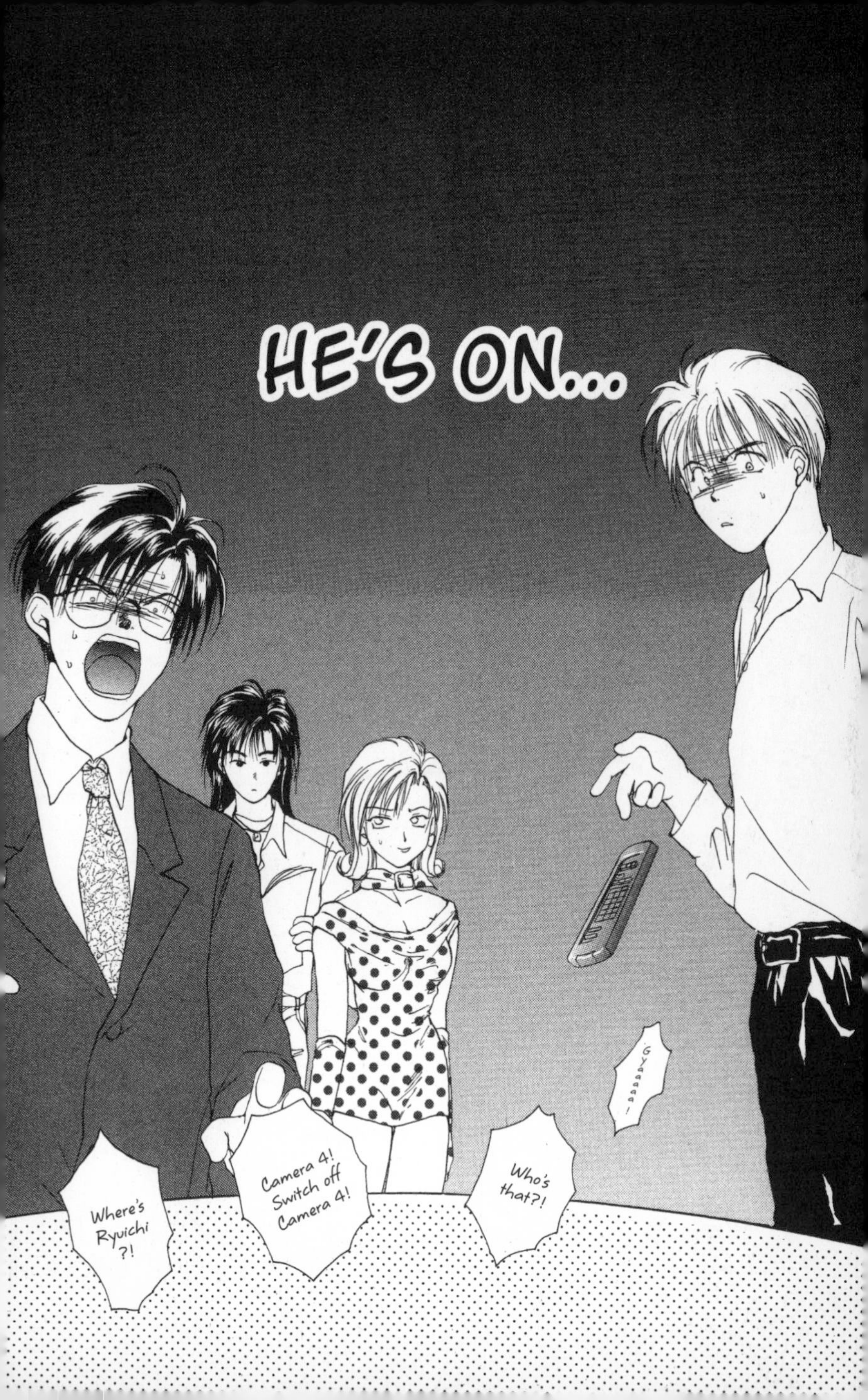
HE'S ON...
GYaaaaa!
Who's that?!
Camera 4! Switch off Camera 4!
Where's Ryuichi ?!

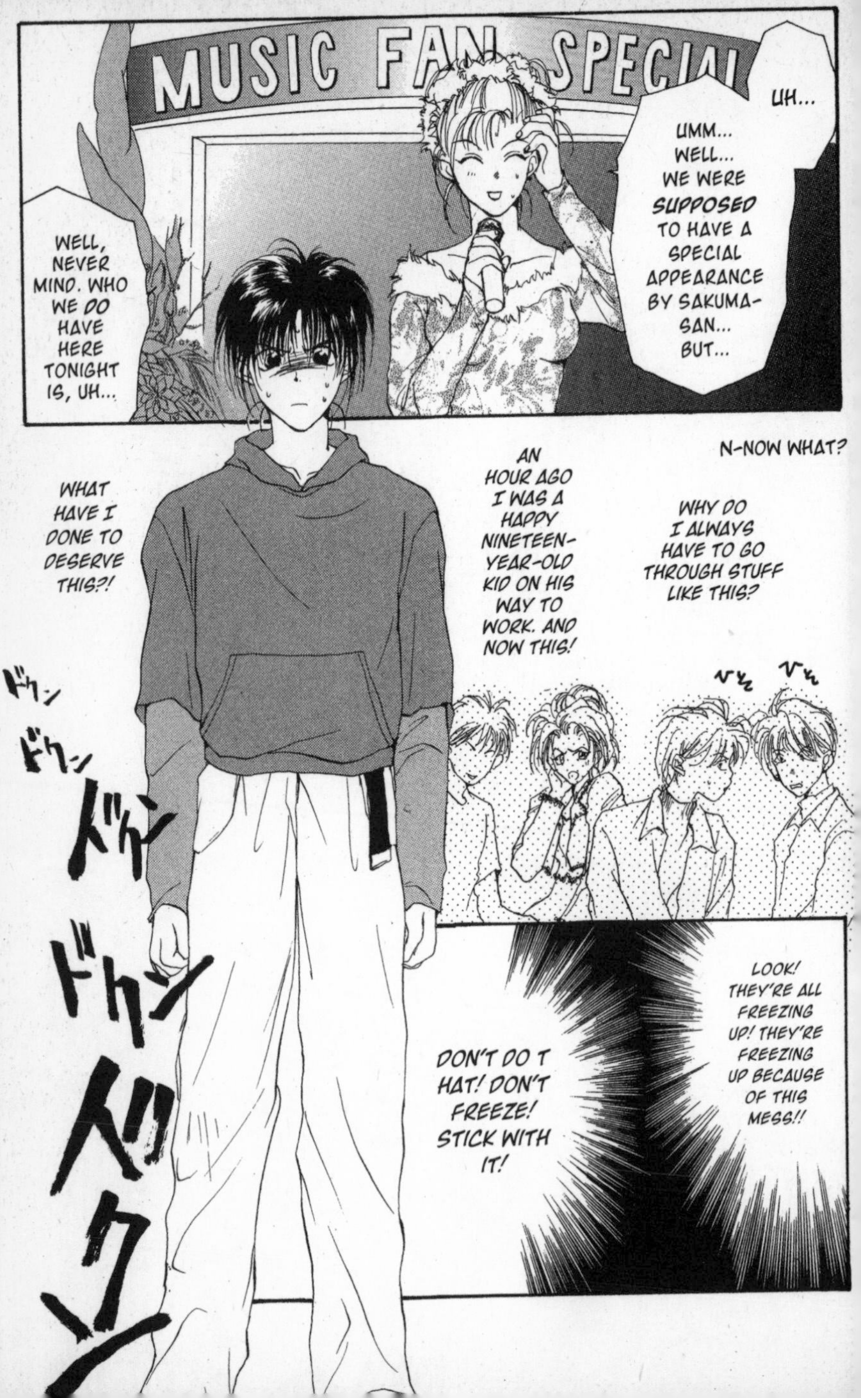
MUSIC FAN SPECIAL
UH...
UMM... WELL... WE WERE SUPPOSED TO HAVE A SPECIAL APPEARANCE BY SAKUMA-SAN... BUT...
WELL, NEVER MIND. WHO WE DO HAVE HERE TONIGHT IS, UH...
N-NOW WHAT?
WHY DO I ALWAYS HAVE TO GO THROUGH STUFF LIKE THIS?
AN HOUR AGO I WAS A HAPPY NINETEEN-YEAR-OLD KID ON HIS WAY TO WORK. AND NOW THIS!
WHAT HAVE I DONE TO DESERVE THIS?!
LOOK! THEY'RE ALL FREEZING UP! THEY'RE FREEZING UP BECAUSE OF THIS MESS!!
DON'T DO T HAT! DON'T FREEZE! STICK WITH IT!
ドクン
ドクン
ドクン
ドクン
バクン

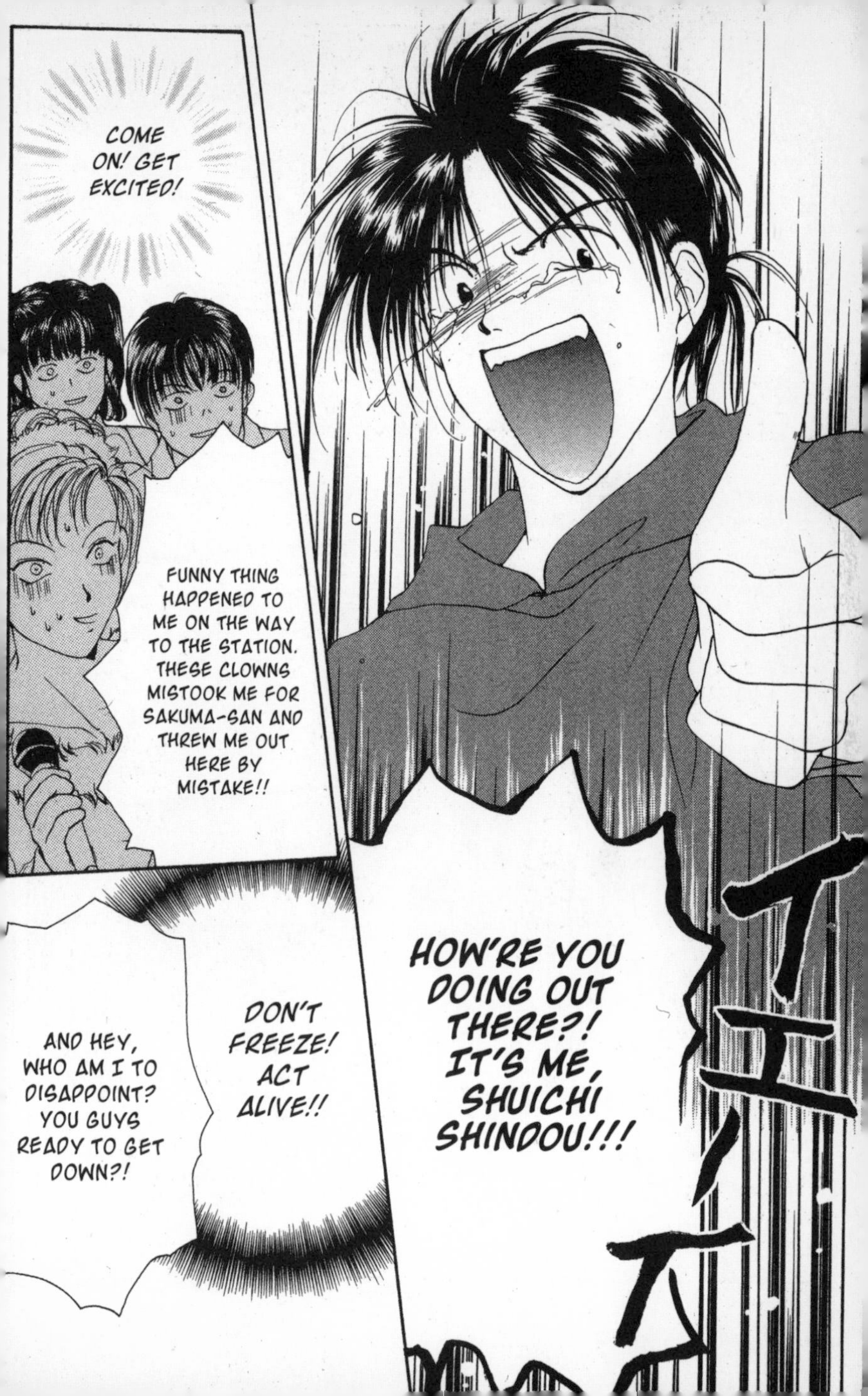
HOW'RE YOU DOING OUT THERE?! IT'S ME, SHUICHI SHINDOU!!!
イエーイ
COME ON! GET EXCITED!
FUNNY THING HAPPENED TO ME ON THE WAY TO THE STATION. THESE CLOWNS MISTOOK ME FOR SAKUMA-SAN AND THREW ME OUT HERE BY MISTAKE!!
DON'T FREEZE! ACT ALIVE!!
AND HEY, WHO AM I TO DISAPPOINT? YOU GUYS READY TO GET DOWN?!

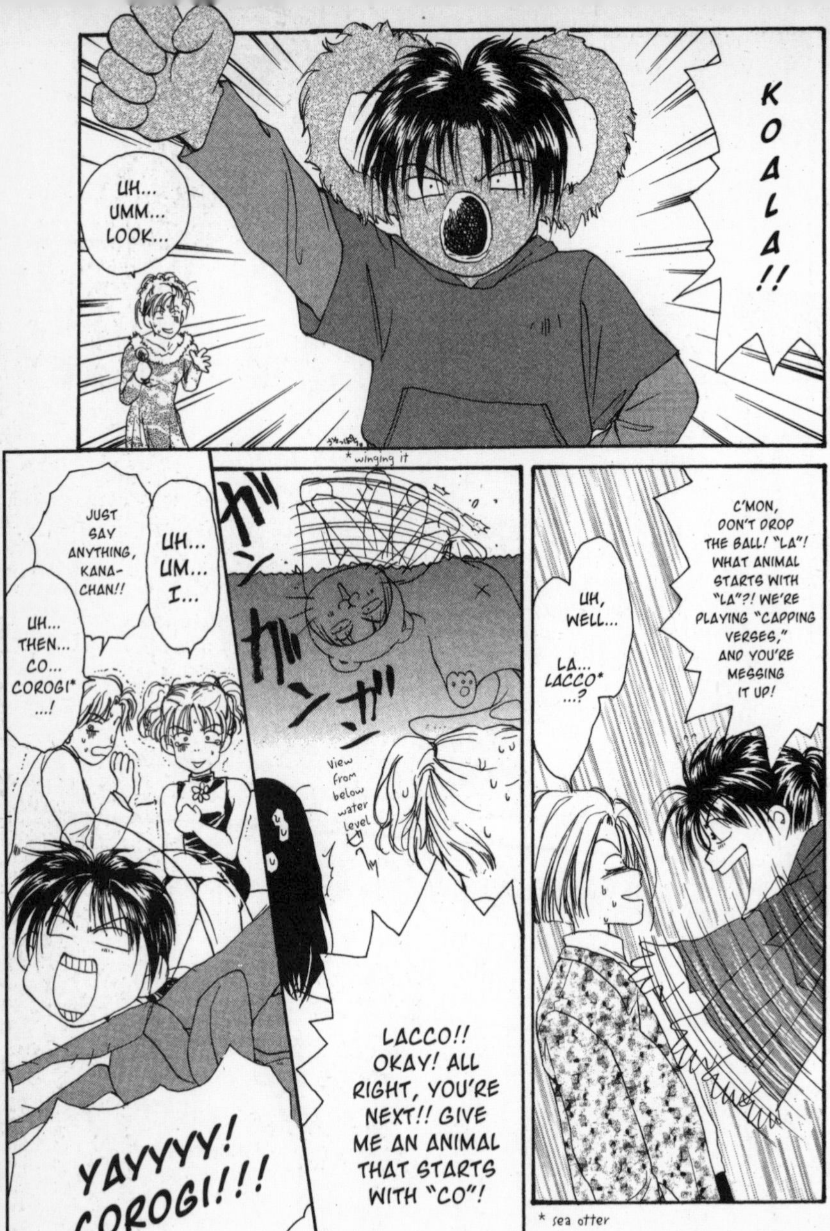
KOALA!!
UH... UMM... LOOK...
C'MON, DON'T DROP THE BALL! "LA"! WHAT ANIMAL STARTS WITH "LA"?! WE'RE PLAYING "CAPPING VERSES," AND YOU'RE MESSING IT UP!
UH, WELL...
LA... LACCO* ...?
View from below water level
LACCO!! OKAY! ALL RIGHT, YOU'RE NEXT!! GIVE ME AN ANIMAL THAT STARTS WITH "CO"!
UH... UM... I...
JUST SAY ANYTHING, KANA-CHAN!!
UH... THEN... CO... COROGI* ...!
YAYYYY! COROGI!!!

* winging it

* sea otter

* cricket

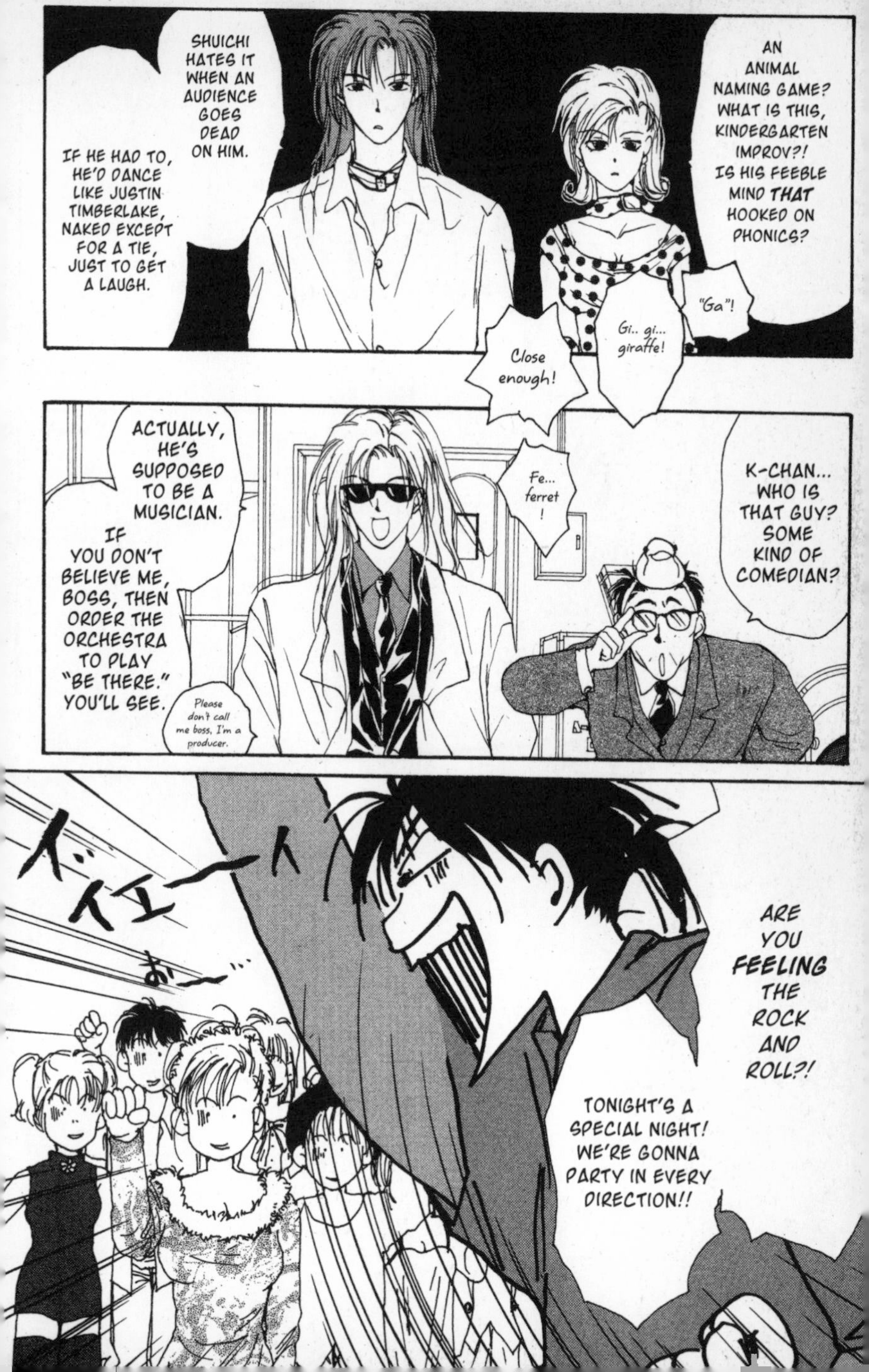
AN ANIMAL NAMING GAME? WHAT IS THIS, KINDERGARTEN IMPROV?! IS HIS FEEBLE MIND **THAT** HOOKED ON PHONICS?
SHUICHI HATES IT WHEN AN AUDIENCE GOES DEAD ON HIM.
IF HE HAD TO, HE'D DANCE LIKE JUSTIN TIMBERLAKE, NAKED EXCEPT FOR A TIE, JUST TO GET A LAUGH.
"Ga"!
Gi.. gi... giraffe!
Close enough!
K-CHAN... WHO IS THAT GUY? SOME KIND OF COMEDIAN?
Fe... ferret!
ACTUALLY, HE'S SUPPOSED TO BE A MUSICIAN.
IF YOU DON'T BELIEVE ME, BOSS, THEN ORDER THE ORCHESTRA TO PLAY "BE THERE." YOU'LL SEE.
Please don't call me boss, I'm a producer.
ARE YOU **FEELING** THE ROCK AND ROLL?!
TONIGHT'S A SPECIAL NIGHT! WE'RE GONNA PARTY IN EVERY DIRECTION!!
イイエーーイ
おー…

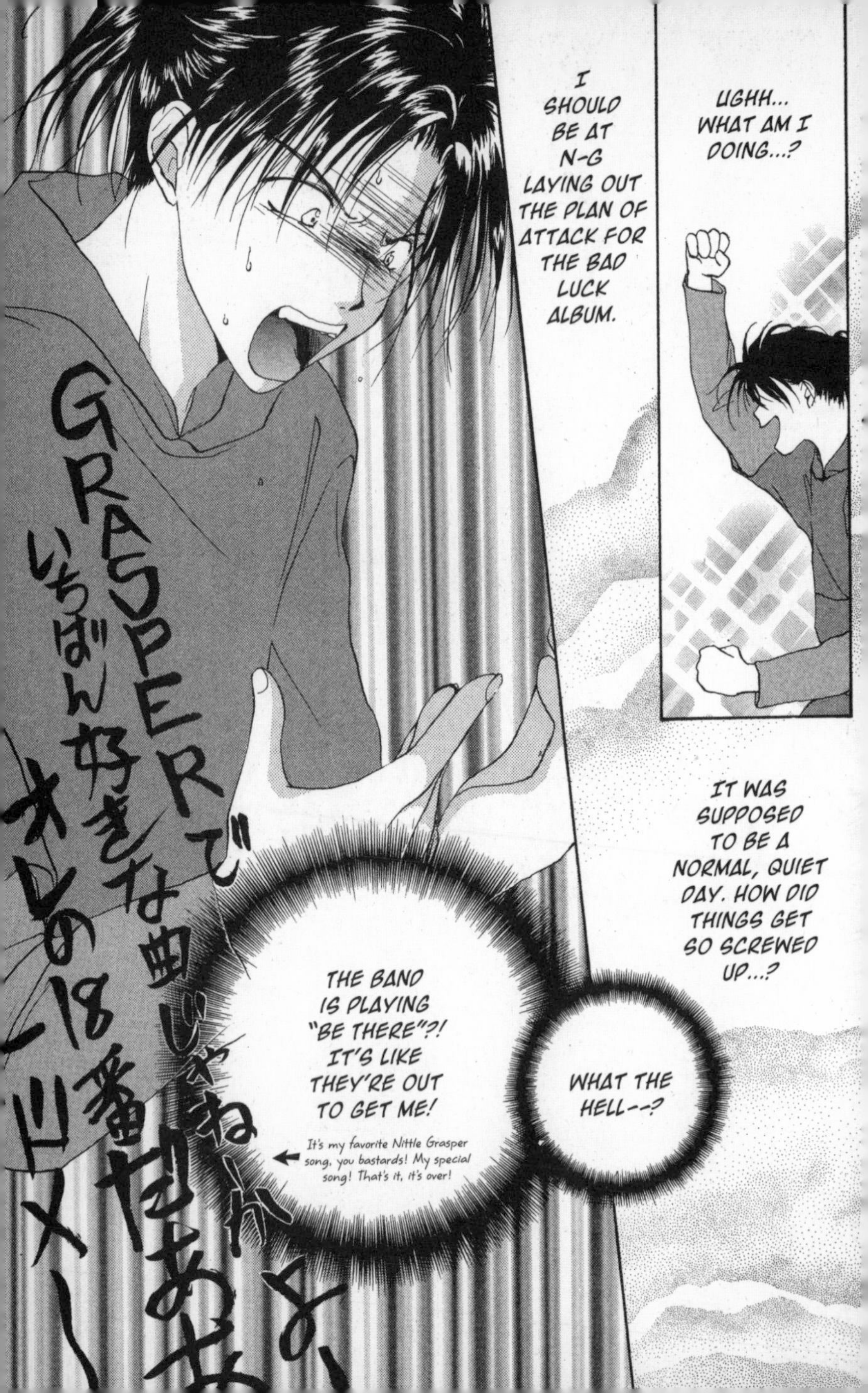
UGHH... WHAT AM I DOING...?
I SHOULD BE AT N-G LAYING OUT THE PLAN OF ATTACK FOR THE BAD LUCK ALBUM.
IT WAS SUPPOSED TO BE A NORMAL, QUIET DAY. HOW DID THINGS GET SO SCREWED UP...?
WHAT THE HELL--?
THE BAND IS PLAYING "BE THERE"?! IT'S LIKE THEY'RE OUT TO GET ME!
It's my favorite Nittle Grasper song, you bastards! My special song! That's it, it's over!

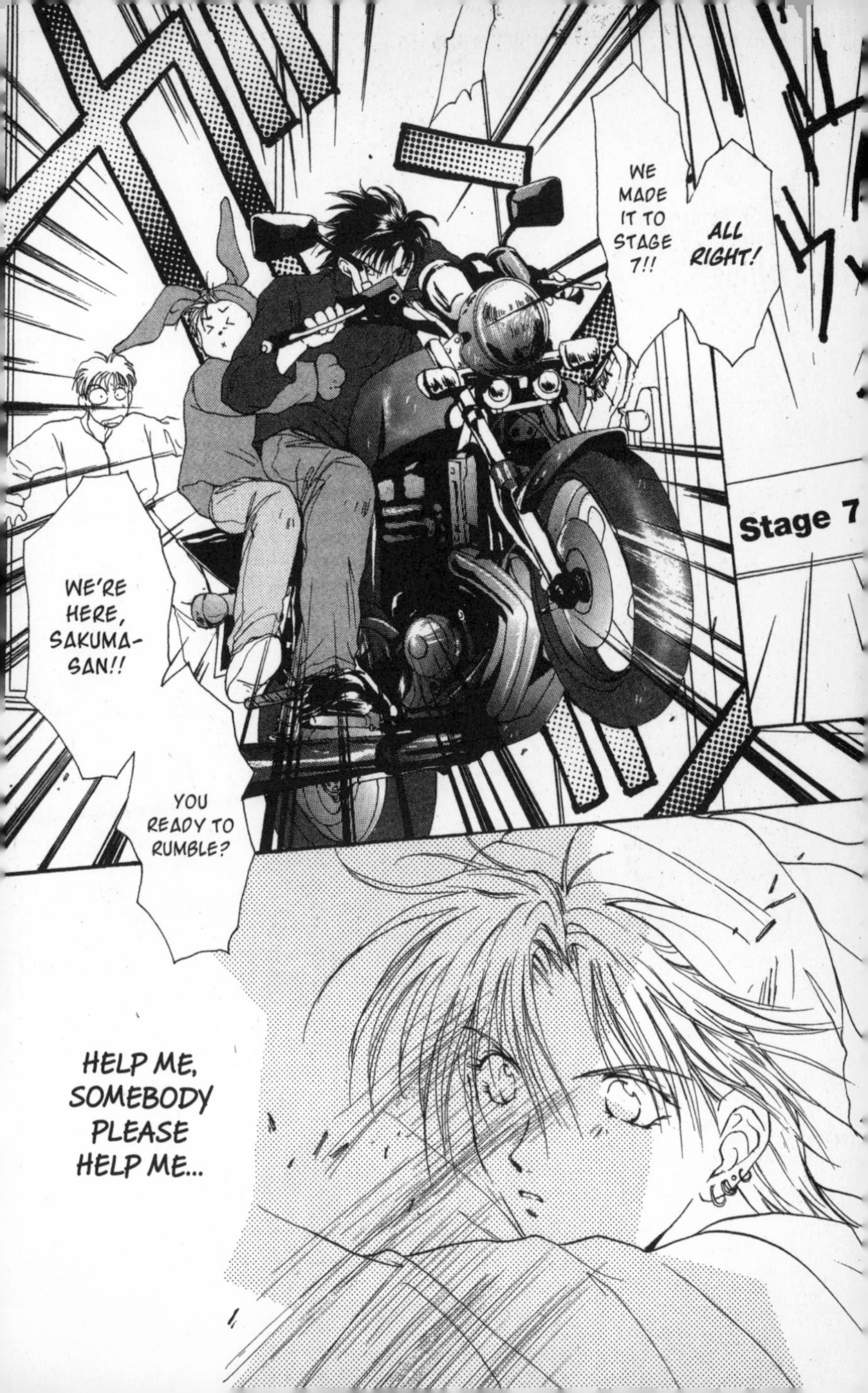
ALL RIGHT!
WE MADE IT TO STAGE 7!!
Stage 7
WE'RE HERE, SAKUMA-SAN!!
YOU READY TO RUMBLE?
HELP ME, SOMEBODY PLEASE HELP ME...

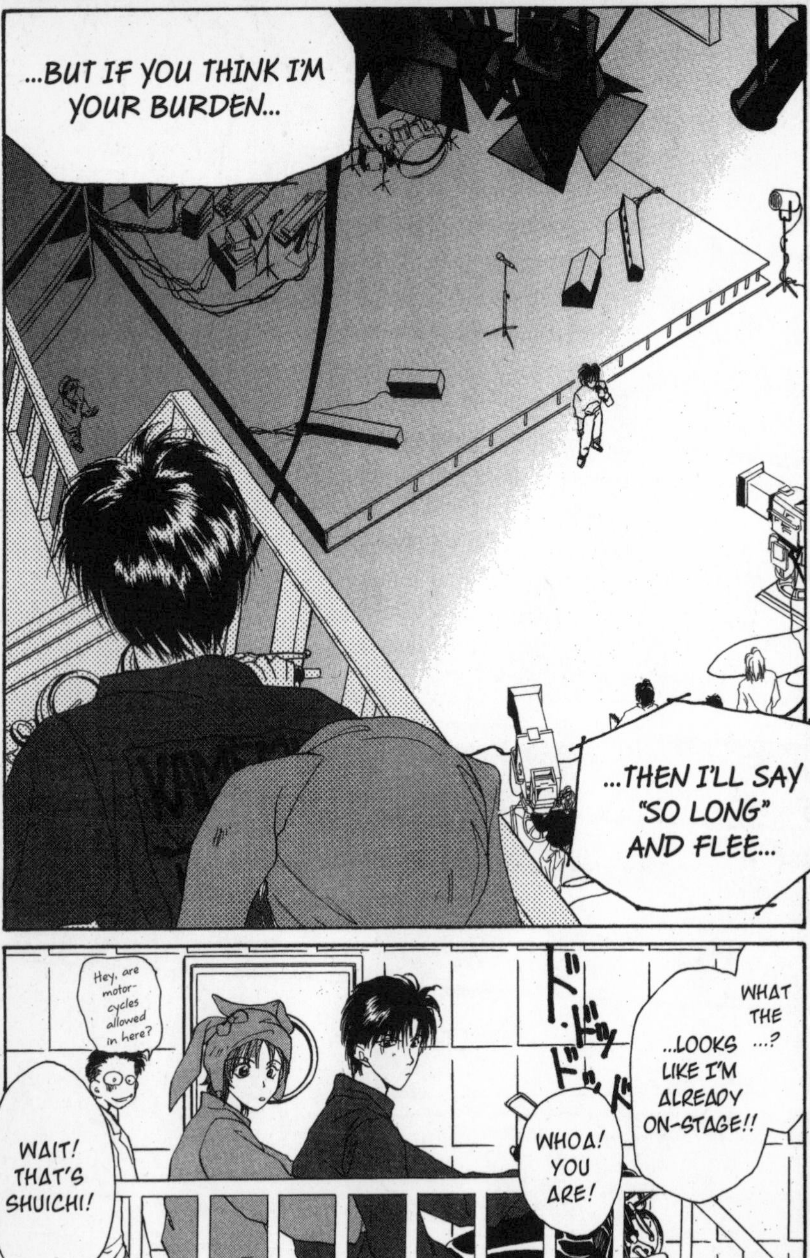
...BUT IF YOU THINK I'M YOUR BURDEN...
...THEN I'LL SAY "SO LONG" AND FLEE...
WHAT THE ...?
...LOOKS LIKE I'M ALREADY ON-STAGE!!
WHOA! YOU ARE!
Hey, are motor-cycles allowed in here?
WAIT! THAT'S SHUICHI!

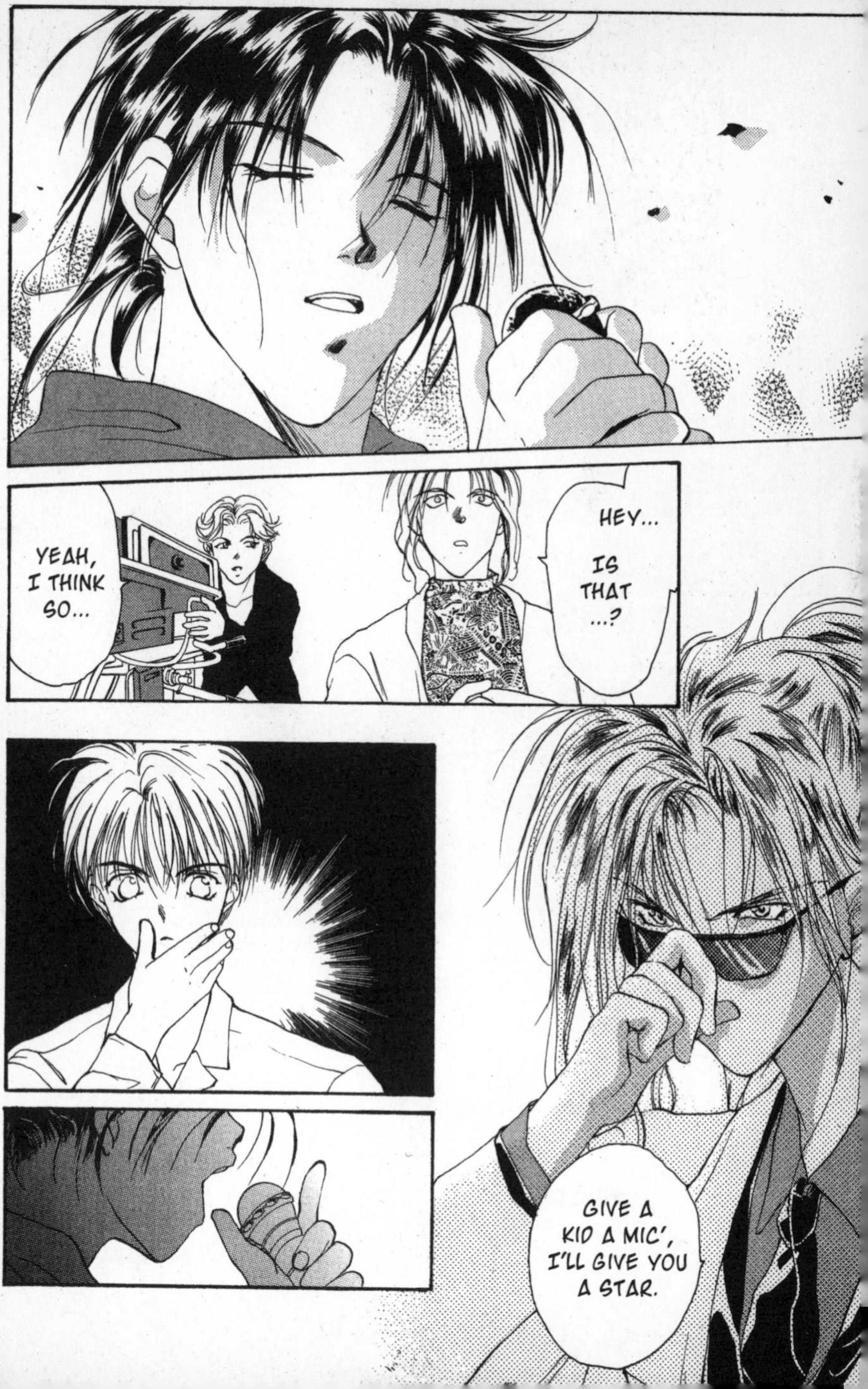
HEY...
IS THAT ...?
YEAH, I THINK SO...
GIVE A KID A MIC', I'LL GIVE YOU A STAR.

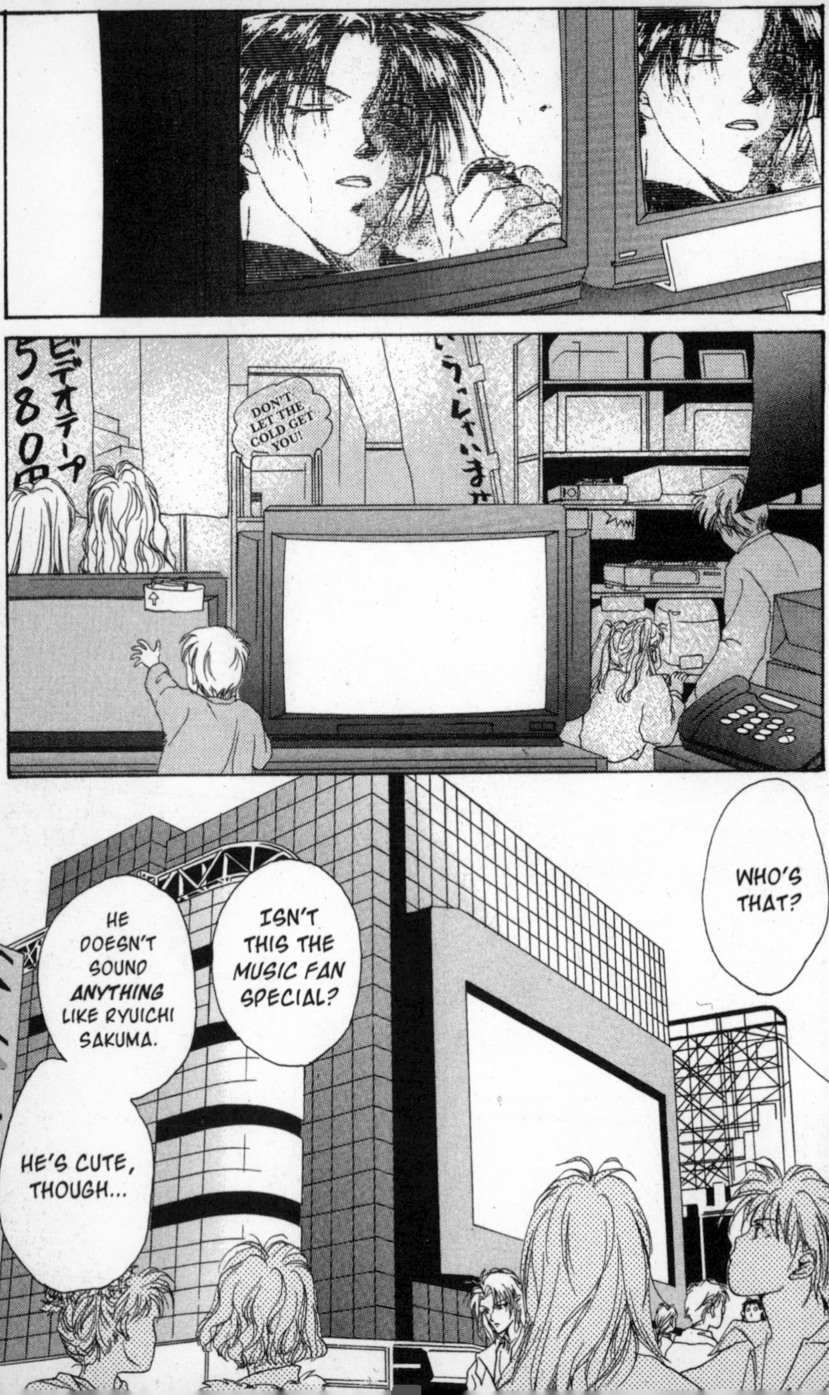
ビデオテープ
580
DON'T LET THE COLD GET YOU!
WHO'S THAT?
ISN'T THIS THE *MUSIC FAN SPECIAL*?
HE DOESN'T SOUND **ANYTHING** LIKE RYUICHI SAKUMA.
HE'S CUTE, THOUGH...

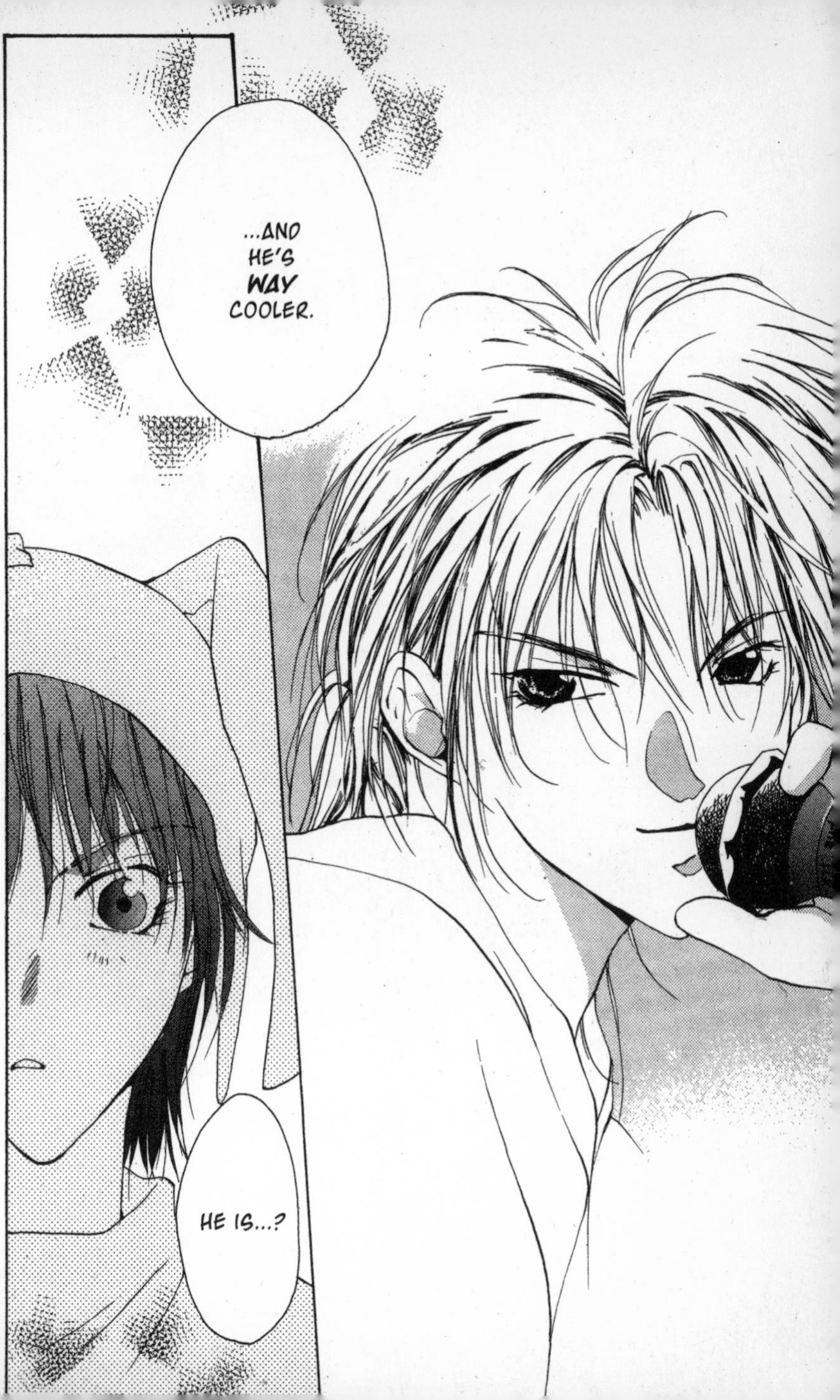
...AND HE'S **WAY** COOLER.
HE IS...?

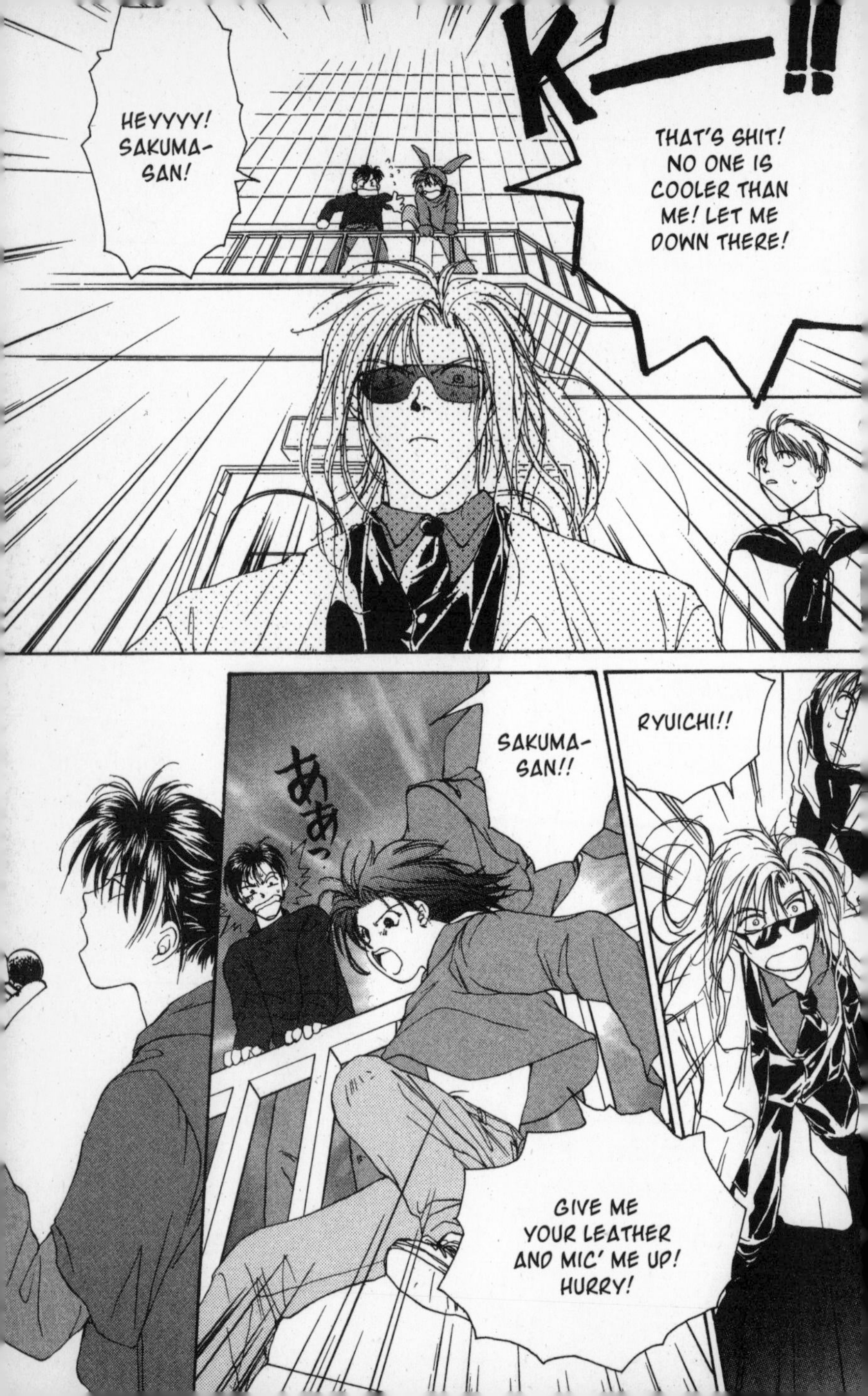
K—!!
THAT'S SHIT! NO ONE IS COOLER THAN ME! LET ME DOWN THERE!
HEYYYY! SAKUMA-SAN!
RYUICHI!!
SAKUMA-SAN!!
ああっ
GIVE ME YOUR LEATHER AND MIC' ME UP! HURRY!

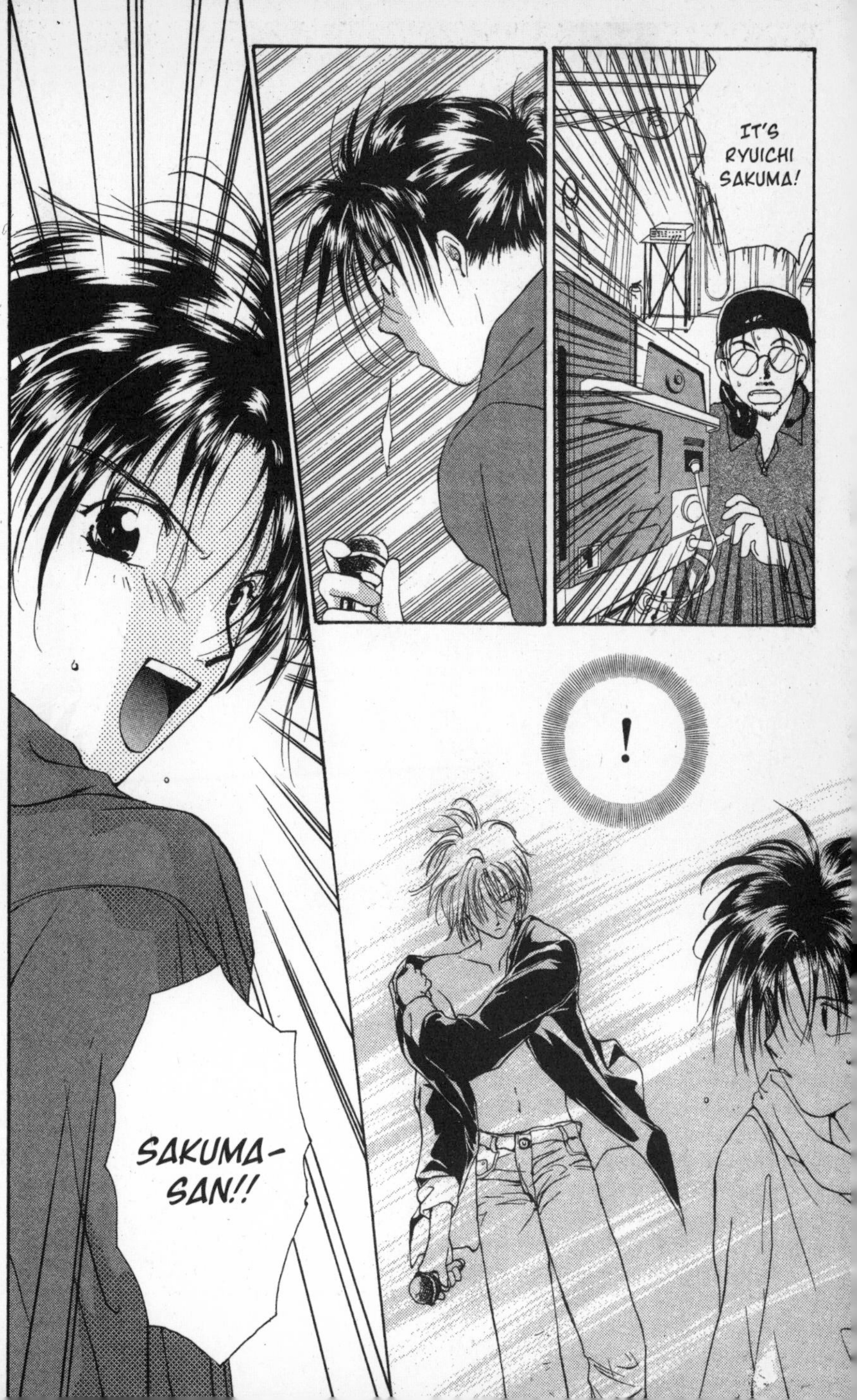
IT'S RYUICHI SAKUMA!
!
SAKUMA-SAN!!

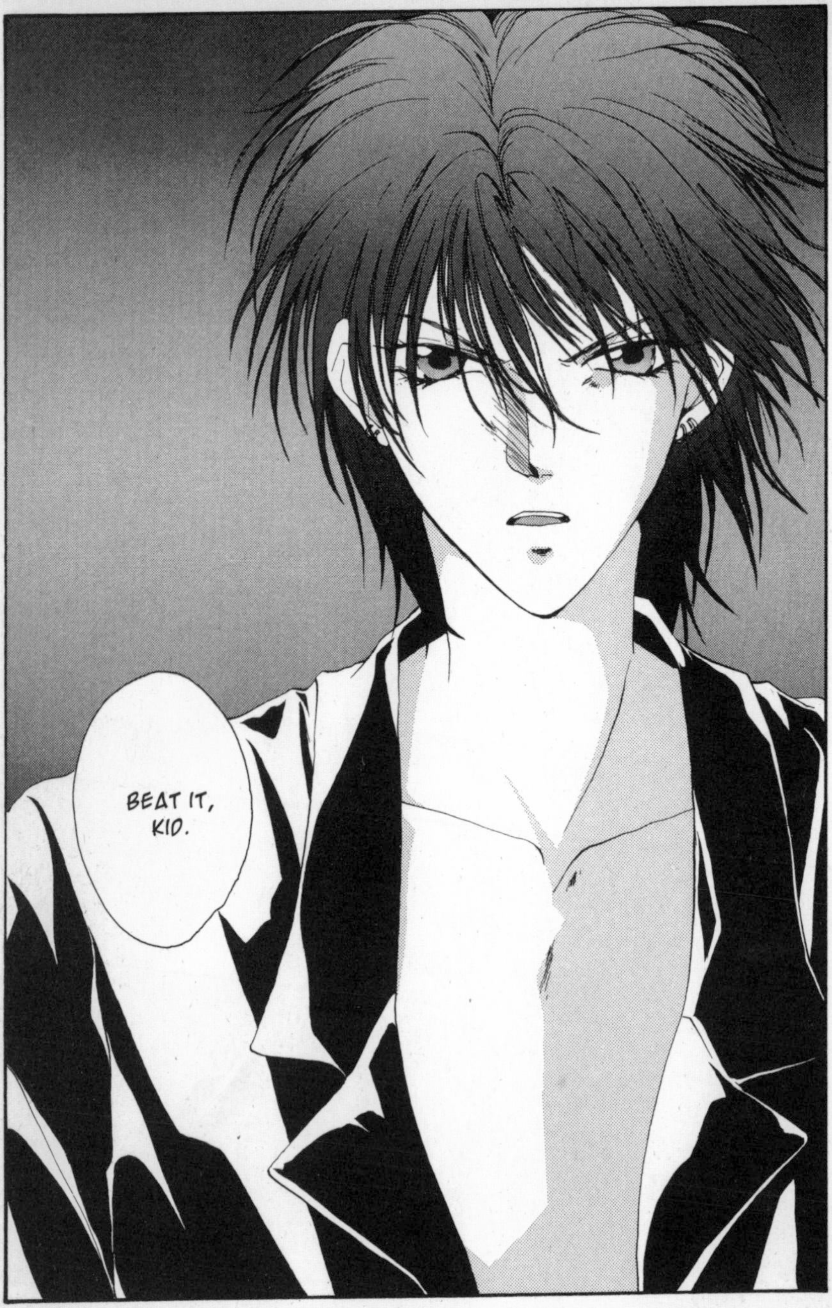
BEAT IT, KID.

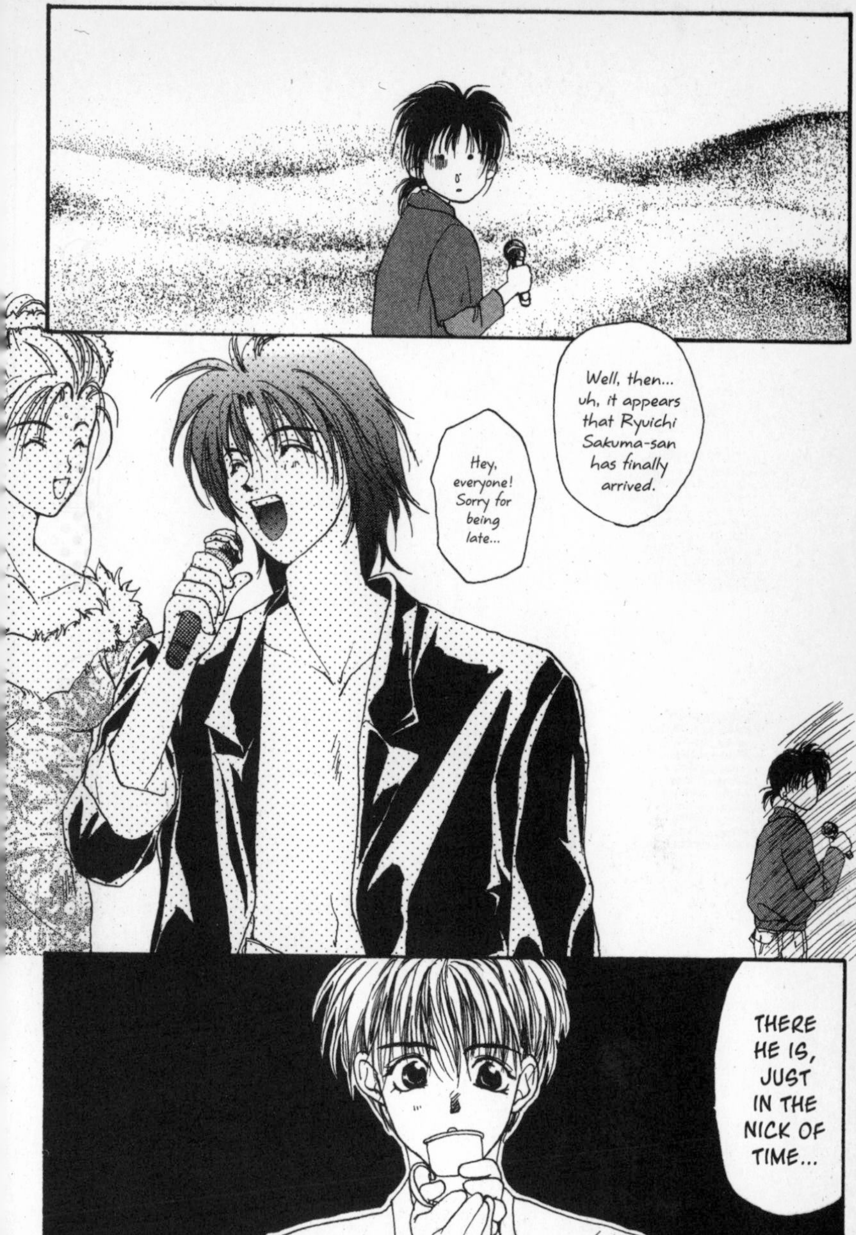
Well, then... uh, it appears that Ryuichi Sakuma-san has finally arrived.
Hey, everyone! Sorry for being late...
THERE HE IS, JUST IN THE NICK OF TIME...

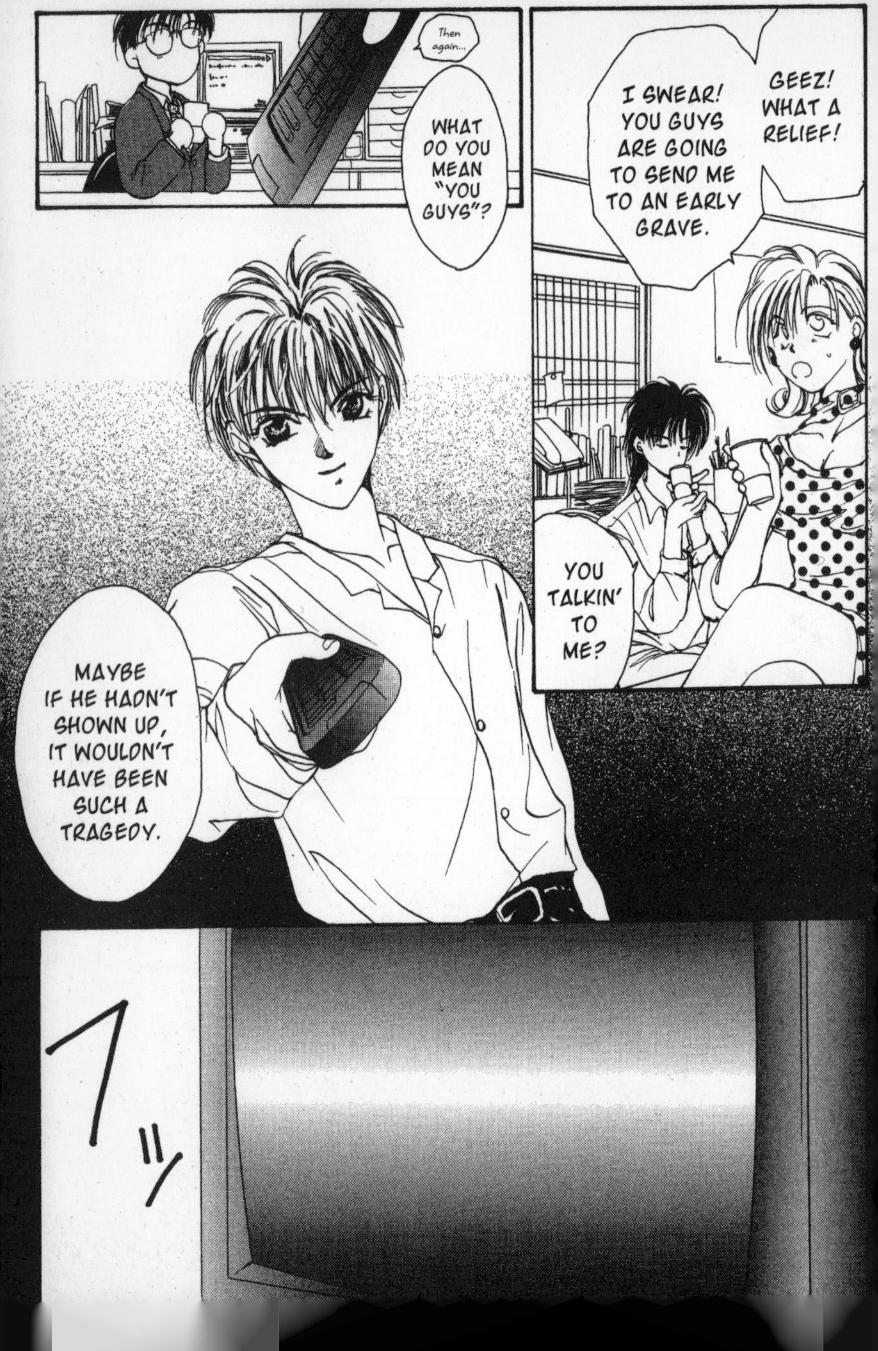
GEEZ! WHAT A RELIEF!
I SWEAR! YOU GUYS ARE GOING TO SEND ME TO AN EARLY GRAVE.
YOU TALKIN' TO ME?
Then again...
WHAT DO YOU MEAN "YOU GUYS"?
MAYBE IF HE HADN'T SHOWN UP, IT WOULDN'T HAVE BEEN SUCH A TRAGEDY.

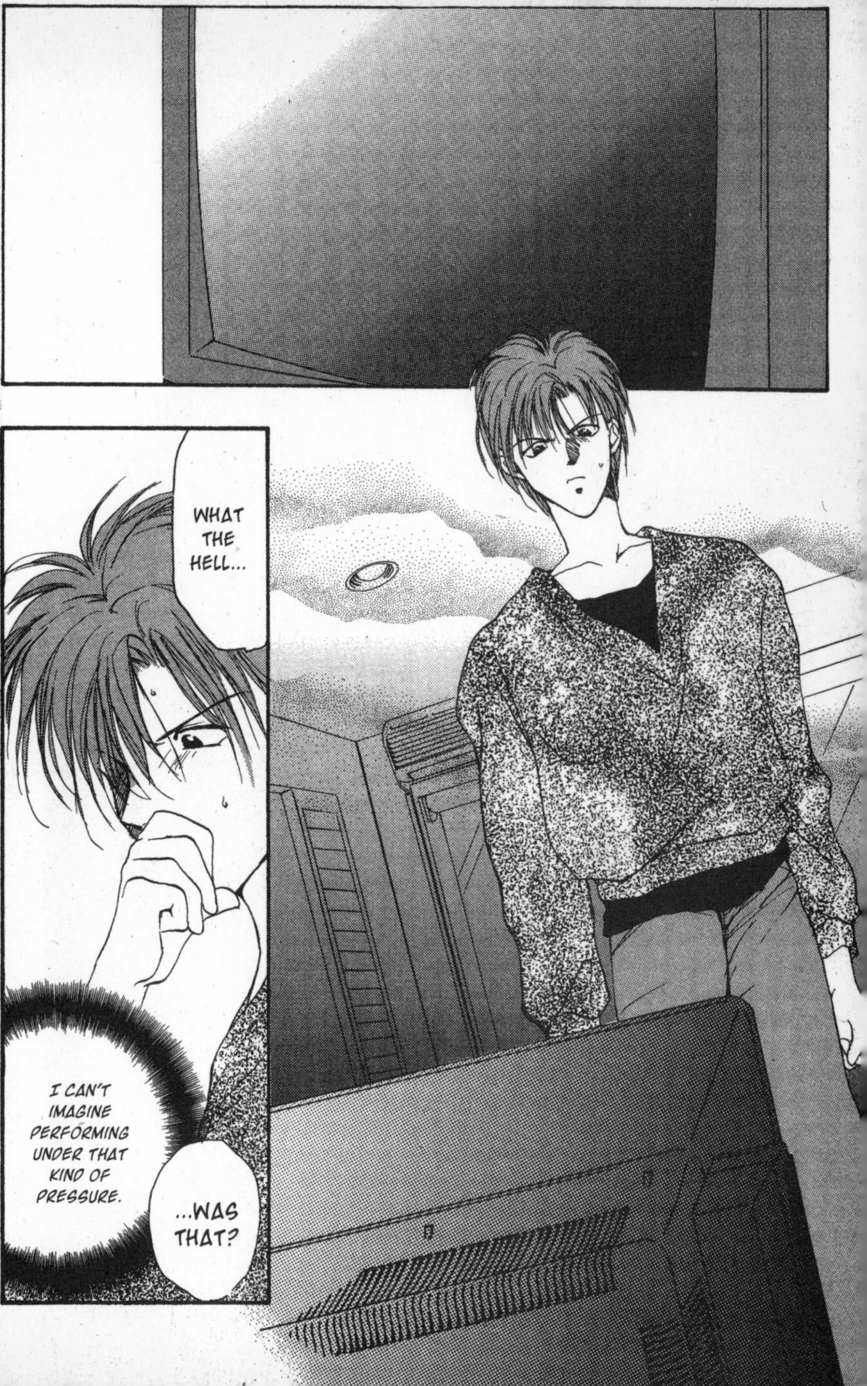
WHAT THE HELL...
...WAS THAT?
I CAN'T IMAGINE PERFORMING UNDER THAT KIND OF PRESSURE.

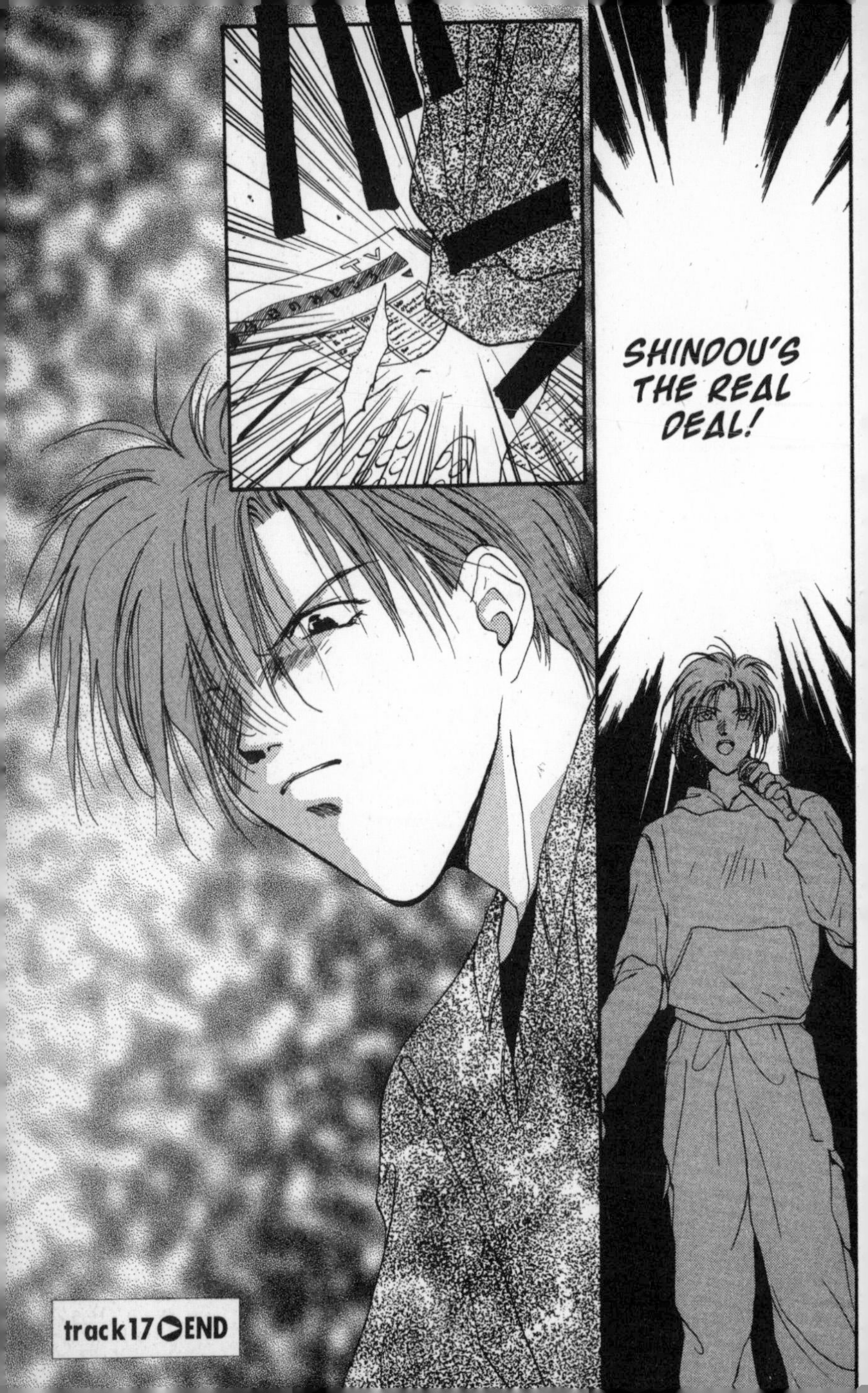
SHINDOU'S THE REAL DEAL!
track17 END

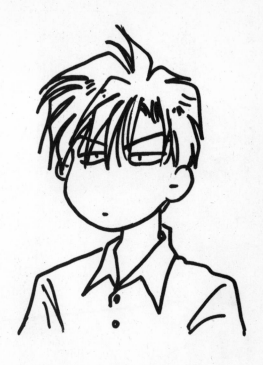

My dream... is to one day...
draw the sexiest,
nastiest erotic scene of all time.
(And to do it during this series' run!)
You've gotta be kidding! They'll kill you!
Yeah, I know. It's impossible...
Heh-heh... I know.

Gravitation

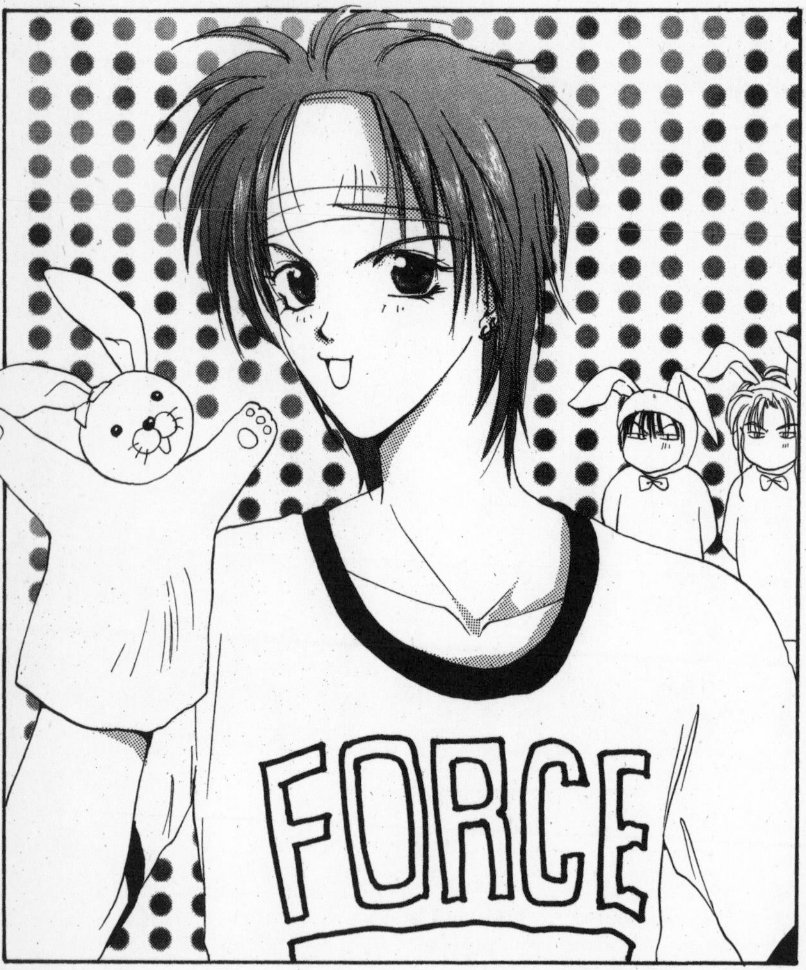
FORCE

track 18

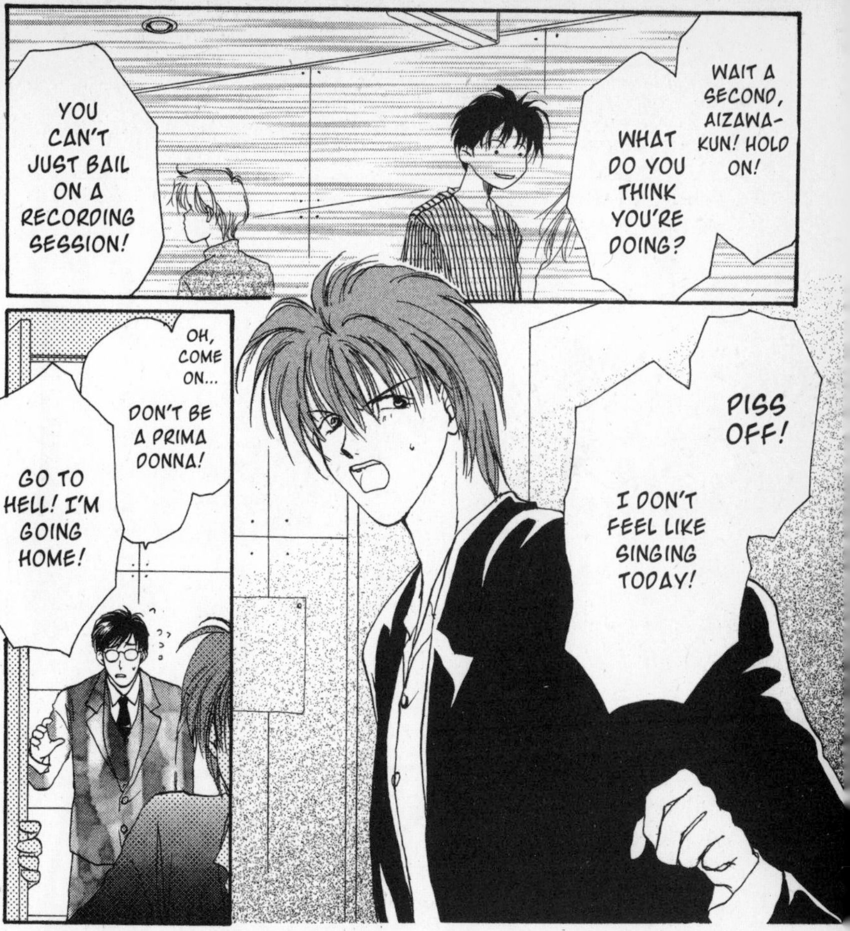
WAIT A SECOND, AIZAWA-KUN! HOLD ON!
WHAT DO YOU THINK YOU'RE DOING?
YOU CAN'T JUST BAIL ON A RECORDING SESSION!
PISS OFF!
I DON'T FEEL LIKE SINGING TODAY!
OH, COME ON...
DON'T BE A PRIMA DONNA!
GO TO HELL! I'M GOING HOME!

ABOUT GRAVITATION TRACK 18

Taki...I don't think we can call him by such a cute name anymore, not with how he's been acting... Then again, some people have been saying that he's such an asshole, they like him in a whole new way now... I guess this thuggish behavior is what everyone's been hoping to see, so I'm happy. I was beginning to wonder if I was making him too mean, but it appears not.

By the way, when we get to the pivotal scene, some people have been saying that the car comes by too conveniently—that maybe Sakano was the driver? Well, that may well be the case. I think you can pretty much assume that to be true. I won't dispute it.

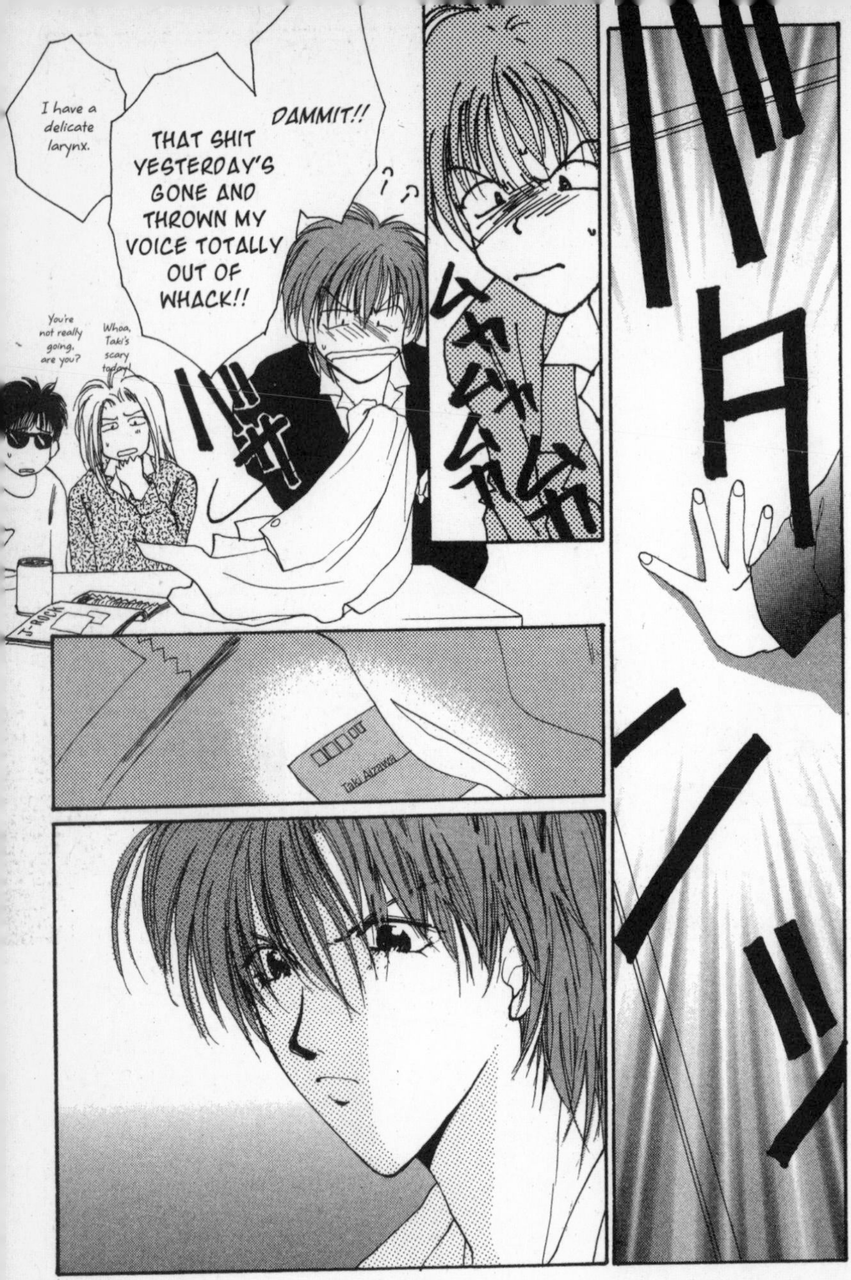

ムカムカ
DAMMIT!!
THAT SHIT YESTERDAY'S GONE AND THROWN MY VOICE TOTALLY OUT OF WHACK!!
I have a delicate larynx.
Whoa, Taki's scary today!
You're not really going, are you?
J-ROCK
Taki Aizawa

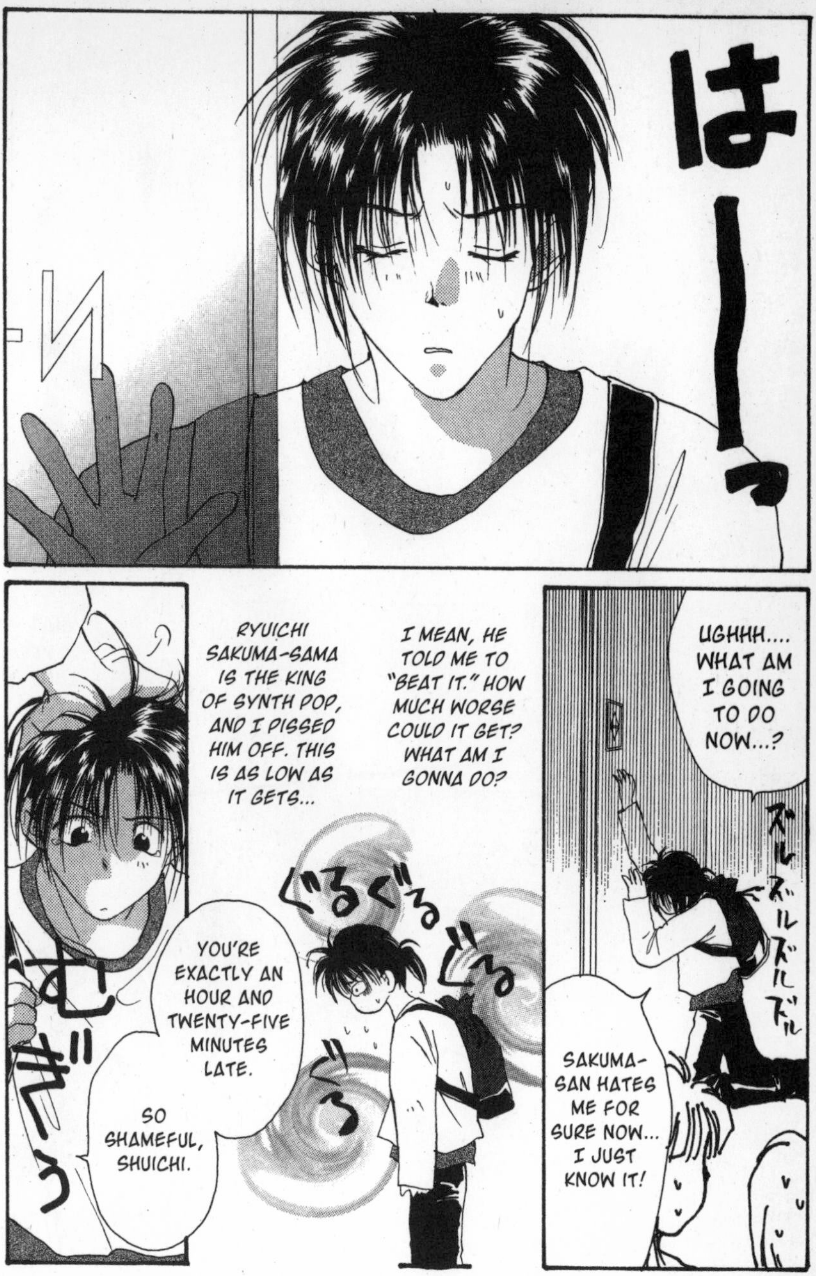
はーーっ
UGHHH.... WHAT AM I GOING TO DO NOW...?
SAKUMA-SAN HATES ME FOR SURE NOW... I JUST KNOW IT!
I MEAN, HE TOLD ME TO "BEAT IT." HOW MUCH WORSE COULD IT GET? WHAT AM I GONNA DO?
RYUICHI SAKUMA-SAMA IS THE KING OF SYNTH POP, AND I PISSED HIM OFF. THIS IS AS LOW AS IT GETS...
YOU'RE EXACTLY AN HOUR AND TWENTY-FIVE MINUTES LATE.
SO SHAMEFUL, SHUICHI.

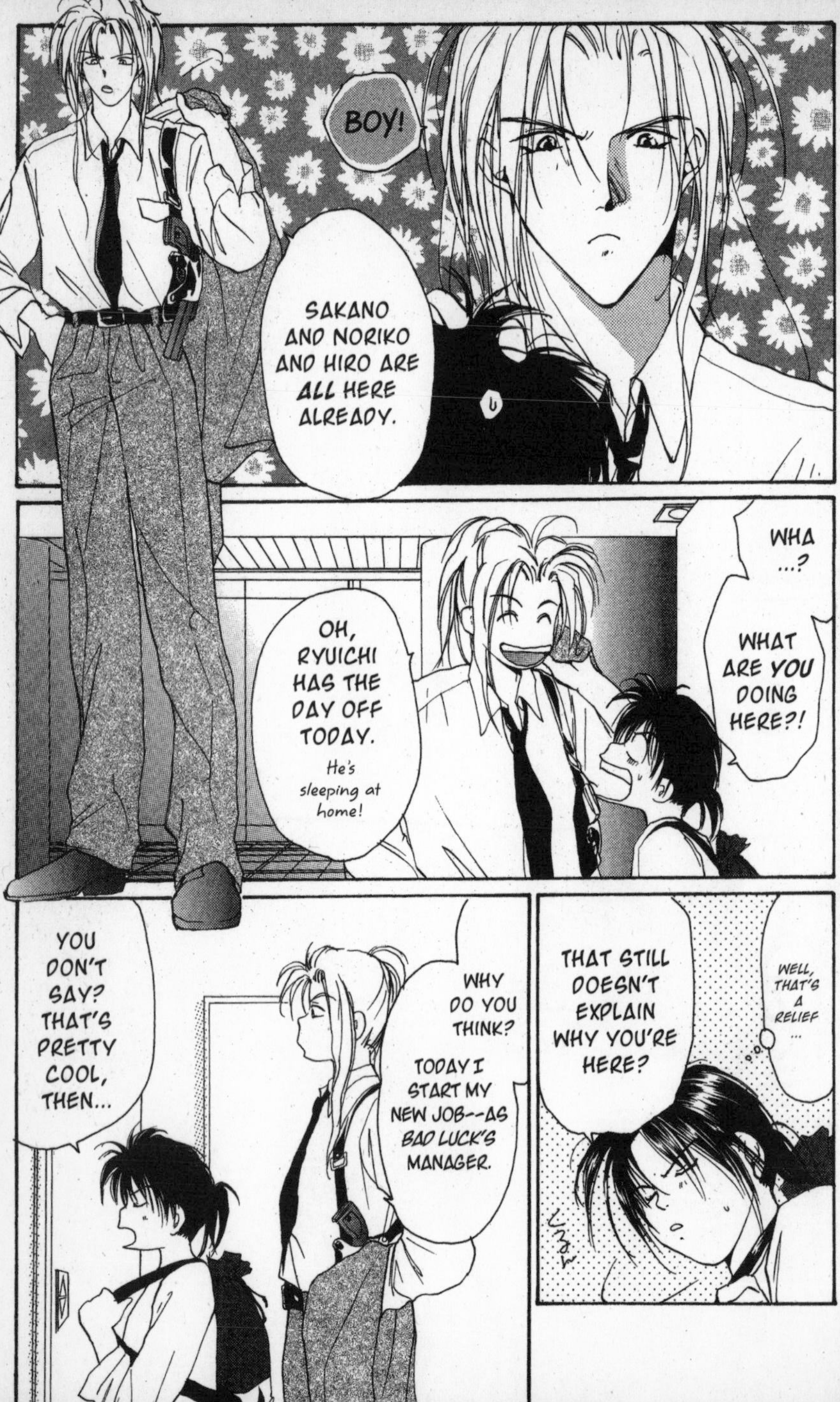
BOY!
SAKANO AND NORIKO AND HIRO ARE ALL HERE ALREADY.
WHA ...?
WHAT ARE YOU DOING HERE?!
OH, RYUICHI HAS THE DAY OFF TODAY.
He's sleeping at home!
WELL, THAT'S A RELIEF ...
THAT STILL DOESN'T EXPLAIN WHY YOU'RE HERE?
WHY DO YOU THINK?
TODAY I START MY NEW JOB--AS BAD LUCK'S MANAGER.
YOU DON'T SAY? THAT'S PRETTY COOL, THEN...

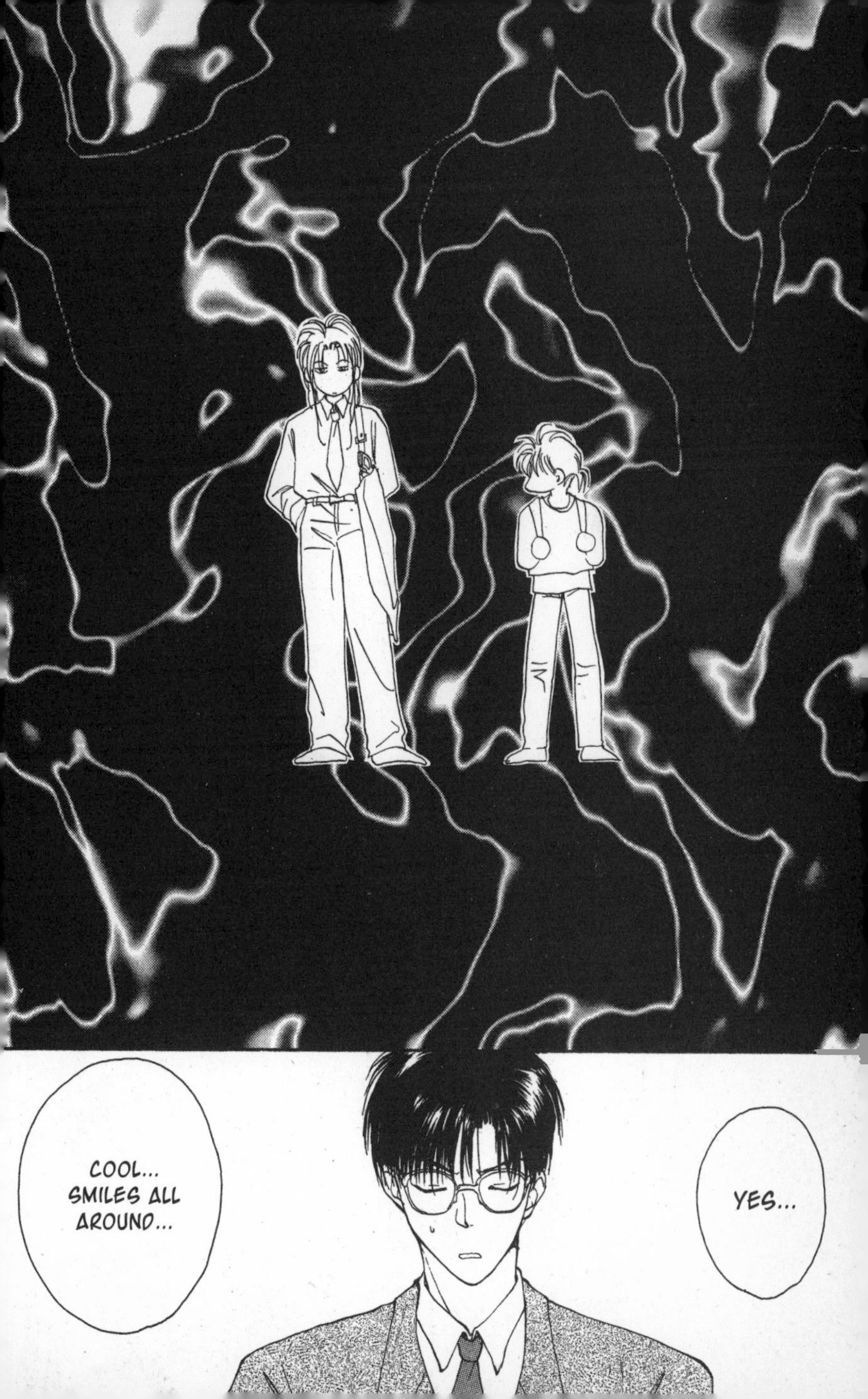
YES...
COOL... SMILES ALL AROUND...

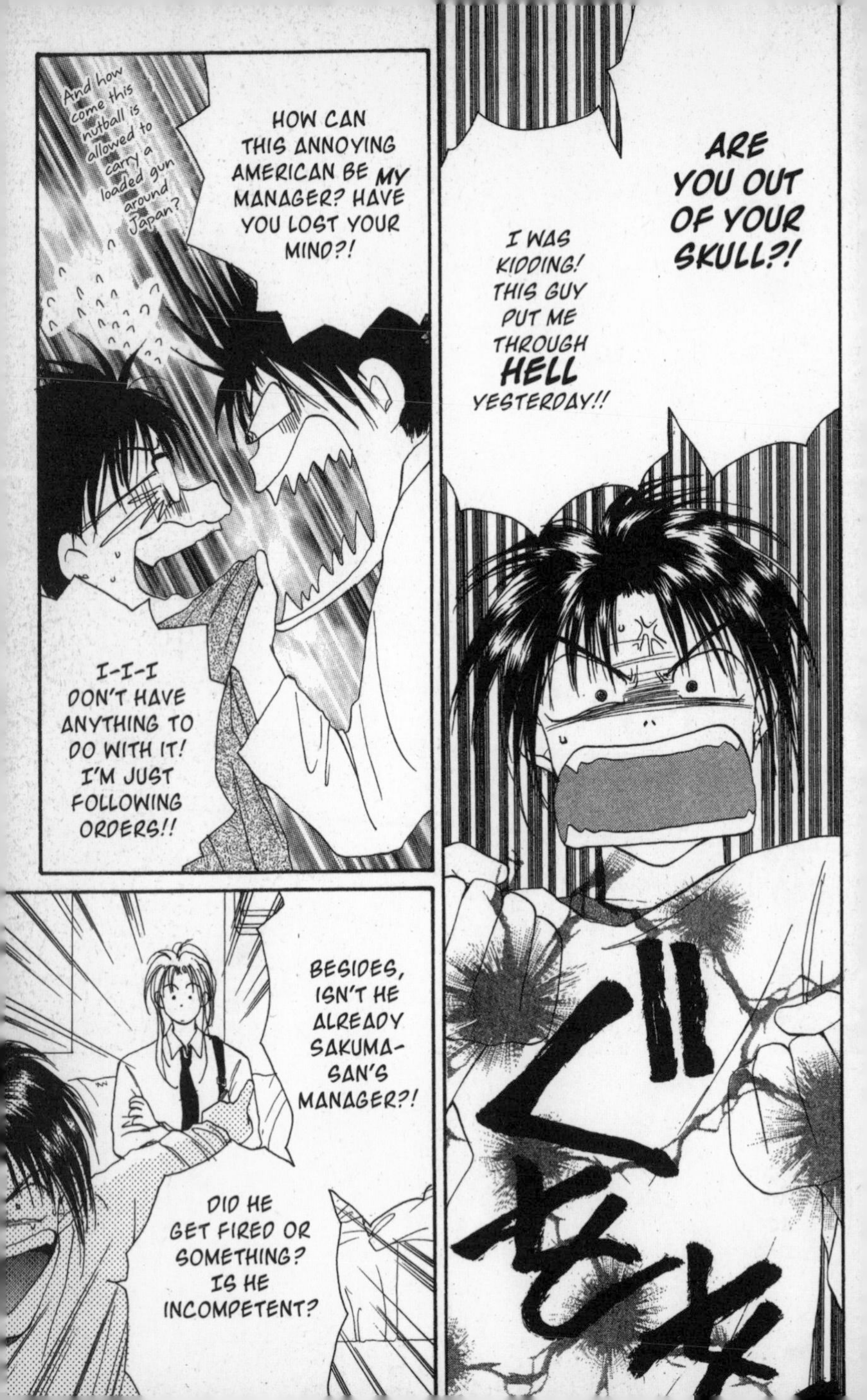
ARE YOU OUT OF YOUR SKULL?!
I WAS KIDDING! THIS GUY PUT ME THROUGH HELL YESTERDAY!!
HOW CAN THIS ANNOYING AMERICAN BE MY MANAGER? HAVE YOU LOST YOUR MIND?!
And how come this nutball is allowed to carry a loaded gun around Japan?
I-I-I DON'T HAVE ANYTHING TO DO WITH IT! I'M JUST FOLLOWING ORDERS!!
BESIDES, ISN'T HE ALREADY SAKUMA-SAN'S MANAGER?!
DID HE GET FIRED OR SOMETHING? IS HE INCOMPETENT?

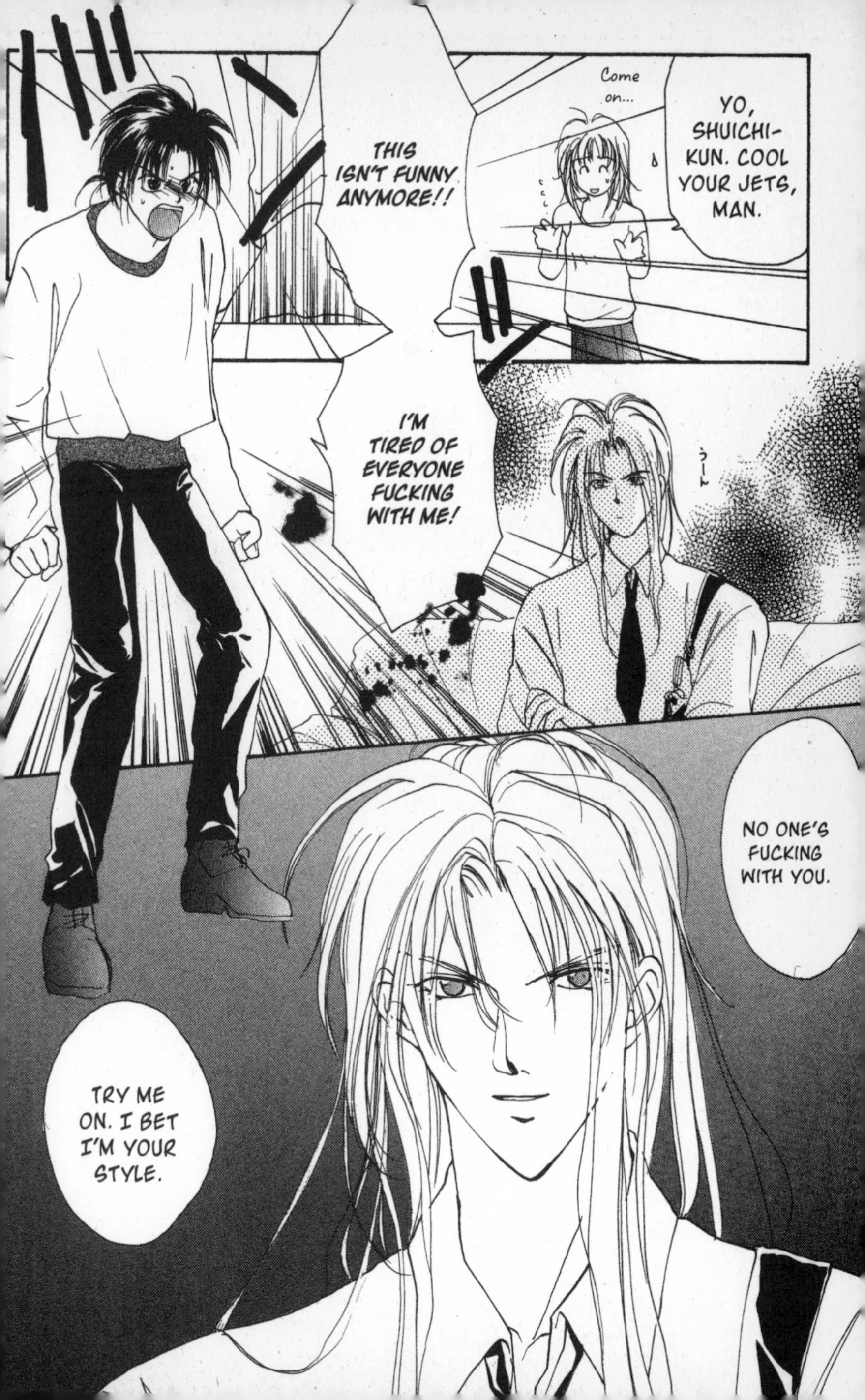

YO, SHUICHI-KUN. COOL YOUR JETS, MAN.
Come on...
THIS ISN'T FUNNY ANYMORE!!
I'M TIRED OF EVERYONE FUCKING WITH ME!
NO ONE'S FUCKING WITH YOU.
TRY ME ON. I BET I'M YOUR STYLE.

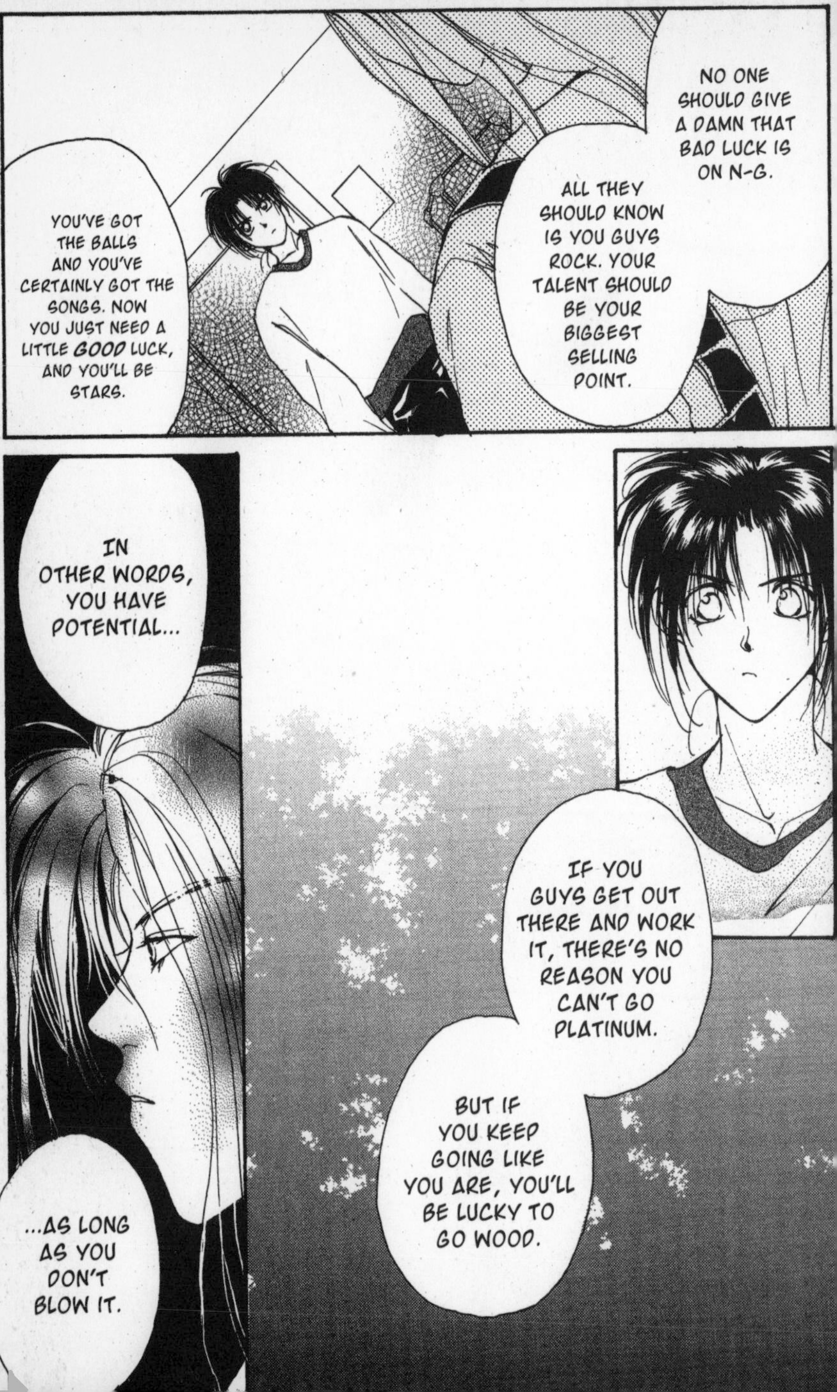
NO ONE SHOULD GIVE A DAMN THAT BAD LUCK IS ON N-G.
ALL THEY SHOULD KNOW IS YOU GUYS ROCK. YOUR TALENT SHOULD BE YOUR BIGGEST SELLING POINT.
YOU'VE GOT THE BALLS AND YOU'VE CERTAINLY GOT THE SONGS. NOW YOU JUST NEED A LITTLE *GOOD* LUCK, AND YOU'LL BE STARS.
IF YOU GUYS GET OUT THERE AND WORK IT, THERE'S NO REASON YOU CAN'T GO PLATINUM.
BUT IF YOU KEEP GOING LIKE YOU ARE, YOU'LL BE LUCKY TO GO WOOD.
IN OTHER WORDS, YOU HAVE POTENTIAL...
...AS LONG AS YOU DON'T BLOW IT.

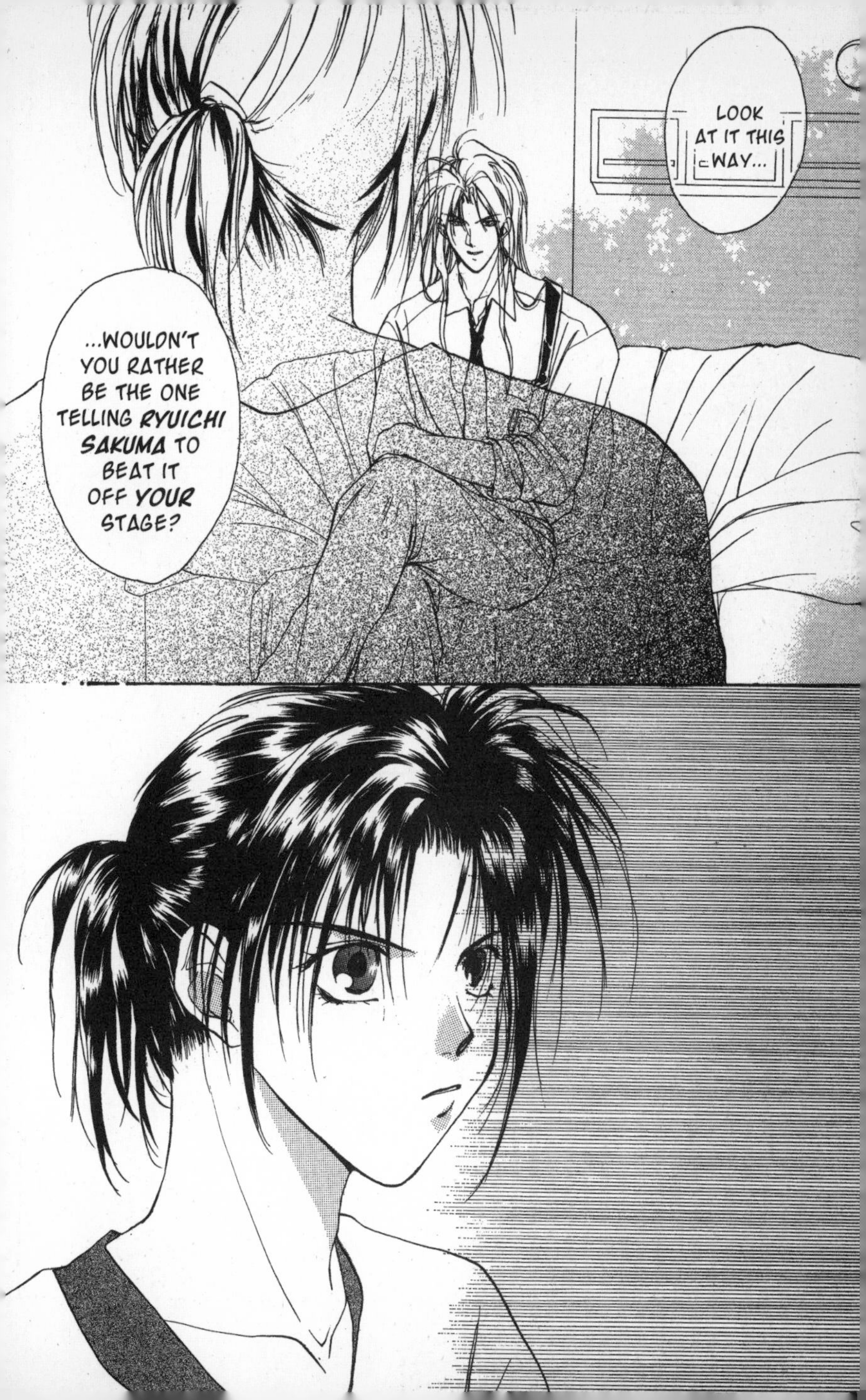
LOOK AT IT THIS WAY...
...WOULDN'T YOU RATHER BE THE ONE TELLING RYUICHI SAKUMA TO BEAT IT OFF YOUR STAGE?

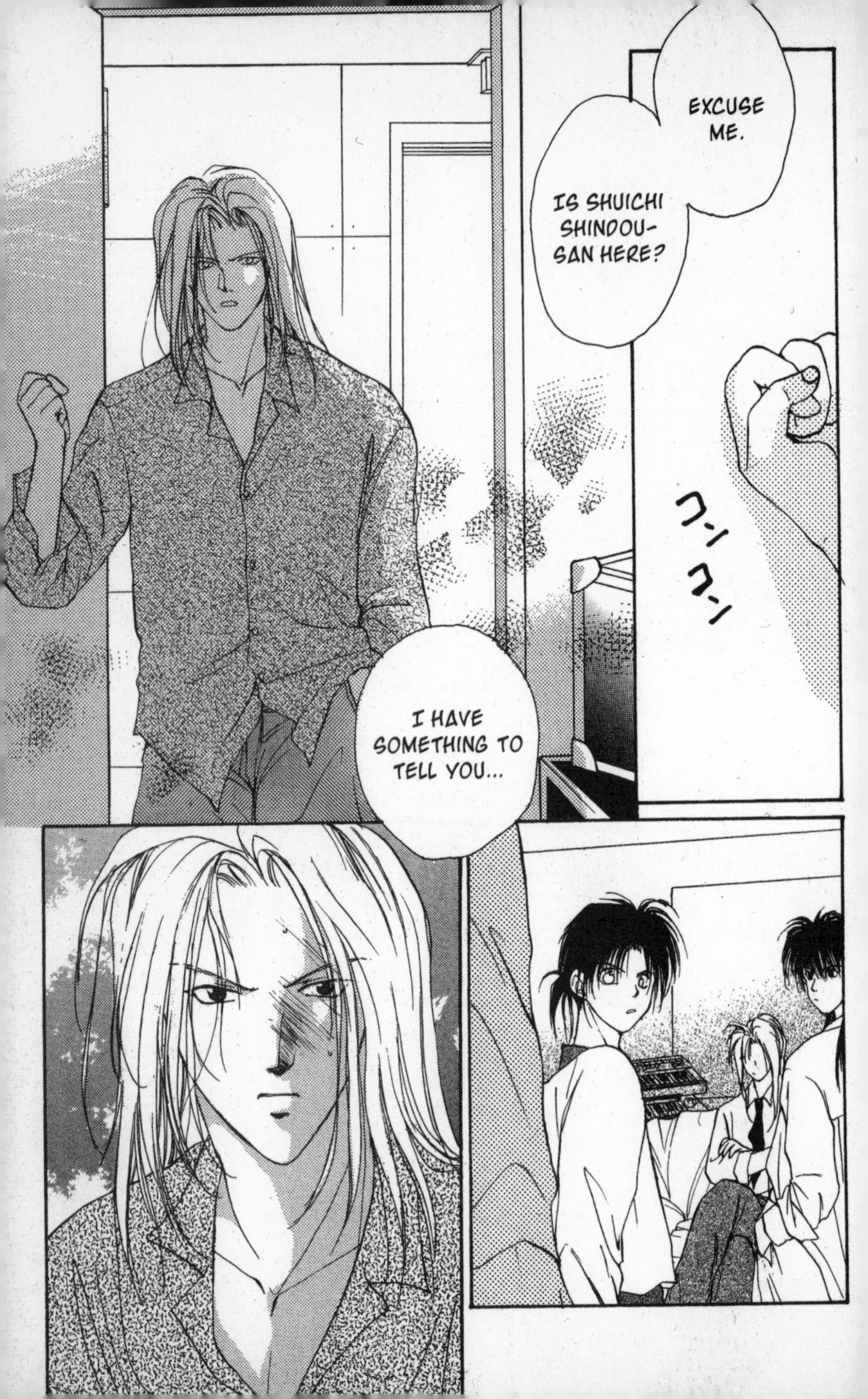
EXCUSE ME.
IS SHUICHI SHINDOU-SAN HERE?
コンコン
I HAVE SOMETHING TO TELL YOU...

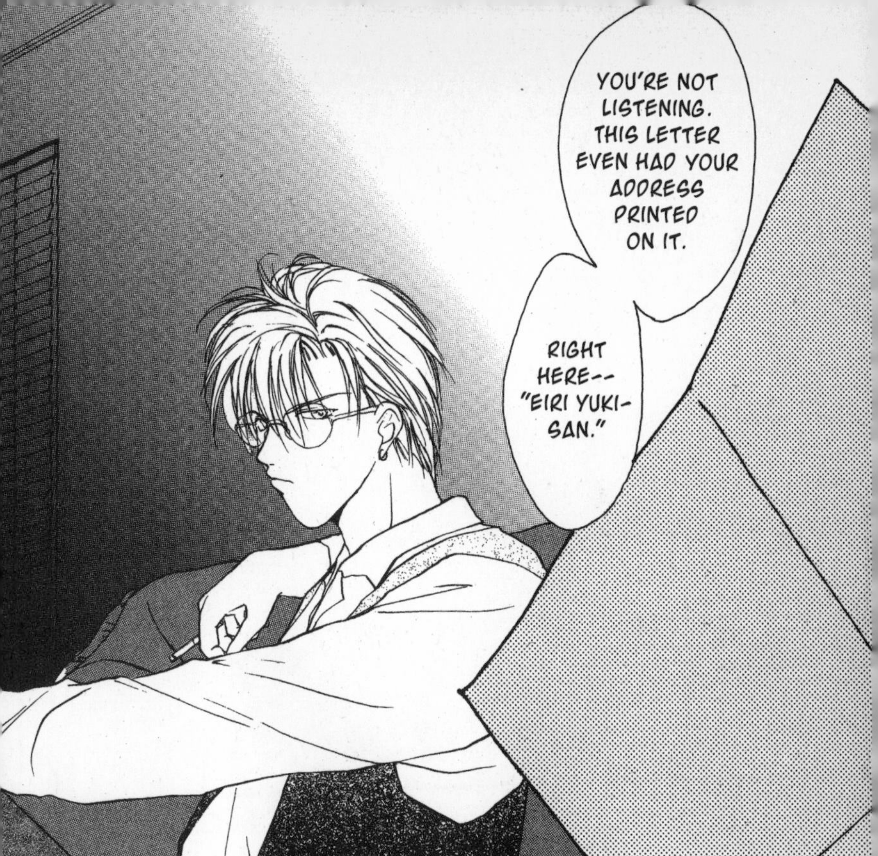
YOU'RE NOT LISTENING. THIS LETTER EVEN HAD YOUR ADDRESS PRINTED ON IT.
RIGHT HERE-- "EIRI YUKI-SAN."
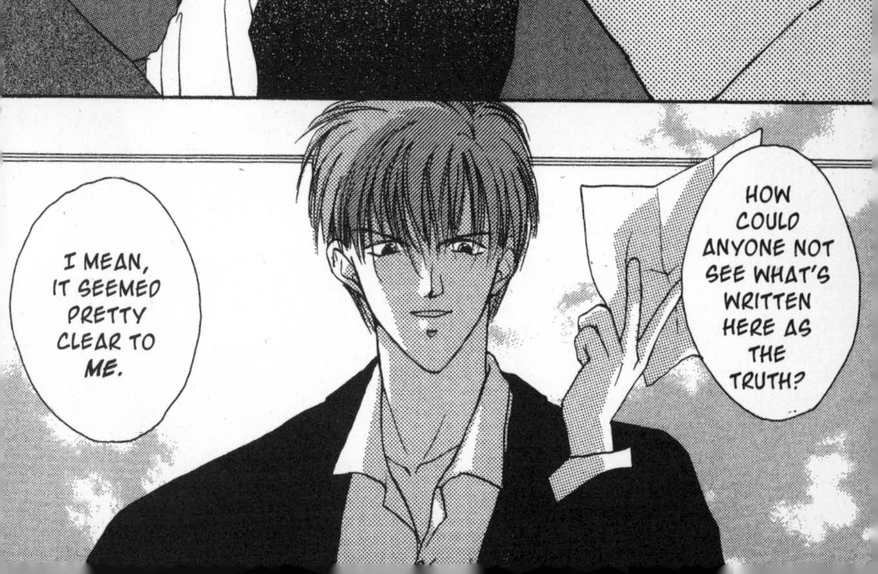
HOW COULD ANYONE NOT SEE WHAT'S WRITTEN HERE AS THE TRUTH?
I MEAN, IT SEEMED PRETTY CLEAR TO ME.

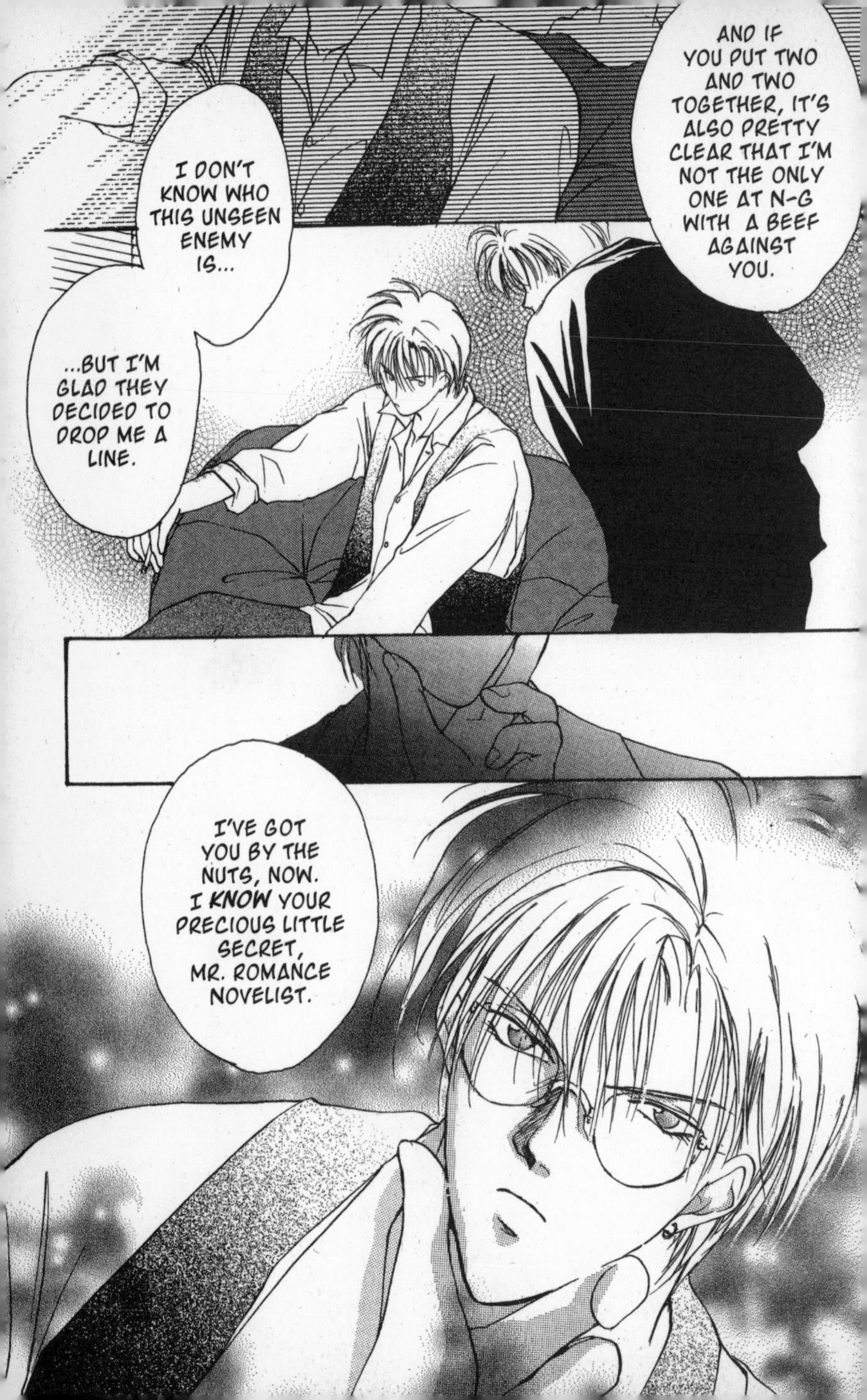
AND IF YOU PUT TWO AND TWO TOGETHER, IT'S ALSO PRETTY CLEAR THAT I'M NOT THE ONLY ONE AT N-G WITH A BEEF AGAINST YOU.
I DON'T KNOW WHO THIS UNSEEN ENEMY IS...
...BUT I'M GLAD THEY DECIDED TO DROP ME A LINE.
I'VE GOT YOU BY THE NUTS, NOW. I *KNOW* YOUR PRECIOUS LITTLE SECRET, MR. ROMANCE NOVELIST.

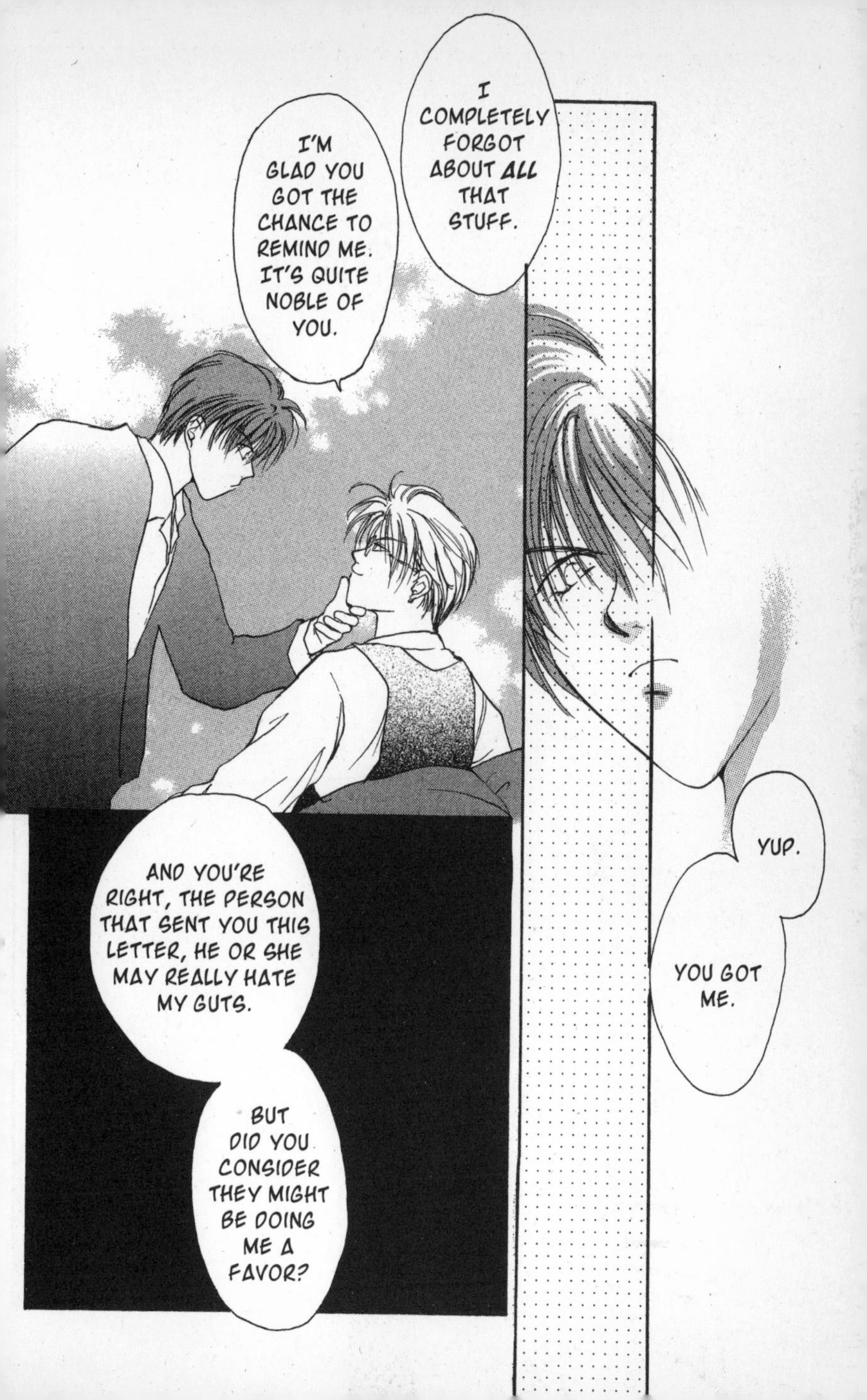

I COMPLETELY FORGOT ABOUT ALL THAT STUFF.
I'M GLAD YOU GOT THE CHANCE TO REMIND ME. IT'S QUITE NOBLE OF YOU.
AND YOU'RE RIGHT, THE PERSON THAT SENT YOU THIS LETTER, HE OR SHE MAY REALLY HATE MY GUTS.
BUT DID YOU CONSIDER THEY MIGHT BE DOING ME A FAVOR?
YUP.
YOU GOT ME.

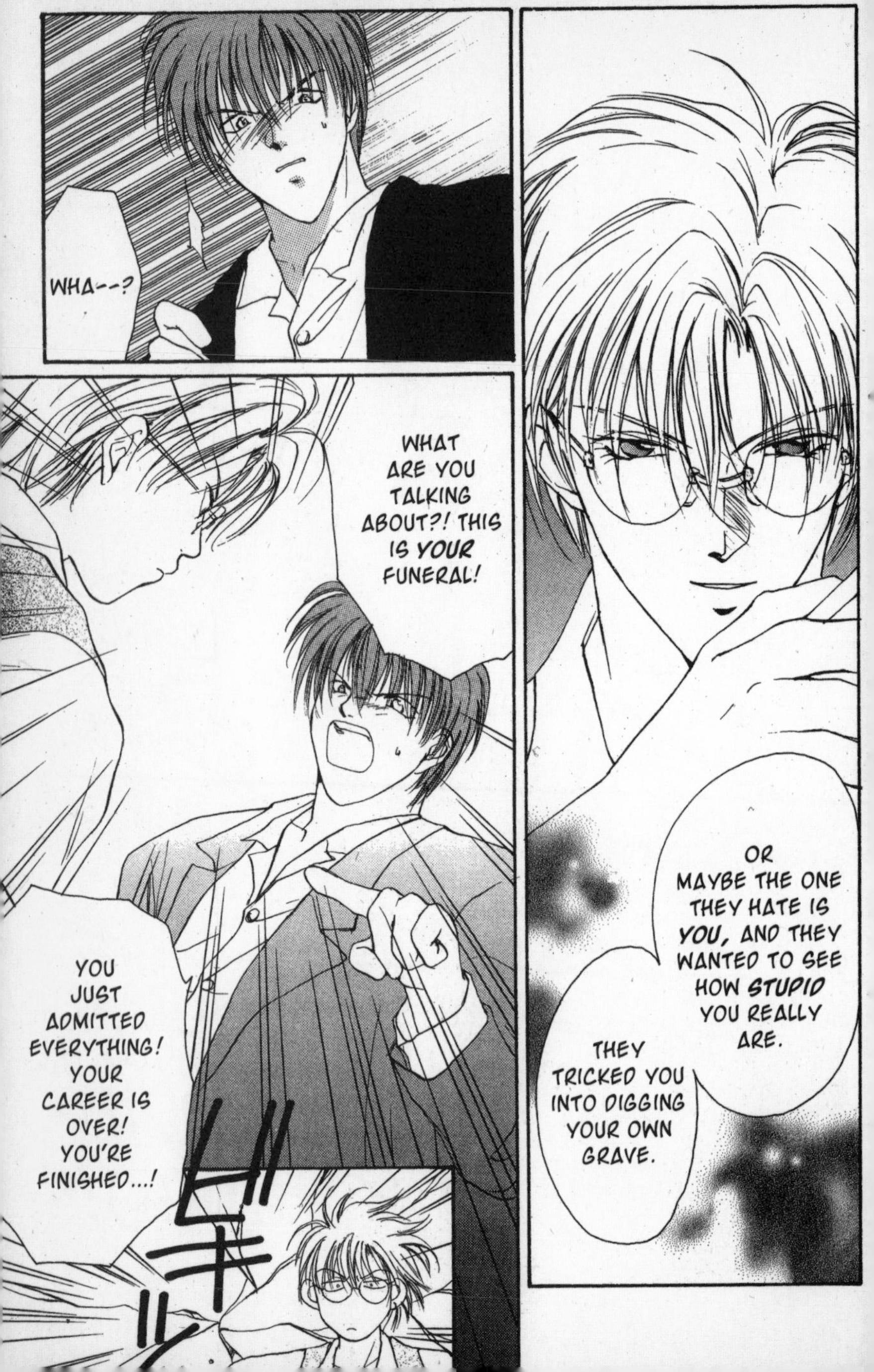

OR MAYBE THE ONE THEY HATE IS *YOU*, AND THEY WANTED TO SEE HOW *STUPID* YOU REALLY ARE.
THEY TRICKED YOU INTO DIGGING YOUR OWN GRAVE.
WHA--?
WHAT ARE YOU TALKING ABOUT?! THIS IS *YOUR* FUNERAL!
YOU JUST ADMITTED EVERYTHING! YOUR CAREER IS OVER! YOU'RE FINISHED...!
ビキッ

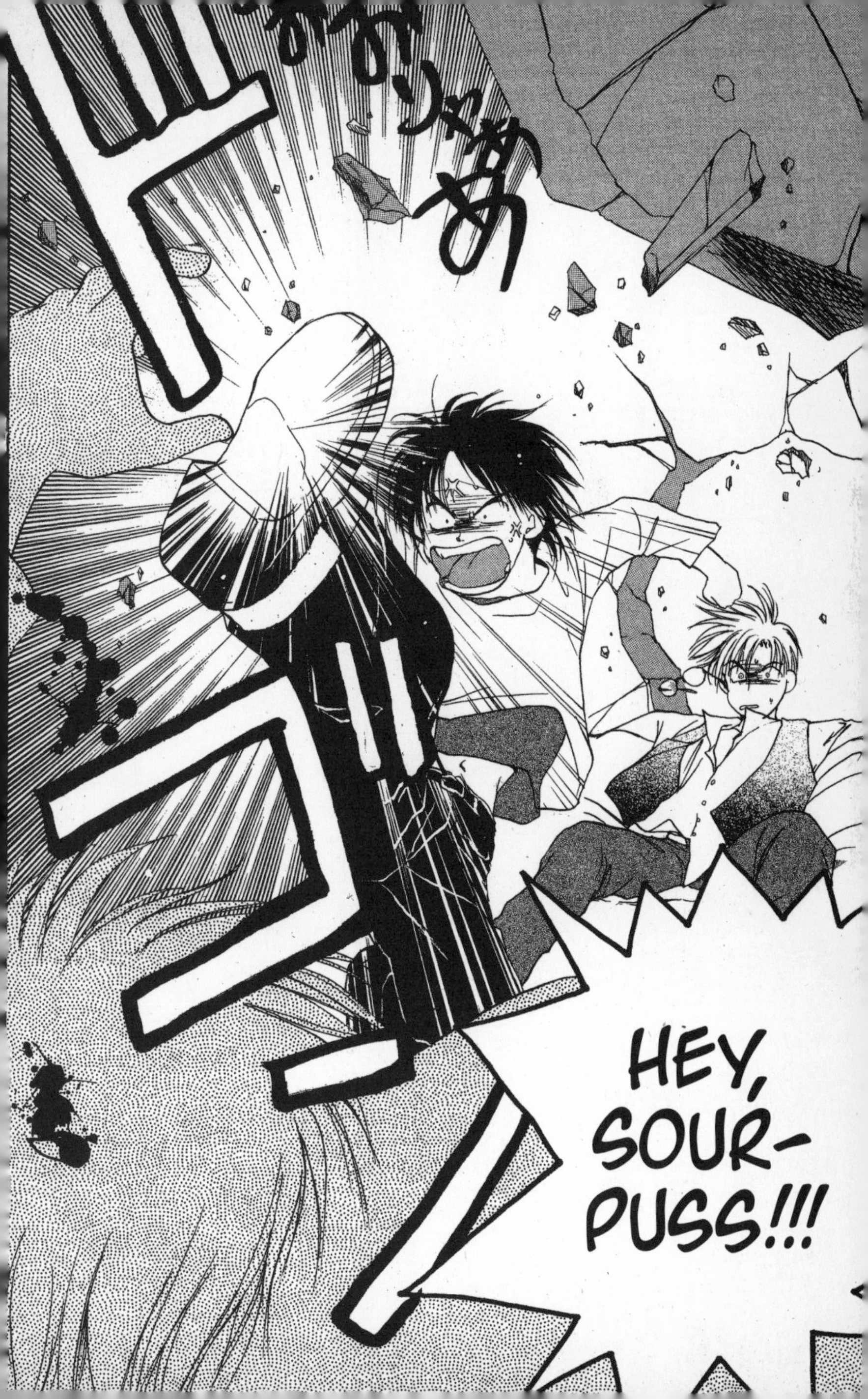
HEY, SOUR-PUSS!!!

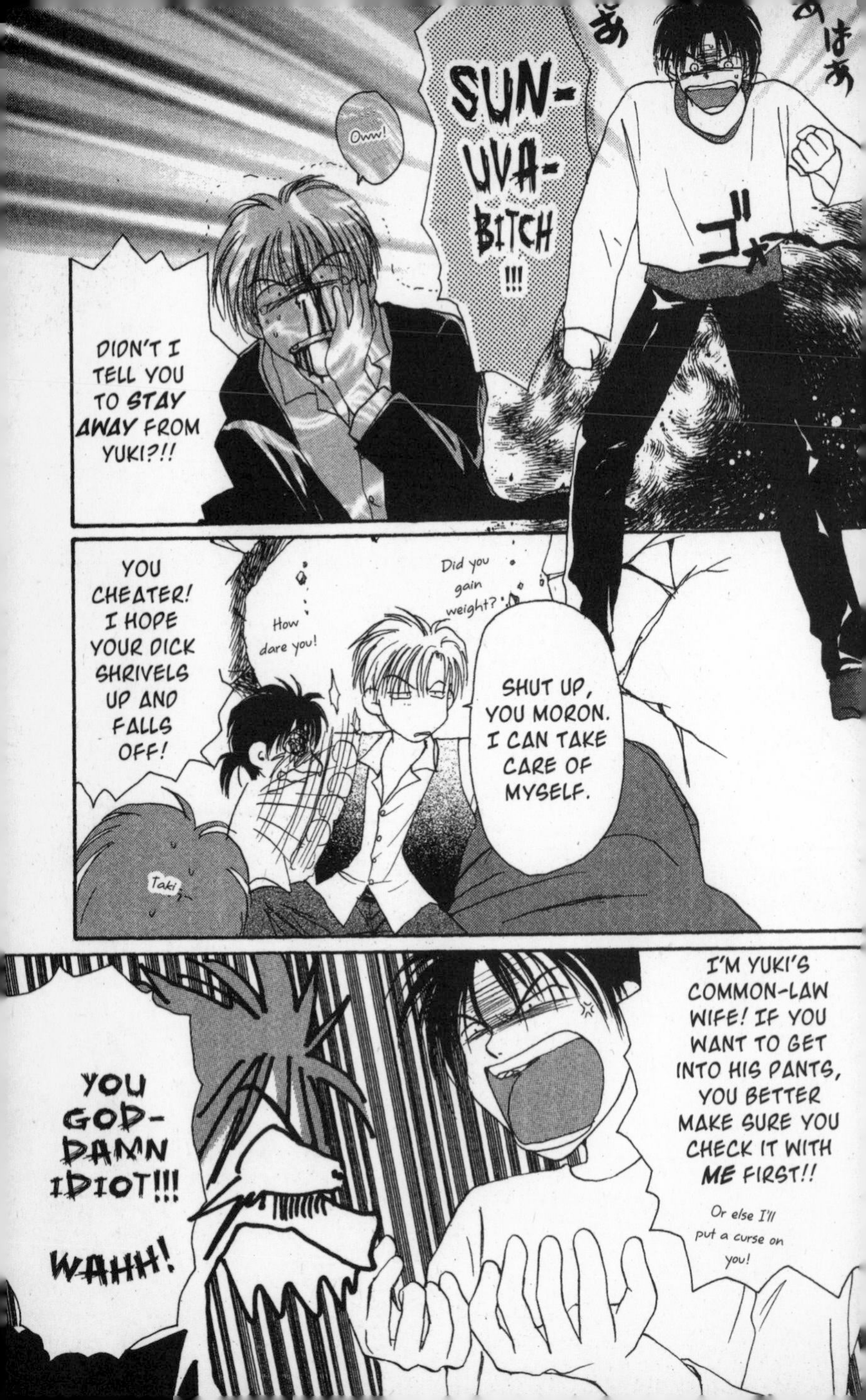
SUN-UVA-BITCH!!!
ゴォ
Oww!
DIDN'T I TELL YOU TO STAY AWAY FROM YUKI?!!
SHUT UP, YOU MORON. I CAN TAKE CARE OF MYSELF.
Did you gain weight?
How dare you!
YOU CHEATER! I HOPE YOUR DICK SHRIVELS UP AND FALLS OFF!
Taki,
I'M YUKI'S COMMON-LAW WIFE! IF YOU WANT TO GET INTO HIS PANTS, YOU BETTER MAKE SURE YOU CHECK IT WITH ME FIRST!!
Or else I'll put a curse on you!
YOU GOD-DAMN IDIOT!!!
WAHH!

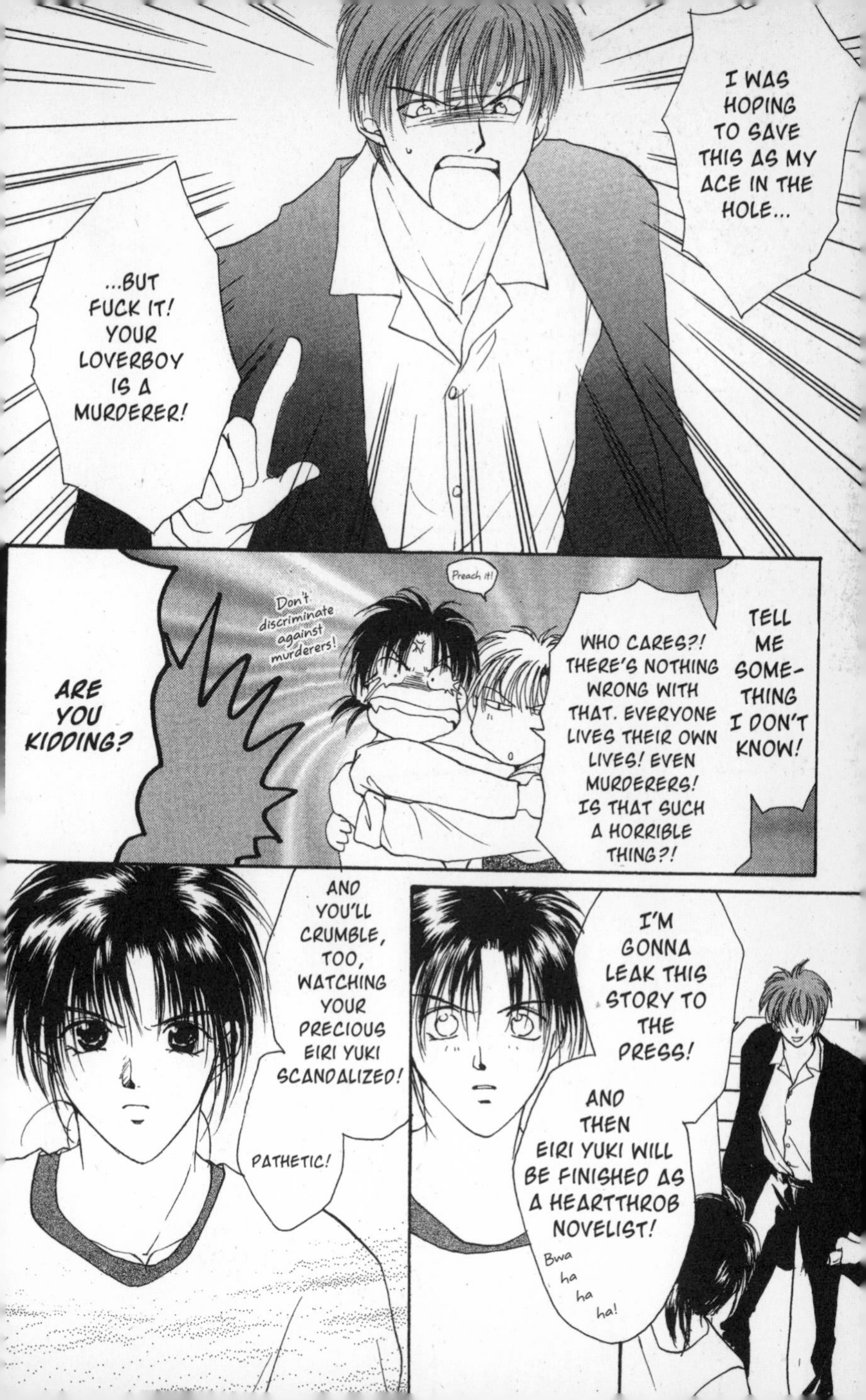

I WAS HOPING TO SAVE THIS AS MY ACE IN THE HOLE...
...BUT FUCK IT! YOUR LOVERBOY IS A MURDERER!
TELL ME SOME-THING I DON'T KNOW!
WHO CARES?! THERE'S NOTHING WRONG WITH THAT. EVERYONE LIVES THEIR OWN LIVES! EVEN MURDERERS! IS THAT SUCH A HORRIBLE THING?!
Preach it!
Don't discriminate against murderers!
ARE YOU KIDDING?
I'M GONNA LEAK THIS STORY TO THE PRESS!
AND THEN EIRI YUKI WILL BE FINISHED AS A HEARTTHROB NOVELIST!
Bwa ha ha ha!
AND YOU'LL CRUMBLE, TOO, WATCHING YOUR PRECIOUS EIRI YUKI SCANDALIZED!
PATHETIC!

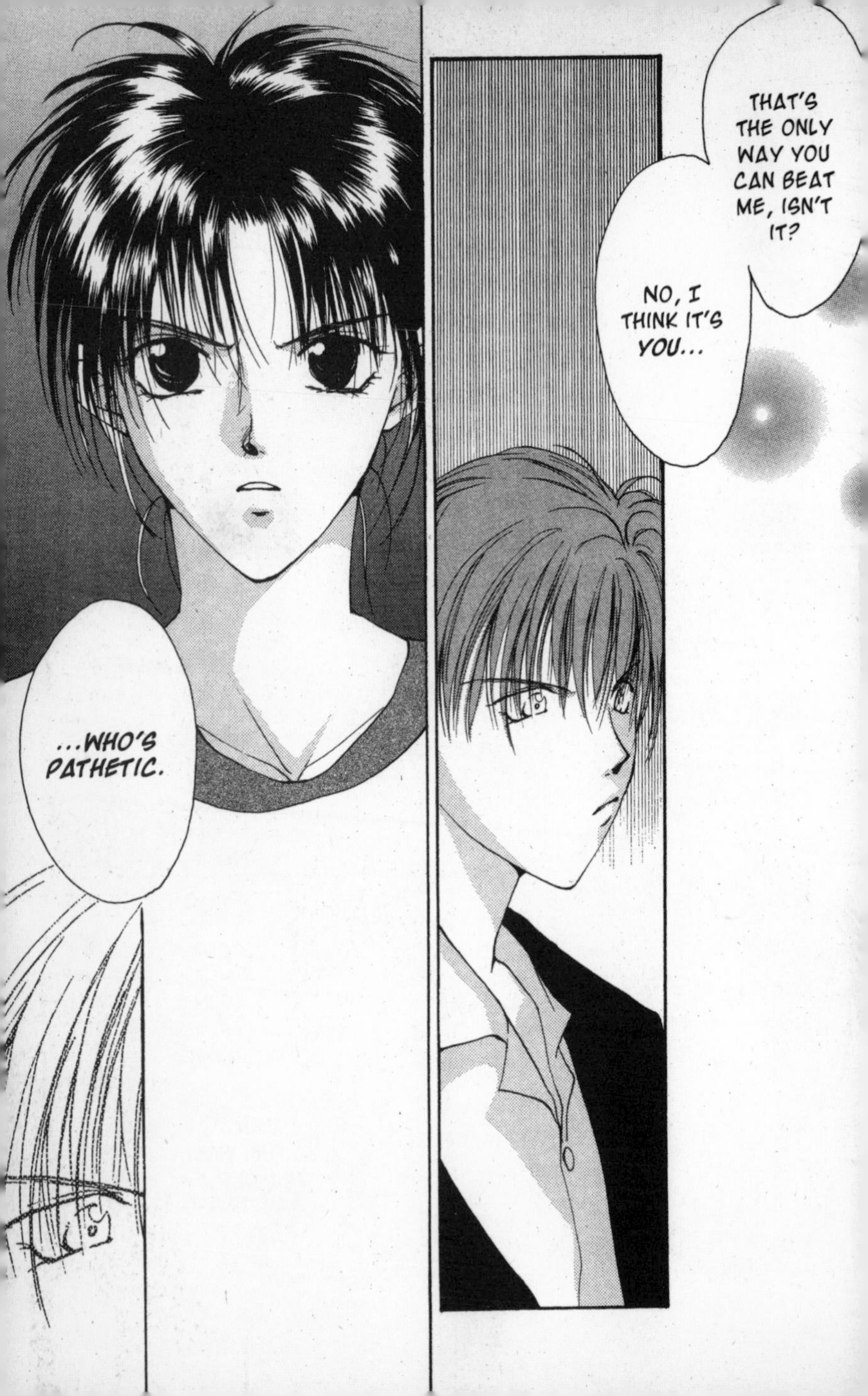
THAT'S THE ONLY WAY YOU CAN BEAT ME, ISN'T IT?
NO, I THINK IT'S YOU...
...WHO'S PATHETIC.

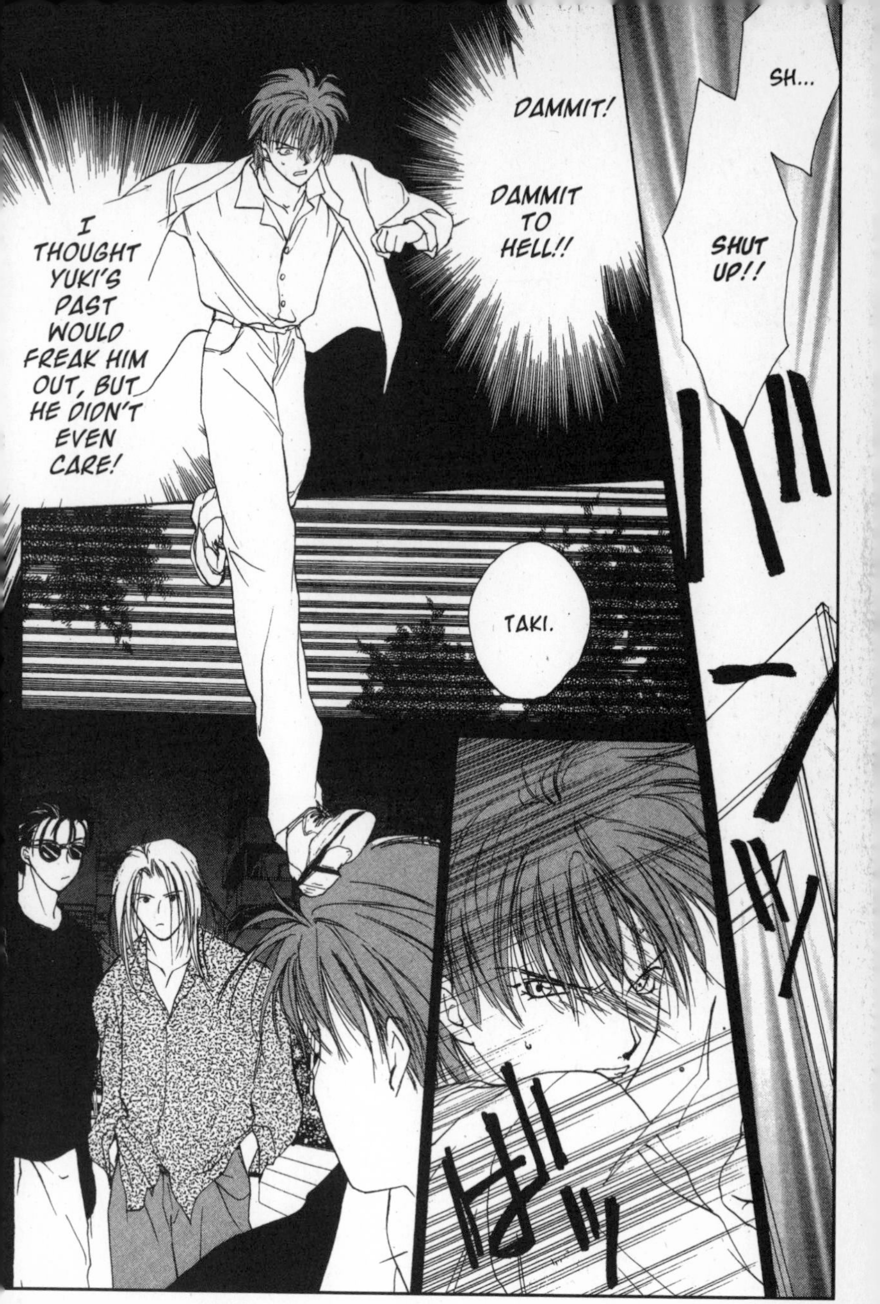
SH...
SHUT UP!!
DAMMIT!
DAMMIT TO HELL!!
I THOUGHT YUKI'S PAST WOULD FREAK HIM OUT, BUT HE DIDN'T EVEN CARE!
TAKI.

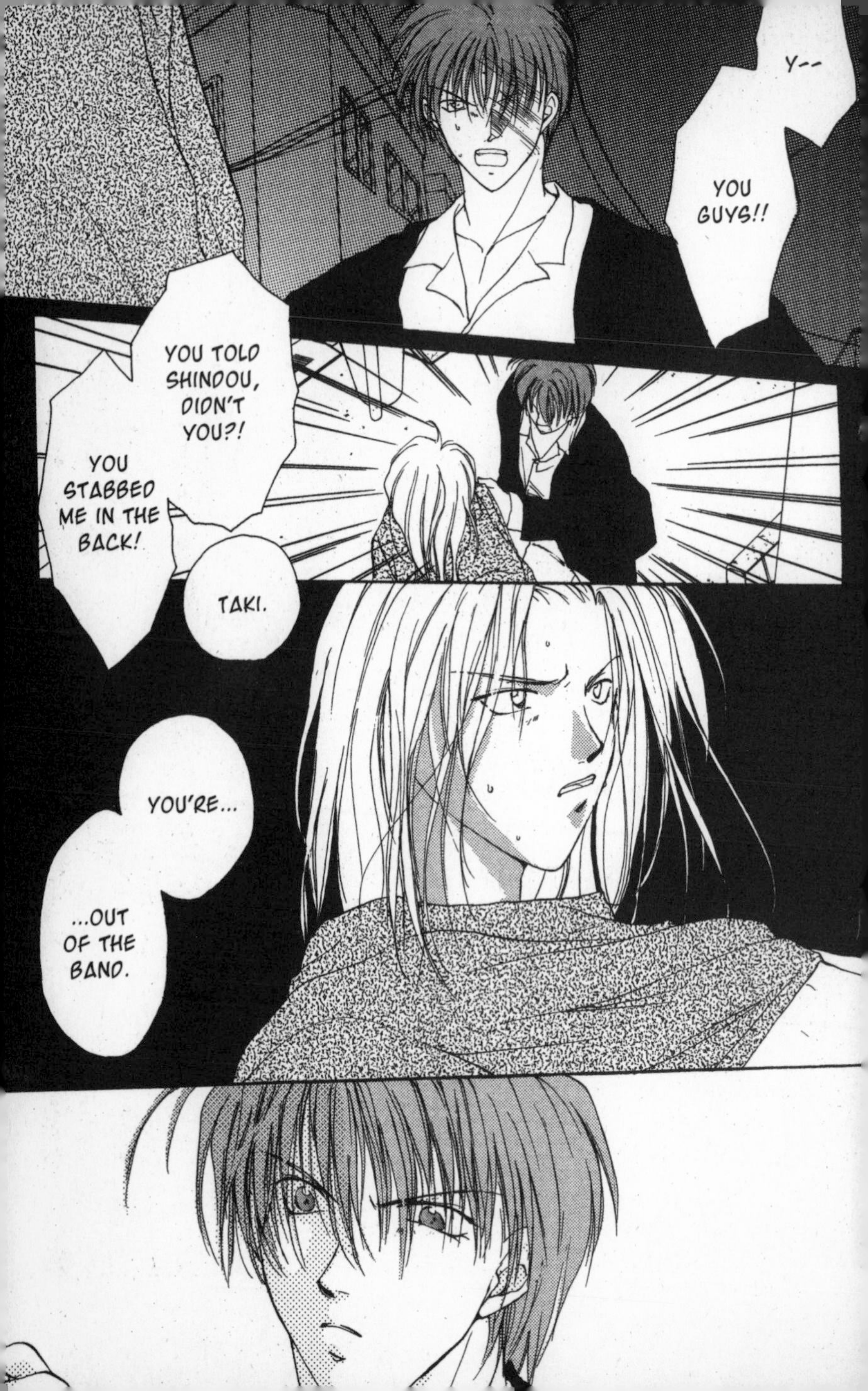
Y--
YOU GUYS!!
YOU TOLD SHINDOU, DIDN'T YOU?!
YOU STABBED ME IN THE BACK!
TAKI.
YOU'RE...
...OUT OF THE BAND.

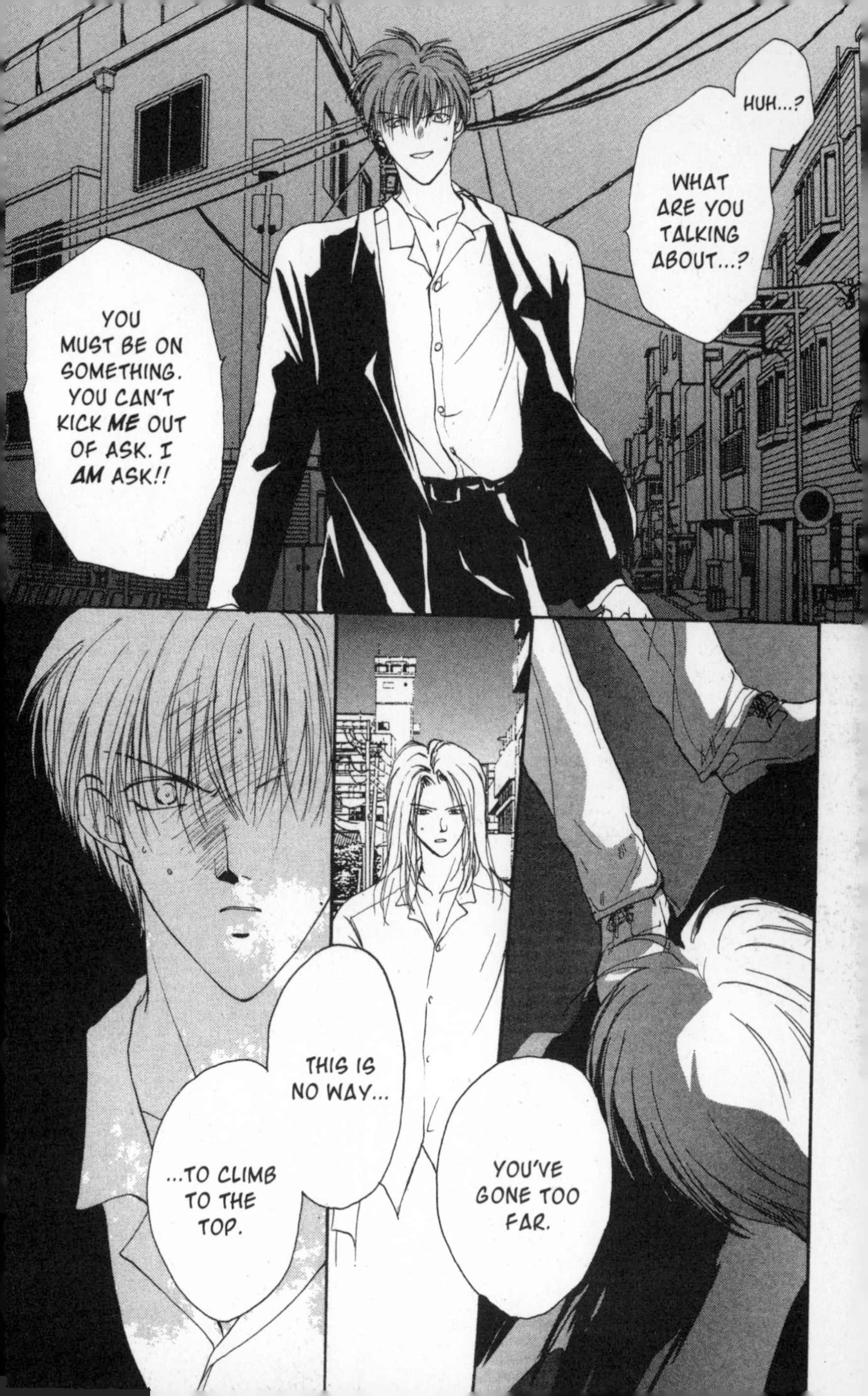
HUH...?
WHAT ARE YOU TALKING ABOUT...?
YOU MUST BE ON SOMETHING. YOU CAN'T KICK **ME** OUT OF ASK. I **AM** ASK!!
YOU'VE GONE TOO FAR.
THIS IS NO WAY...
...TO CLIMB TO THE TOP.

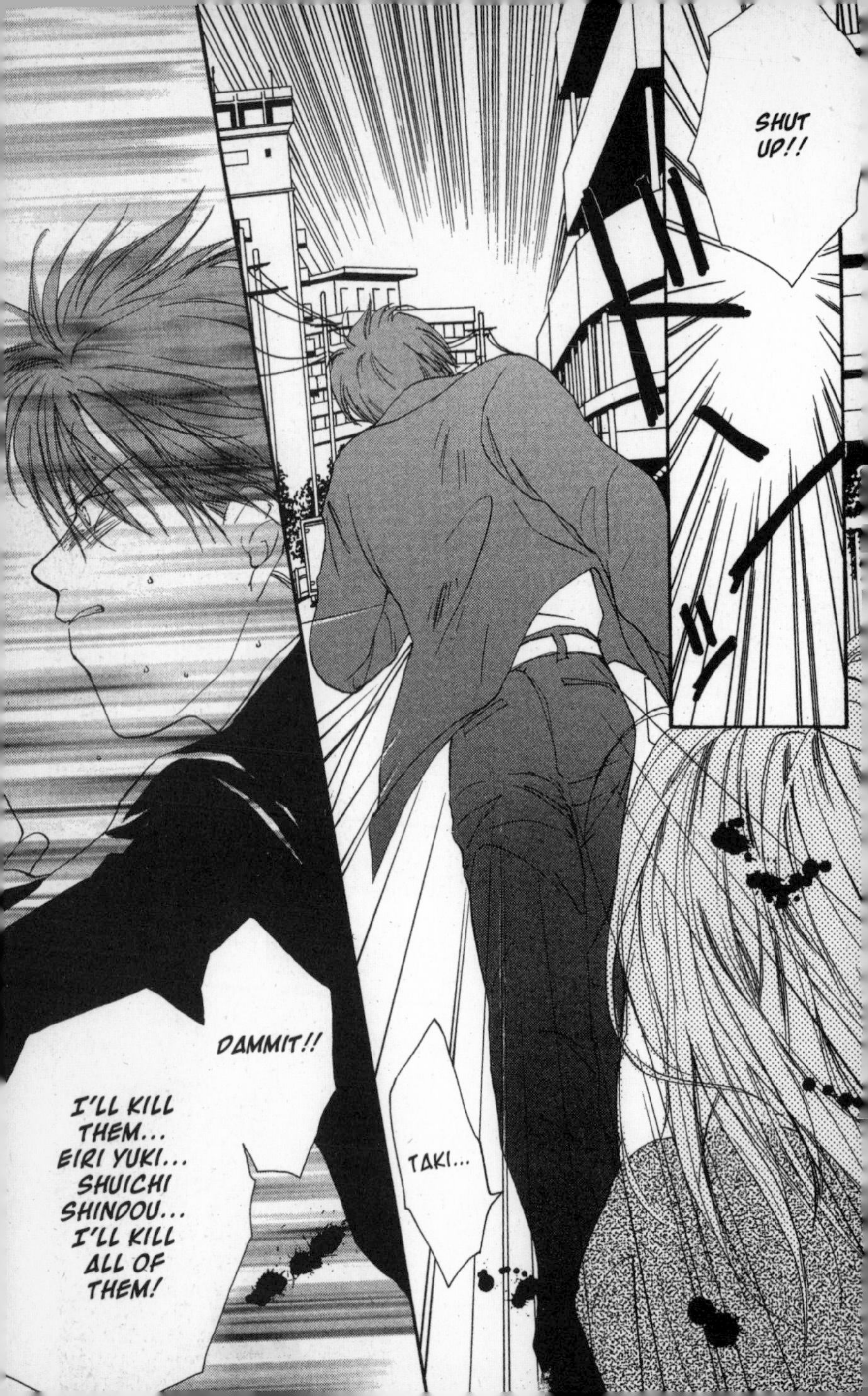
SHUT UP!!
TAKI...
DAMMIT!!
I'LL KILL THEM... EIRI YUKI... SHUICHI SHINDOU... I'LL KILL ALL OF THEM!

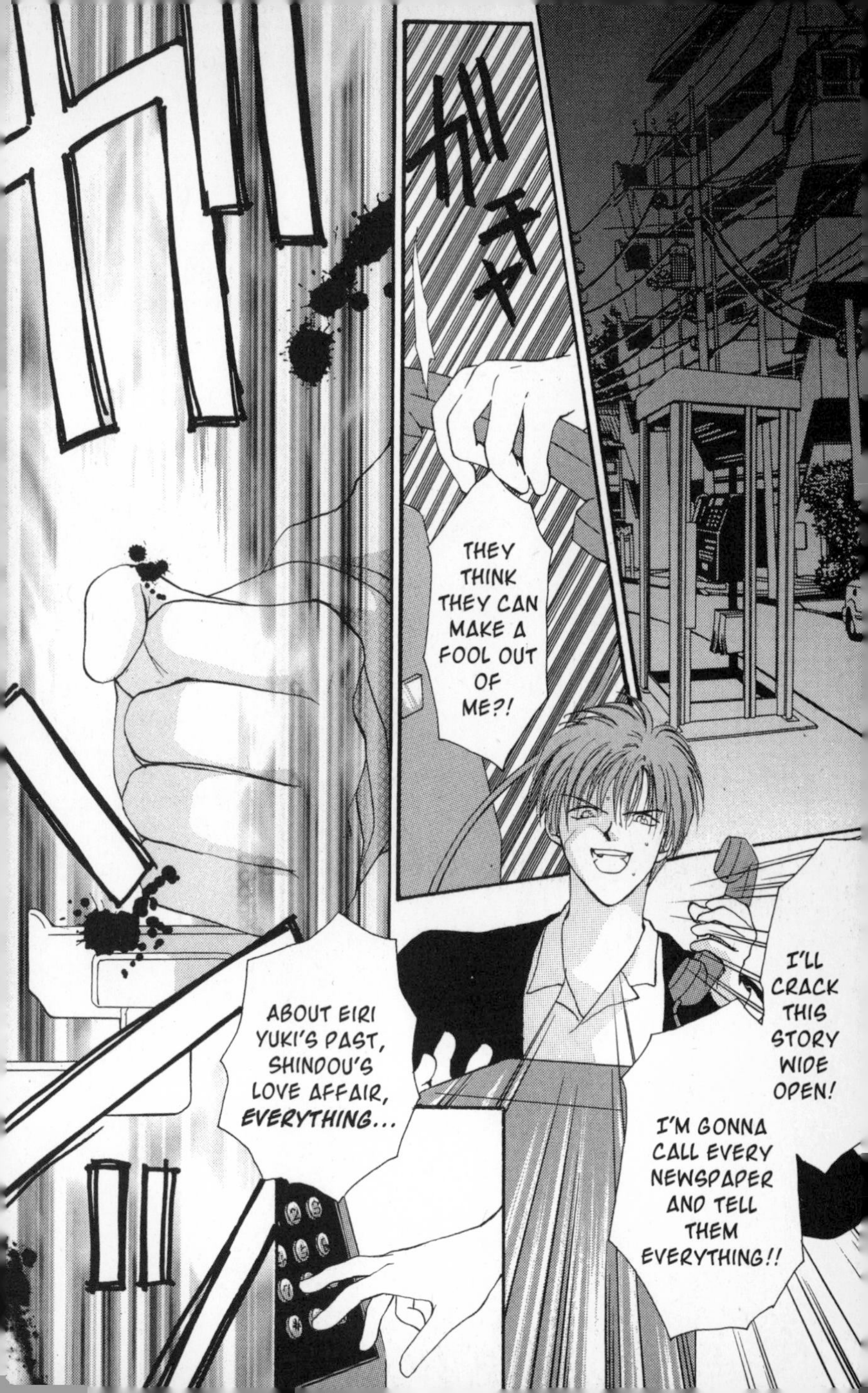
THEY THINK THEY CAN MAKE A FOOL OUT OF ME?!
I'LL CRACK THIS STORY WIDE OPEN!
I'M GONNA CALL EVERY NEWSPAPER AND TELL THEM EVERYTHING!!
ABOUT EIRI YUKI'S PAST, SHINDOU'S LOVE AFFAIR, EVERYTHING...

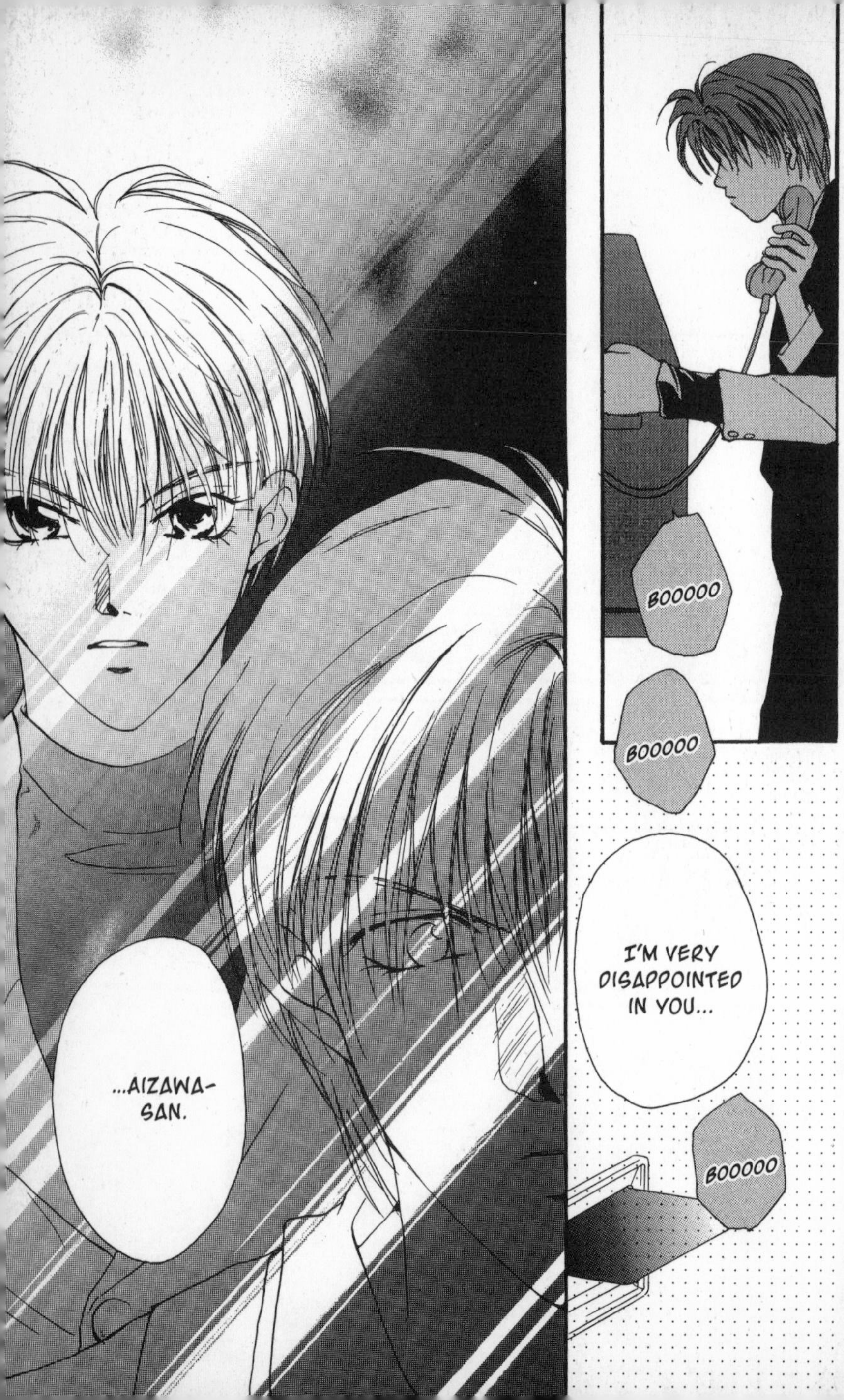
BOOOOO
BOOOOO
I'M VERY DISAPPOINTED IN YOU...
BOOOOO
...AIZAWA-SAN.

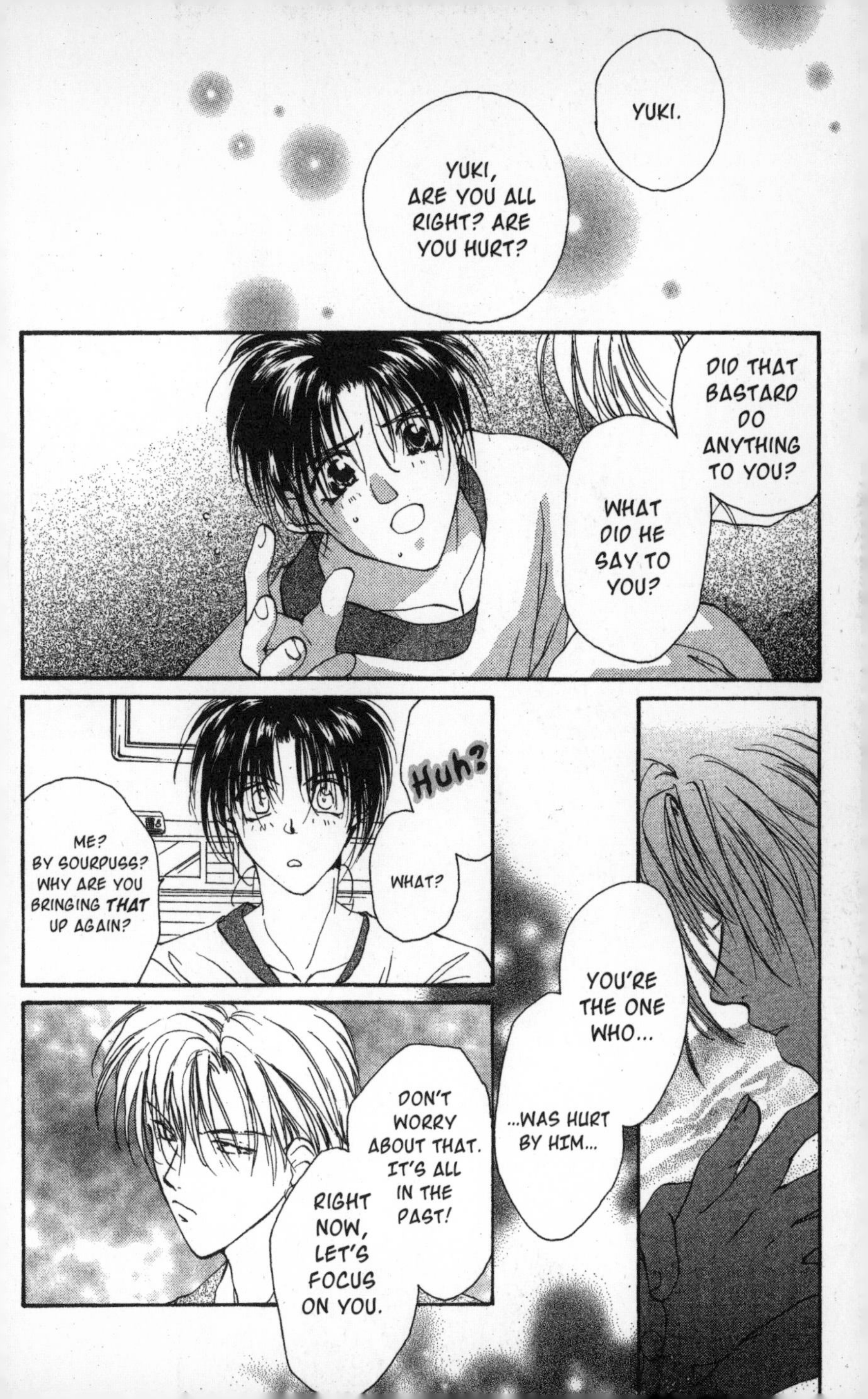
YUKI.
YUKI, ARE YOU ALL RIGHT? ARE YOU HURT?
DID THAT BASTARD DO ANYTHING TO YOU?
WHAT DID HE SAY TO YOU?
YOU'RE THE ONE WHO...
...WAS HURT BY HIM...
Huh?
WHAT?
ME? BY SOURPUSS? WHY ARE YOU BRINGING THAT UP AGAIN?
DON'T WORRY ABOUT THAT. IT'S ALL IN THE PAST!
RIGHT NOW, LET'S FOCUS ON YOU.

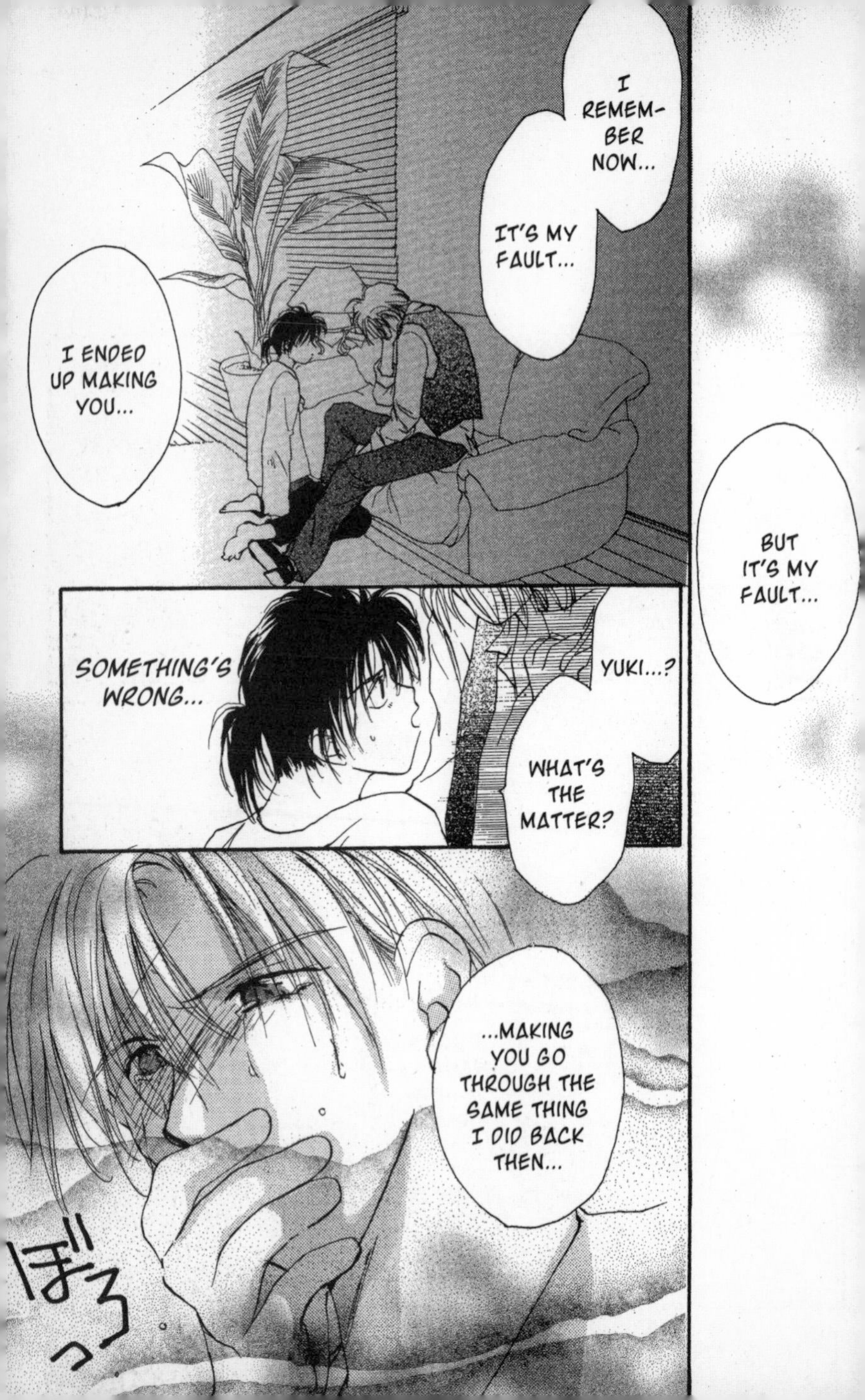
BUT IT'S MY FAULT...
I REMEMBER NOW...
IT'S MY FAULT...
I ENDED UP MAKING YOU...
YUKI...?
WHAT'S THE MATTER?
SOMETHING'S WRONG...
...MAKING YOU GO THROUGH THE SAME THING I DID BACK THEN...
ぼろっ

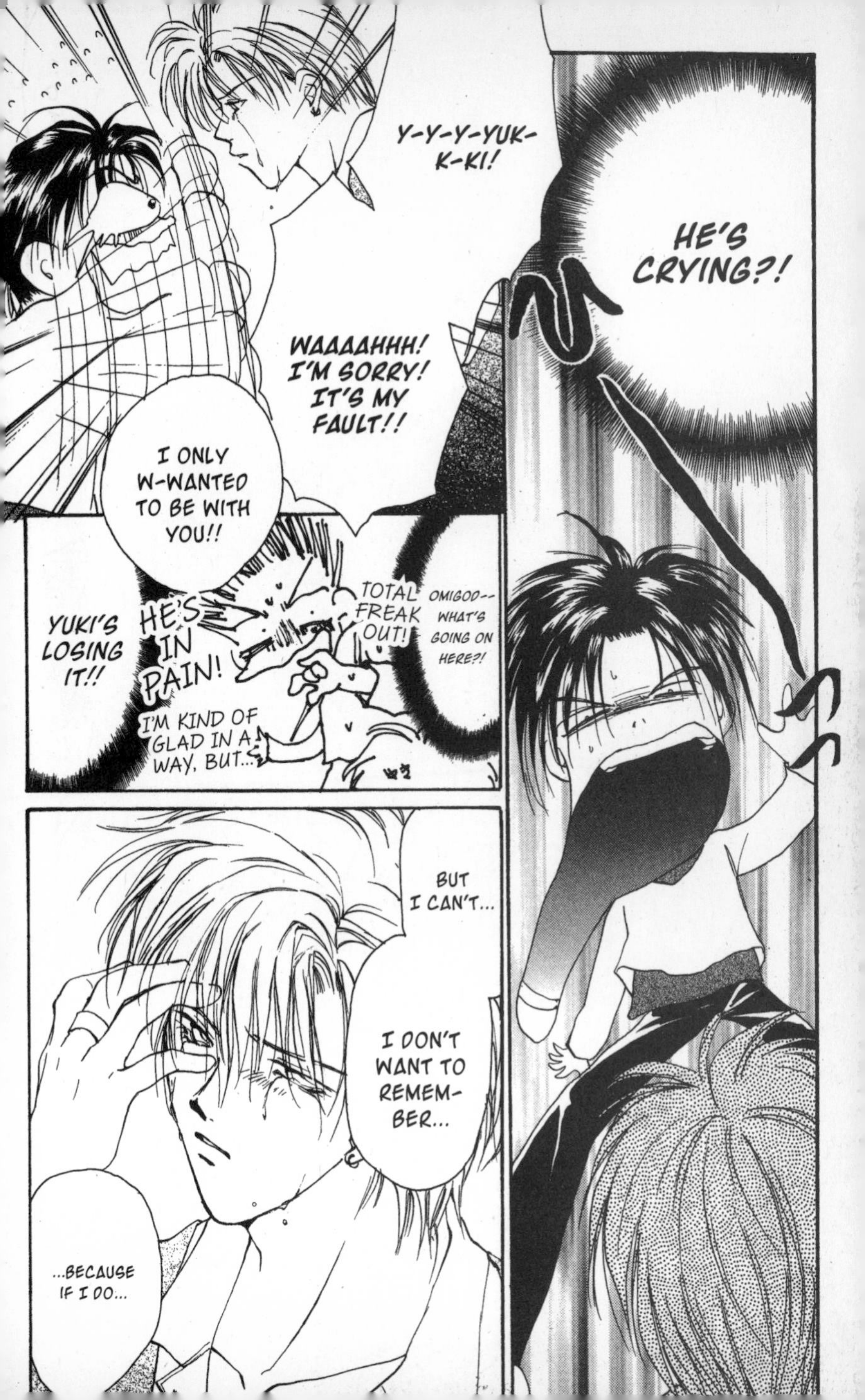
HE'S CRYING?!
Y-Y-Y-YUK-K-KI!
WAAAAHHH! I'M SORRY! IT'S MY FAULT!!
I ONLY W-WANTED TO BE WITH YOU!!
OMIGOD-- WHAT'S GOING ON HERE?!
TOTAL FREAK OUT!
HE'S IN PAIN!
YUKI'S LOSING IT!!
I'M KIND OF GLAD IN A WAY, BUT...
BUT I CAN'T...
I DON'T WANT TO REMEMBER...
...BECAUSE IF I DO...

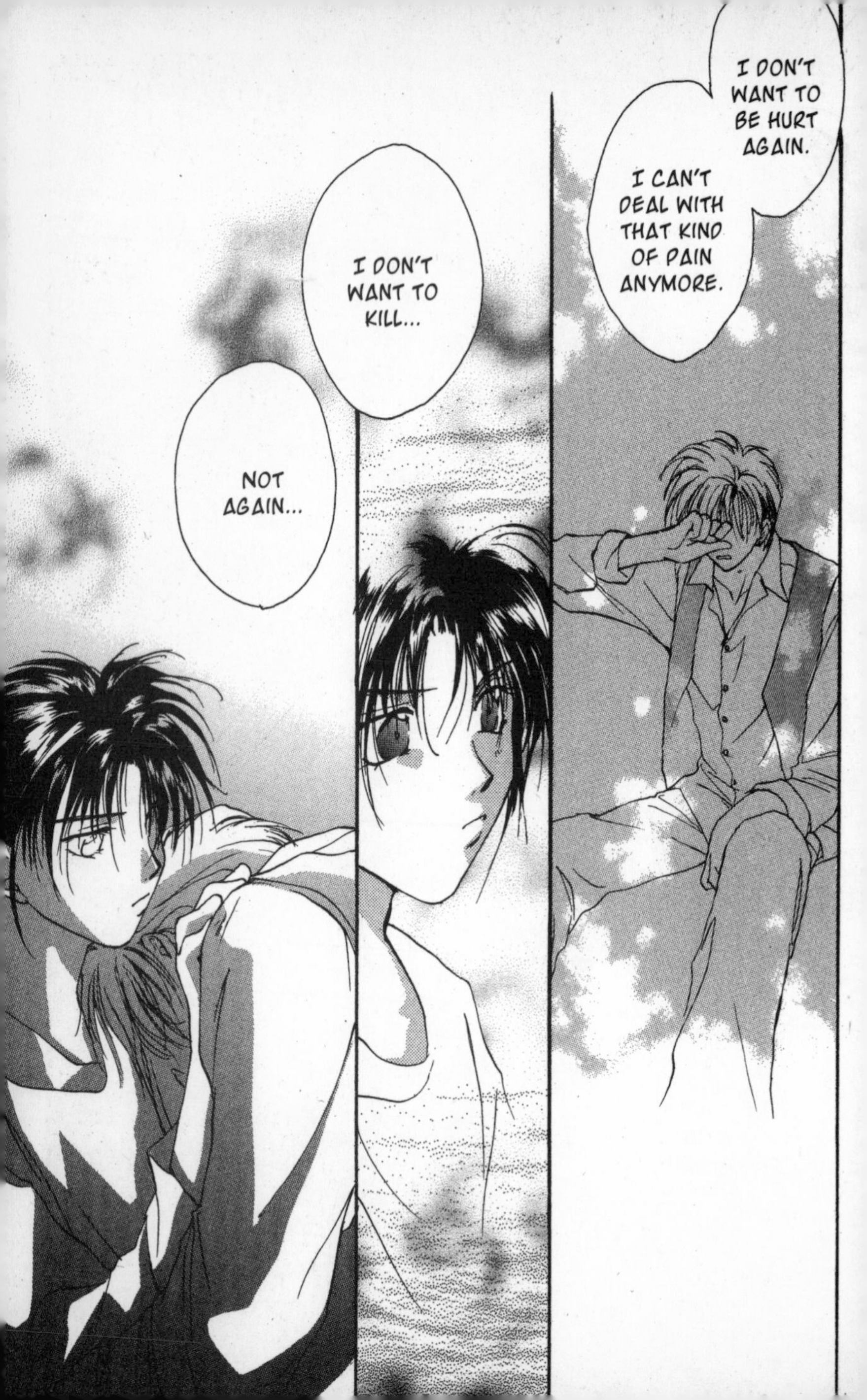
I DON'T WANT TO BE HURT AGAIN.
I CAN'T DEAL WITH THAT KIND OF PAIN ANYMORE.
I DON'T WANT TO KILL...
NOT AGAIN...

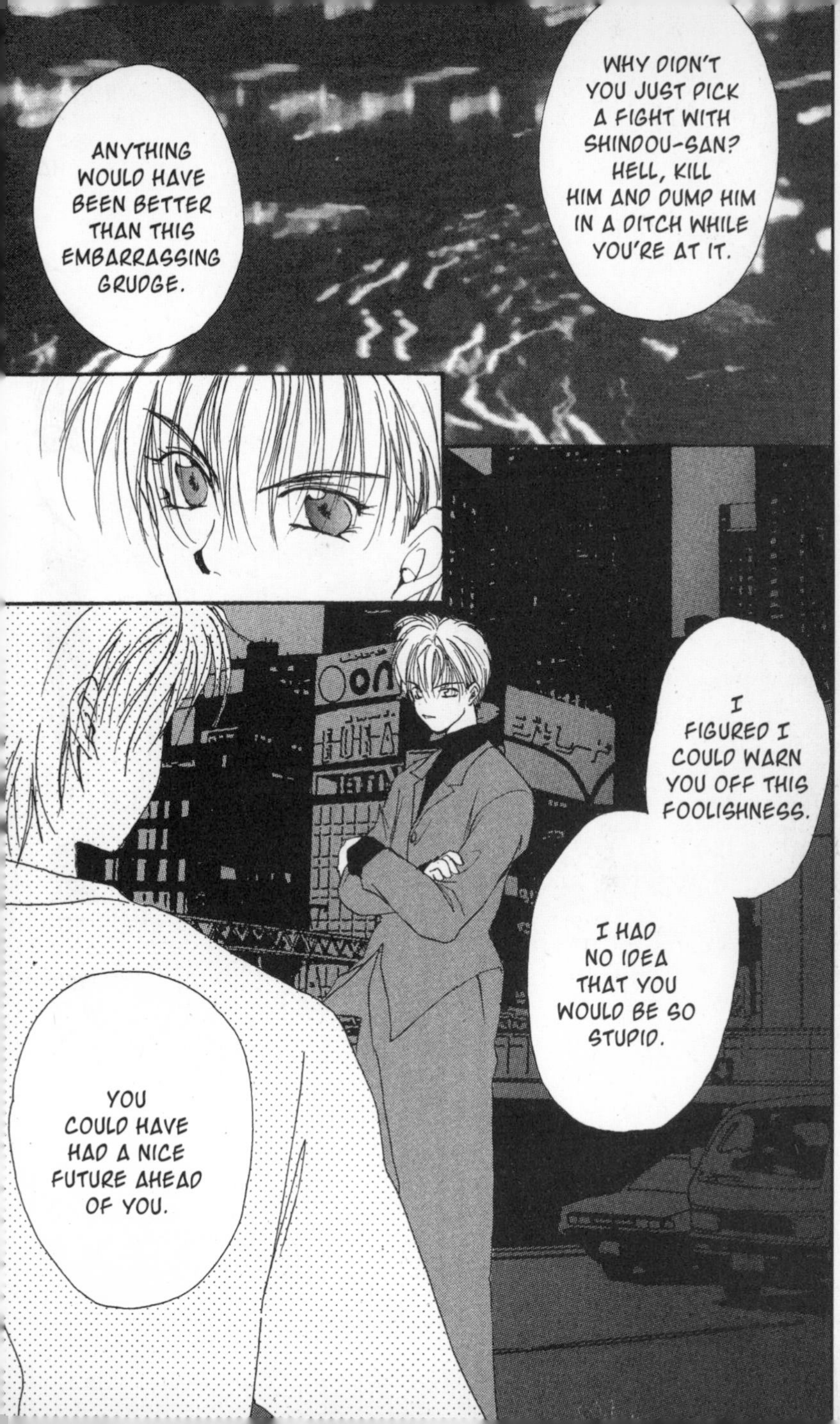
WHY DIDN'T YOU JUST PICK A FIGHT WITH SHINDOU-SAN? HELL, KILL HIM AND DUMP HIM IN A DITCH WHILE YOU'RE AT IT.
ANYTHING WOULD HAVE BEEN BETTER THAN THIS EMBARRASSING GRUDGE.
I FIGURED I COULD WARN YOU OFF THIS FOOLISHNESS.
I HAD NO IDEA THAT YOU WOULD BE SO STUPID.
YOU COULD HAVE HAD A NICE FUTURE AHEAD OF YOU.

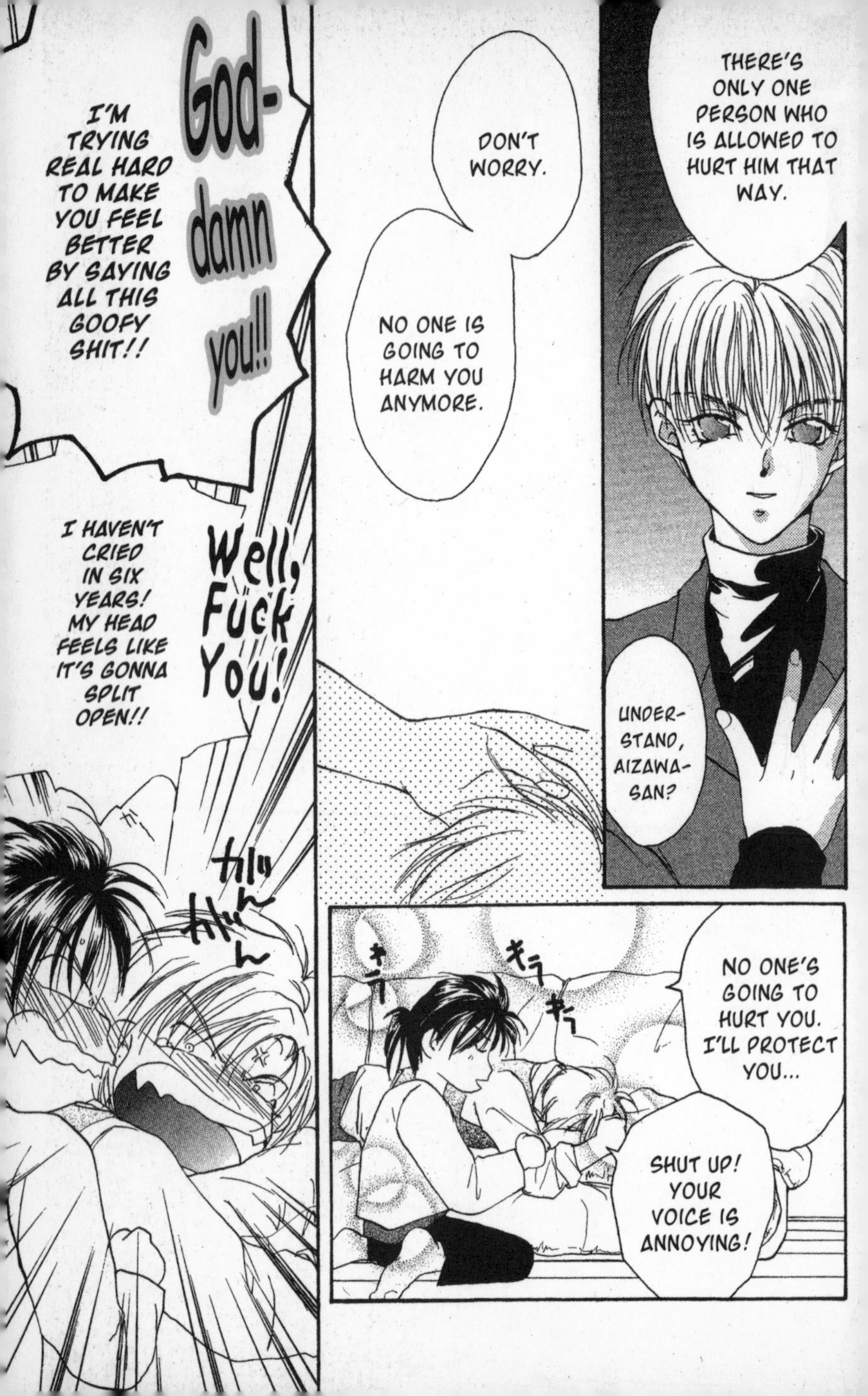
THERE'S ONLY ONE PERSON WHO IS ALLOWED TO HURT HIM THAT WAY.
UNDER-STAND, AIZAWA-SAN?
DON'T WORRY.
NO ONE IS GOING TO HARM YOU ANYMORE.
NO ONE'S GOING TO HURT YOU. I'LL PROTECT YOU...
SHUT UP! YOUR VOICE IS ANNOYING!
God-damn you!!
I'M TRYING REAL HARD TO MAKE YOU FEEL BETTER BY SAYING ALL THIS GOOFY SHIT!!
Well, Fuck You!
I HAVEN'T CRIED IN SIX YEARS! MY HEAD FEELS LIKE IT'S GONNA SPLIT OPEN!!

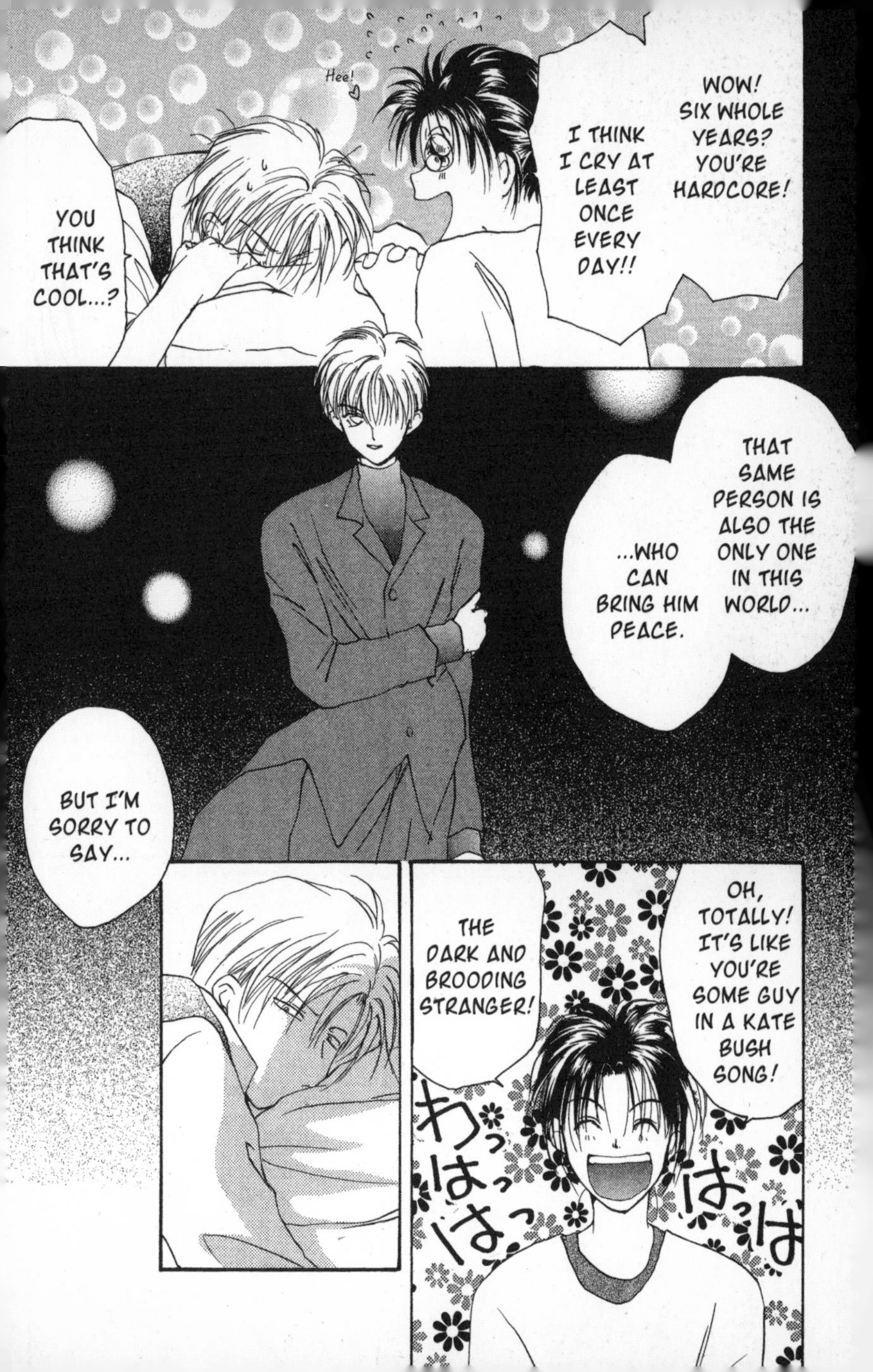
WOW! SIX WHOLE YEARS? YOU'RE HARDCORE!
I THINK I CRY AT LEAST ONCE EVERY DAY!!
Hee!
YOU THINK THAT'S COOL...?
THAT SAME PERSON IS ALSO THE ONLY ONE IN THIS WORLD...
...WHO CAN BRING HIM PEACE.
BUT I'M SORRY TO SAY...
OH, TOTALLY! IT'S LIKE YOU'RE SOME GUY IN A KATE BUSH SONG!
THE DARK AND BROODING STRANGER!
はっはっ
わっはっはっ

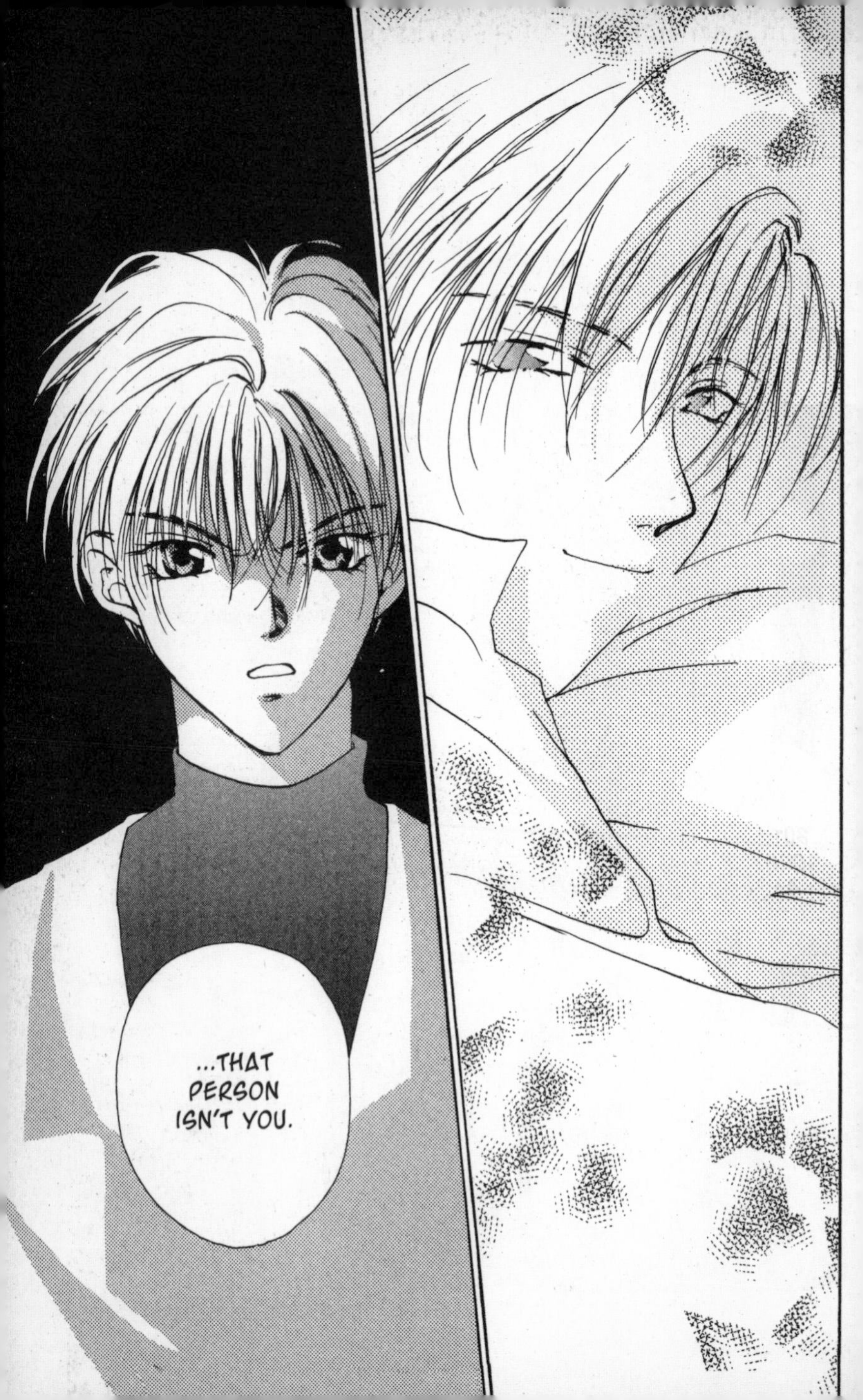
...THAT PERSON ISN'T YOU.

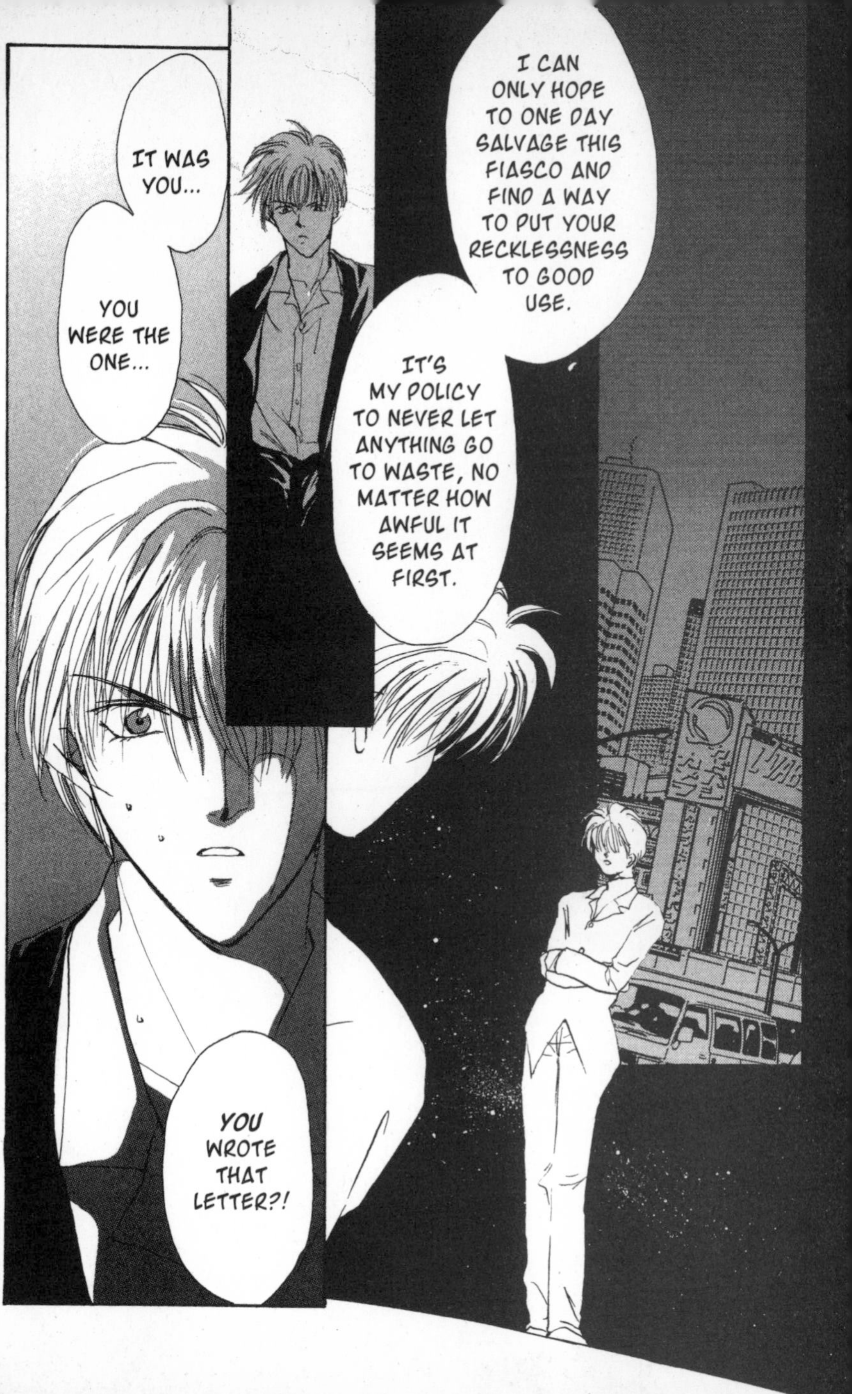
I CAN ONLY HOPE TO ONE DAY SALVAGE THIS FIASCO AND FIND A WAY TO PUT YOUR RECKLESSNESS TO GOOD USE.
IT'S MY POLICY TO NEVER LET ANYTHING GO TO WASTE, NO MATTER HOW AWFUL IT SEEMS AT FIRST.
IT WAS YOU...
YOU WERE THE ONE...
YOU WROTE THAT LETTER?!

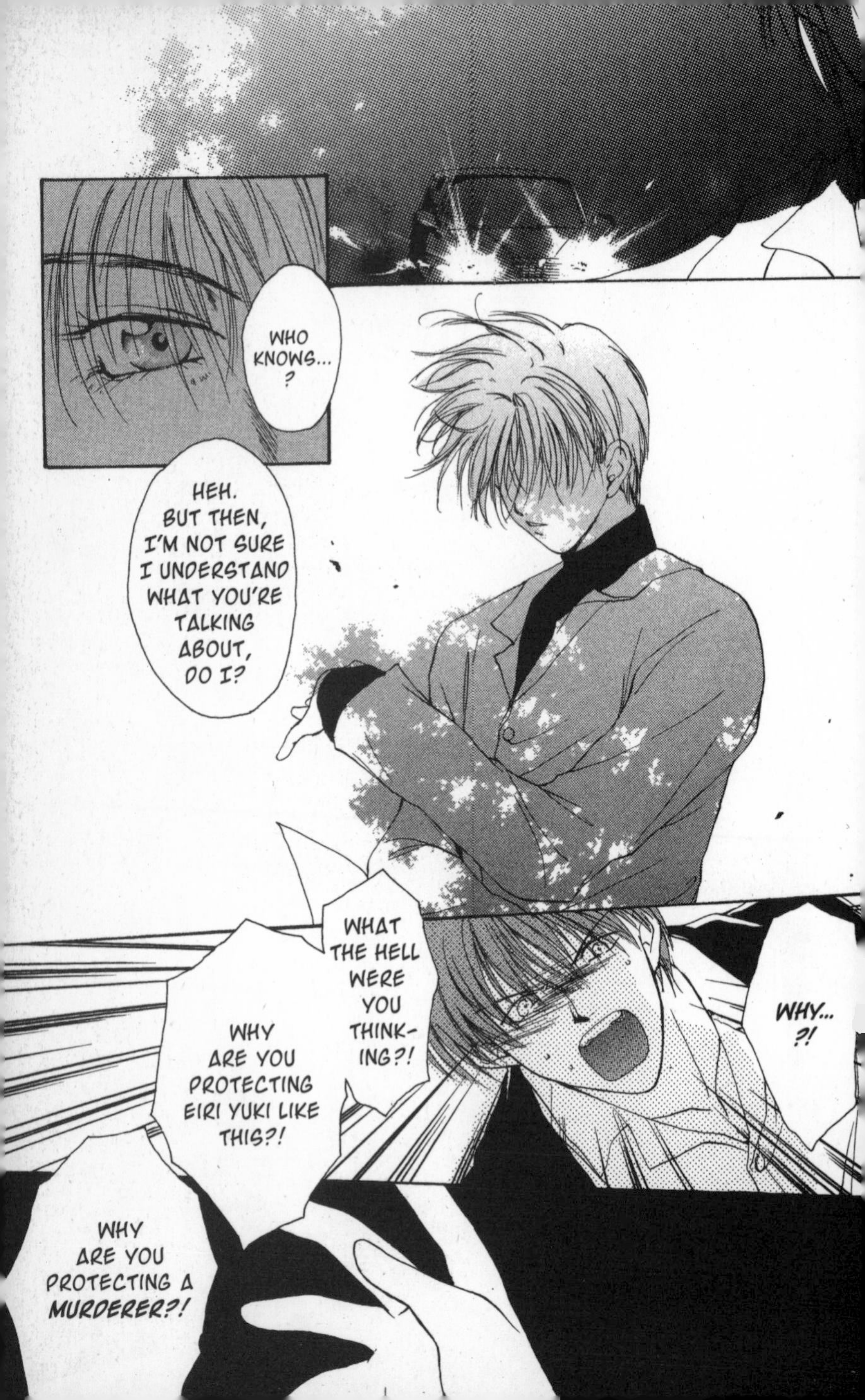
WHO KNOWS... ?
HEH. BUT THEN, I'M NOT SURE I UNDERSTAND WHAT YOU'RE TALKING ABOUT, DO I?
WHY... ?!
WHAT THE HELL WERE YOU THINKING?!
WHY ARE YOU PROTECTING EIRI YUKI LIKE THIS?!
WHY ARE YOU PROTECTING A *MURDERER*?!

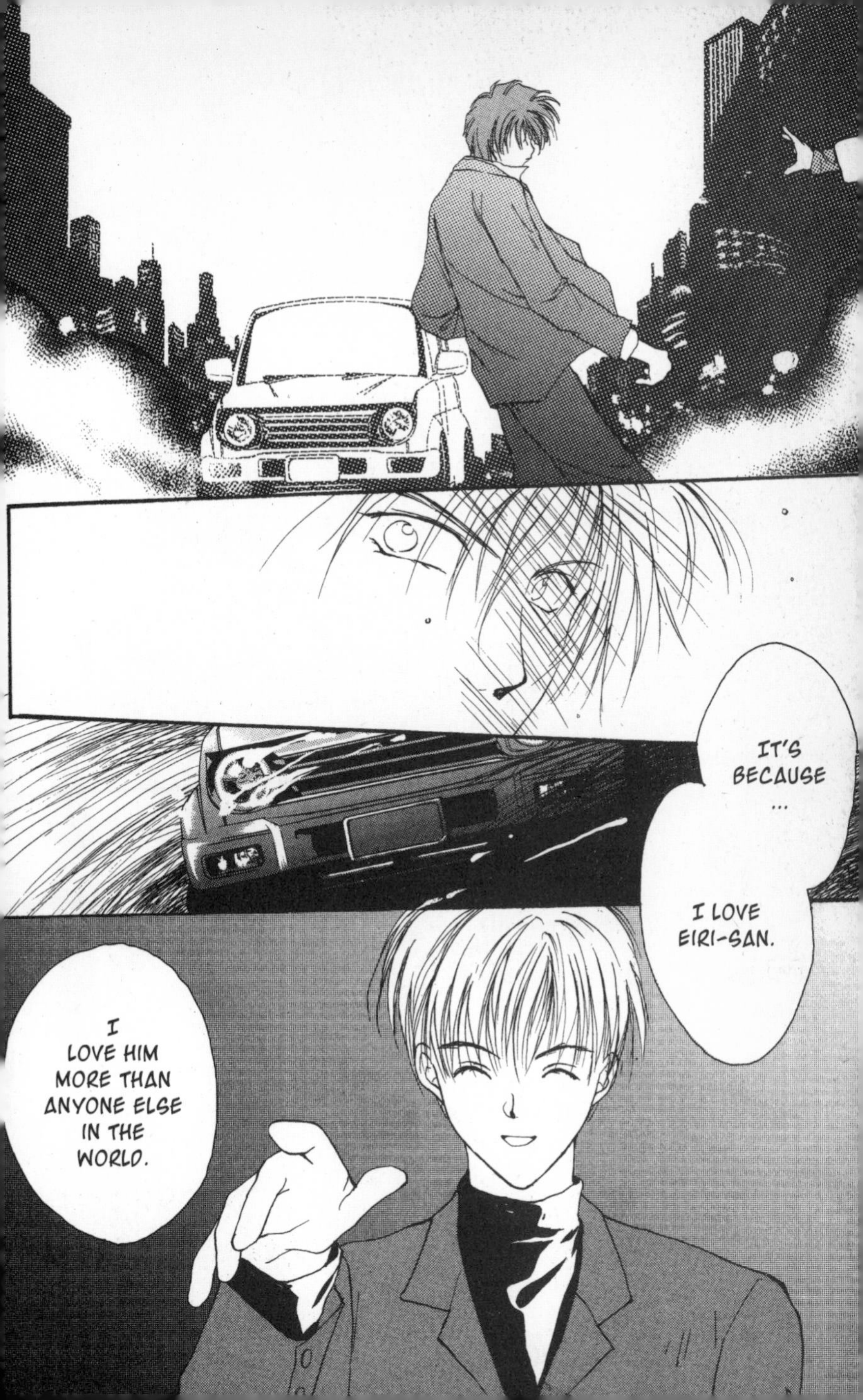
IT'S BECAUSE ...
I LOVE EIRI-SAN.
I LOVE HIM MORE THAN ANYONE ELSE IN THE WORLD.

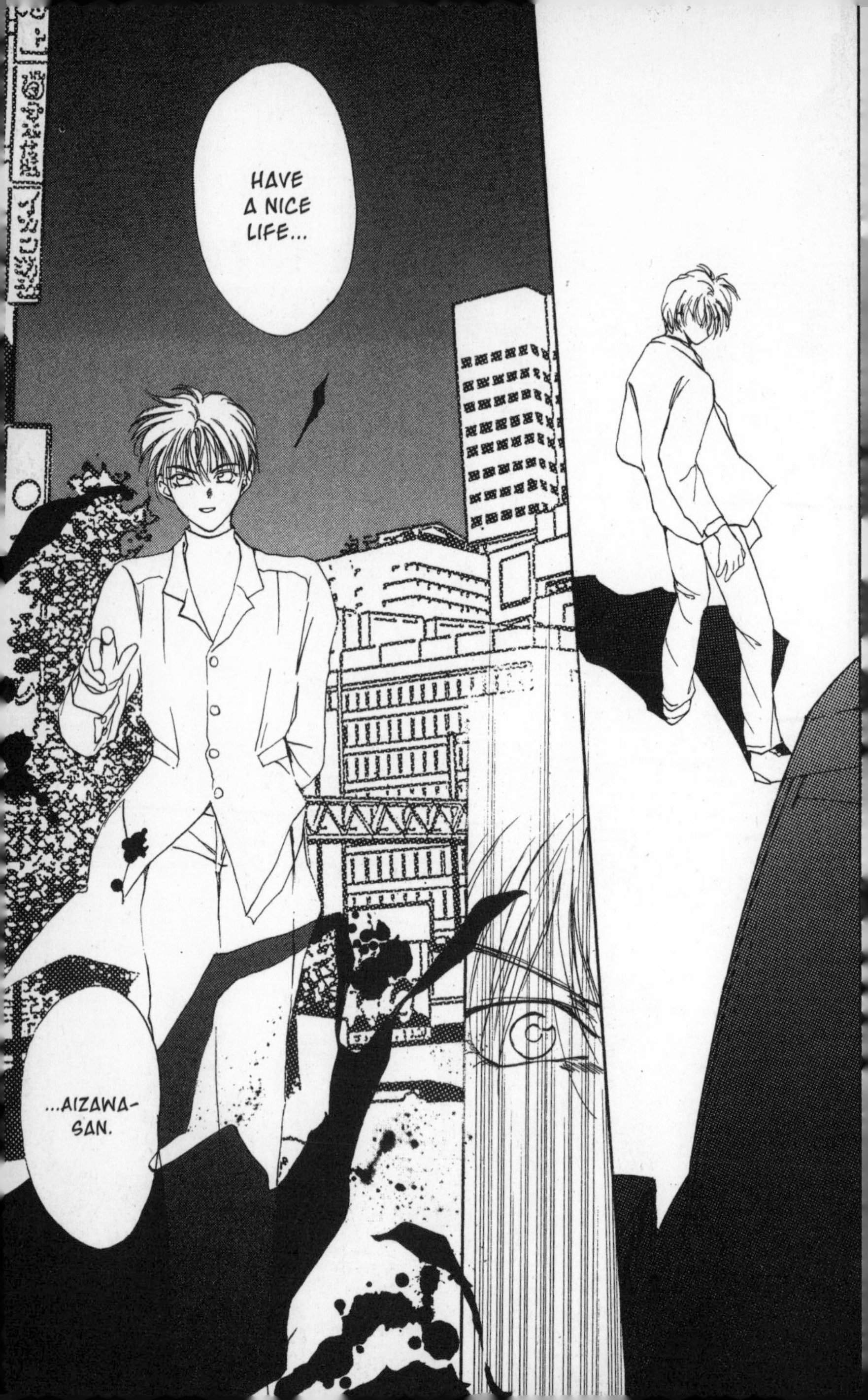
HAVE A NICE LIFE...
...AIZAWA-SAN.

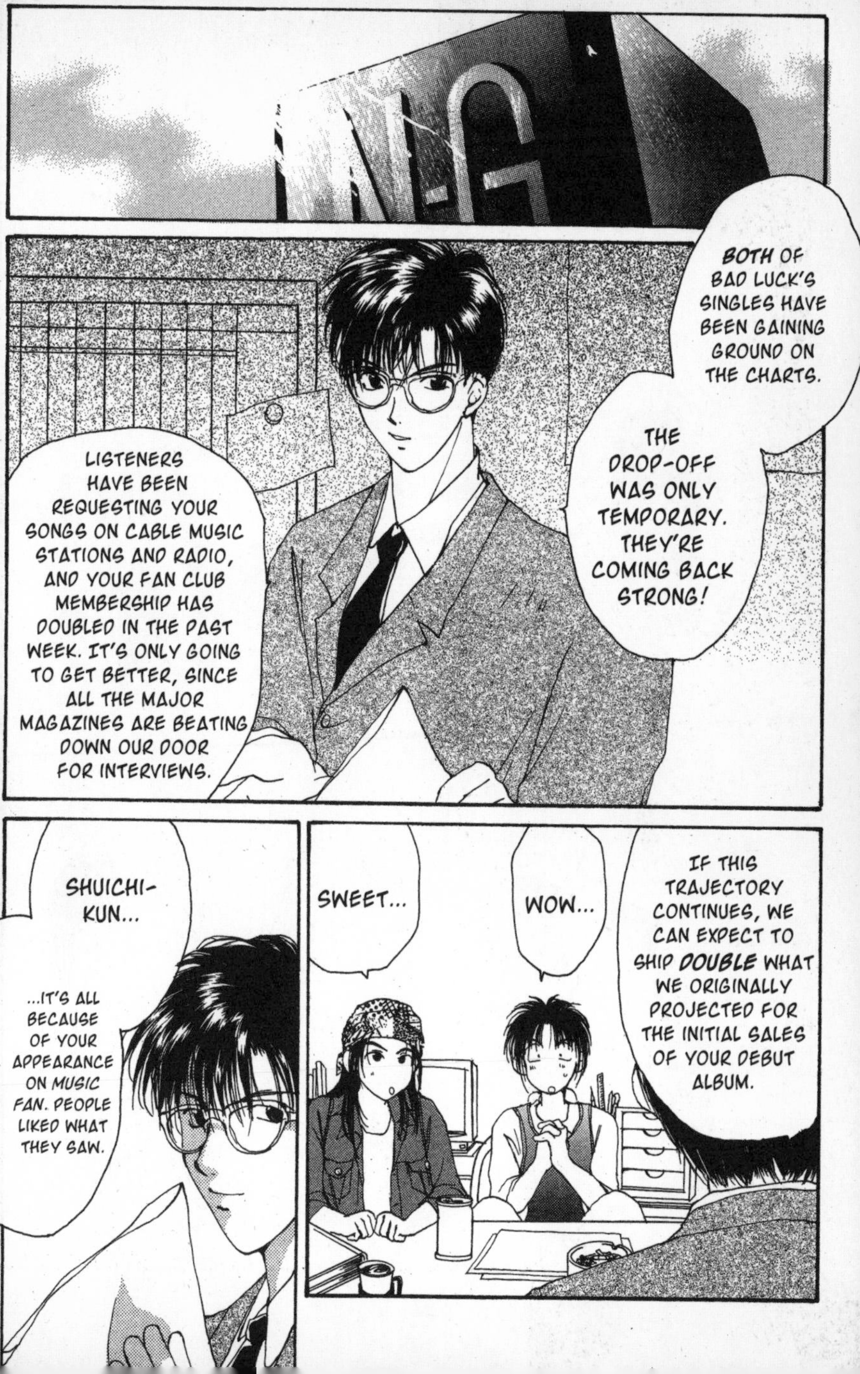

BOTH OF BAD LUCK'S SINGLES HAVE BEEN GAINING GROUND ON THE CHARTS.
THE DROP-OFF WAS ONLY TEMPORARY. THEY'RE COMING BACK STRONG!
LISTENERS HAVE BEEN REQUESTING YOUR SONGS ON CABLE MUSIC STATIONS AND RADIO, AND YOUR FAN CLUB MEMBERSHIP HAS DOUBLED IN THE PAST WEEK. IT'S ONLY GOING TO GET BETTER, SINCE ALL THE MAJOR MAGAZINES ARE BEATING DOWN OUR DOOR FOR INTERVIEWS.
IF THIS TRAJECTORY CONTINUES, WE CAN EXPECT TO SHIP DOUBLE WHAT WE ORIGINALLY PROJECTED FOR THE INITIAL SALES OF YOUR DEBUT ALBUM.
WOW...
SWEET...
SHUICHI-KUN...
...IT'S ALL BECAUSE OF YOUR APPEARANCE ON MUSIC FAN. PEOPLE LIKED WHAT THEY SAW.

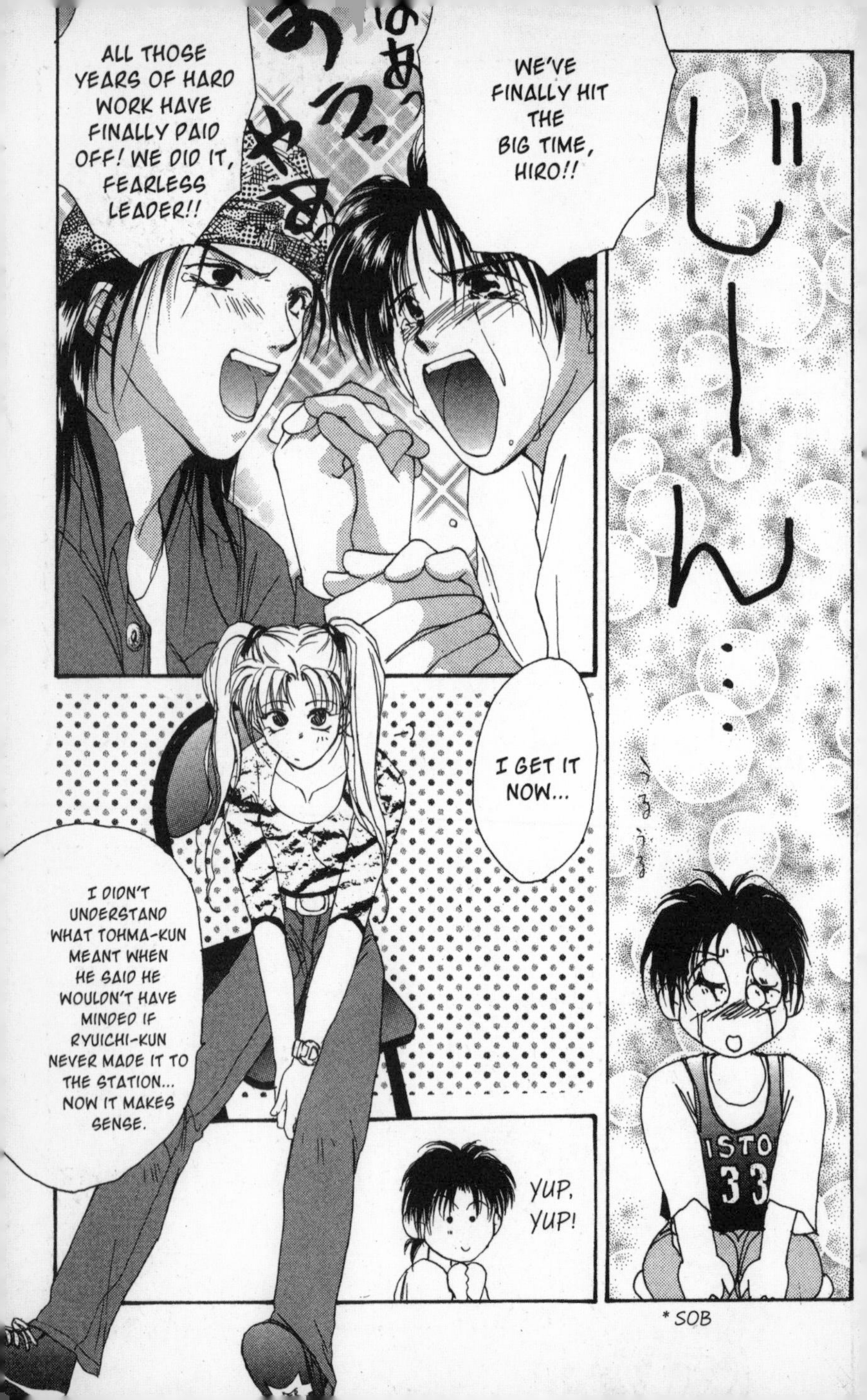
じーん…
* SOB
WE'VE FINALLY HIT THE BIG TIME, HIRO!!
ALL THOSE YEARS OF HARD WORK HAVE FINALLY PAID OFF! WE DID IT, FEARLESS LEADER!!
I GET IT NOW...
I DIDN'T UNDERSTAND WHAT TOHMA-KUN MEANT WHEN HE SAID HE WOULDN'T HAVE MINDED IF RYUICHI-KUN NEVER MADE IT TO THE STATION... NOW IT MAKES SENSE.
YUP, YUP!
ISTO 33

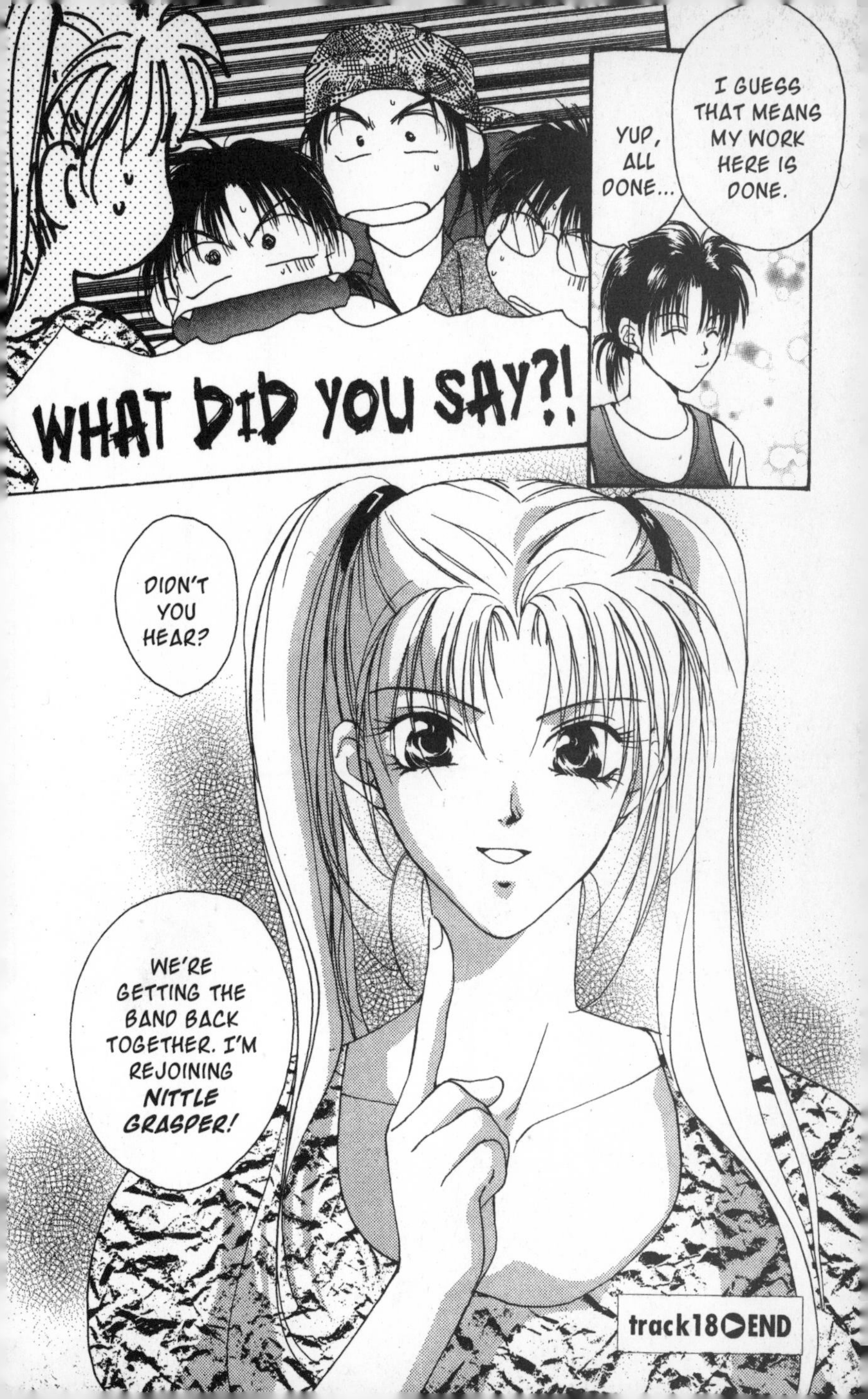
I GUESS THAT MEANS MY WORK HERE IS DONE.
YUP, ALL DONE...
WHAT DID YOU SAY?!
DIDN'T YOU HEAR?
WE'RE GETTING THE BAND BACK TOGETHER. I'M REJOINING NITTLE GRASPER!
track18▶END

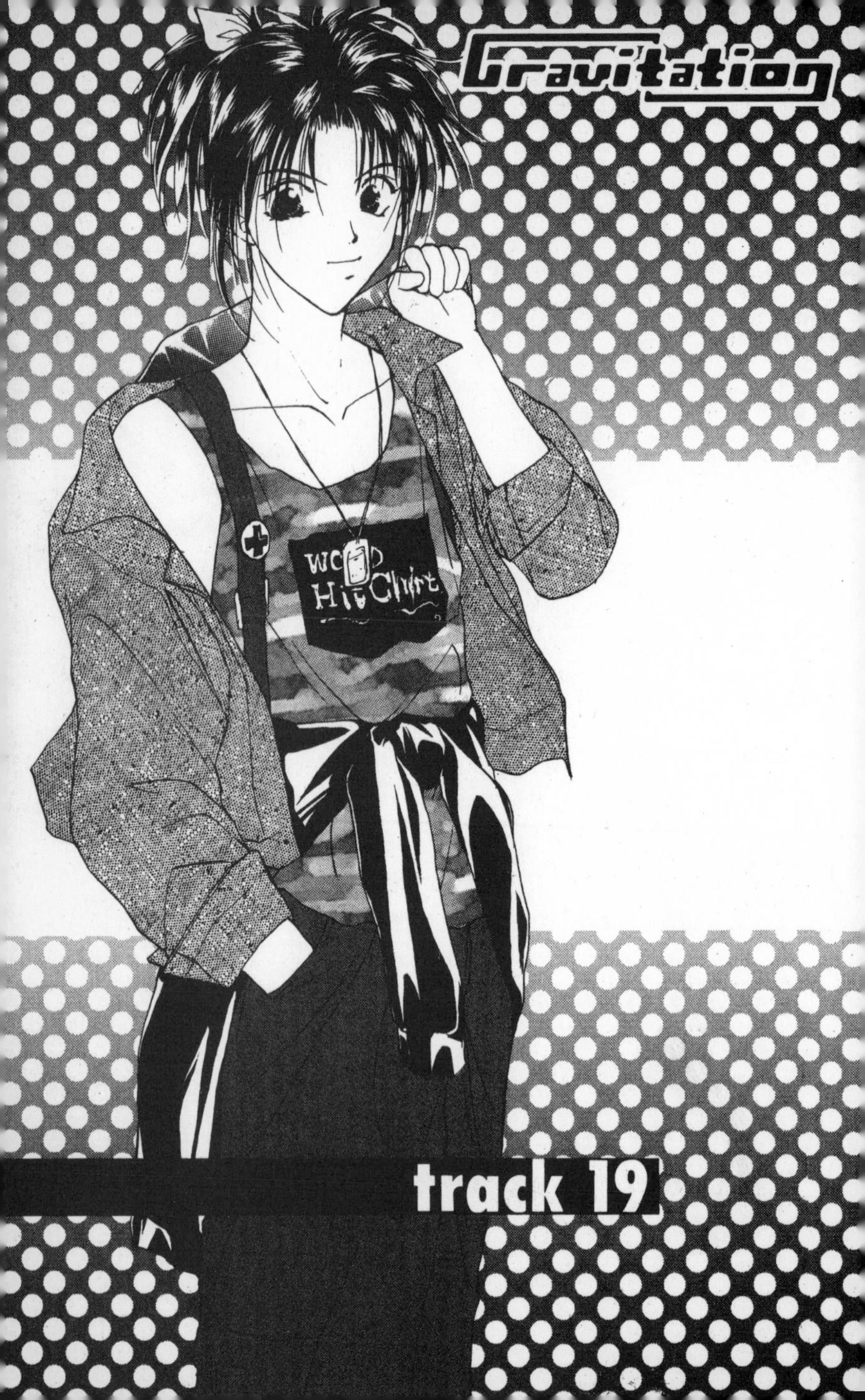
Gravitation
track 19

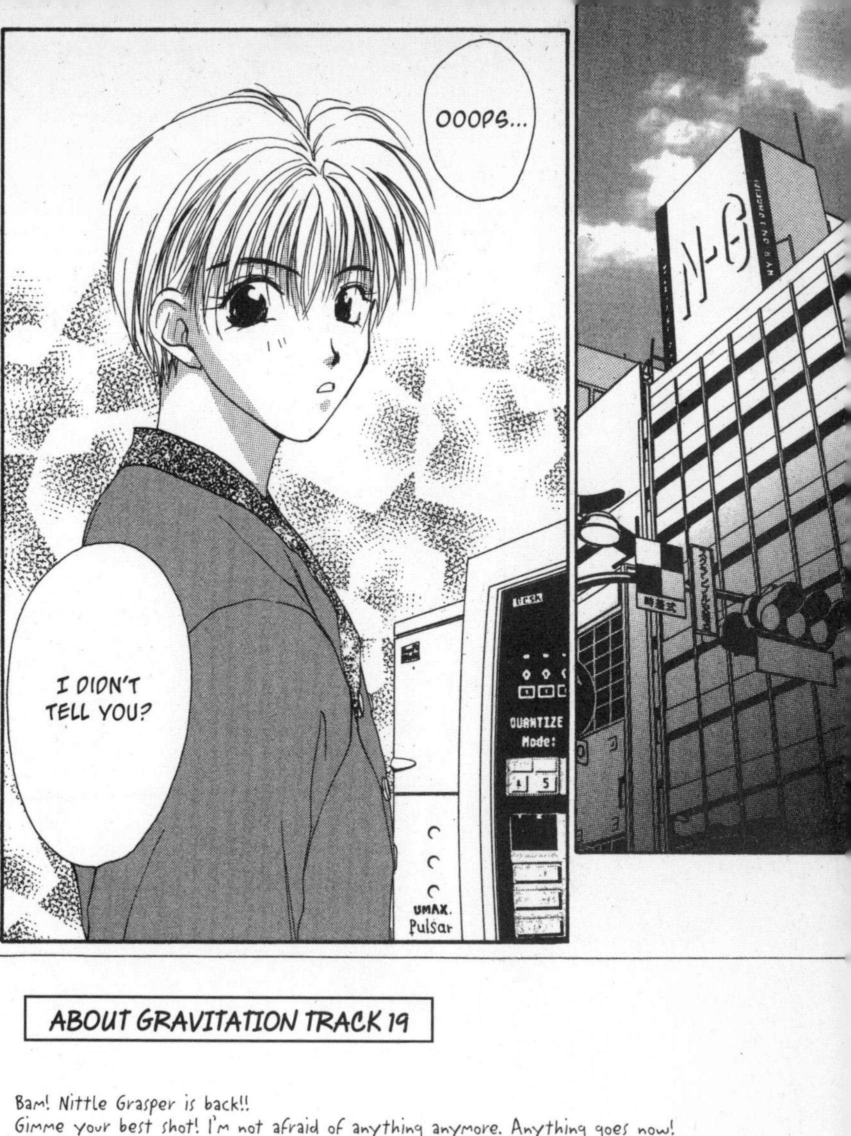
N-G
OOOPS...
I DIDN'T TELL YOU?
QUANTIZE
Mode:
UMAX.
Pulsar

ABOUT GRAVITATION TRACK 19

Bam! Nittle Grasper is back!!
Gimme your best shot! I'm not afraid of anything anymore. Anything goes now!
Then again, that shouldn't be news to anybody at this point. This picture of the N-G building is a reference photo that I altered to my own purposes! Track 19 isn't one of my favorites, but with K-chan getting more involved in the story, some sexy new lovemaking scenes, and the introduction of new characters, it's still pretty loaded as far as chapters go. In a lot of ways, I think of it as a brand new piece of work. (Although I ain't even finished with the old one yet!)

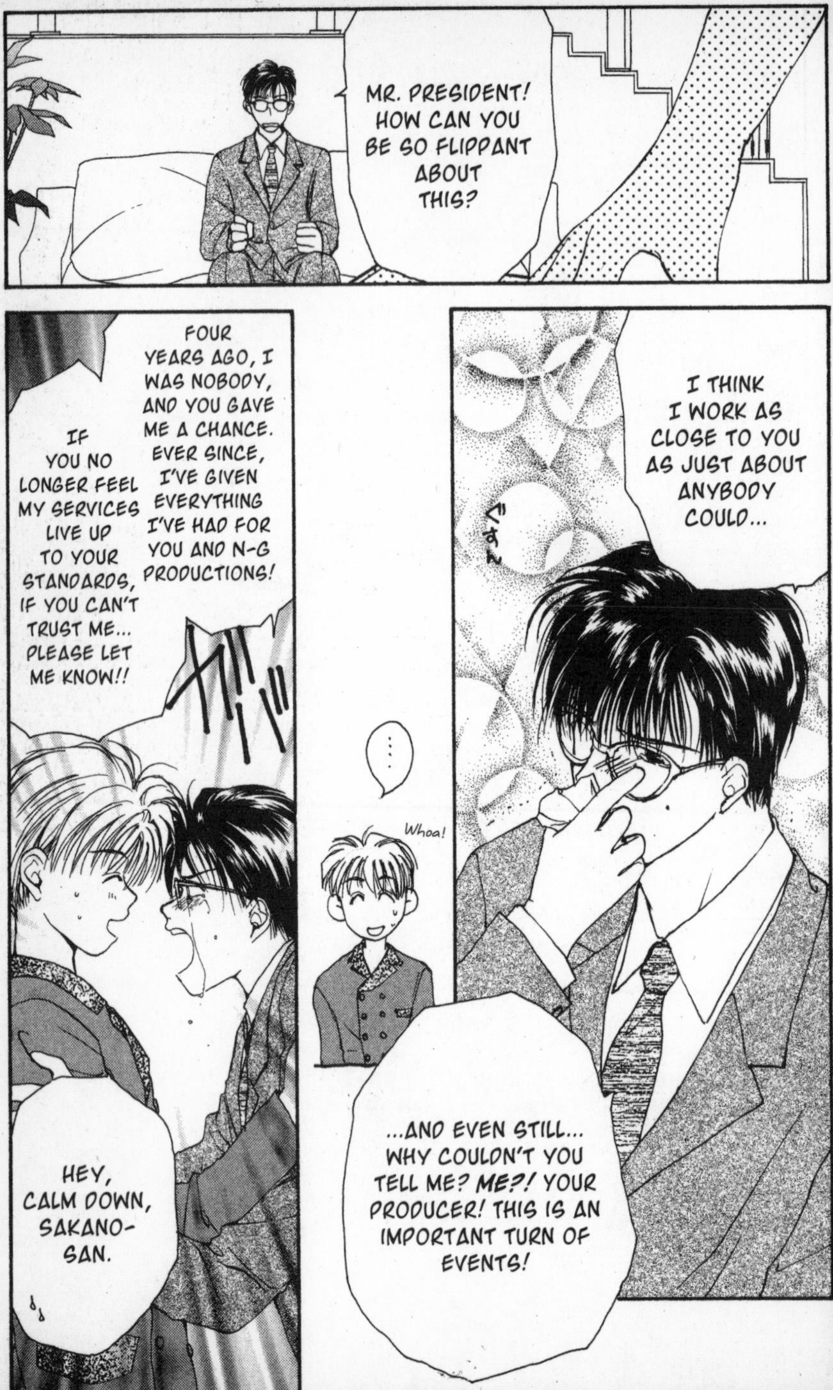
MR. PRESIDENT! HOW CAN YOU BE SO FLIPPANT ABOUT THIS?
I THINK I WORK AS CLOSE TO YOU AS JUST ABOUT ANYBODY COULD...
ぐす
...AND EVEN STILL... WHY COULDN'T YOU TELL ME? ***ME?!*** YOUR PRODUCER! THIS IS AN IMPORTANT TURN OF EVENTS!
....
Whoa!
FOUR YEARS AGO, I WAS NOBODY, AND YOU GAVE ME A CHANCE. EVER SINCE, I'VE GIVEN EVERYTHING I'VE HAD FOR YOU AND N-G PRODUCTIONS!
IF YOU NO LONGER FEEL MY SERVICES LIVE UP TO YOUR STANDARDS, IF YOU CAN'T TRUST ME... PLEASE LET ME KNOW!!
HEY, CALM DOWN, SAKANO-SAN.

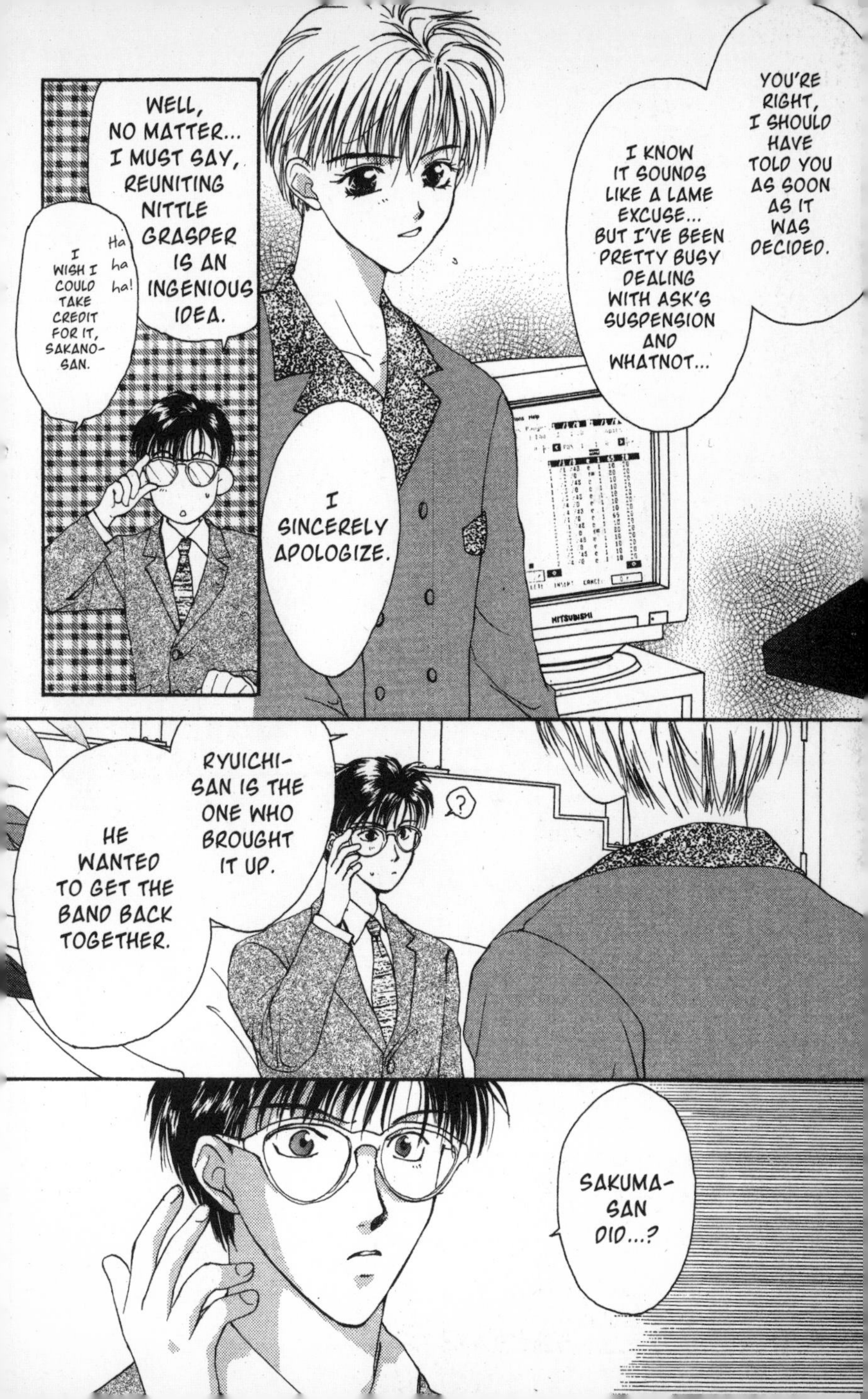
YOU'RE RIGHT, I SHOULD HAVE TOLD YOU AS SOON AS IT WAS DECIDED.
I KNOW IT SOUNDS LIKE A LAME EXCUSE... BUT I'VE BEEN PRETTY BUSY DEALING WITH ASK'S SUSPENSION AND WHATNOT...
I SINCERELY APOLOGIZE.
WELL, NO MATTER... I MUST SAY, REUNITING NITTLE GRASPER IS AN INGENIOUS IDEA.
Ha ha ha!
I WISH I COULD TAKE CREDIT FOR IT, SAKANO-SAN.
RYUICHI-SAN IS THE ONE WHO BROUGHT IT UP.
?
HE WANTED TO GET THE BAND BACK TOGETHER.
SAKUMA-SAN DID...?

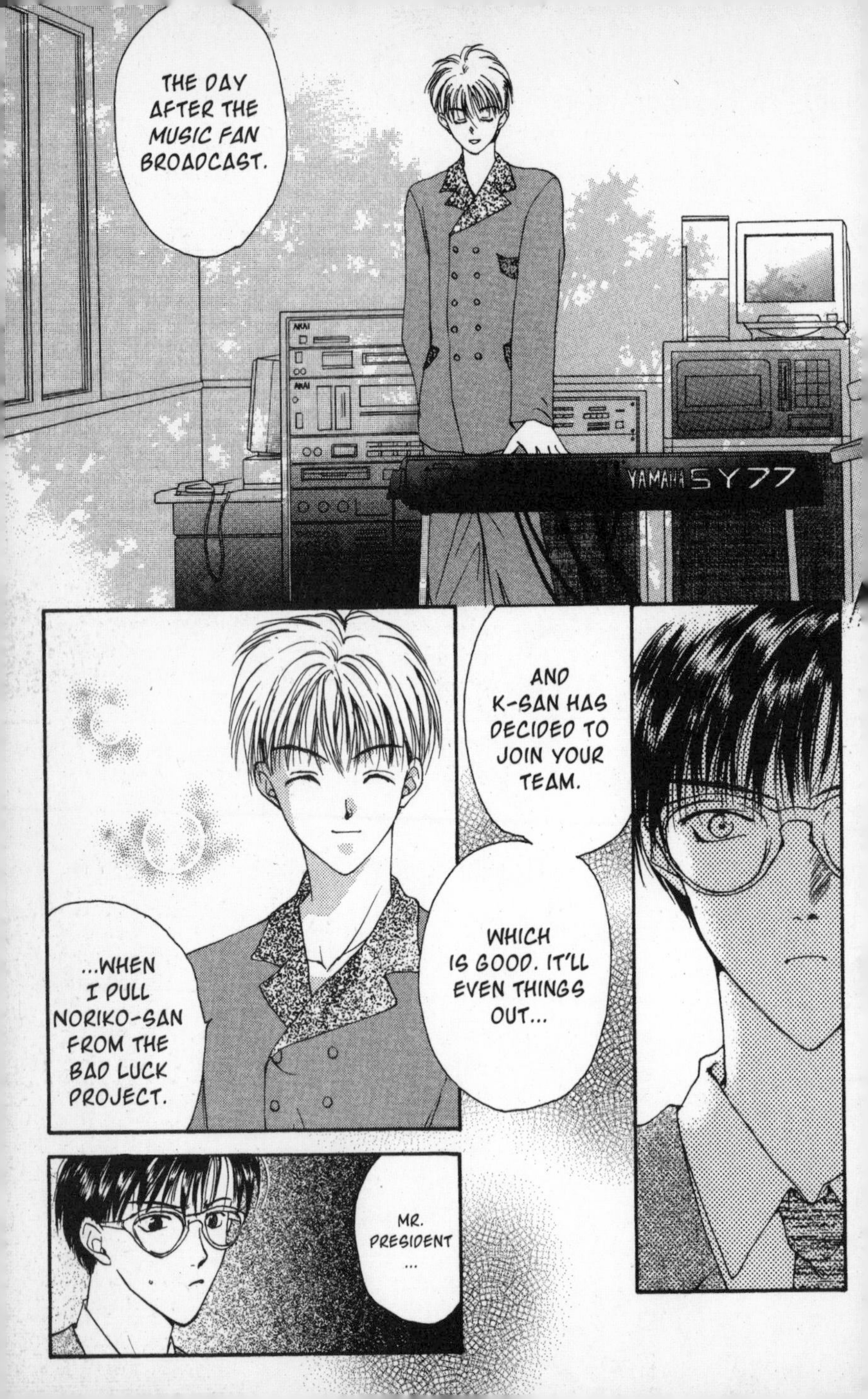
THE DAY AFTER THE MUSIC FAN BROADCAST.
YAMAHA SY77
AND K-SAN HAS DECIDED TO JOIN YOUR TEAM.
WHICH IS GOOD. IT'LL EVEN THINGS OUT...
...WHEN I PULL NORIKO-SAN FROM THE BAD LUCK PROJECT.
MR. PRESIDENT ...

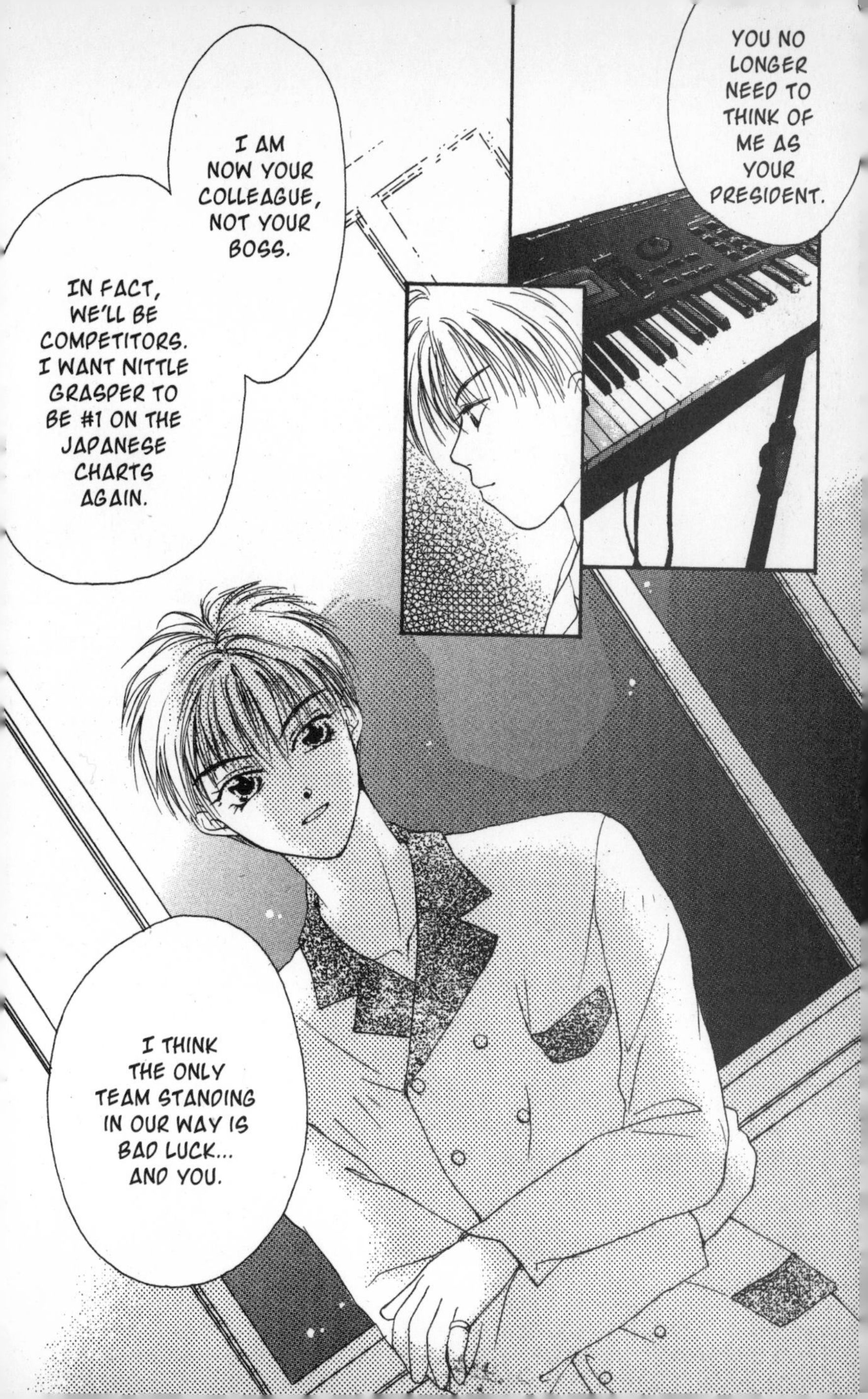
YOU NO LONGER NEED TO THINK OF ME AS YOUR PRESIDENT.
I AM NOW YOUR COLLEAGUE, NOT YOUR BOSS.
IN FACT, WE'LL BE COMPETITORS. I WANT NITTLE GRASPER TO BE #1 ON THE JAPANESE CHARTS AGAIN.
I THINK THE ONLY TEAM STANDING IN OUR WAY IS BAD LUCK... AND YOU.

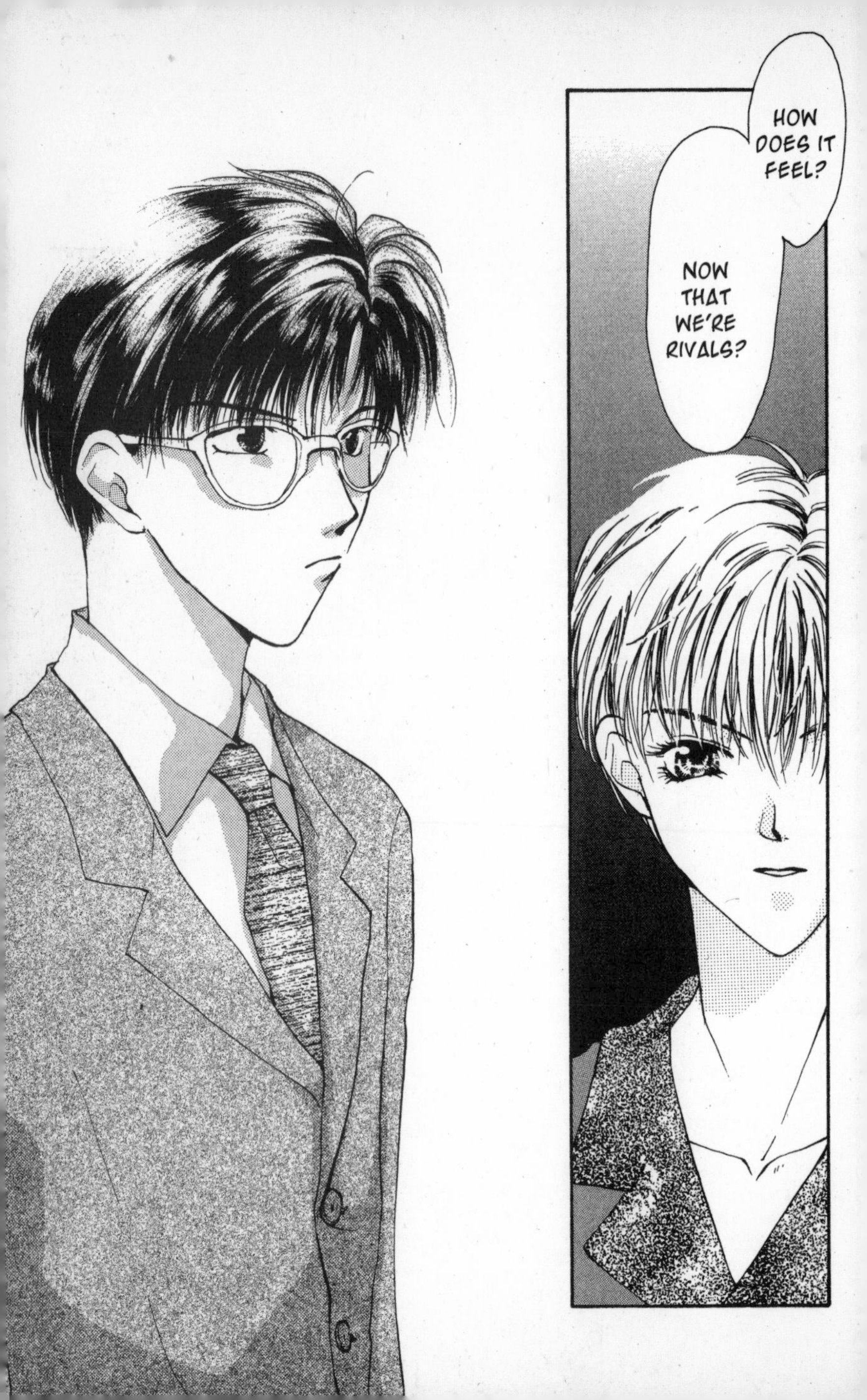
HOW DOES IT FEEL?
NOW THAT WE'RE RIVALS?

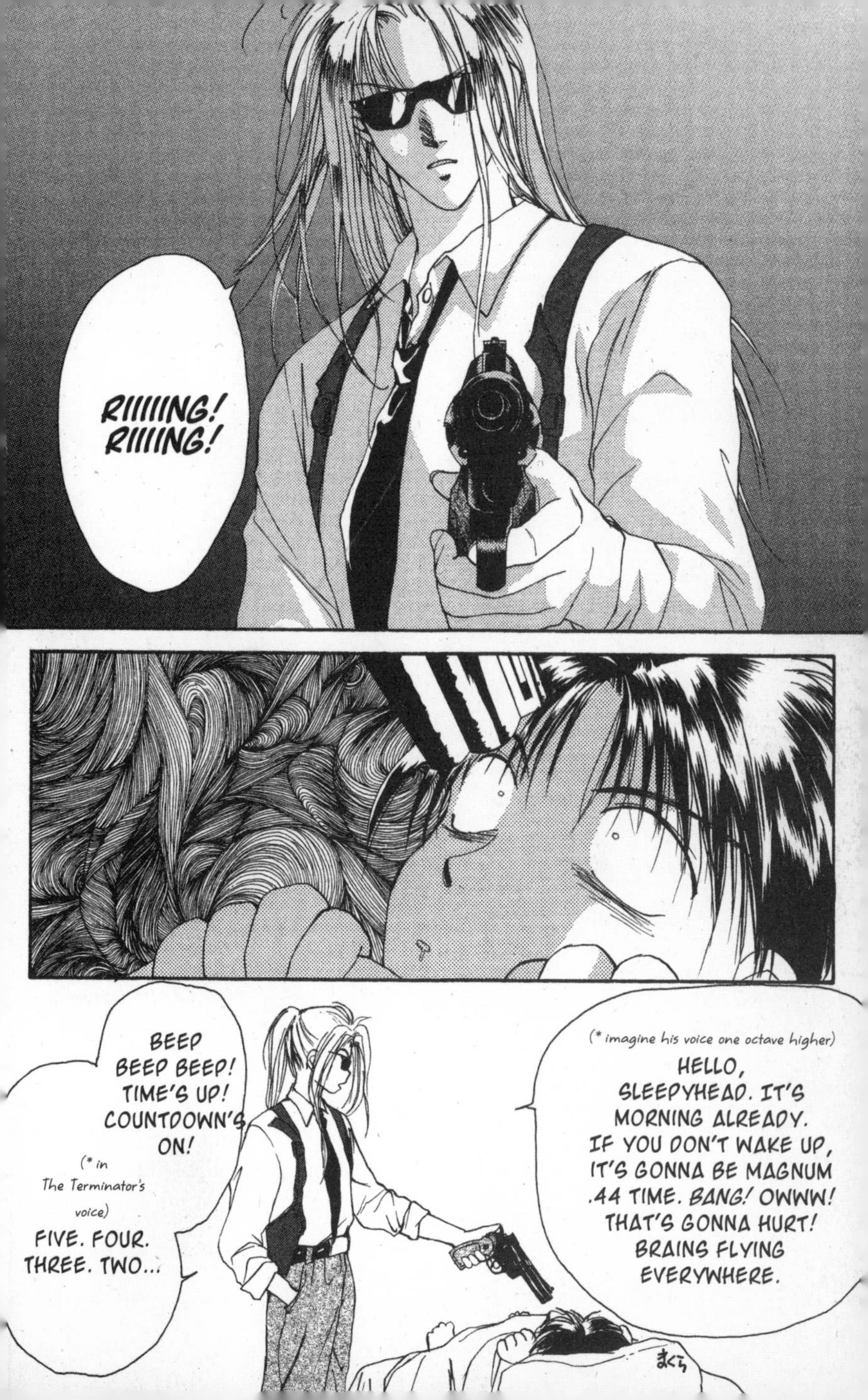
RIIIIING! RIIIING!
(* imagine his voice one octave higher)
HELLO, SLEEPYHEAD. IT'S MORNING ALREADY. IF YOU DON'T WAKE UP, IT'S GONNA BE MAGNUM .44 TIME. *BANG!* OWWW! THAT'S GONNA HURT! BRAINS FLYING EVERYWHERE.
BEEP BEEP BEEP! TIME'S UP! COUNTDOWN'S ON!
(* in The Terminator's voice)
FIVE. FOUR. THREE. TWO...
まくら

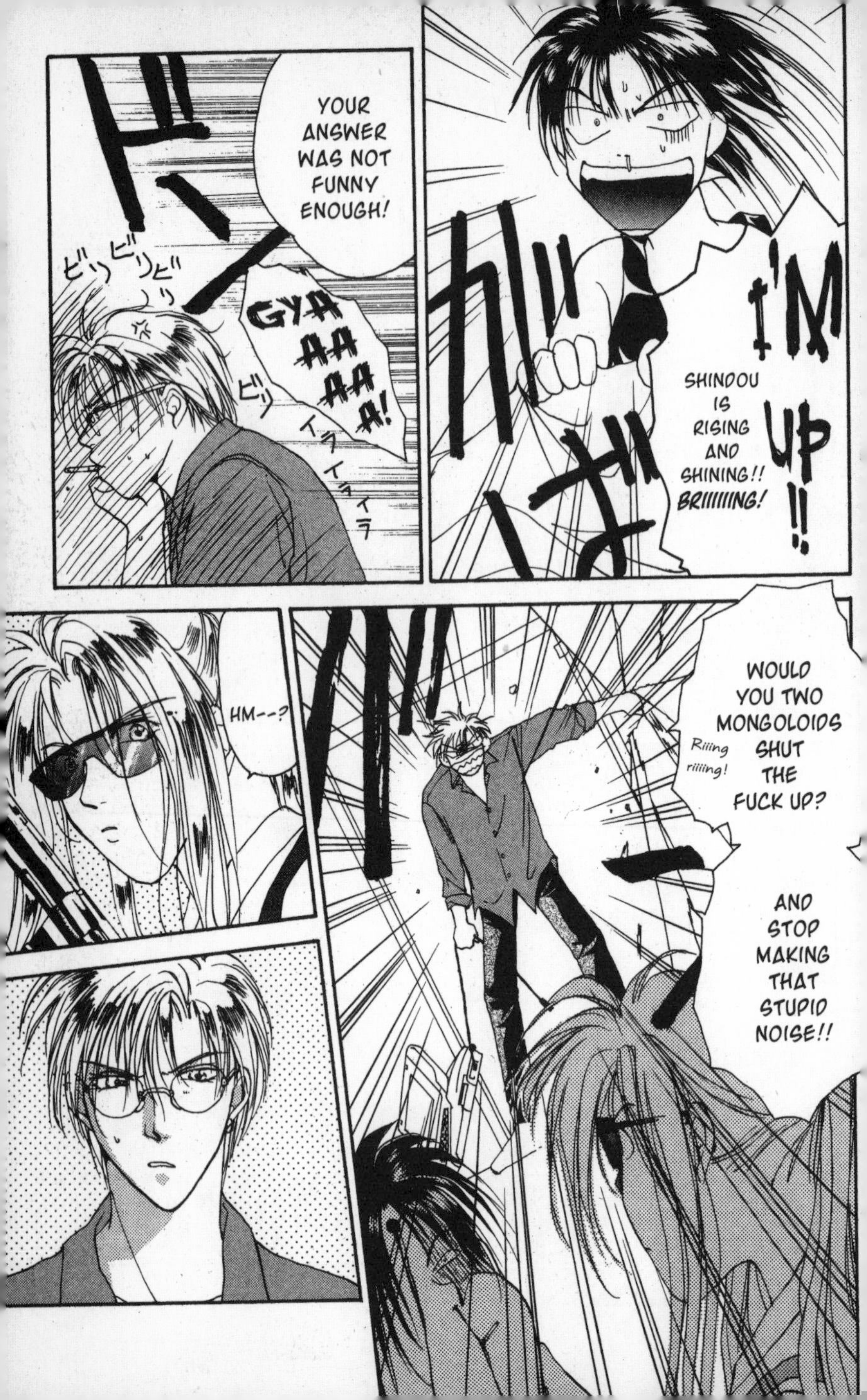
I'M UP!!
SHINDOU IS RISING AND SHINING!! BRIIIIIING!
YOUR ANSWER WAS NOT FUNNY ENOUGH!
GYAAAAAAA!
WOULD YOU TWO MONGOLOIDS SHUT THE FUCK UP?
Riiing riiiing!
AND STOP MAKING THAT STUPID NOISE!!
HM--?

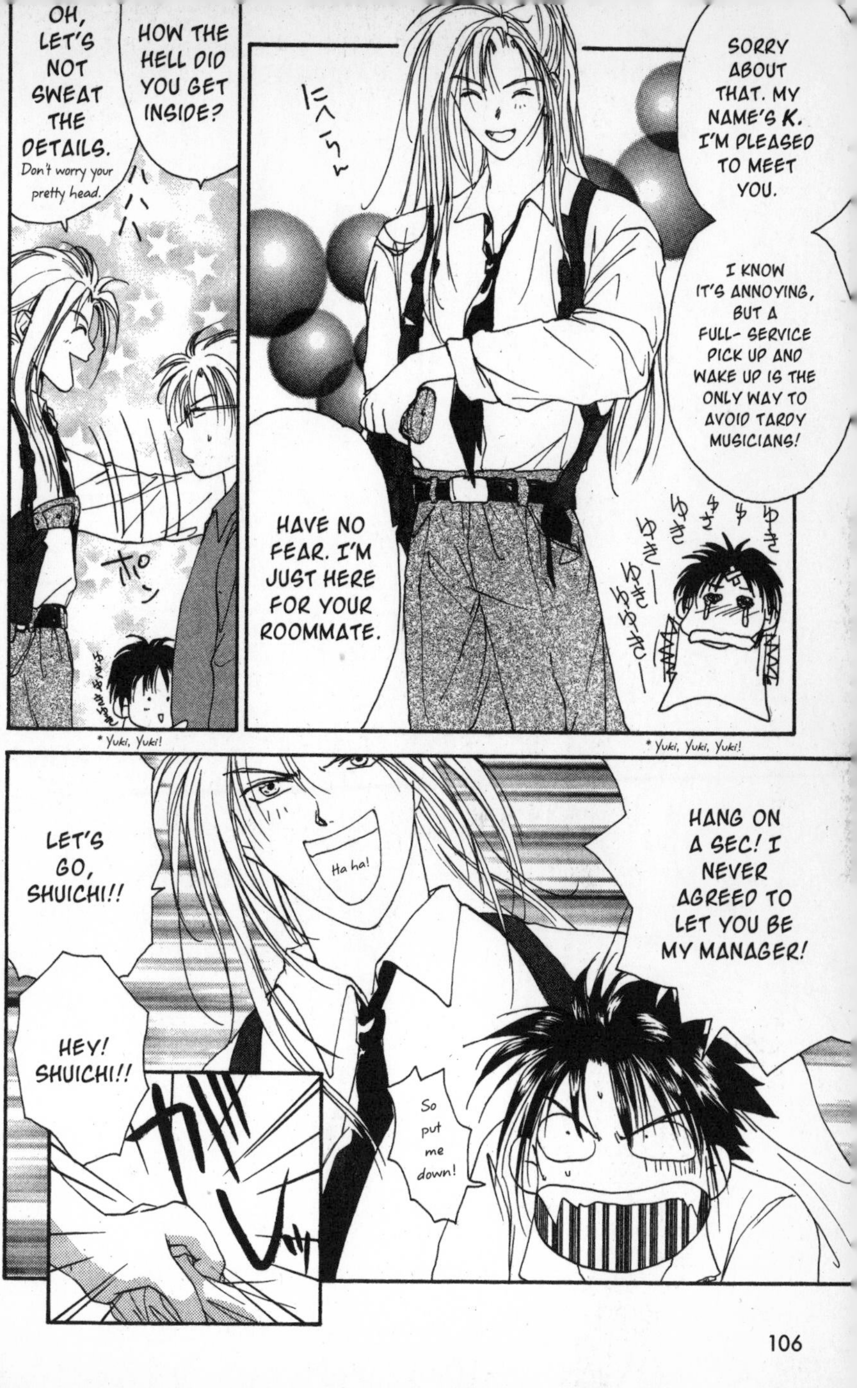
SORRY ABOUT THAT. MY NAME'S K. I'M PLEASED TO MEET YOU.
I KNOW IT'S ANNOYING, BUT A FULL- SERVICE PICK UP AND WAKE UP IS THE ONLY WAY TO AVOID TARDY MUSICIANS!
HAVE NO FEAR. I'M JUST HERE FOR YOUR ROOMMATE.
* Yuki, Yuki, Yuki!
HOW THE HELL DID YOU GET INSIDE?
OH, LET'S NOT SWEAT THE DETAILS.
Don't worry your pretty head.
ハハハ
ポン
* Yuki, Yuki!
HANG ON A SEC! I NEVER AGREED TO LET YOU BE MY MANAGER!
LET'S GO, SHUICHI!!
Ha ha!
So put me down!
HEY! SHUICHI!!

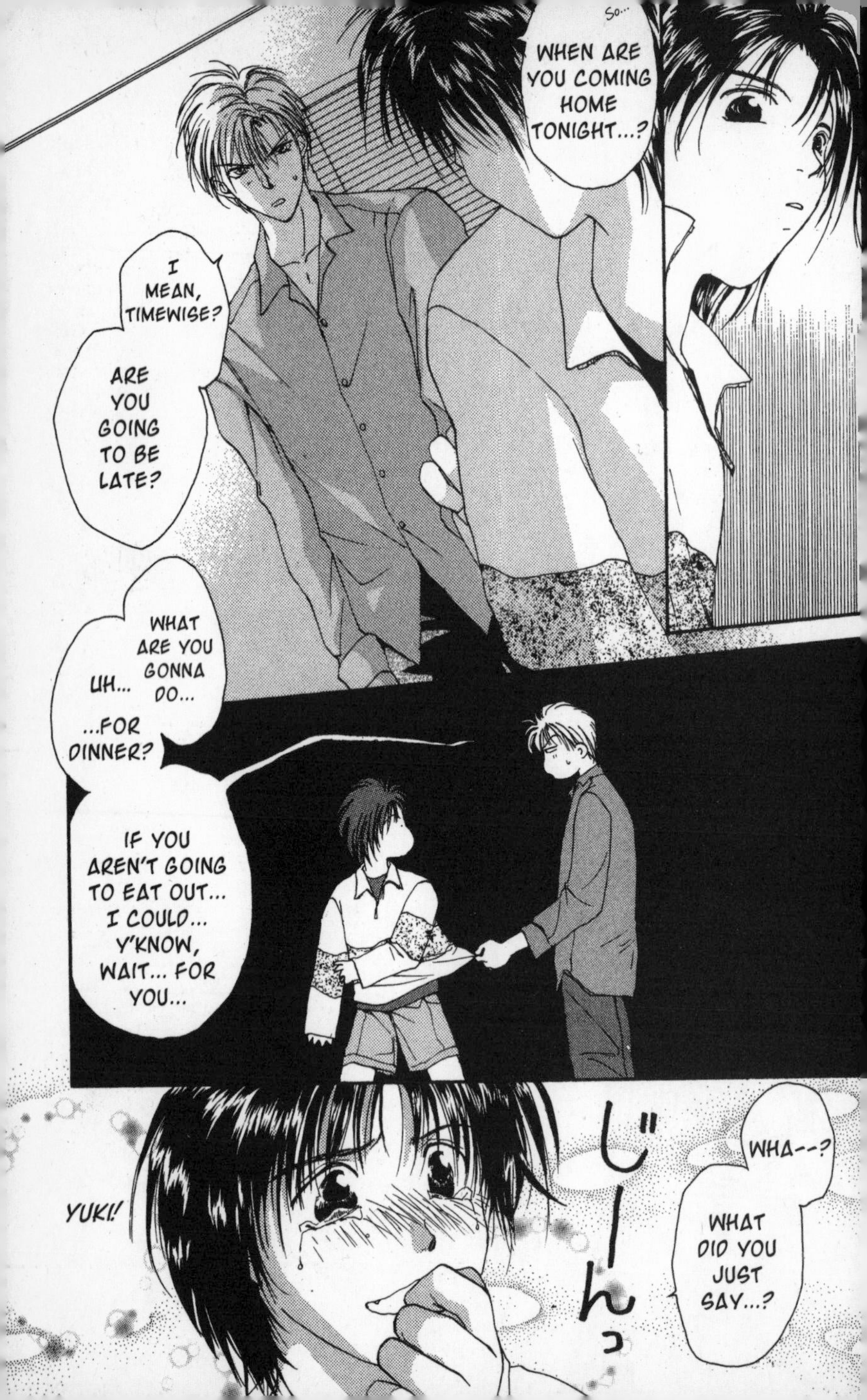
So...
WHEN ARE YOU COMING HOME TONIGHT...?
I MEAN, TIMEWISE?
ARE YOU GOING TO BE LATE?
WHAT ARE YOU GONNA DO...
UH...
...FOR DINNER?
IF YOU AREN'T GOING TO EAT OUT... I COULD... Y'KNOW, WAIT... FOR YOU...
じーんっ
WHA--?
WHAT DID YOU JUST SAY...?
YUKI!

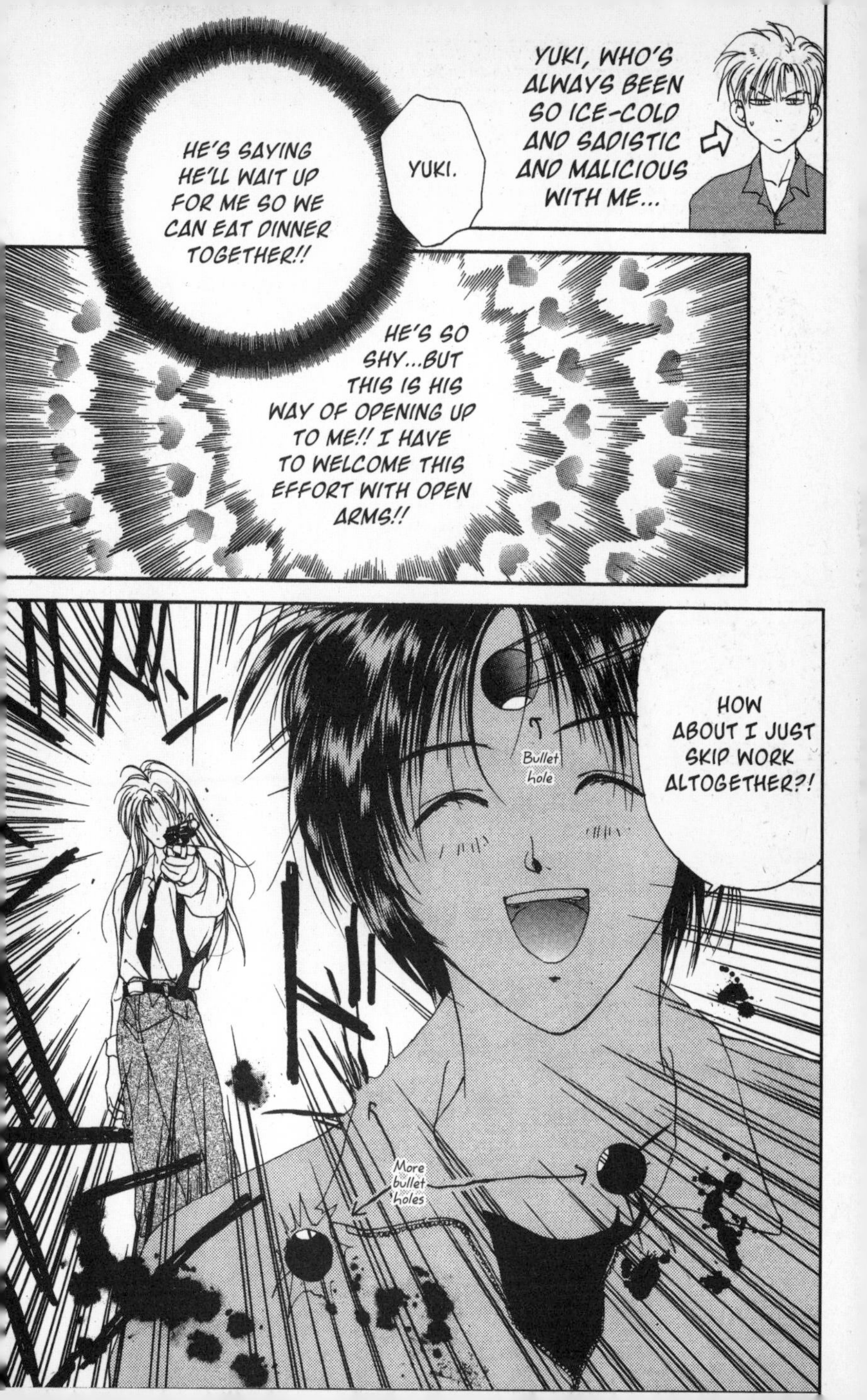
YUKI, WHO'S ALWAYS BEEN SO ICE-COLD AND SADISTIC AND MALICIOUS WITH ME...
YUKI.
HE'S SAYING HE'LL WAIT UP FOR ME SO WE CAN EAT DINNER TOGETHER!!
HE'S SO SHY...BUT THIS IS HIS WAY OF OPENING UP TO ME!! I HAVE TO WELCOME THIS EFFORT WITH OPEN ARMS!!
HOW ABOUT I JUST SKIP WORK ALTOGETHER?!
Bullet hole
More bullet holes

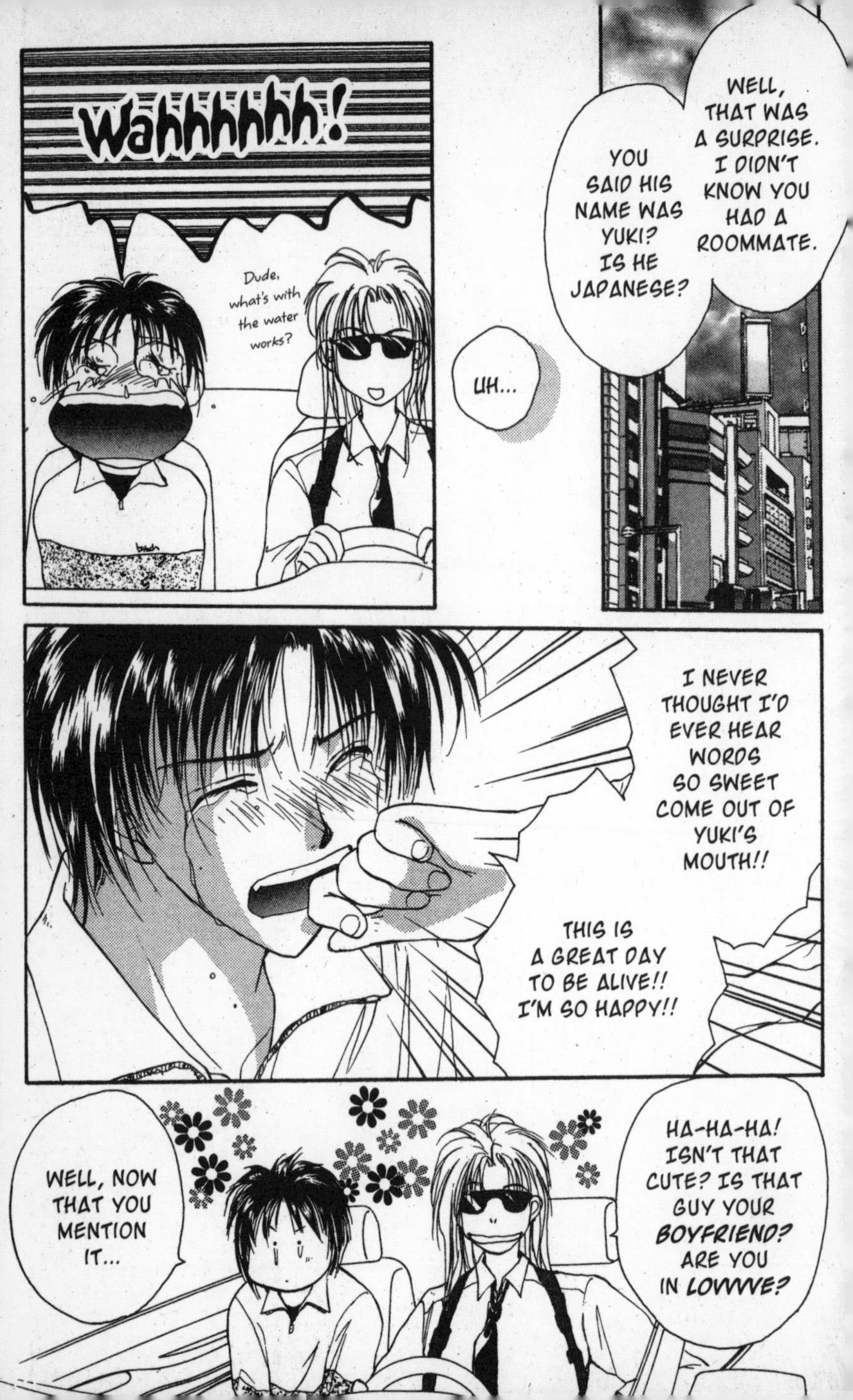
WELL, THAT WAS A SURPRISE. I DIDN'T KNOW YOU HAD A ROOMMATE.
YOU SAID HIS NAME WAS YUKI? IS HE JAPANESE?
UH...
Wahhhhhh!
Dude, what's with the water works?
I NEVER THOUGHT I'D EVER HEAR WORDS SO SWEET COME OUT OF YUKI'S MOUTH!!
THIS IS A GREAT DAY TO BE ALIVE!! I'M SO HAPPY!!
HA-HA-HA! ISN'T THAT CUTE? IS THAT GUY YOUR *BOYFRIEND?* ARE YOU IN *LOVVVVE?*
WELL, NOW THAT YOU MENTION IT...

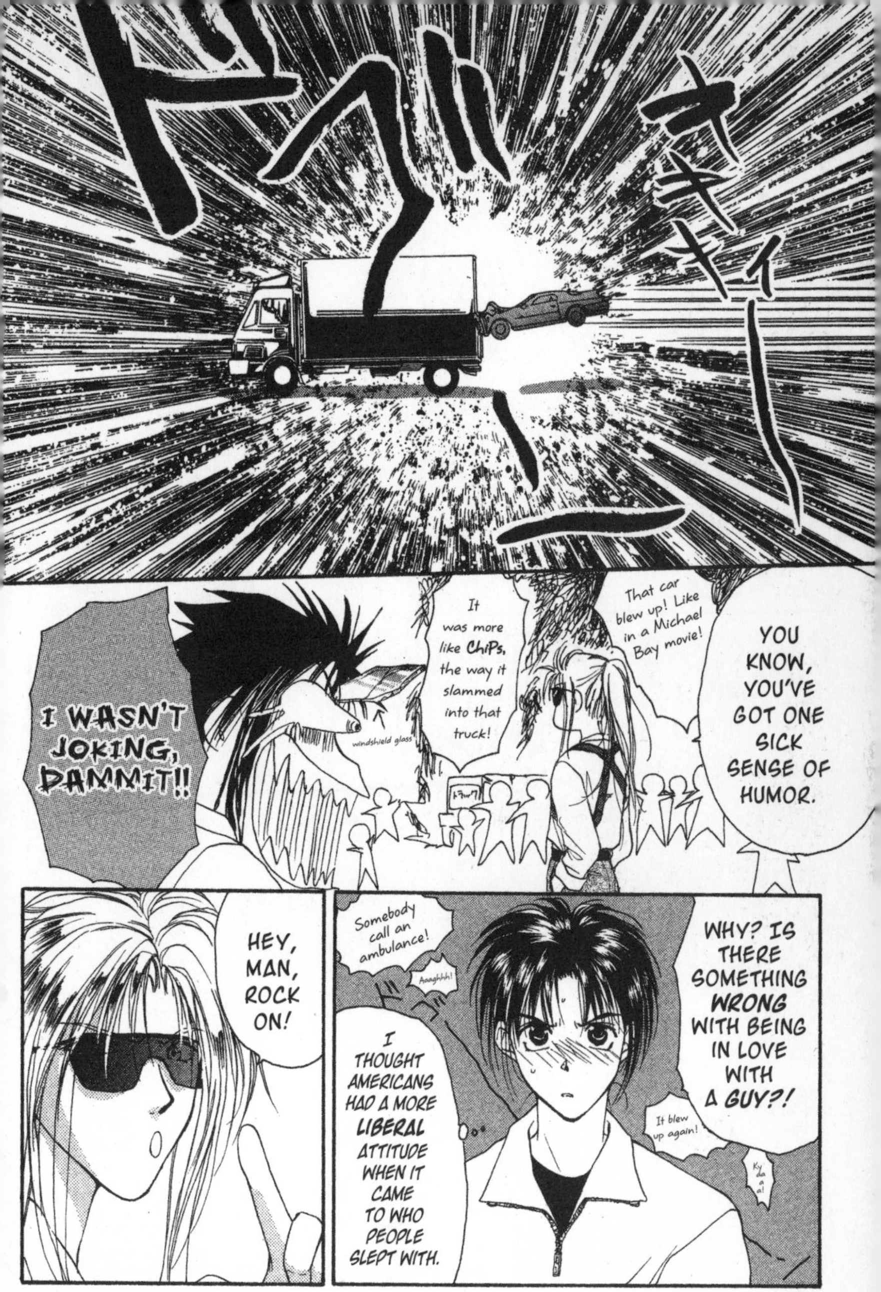
YOU KNOW, YOU'VE GOT ONE SICK SENSE OF HUMOR.
That car blew up! Like in a Michael Bay movie!
It was more like ChiPs, the way it slammed into that truck!
windshield glass
I WASN'T JOKING, DAMMIT!!
WHY? IS THERE SOMETHING WRONG WITH BEING IN LOVE WITH A GUY?!
Somebody call an ambulance!
Aaaghhh!
It blew up again!
Ky da a a!
I THOUGHT AMERICANS HAD A MORE LIBERAL ATTITUDE WHEN IT CAME TO WHO PEOPLE SLEPT WITH.
HEY, MAN, ROCK ON!

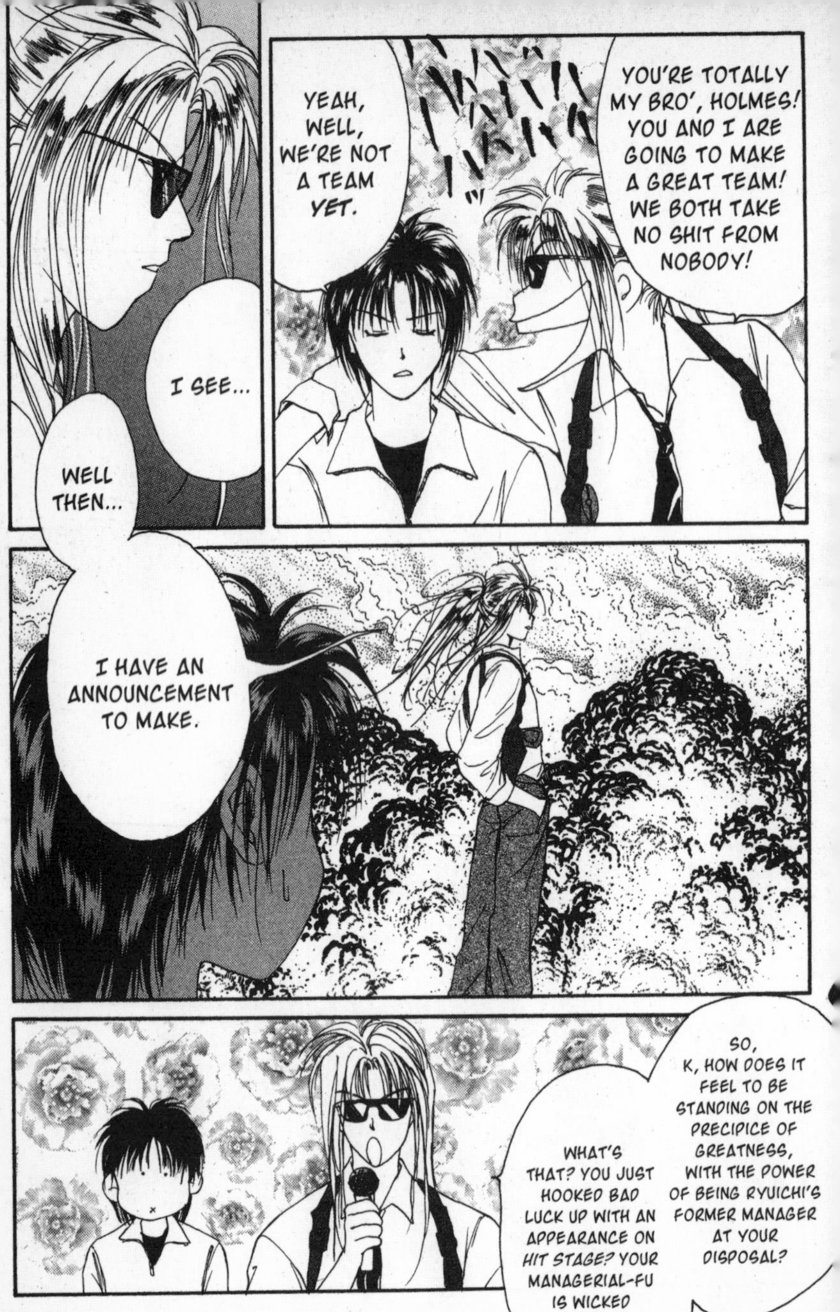
YOU'RE TOTALLY MY BRO', HOLMES! YOU AND I ARE GOING TO MAKE A GREAT TEAM! WE BOTH TAKE NO SHIT FROM NOBODY!
YEAH, WELL, WE'RE NOT A TEAM *YET.*
I SEE...
WELL THEN...
I HAVE AN ANNOUNCEMENT TO MAKE.
SO, K, HOW DOES IT FEEL TO BE STANDING ON THE PRECIPICE OF GREATNESS, WITH THE POWER OF BEING RYUICHI'S FORMER MANAGER AT YOUR DISPOSAL?
WHAT'S THAT? YOU JUST HOOKED BAD LUCK UP WITH AN APPEARANCE ON *HIT STAGE?* YOUR MANAGERIAL-FU IS WICKED FIERCE!

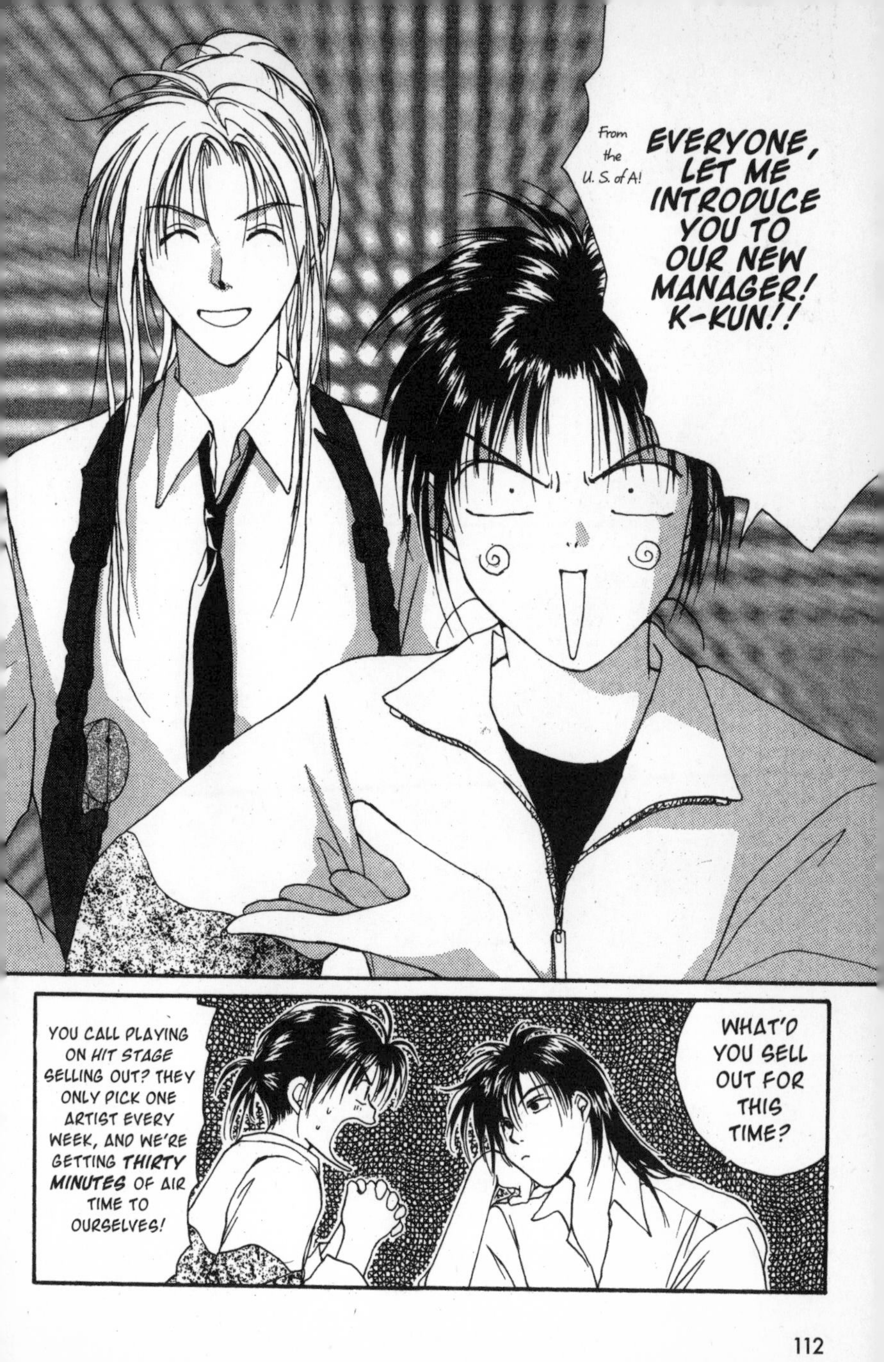
EVERYONE, LET ME INTRODUCE YOU TO OUR NEW MANAGER! K-KUN!!
From the U. S. of A!
WHAT'D YOU SELL OUT FOR THIS TIME?
YOU CALL PLAYING ON HIT STAGE SELLING OUT? THEY ONLY PICK ONE ARTIST EVERY WEEK, AND WE'RE GETTING **THIRTY MINUTES** OF AIR TIME TO OURSELVES!

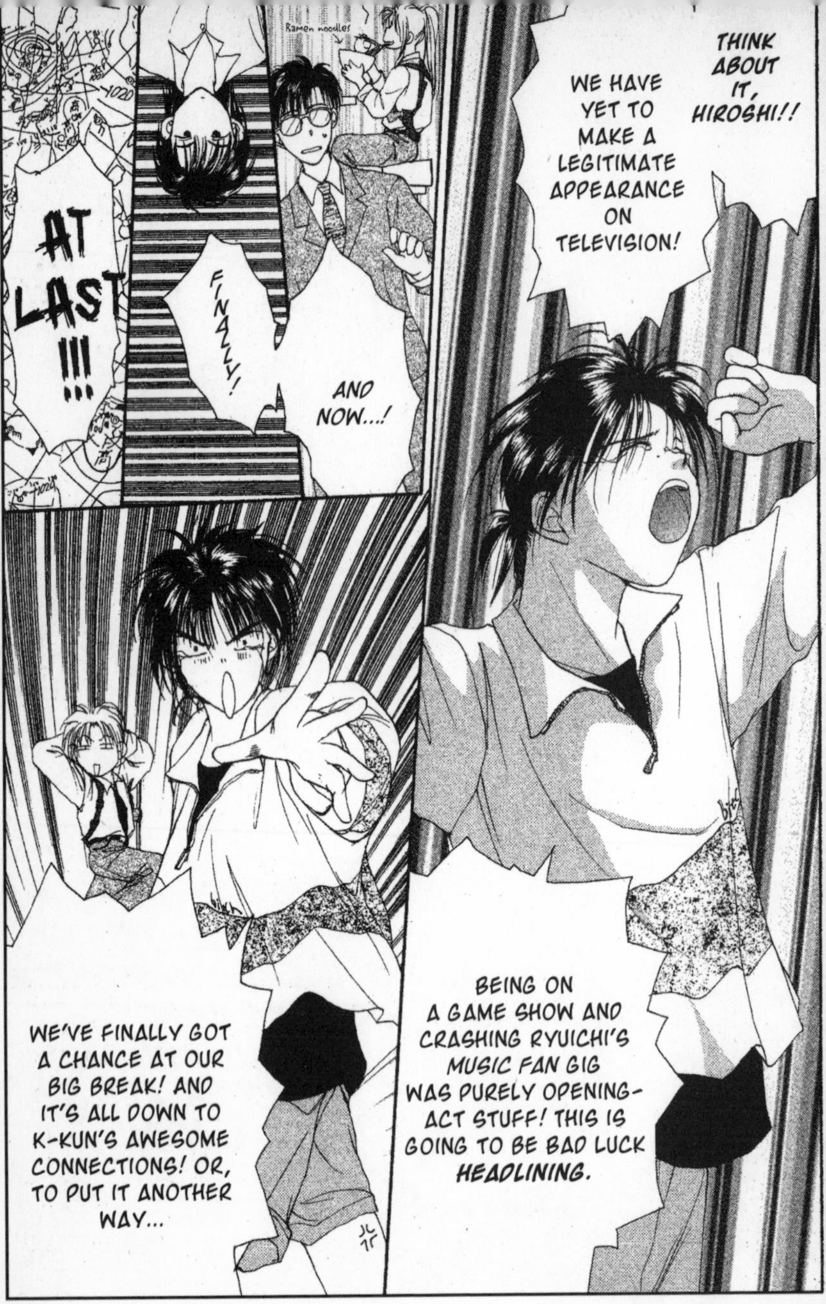
THINK ABOUT IT, HIROSHI!!
WE HAVE YET TO MAKE A LEGITIMATE APPEARANCE ON TELEVISION!
BEING ON A GAME SHOW AND CRASHING RYUICHI'S MUSIC FAN GIG WAS PURELY OPENING-ACT STUFF! THIS IS GOING TO BE BAD LUCK **HEADLINING.**
Ramen noodles
AND NOW...!
FINALLY!
AT LAST!!!
WE'VE FINALLY GOT A CHANCE AT OUR BIG BREAK! AND IT'S ALL DOWN TO K-KUN'S AWESOME CONNECTIONS! OR, TO PUT IT ANOTHER WAY...

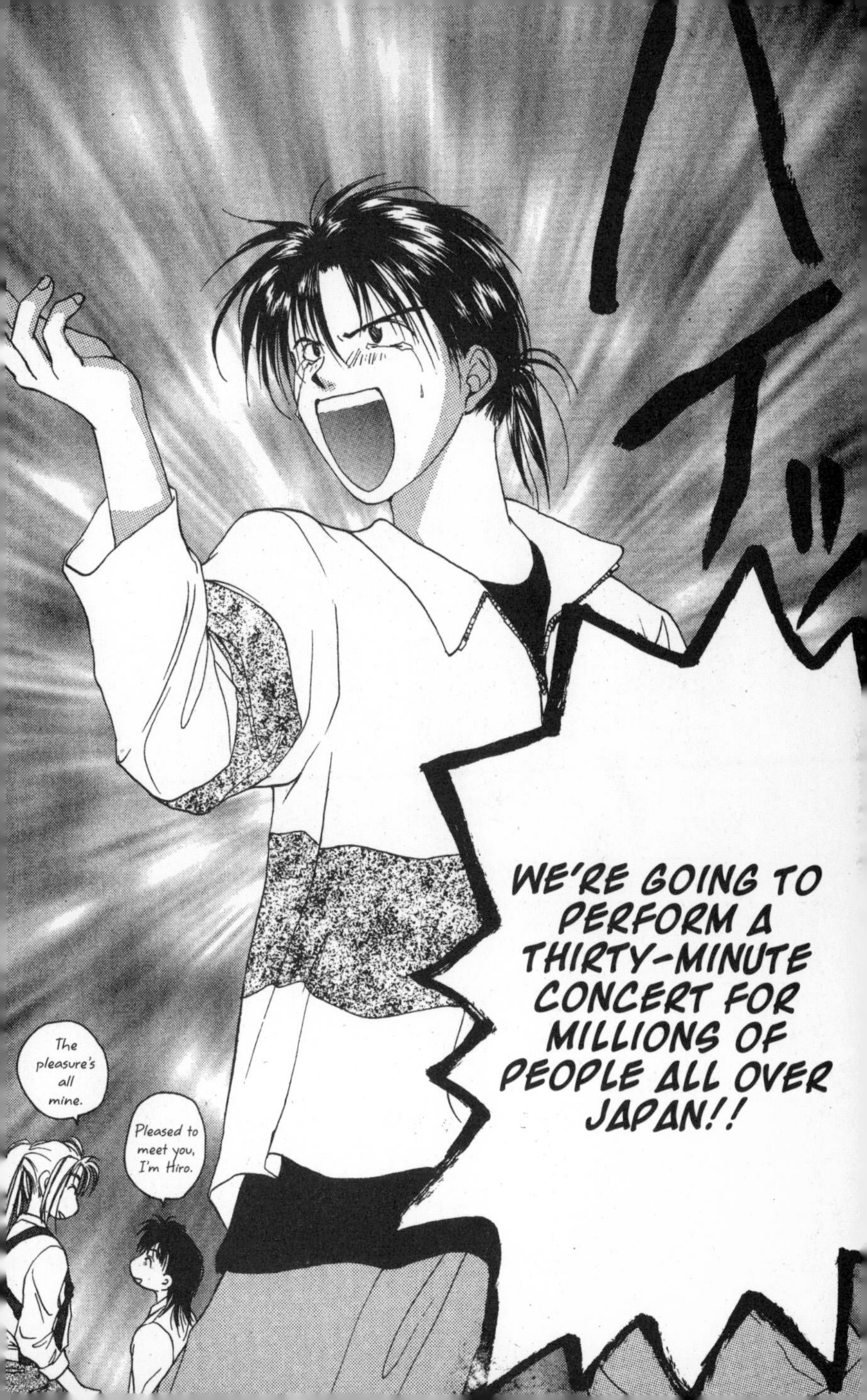
WE'RE GOING TO PERFORM A THIRTY-MINUTE CONCERT FOR MILLIONS OF PEOPLE ALL OVER JAPAN!!
Pleased to meet you, I'm Hiro.
The pleasure's all mine.

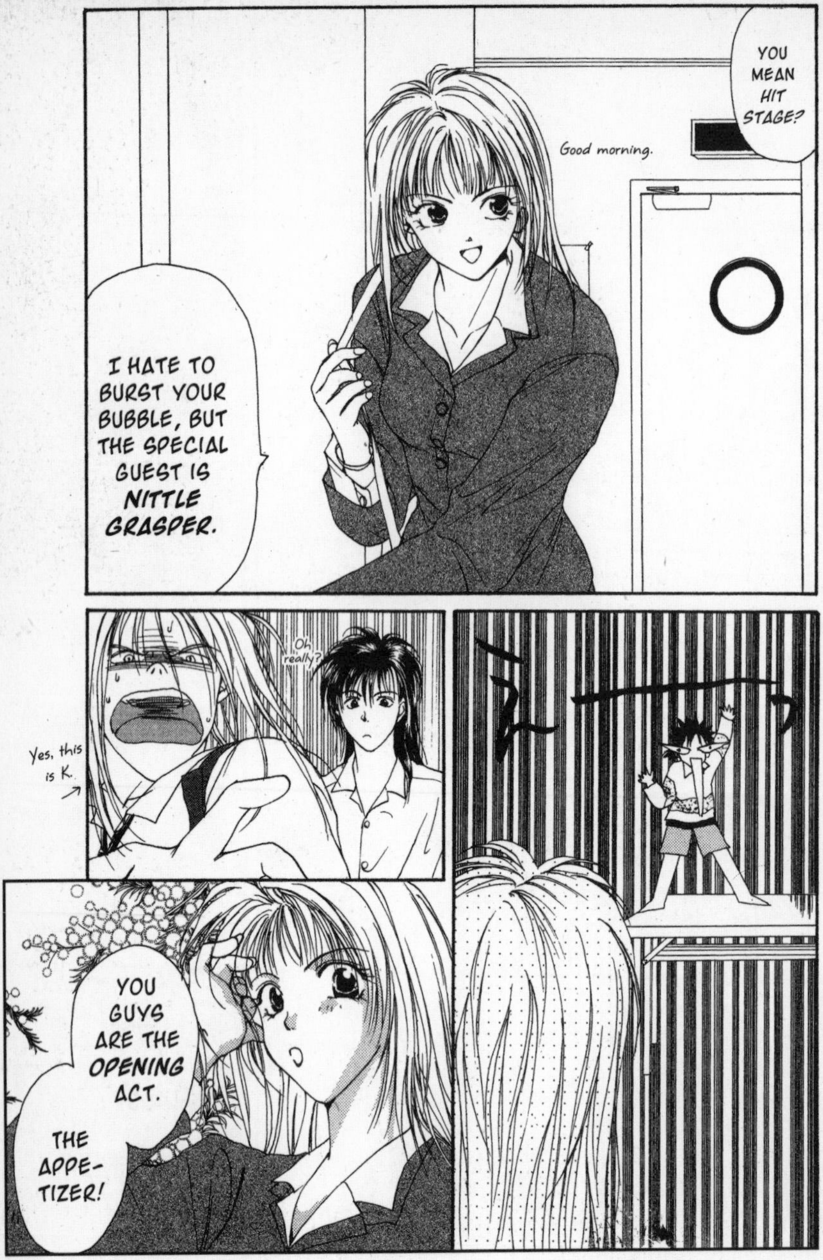
YOU MEAN HIT STAGE?
Good morning.
I HATE TO BURST YOUR BUBBLE, BUT THE SPECIAL GUEST IS NITTLE GRASPER.
Oh really?
YOU GUYS ARE THE OPENING ACT.
THE APPE-TIZER!

Yes, this is K.

* Whaaat?!

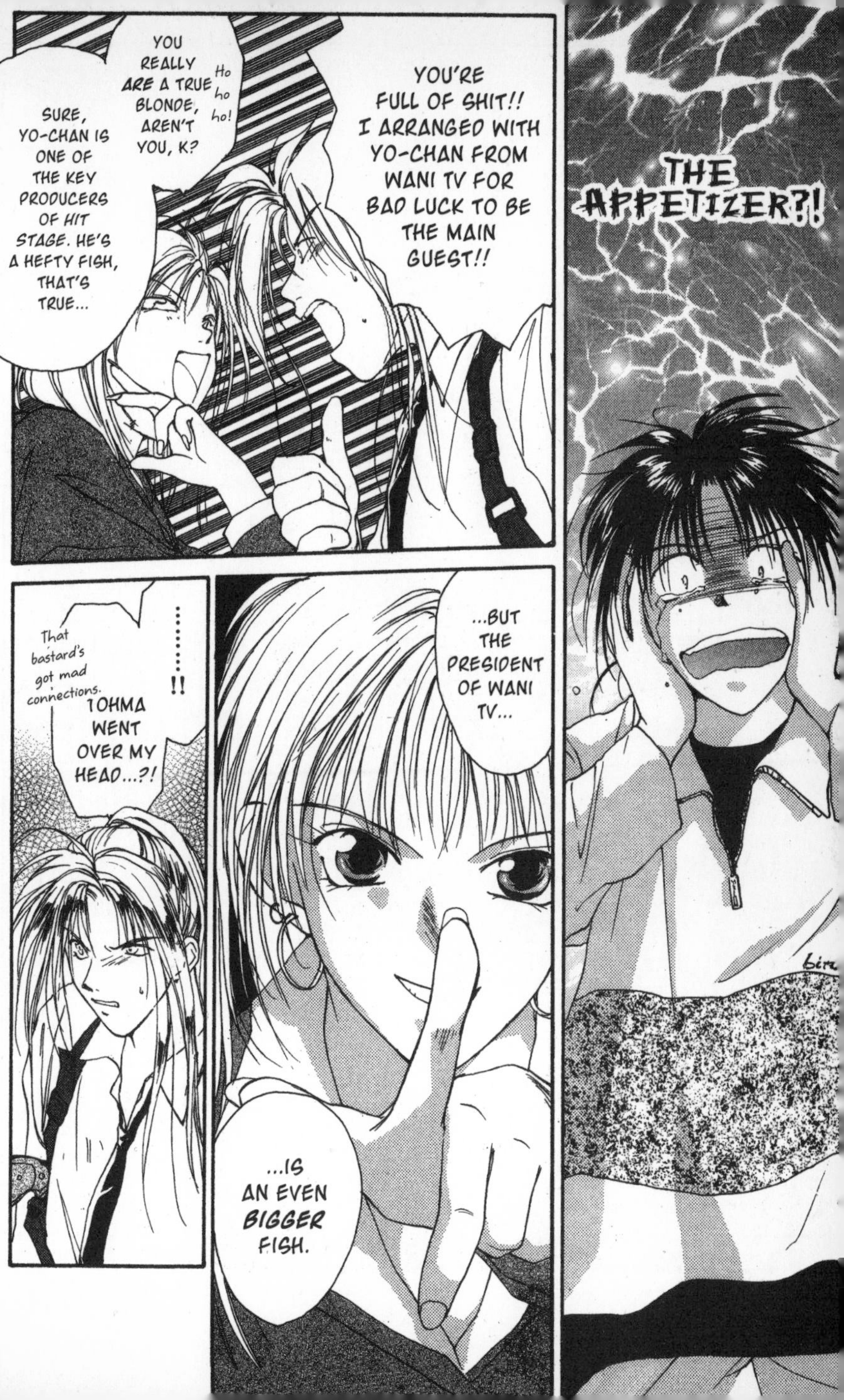
THE APPETIZER?!
YOU'RE FULL OF SHIT!! I ARRANGED WITH YO-CHAN FROM WANI TV FOR BAD LUCK TO BE THE MAIN GUEST!!
YOU REALLY ARE A TRUE BLONDE, AREN'T YOU, K?
Ho ho ho!
SURE, YO-CHAN IS ONE OF THE KEY PRODUCERS OF HIT STAGE. HE'S A HEFTY FISH, THAT'S TRUE...
...BUT THE PRESIDENT OF WANI TV...
...IS AN EVEN BIGGER FISH.
......!!
TOHMA WENT OVER MY HEAD...?!
That bastard's got mad connections.

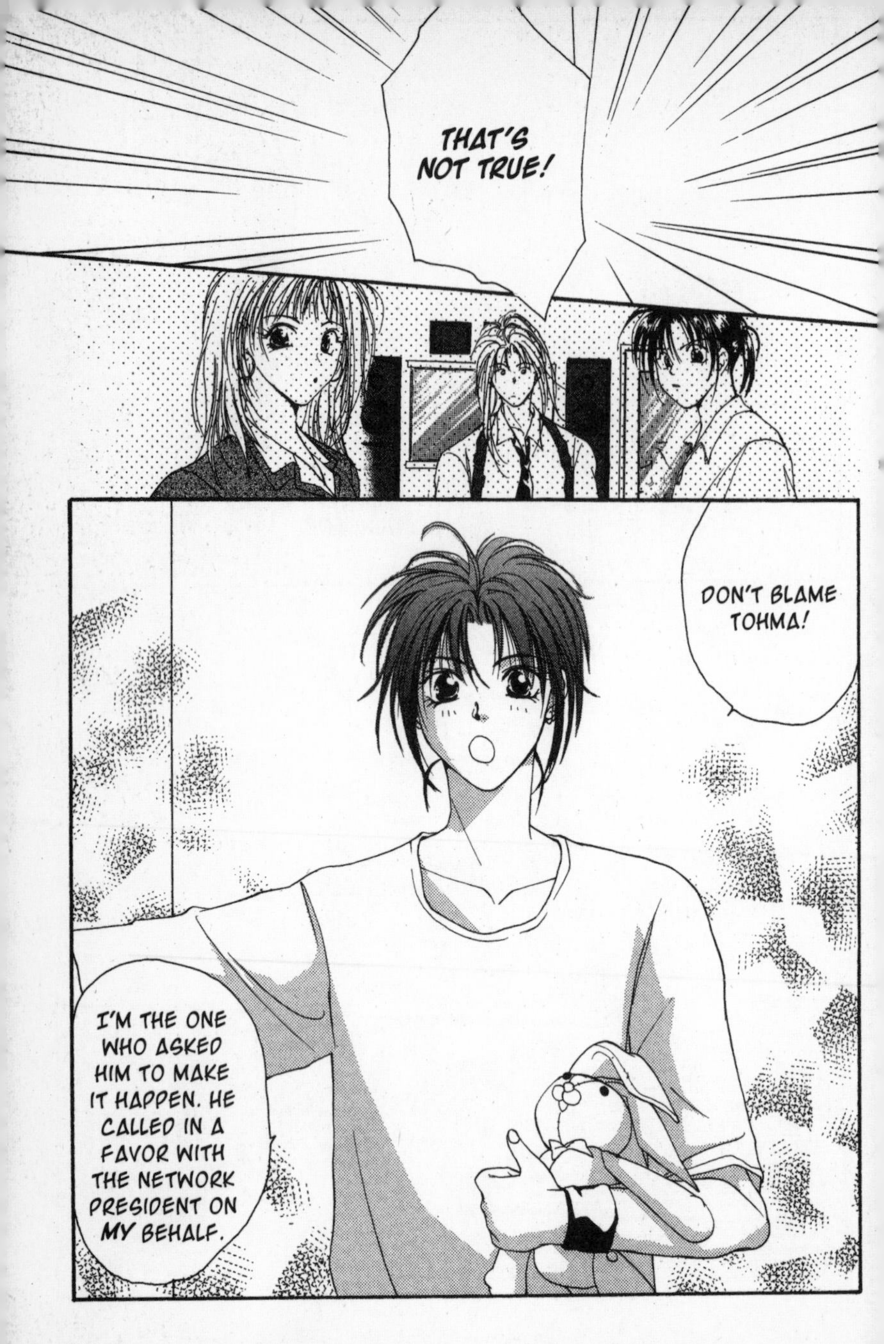
THAT'S NOT TRUE!
DON'T BLAME TOHMA!
I'M THE ONE WHO ASKED HIM TO MAKE IT HAPPEN. HE CALLED IN A FAVOR WITH THE NETWORK PRESIDENT ON *MY* BEHALF.

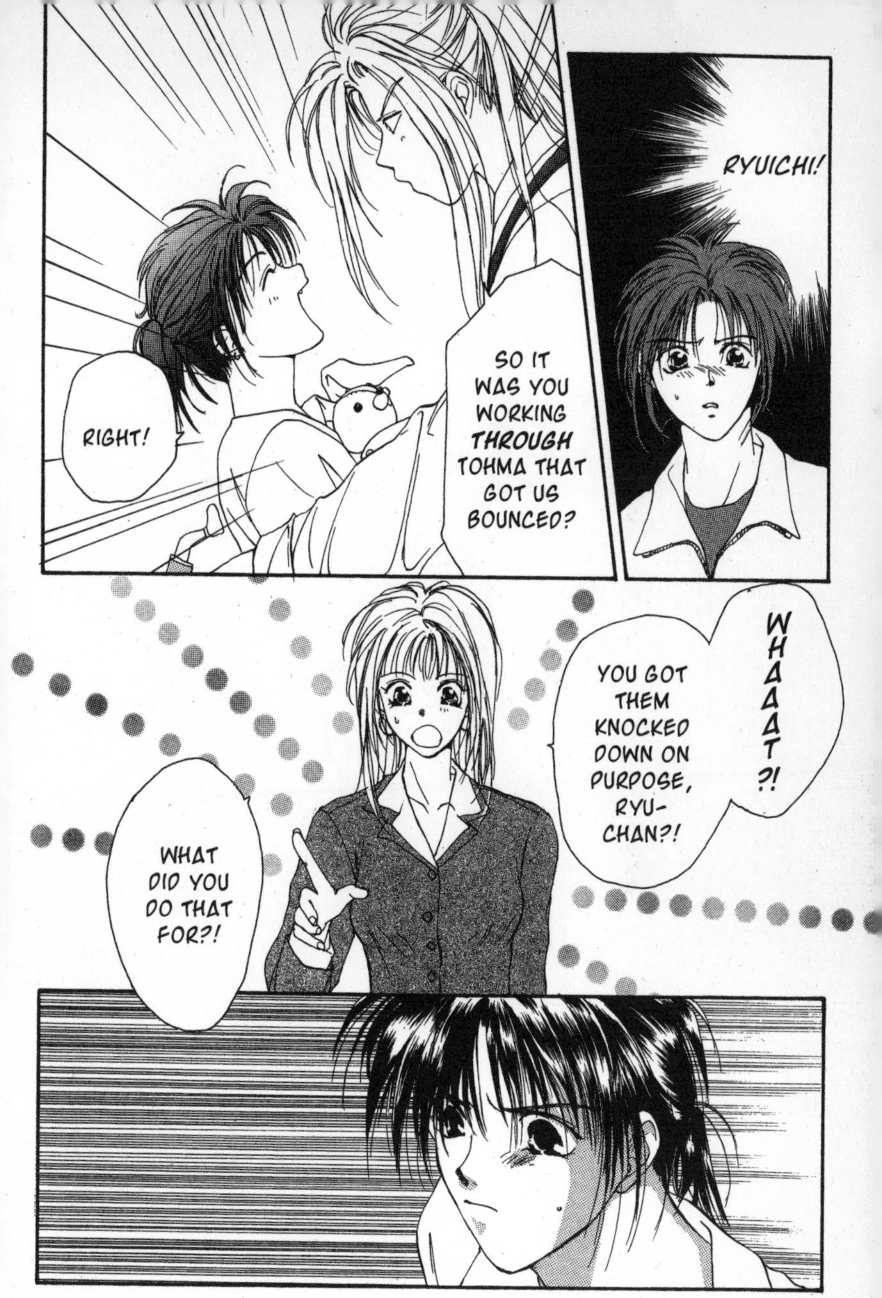
RYUICHI!
SO IT WAS YOU WORKING **THROUGH** TOHMA THAT GOT US BOUNCED?
RIGHT!
WHAAAT?!
YOU GOT THEM KNOCKED DOWN ON PURPOSE, RYU-CHAN?!
WHAT DID YOU DO THAT FOR?!

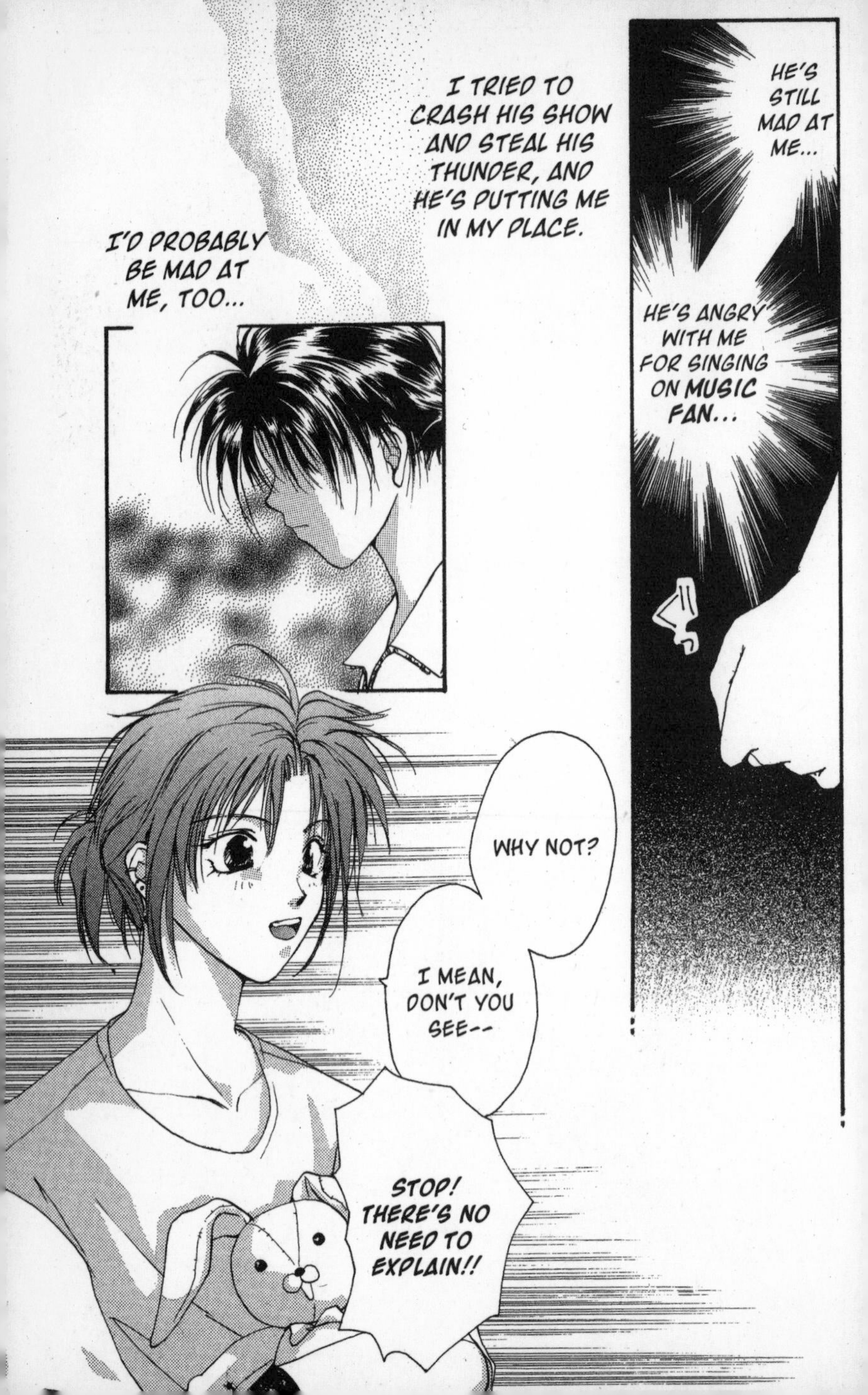
HE'S STILL MAD AT ME...
HE'S ANGRY WITH ME FOR SINGING ON MUSIC FAN...
I TRIED TO CRASH HIS SHOW AND STEAL HIS THUNDER, AND HE'S PUTTING ME IN MY PLACE.
I'D PROBABLY BE MAD AT ME, TOO...
WHY NOT?
I MEAN, DON'T YOU SEE--
STOP! THERE'S NO NEED TO EXPLAIN!!

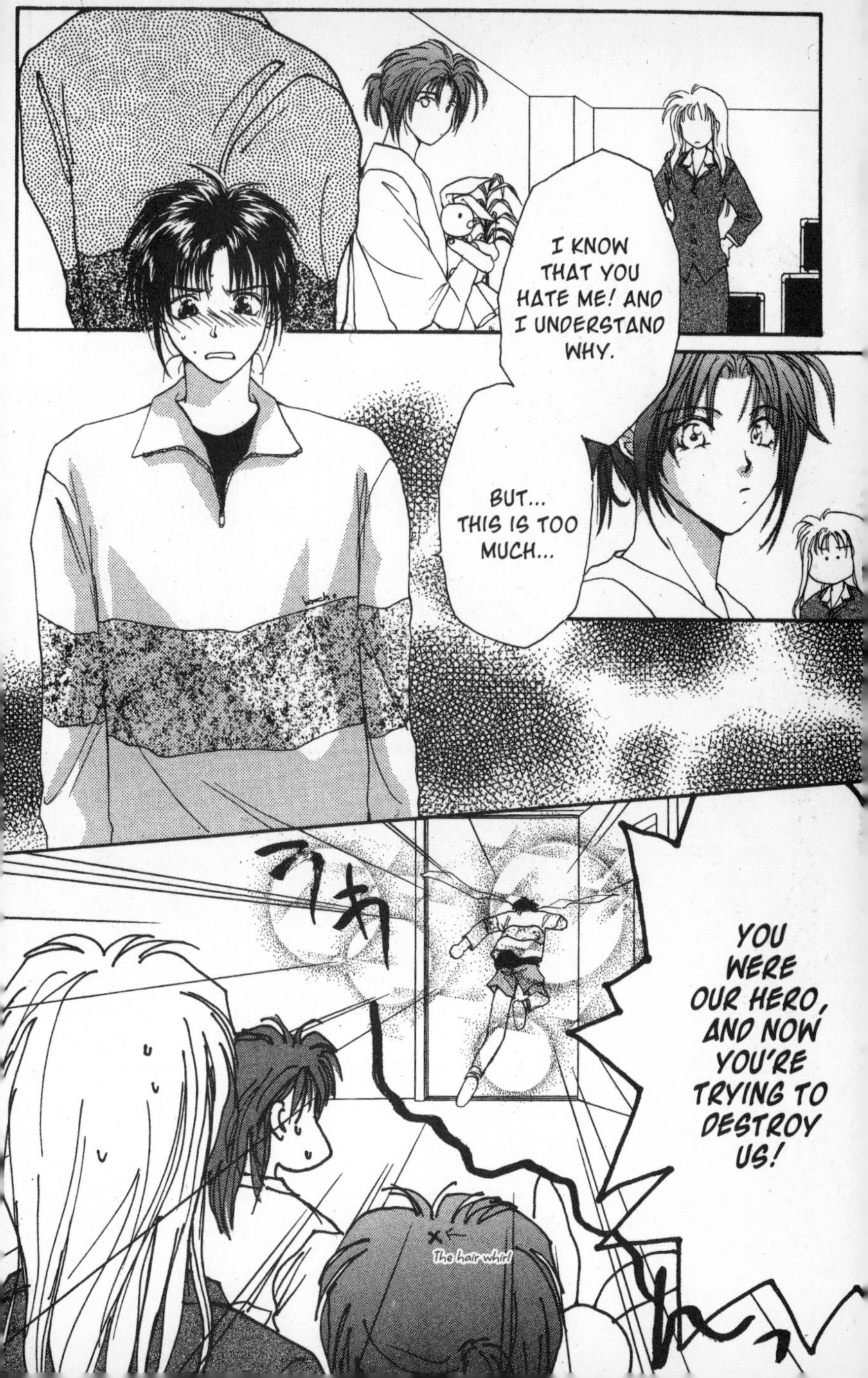
I KNOW THAT YOU HATE ME! AND I UNDERSTAND WHY.
BUT... THIS IS TOO MUCH...
YOU WERE OUR HERO, AND NOW YOU'RE TRYING TO DESTROY US!
The hair whirl

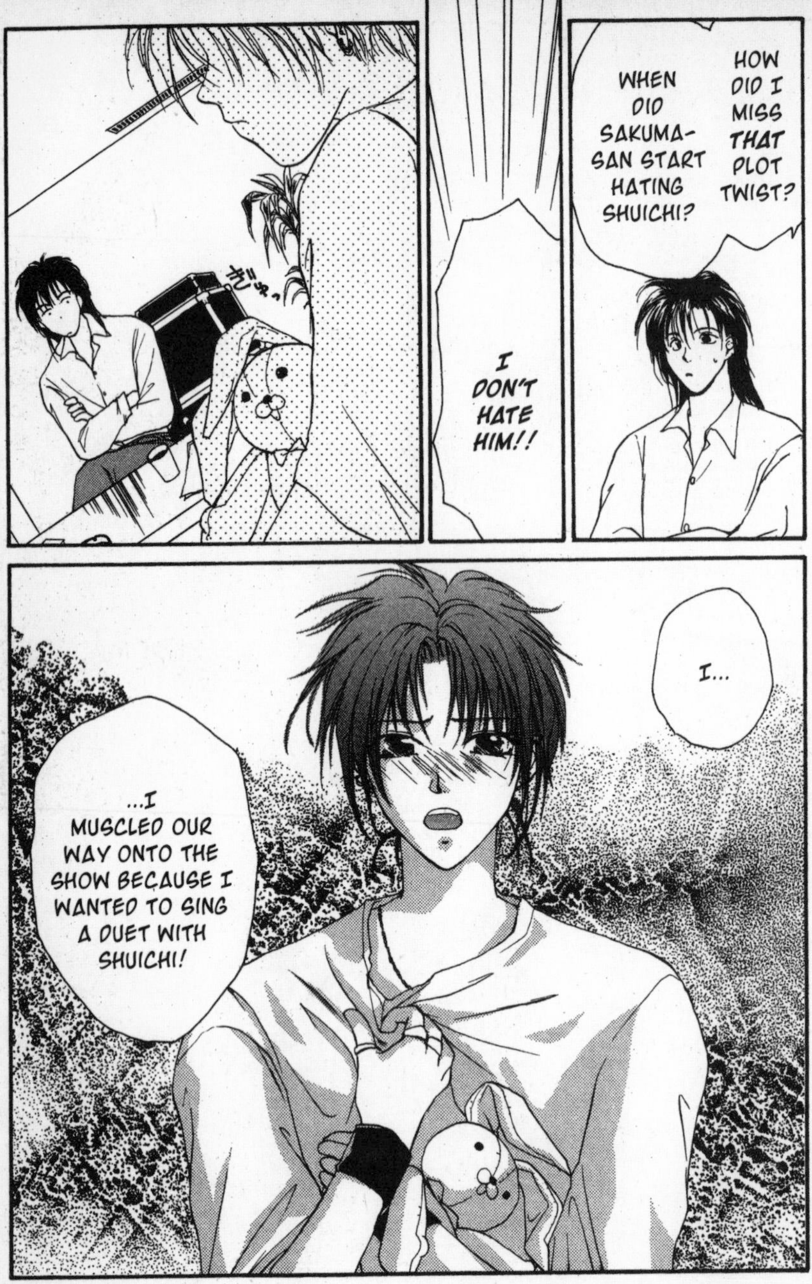
HOW DID I MISS THAT PLOT TWIST?
WHEN DID SAKUMA-SAN START HATING SHUICHI?
I DON'T HATE HIM!!
I...
...I MUSCLED OUR WAY ONTO THE SHOW BECAUSE I WANTED TO SING A DUET WITH SHUICHI!

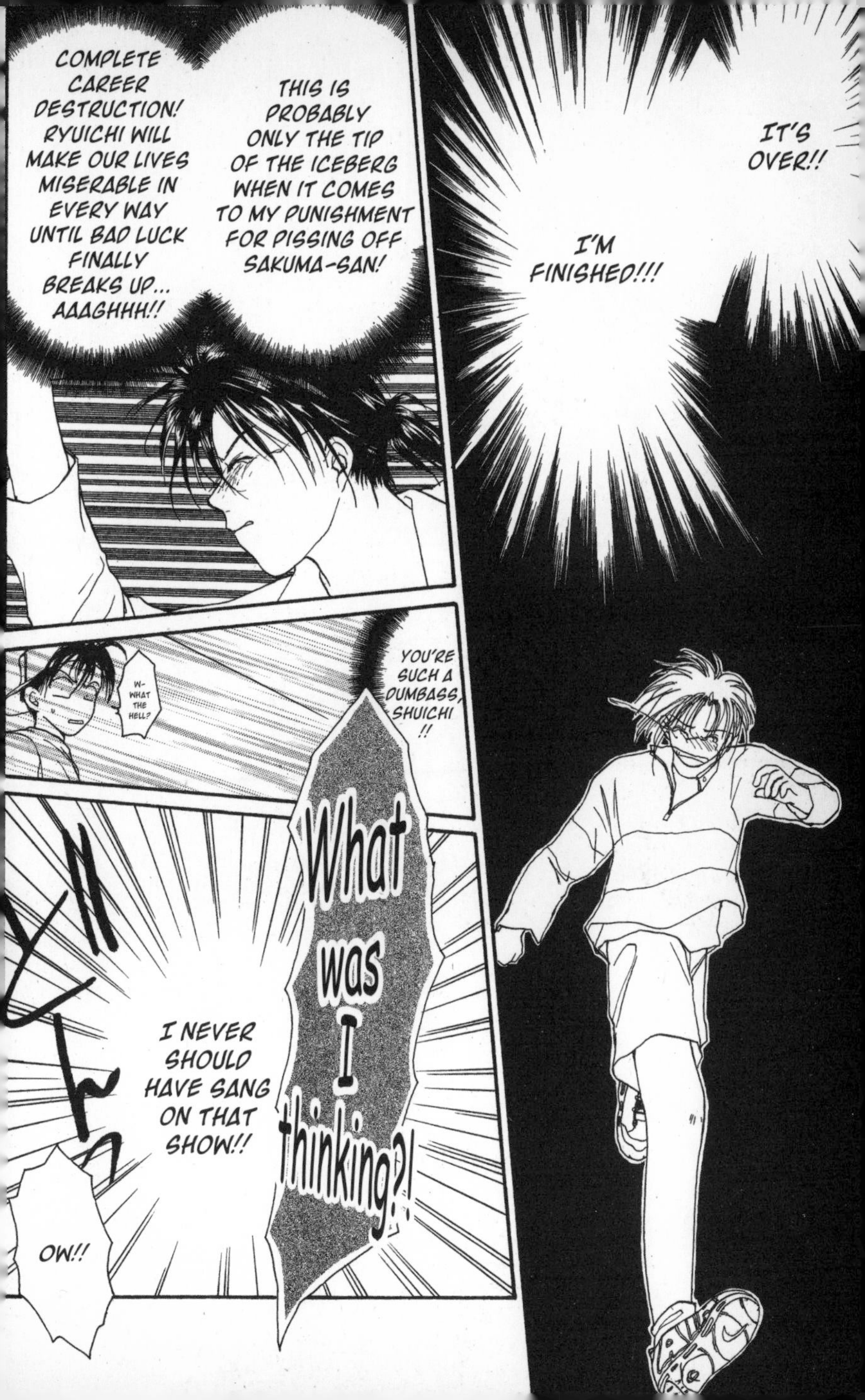
IT'S OVER!!
I'M FINISHED!!!
THIS IS PROBABLY ONLY THE TIP OF THE ICEBERG WHEN IT COMES TO MY PUNISHMENT FOR PISSING OFF SAKUMA-SAN!
COMPLETE CAREER DESTRUCTION! RYUICHI WILL MAKE OUR LIVES MISERABLE IN EVERY WAY UNTIL BAD LUCK FINALLY BREAKS UP... AAAGHHH!!
YOU'RE SUCH A DUMBASS, SHUICHI!!
W-WHAT THE HELL?
What was I thinking?!
I NEVER SHOULD HAVE SANG ON THAT SHOW!!
OW!!

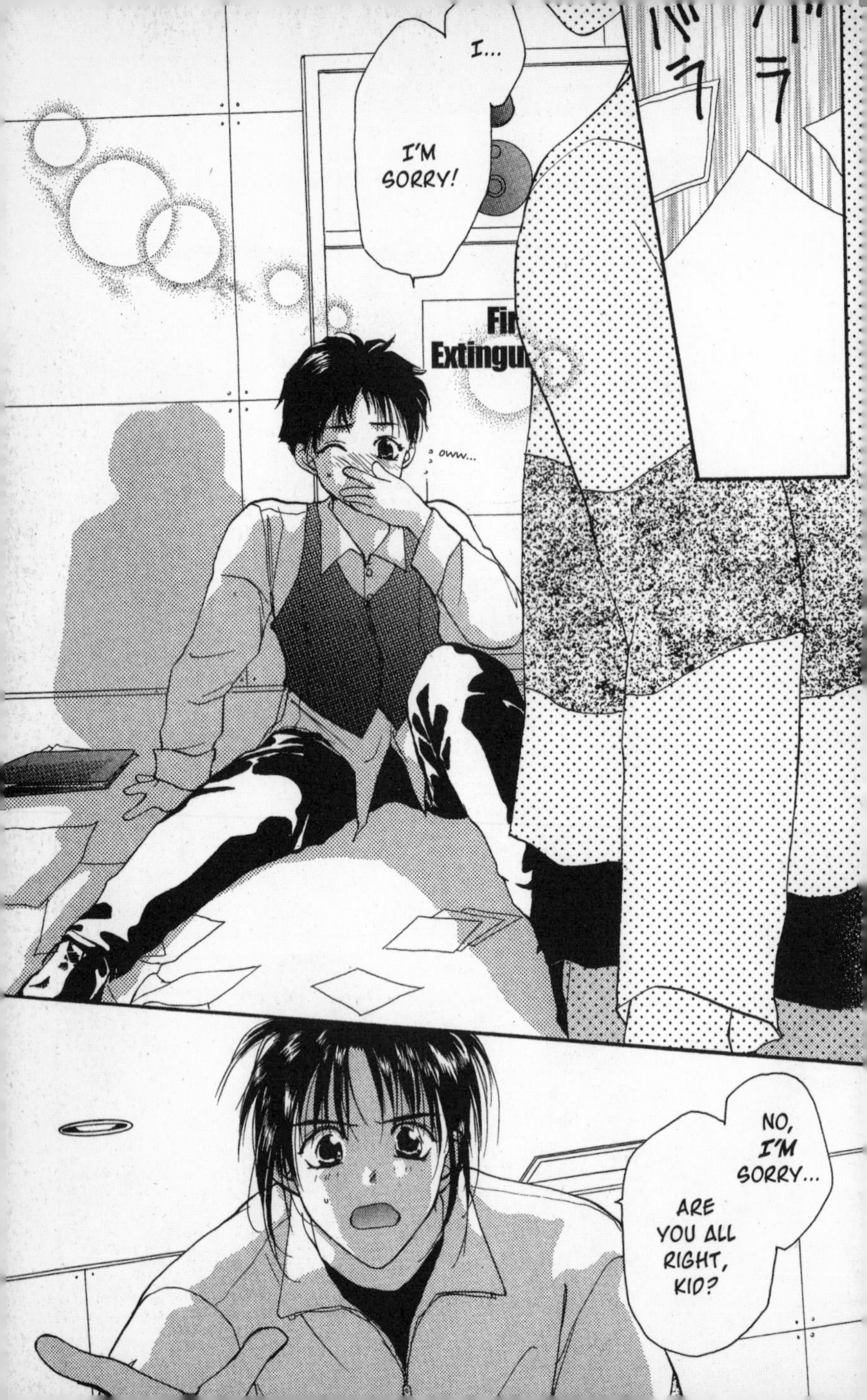
バラ
バラ
I...
I'M SORRY!
Fire
Extingu
oww...
NO, I'M SORRY...
ARE YOU ALL RIGHT, KID?

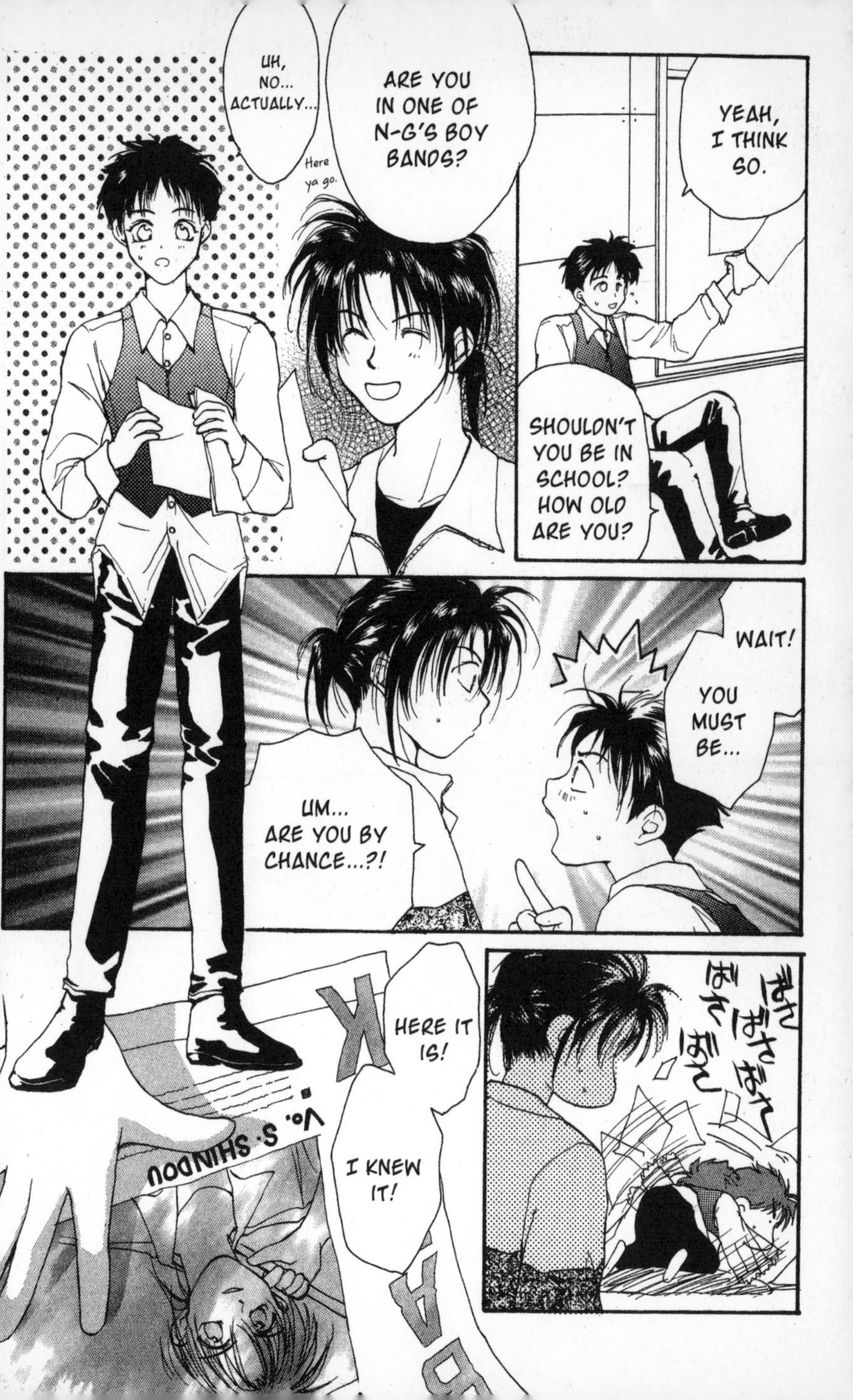
YEAH, I THINK SO.
SHOULDN'T YOU BE IN SCHOOL? HOW OLD ARE YOU?
ARE YOU IN ONE OF N-G'S BOY BANDS?
UH, NO... ACTUALLY...
Here ya go.
WAIT!
YOU MUST BE...
UM... ARE YOU BY CHANCE...?!
ばさ
ばさばさ
ばさばさ
HERE IT IS!
I KNEW IT!
S. SHINDOU

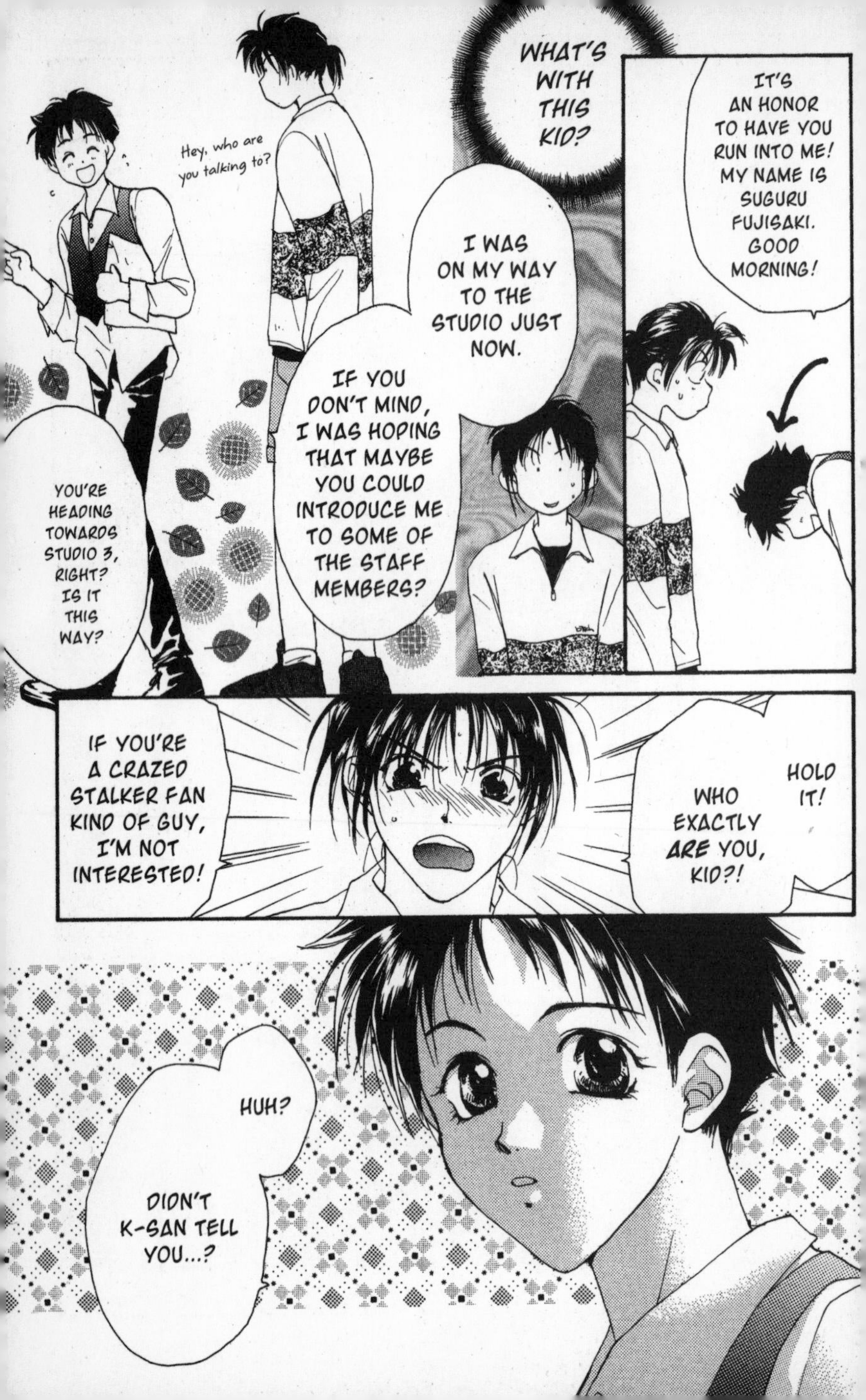
IT'S AN HONOR TO HAVE YOU RUN INTO ME! MY NAME IS SUGURU FUJISAKI. GOOD MORNING!
WHAT'S WITH THIS KID?
I WAS ON MY WAY TO THE STUDIO JUST NOW.
IF YOU DON'T MIND, I WAS HOPING THAT MAYBE YOU COULD INTRODUCE ME TO SOME OF THE STAFF MEMBERS?
Hey, who are you talking to?
YOU'RE HEADING TOWARDS STUDIO 3, RIGHT? IS IT THIS WAY?
HOLD IT!
WHO EXACTLY ARE YOU, KID?!
IF YOU'RE A CRAZED STALKER FAN KIND OF GUY, I'M NOT INTERESTED!
HUH?
DIDN'T K-SAN TELL YOU...?

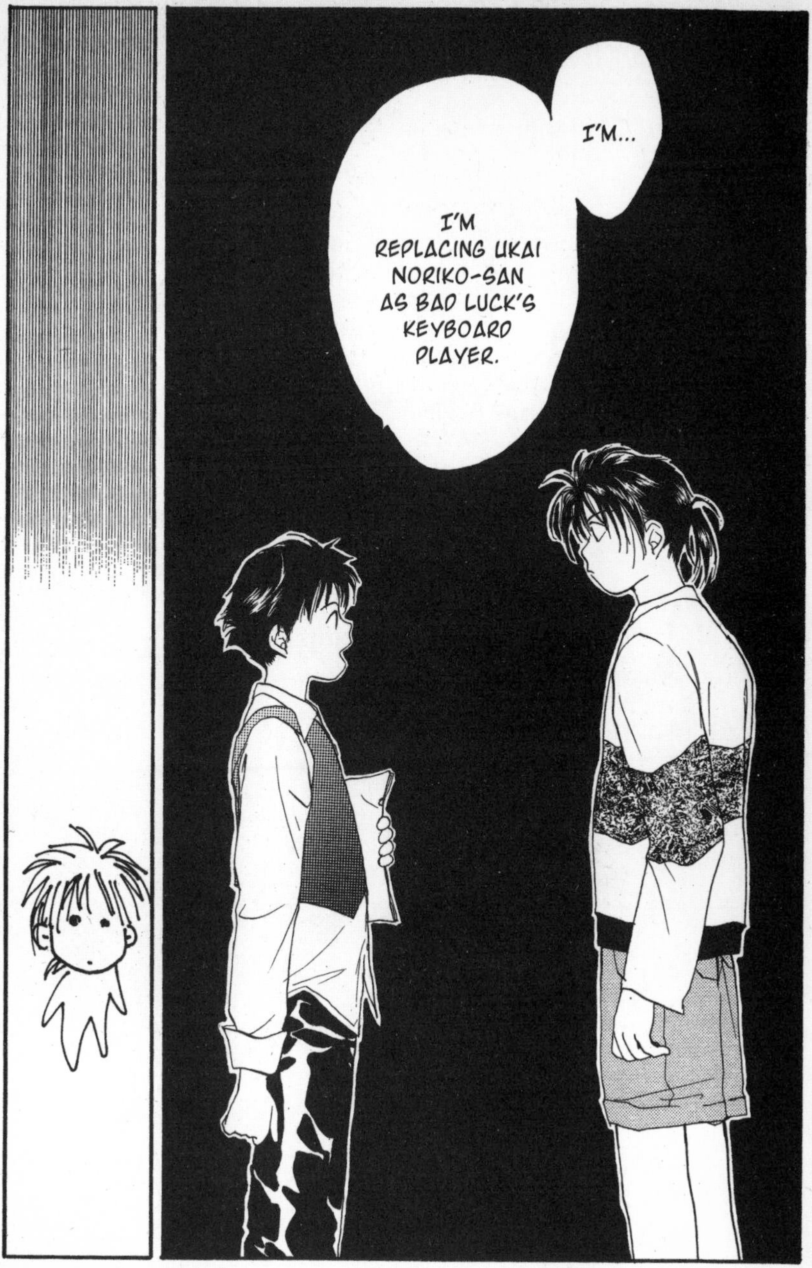
I'M...
I'M REPLACING UKAI NORIKO-SAN AS BAD LUCK'S KEYBOARD PLAYER.

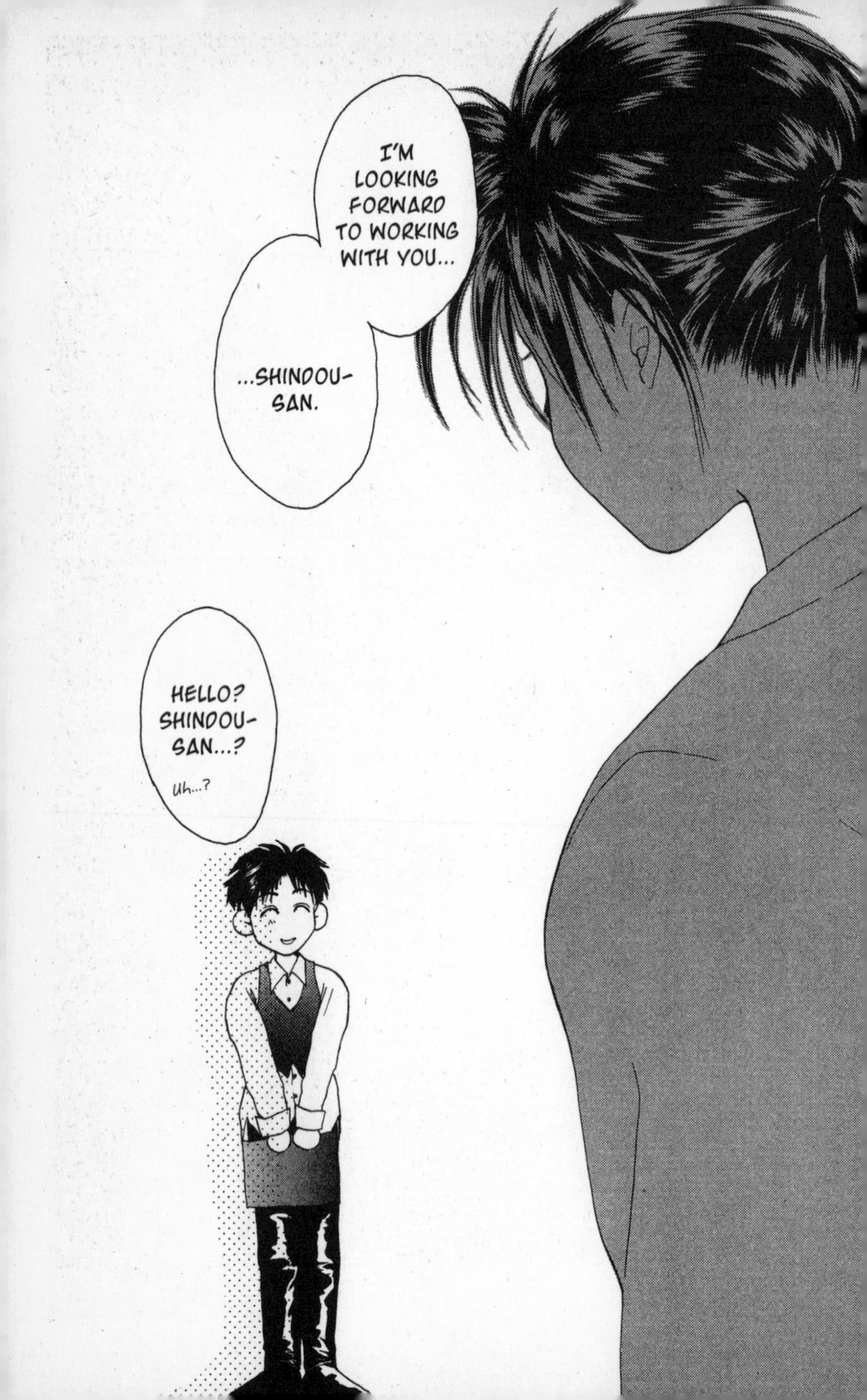
I'M LOOKING FORWARD TO WORKING WITH YOU...
...SHINDOU-SAN.
HELLO? SHINDOU-SAN...?
Uh...?

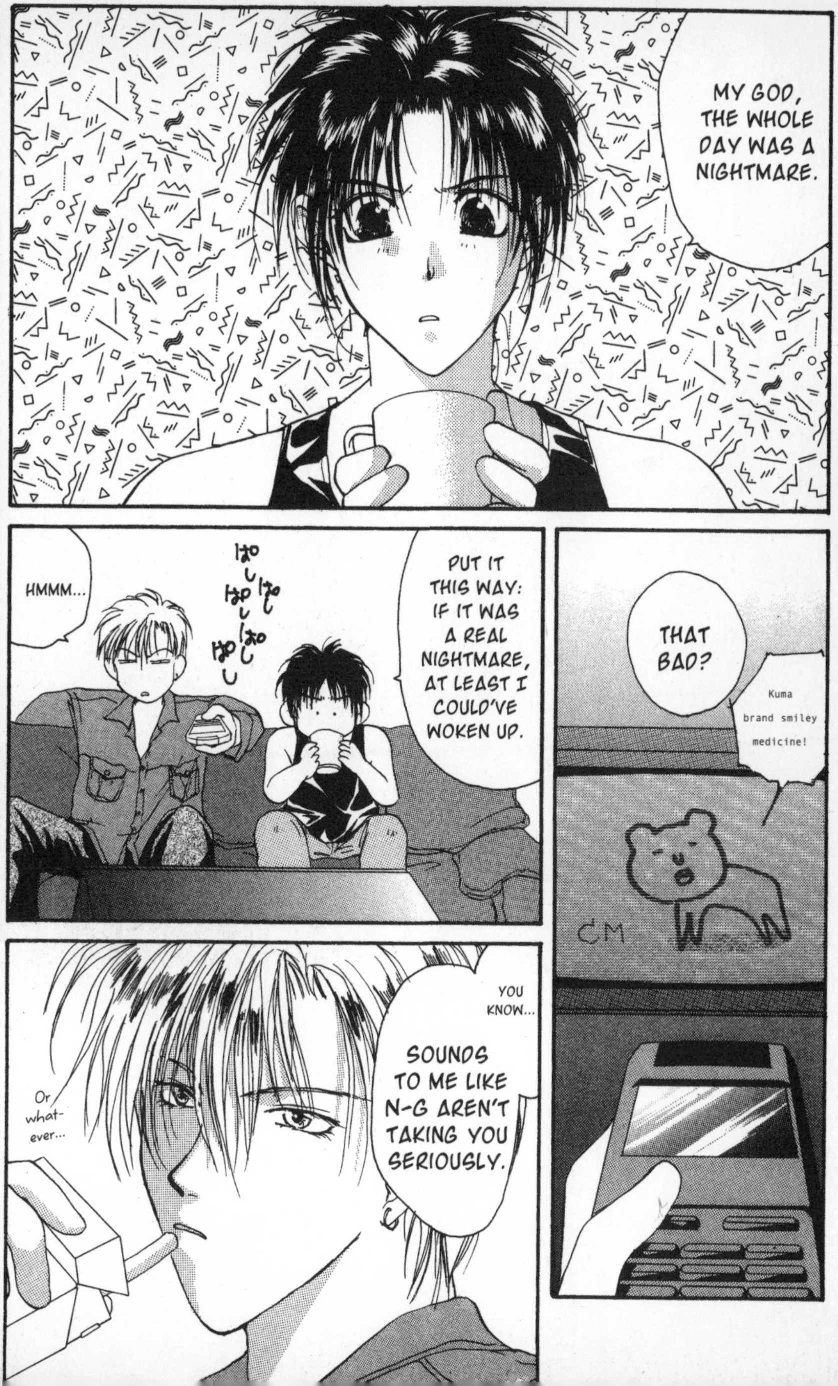
MY GOD, THE WHOLE DAY WAS A NIGHTMARE.
THAT BAD?
Kuma brand smiley medicine!
CM
PUT IT THIS WAY: IF IT WAS A REAL NIGHTMARE, AT LEAST I COULD'VE WOKEN UP.
HMMM...
YOU KNOW...
SOUNDS TO ME LIKE N-G AREN'T TAKING YOU SERIOUSLY.
Or whatever...

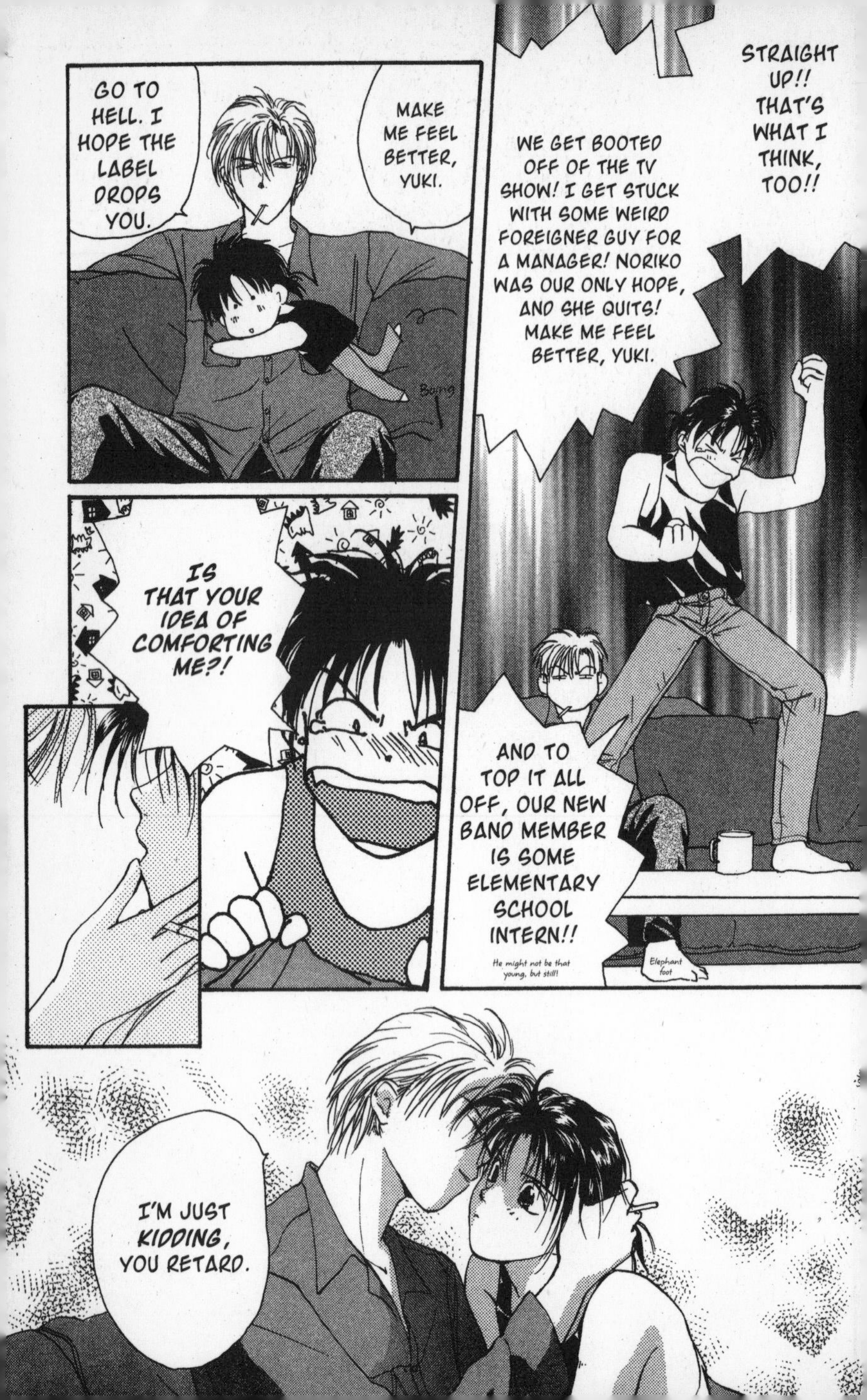
STRAIGHT UP!! THAT'S WHAT I THINK, TOO!!
WE GET BOOTED OFF OF THE TV SHOW! I GET STUCK WITH SOME WEIRD FOREIGNER GUY FOR A MANAGER! NORIKO WAS OUR ONLY HOPE, AND SHE QUITS! MAKE ME FEEL BETTER, YUKI.
AND TO TOP IT ALL OFF, OUR NEW BAND MEMBER IS SOME ELEMENTARY SCHOOL INTERN!!
Elephant foot
He might not be that young, but still!
MAKE ME FEEL BETTER, YUKI.
GO TO HELL. I HOPE THE LABEL DROPS YOU.
Bang
IS THAT YOUR IDEA OF COMFORTING ME?!
I'M JUST KIDDING, YOU RETARD.

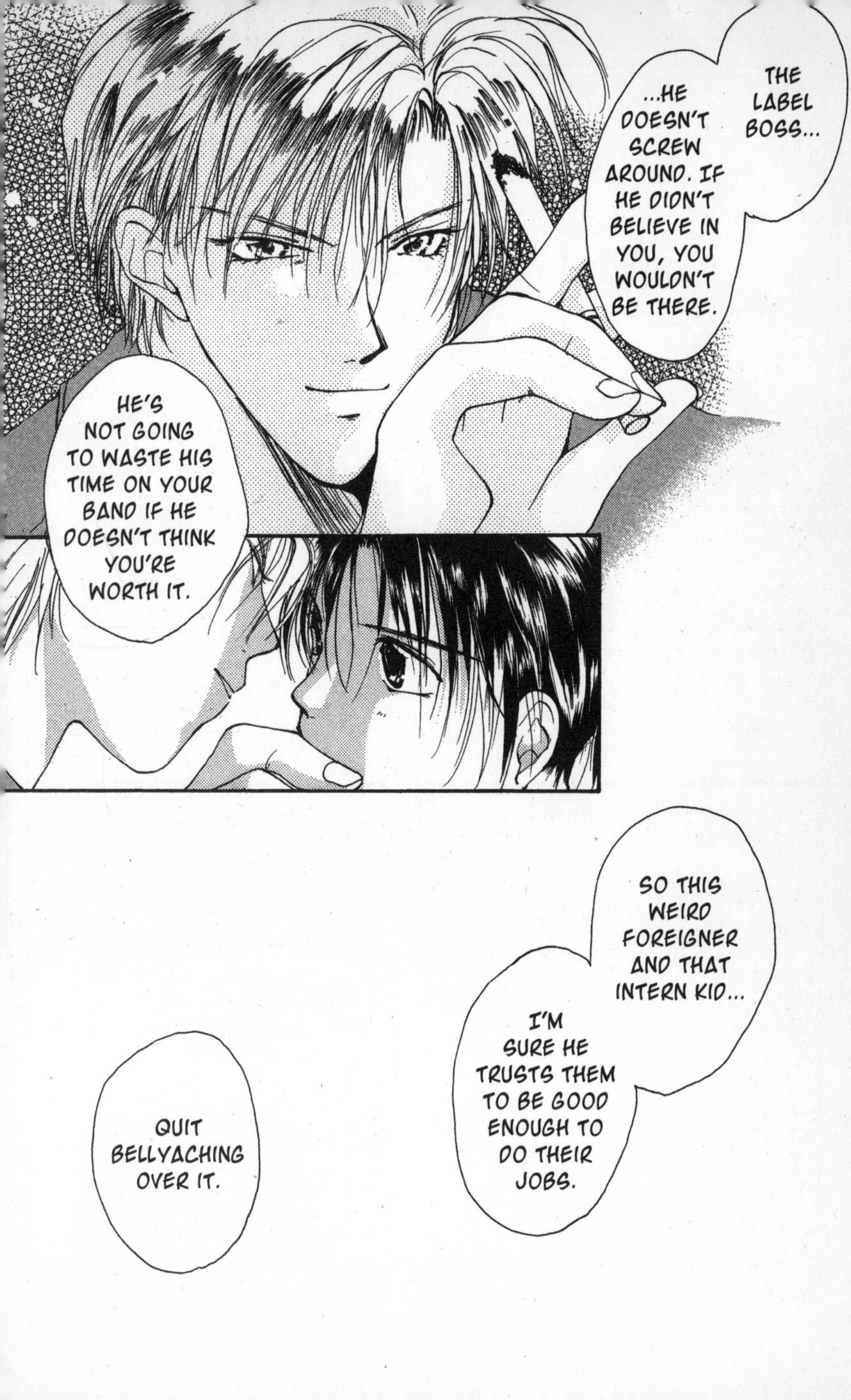
THE LABEL BOSS...
...HE DOESN'T SCREW AROUND. IF HE DIDN'T BELIEVE IN YOU, YOU WOULDN'T BE THERE.
HE'S NOT GOING TO WASTE HIS TIME ON YOUR BAND IF HE DOESN'T THINK YOU'RE WORTH IT.
SO THIS WEIRD FOREIGNER AND THAT INTERN KID...
I'M SURE HE TRUSTS THEM TO BE GOOD ENOUGH TO DO THEIR JOBS.
QUIT BELLYACHING OVER IT.

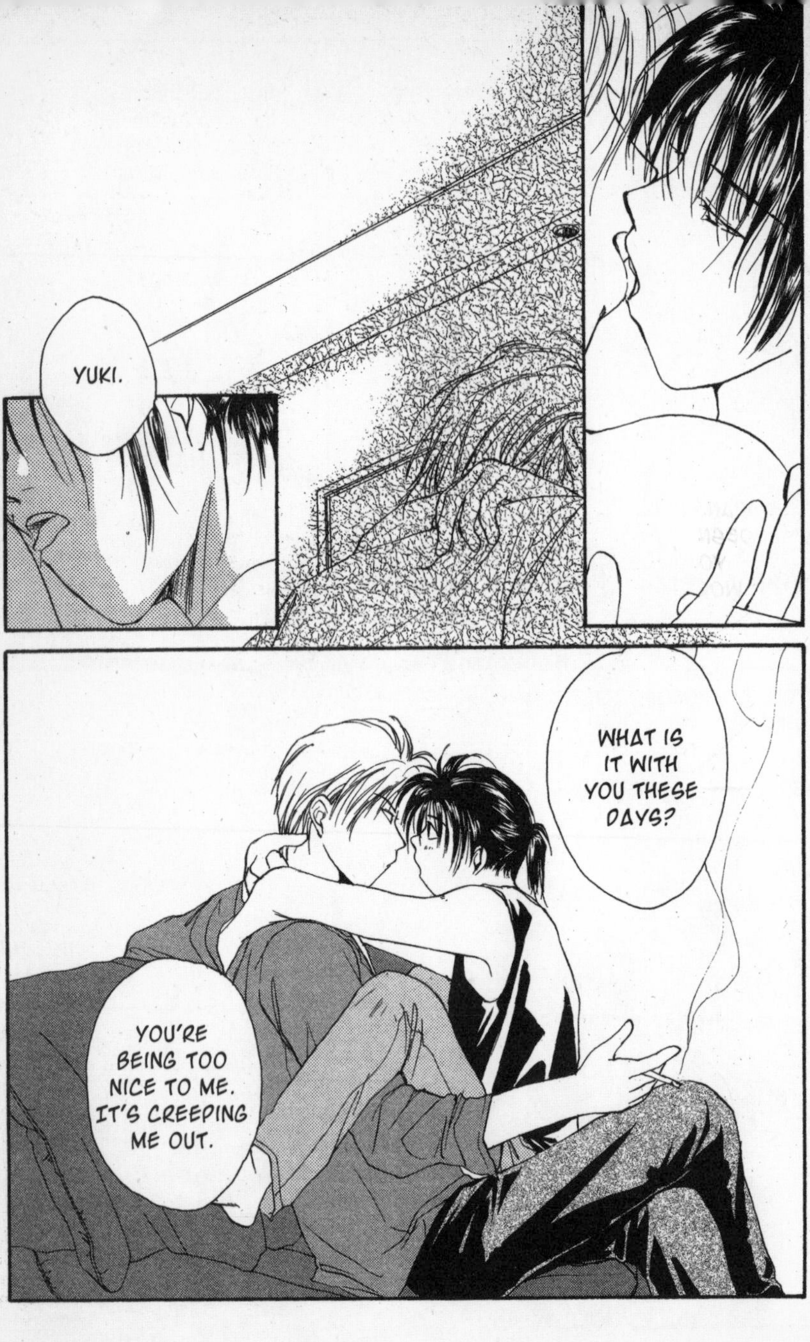
YUKI.
WHAT IS IT WITH YOU THESE DAYS?
YOU'RE BEING TOO NICE TO ME. IT'S CREEPING ME OUT.

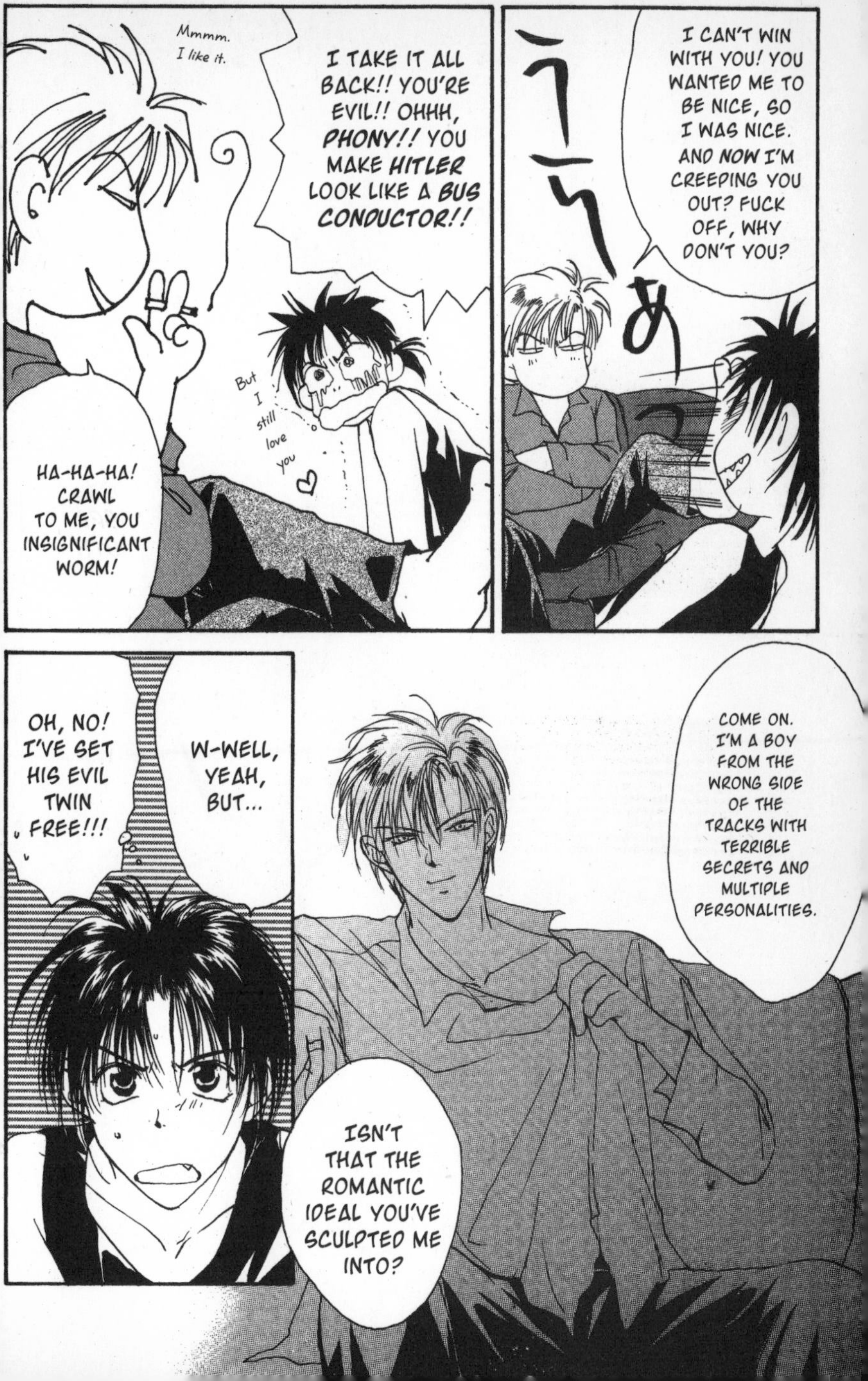
I CAN'T WIN WITH YOU! YOU WANTED ME TO BE NICE, SO I WAS NICE. AND NOW I'M CREEPING YOU OUT? FUCK OFF, WHY DON'T YOU?
う〜あっ
I TAKE IT ALL BACK!! YOU'RE EVIL!! OHHH, PHONY!! YOU MAKE HITLER LOOK LIKE A BUS CONDUCTOR!!
Mmmm. I like it.
But I still love you
HA-HA-HA! CRAWL TO ME, YOU INSIGNIFICANT WORM!
COME ON. I'M A BOY FROM THE WRONG SIDE OF THE TRACKS WITH TERRIBLE SECRETS AND MULTIPLE PERSONALITIES.
ISN'T THAT THE ROMANTIC IDEAL YOU'VE SCULPTED ME INTO?
W-WELL, YEAH, BUT...
OH, NO! I'VE SET HIS EVIL TWIN FREE!!!

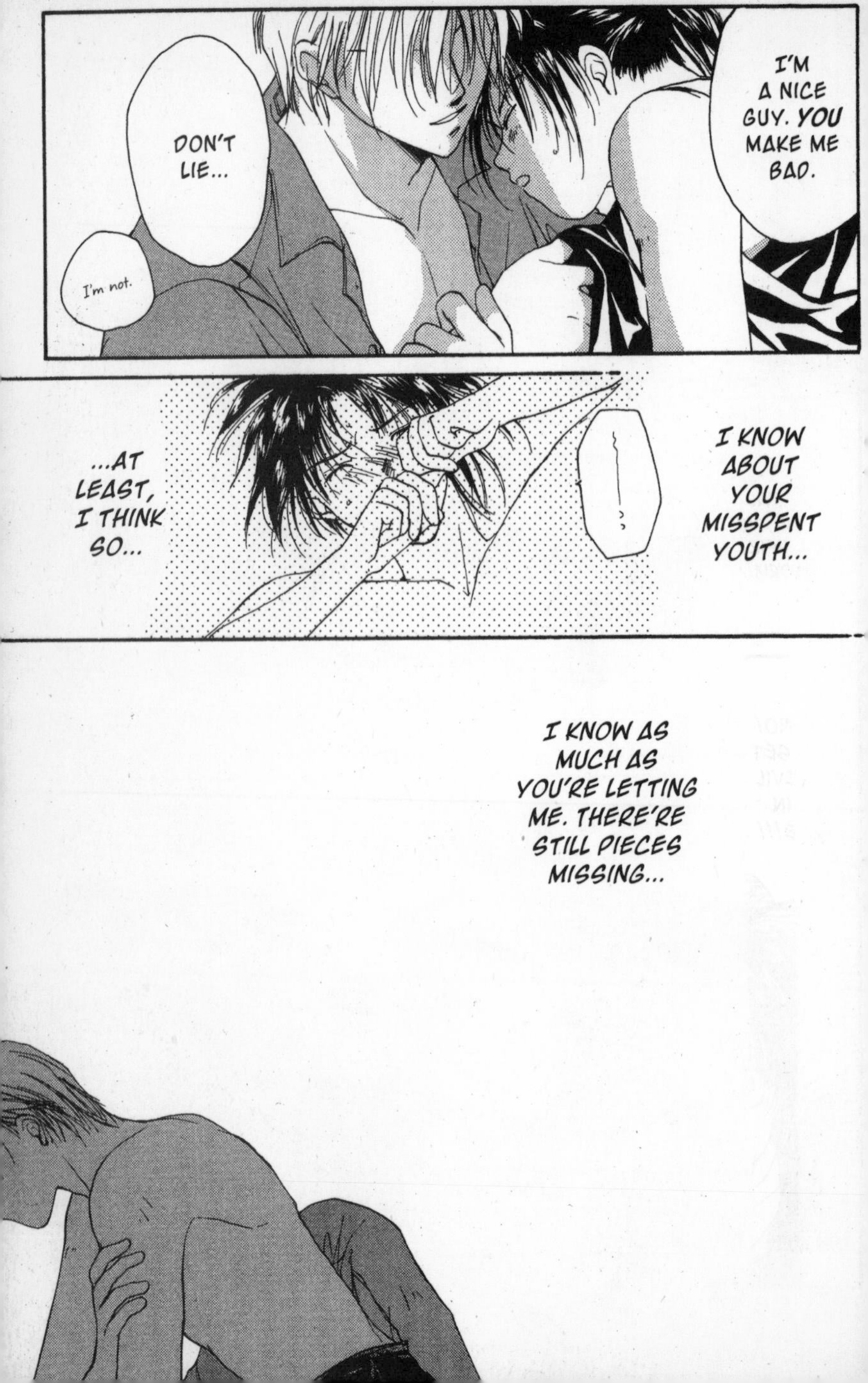
I'M A NICE GUY. YOU MAKE ME BAD.
DON'T LIE...
I'm not.
I KNOW ABOUT YOUR MISSPENT YOUTH...
...AT LEAST, I THINK SO...
I KNOW AS MUCH AS YOU'RE LETTING ME. THERE'RE STILL PIECES MISSING...

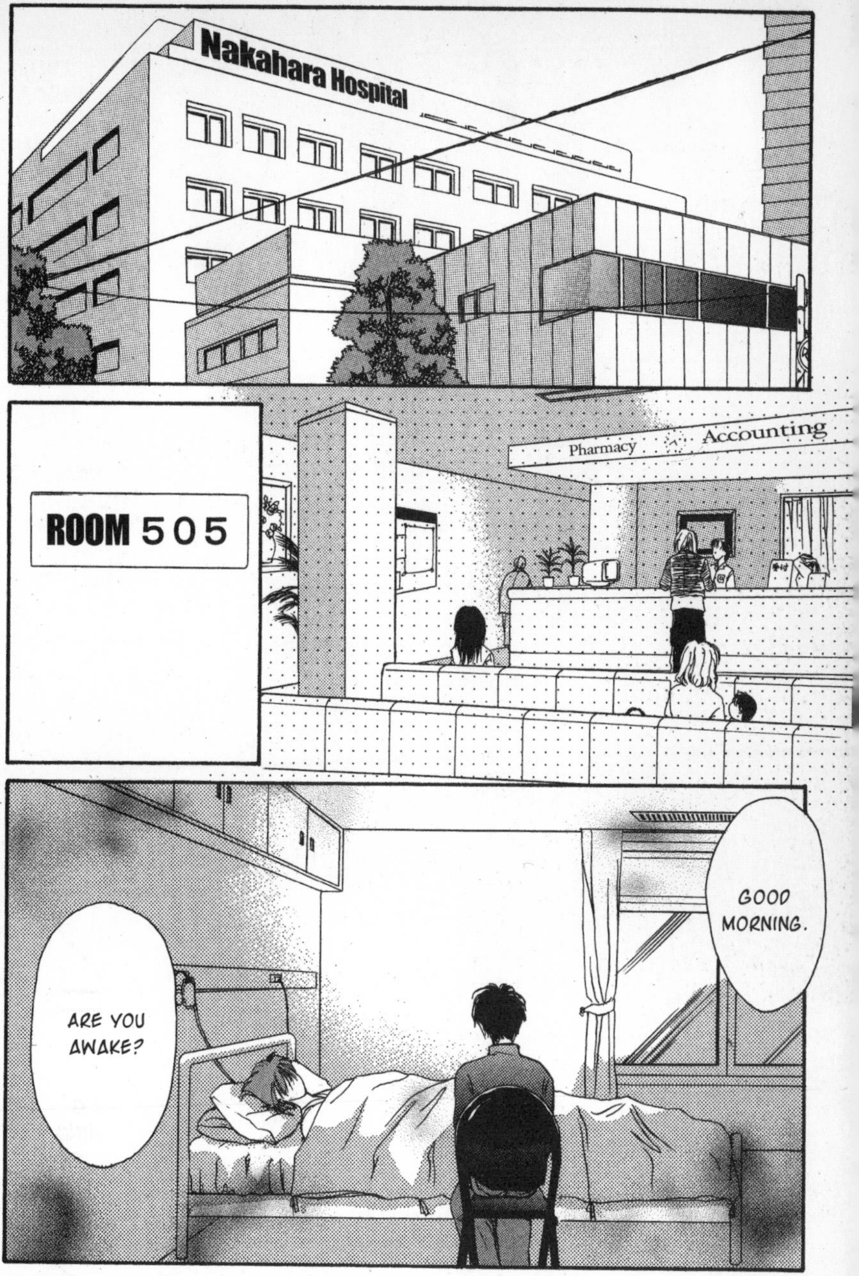
Nakahara Hospital
Pharmacy
Accounting
ROOM 505
GOOD MORNING.
ARE YOU AWAKE?

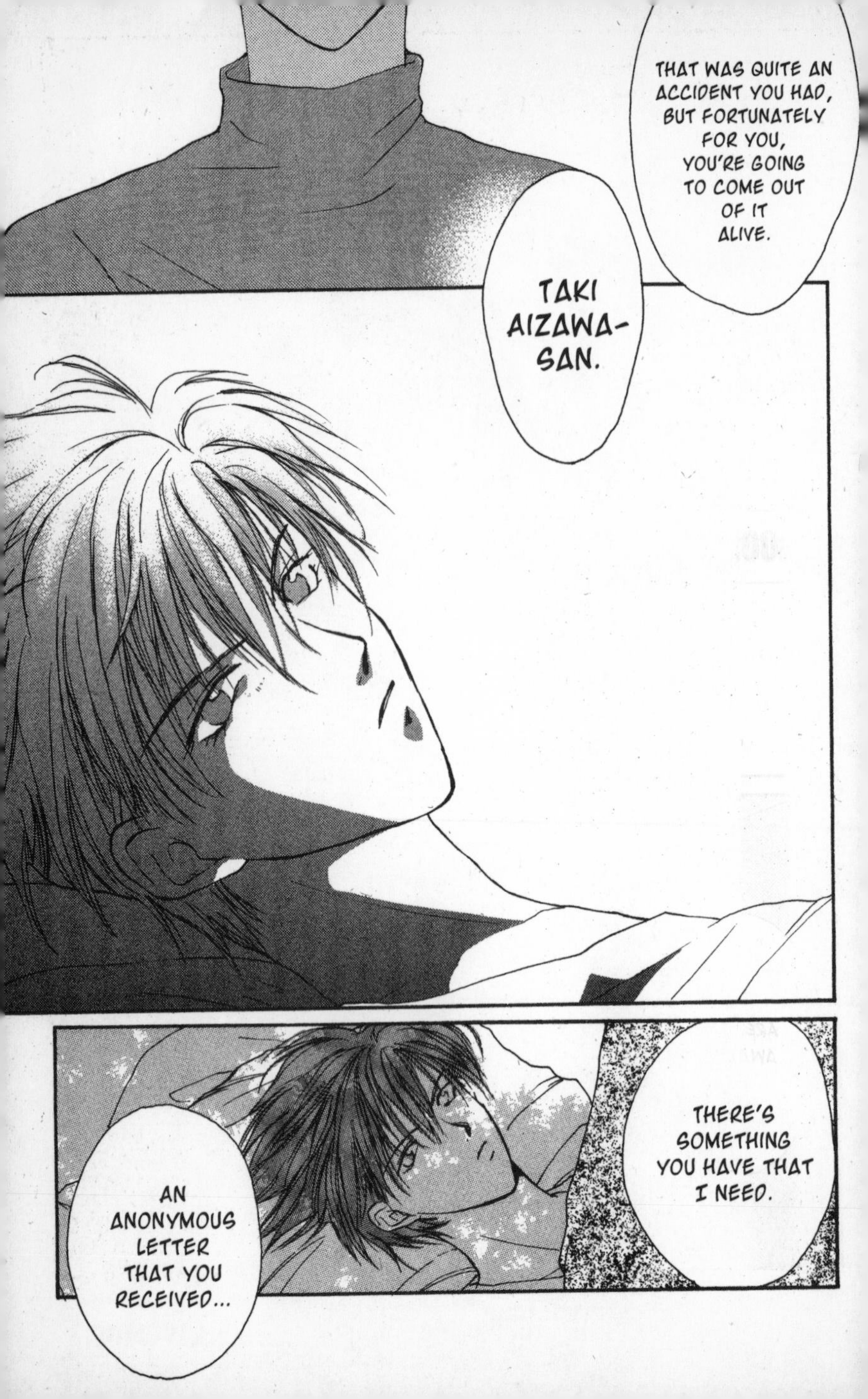
THAT WAS QUITE AN ACCIDENT YOU HAD, BUT FORTUNATELY FOR YOU, YOU'RE GOING TO COME OUT OF IT ALIVE.
TAKI AIZAWA-SAN.
THERE'S SOMETHING YOU HAVE THAT I NEED.
AN ANONYMOUS LETTER THAT YOU RECEIVED...

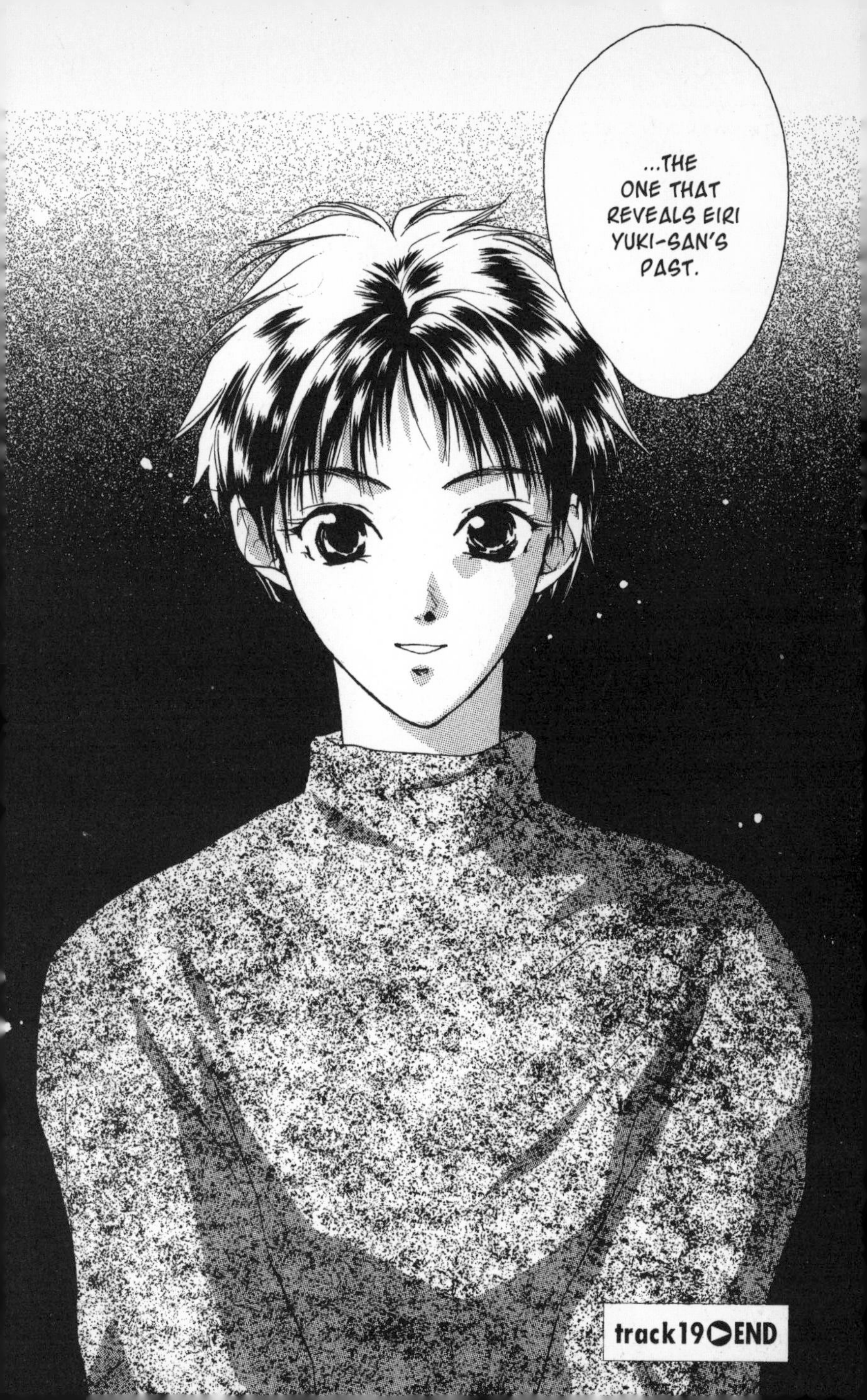
...THE ONE THAT REVEALS EIRI YUKI-SAN'S PAST.
track19 END

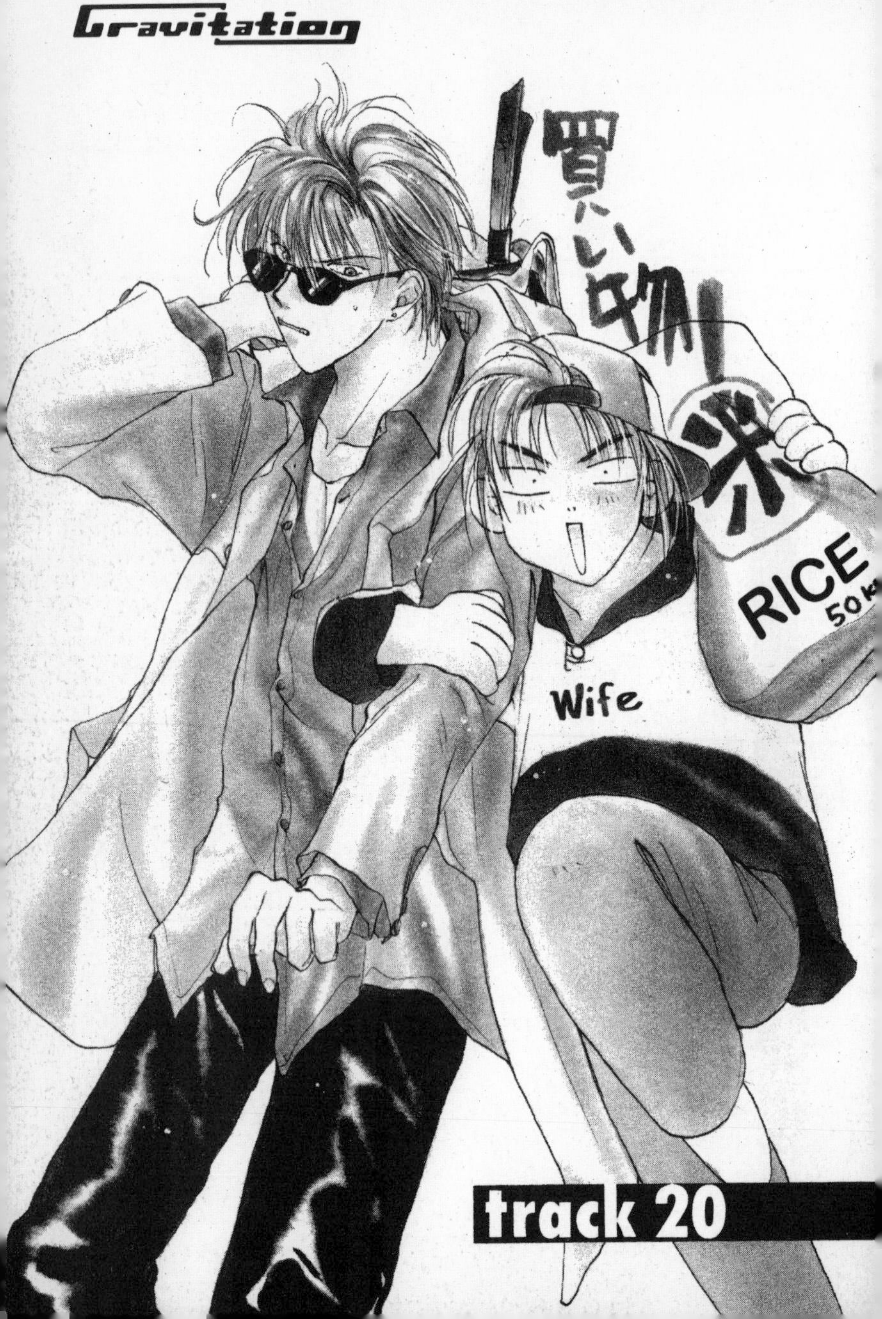
Gravitation
買い物!
米
RICE
50k
Wife
track 20

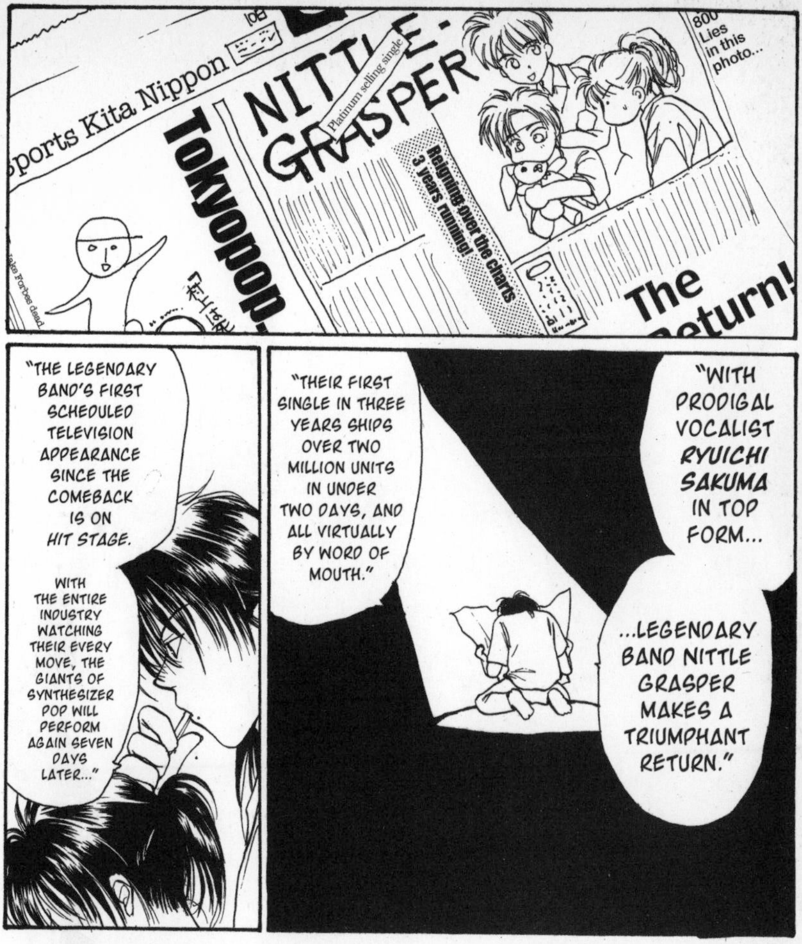
Sports Kita Nippon
Tokyopop
NITTLE-GRASPER
Platinum selling single
Reigning over the charts 3 years running!
800 Lies in this photo...
The Return!
"WITH PRODIGAL VOCALIST RYUICHI SAKUMA IN TOP FORM...
...LEGENDARY BAND NITTLE GRASPER MAKES A TRIUMPHANT RETURN."
"THEIR FIRST SINGLE IN THREE YEARS SHIPS OVER TWO MILLION UNITS IN UNDER TWO DAYS, AND ALL VIRTUALLY BY WORD OF MOUTH."
"THE LEGENDARY BAND'S FIRST SCHEDULED TELEVISION APPEARANCE SINCE THE COMEBACK IS ON HIT STAGE.
WITH THE ENTIRE INDUSTRY WATCHING THEIR EVERY MOVE, THE GIANTS OF SYNTHESIZER POP WILL PERFORM AGAIN SEVEN DAYS LATER..."

ABOUT GRAVITATION TRACK 20

(I wrote all this stuff thinking it was Track 20, but what if it isn't? I'm losing track myself... I think it is, right?) Ryu-chan's back. Even if he appears only as a name to fear. Rumors are going around that this is the last episode, so you may never see him again. Ha ha ha. You guys are way too gullible! Gullible, gullible, gullible! Gobble gobble! Say that three times fast! How about it? Well, if I have to ask, I must be an amateur at tongue twisters myself. I chose a thinner point pen this time. Hey, wasn't the topic of this section supposed to be Ryu-chan?

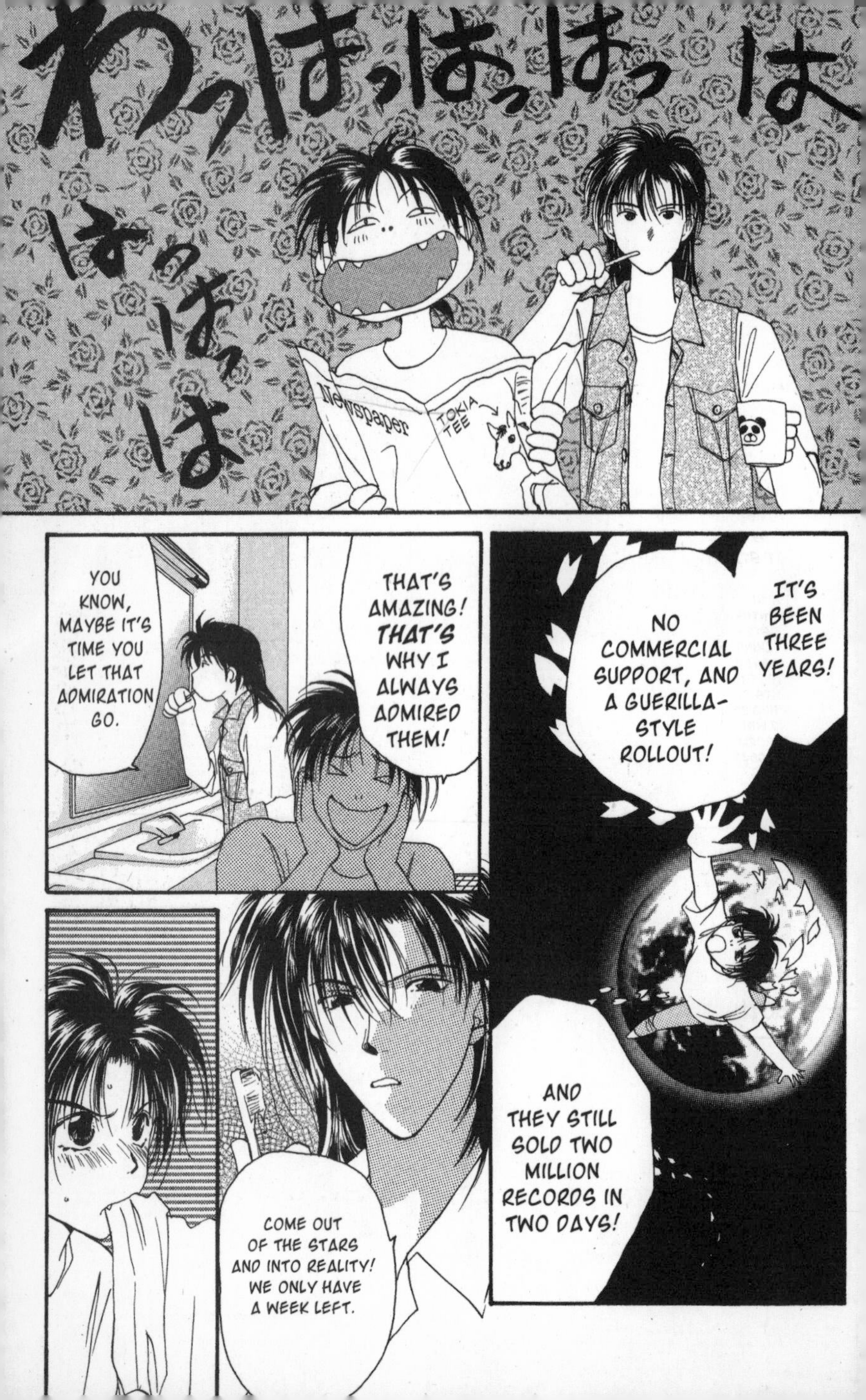
わっはっはっはっは
はっはっは
Newspaper
TOKIA TEE
IT'S BEEN THREE YEARS!
NO COMMERCIAL SUPPORT, AND A GUERILLA-STYLE ROLLOUT!
AND THEY STILL SOLD TWO MILLION RECORDS IN TWO DAYS!
THAT'S AMAZING! *THAT'S* WHY I ALWAYS ADMIRED THEM!
YOU KNOW, MAYBE IT'S TIME YOU LET THAT ADMIRATION GO.
COME OUT OF THE STARS AND INTO REALITY! WE ONLY HAVE A WEEK LEFT.

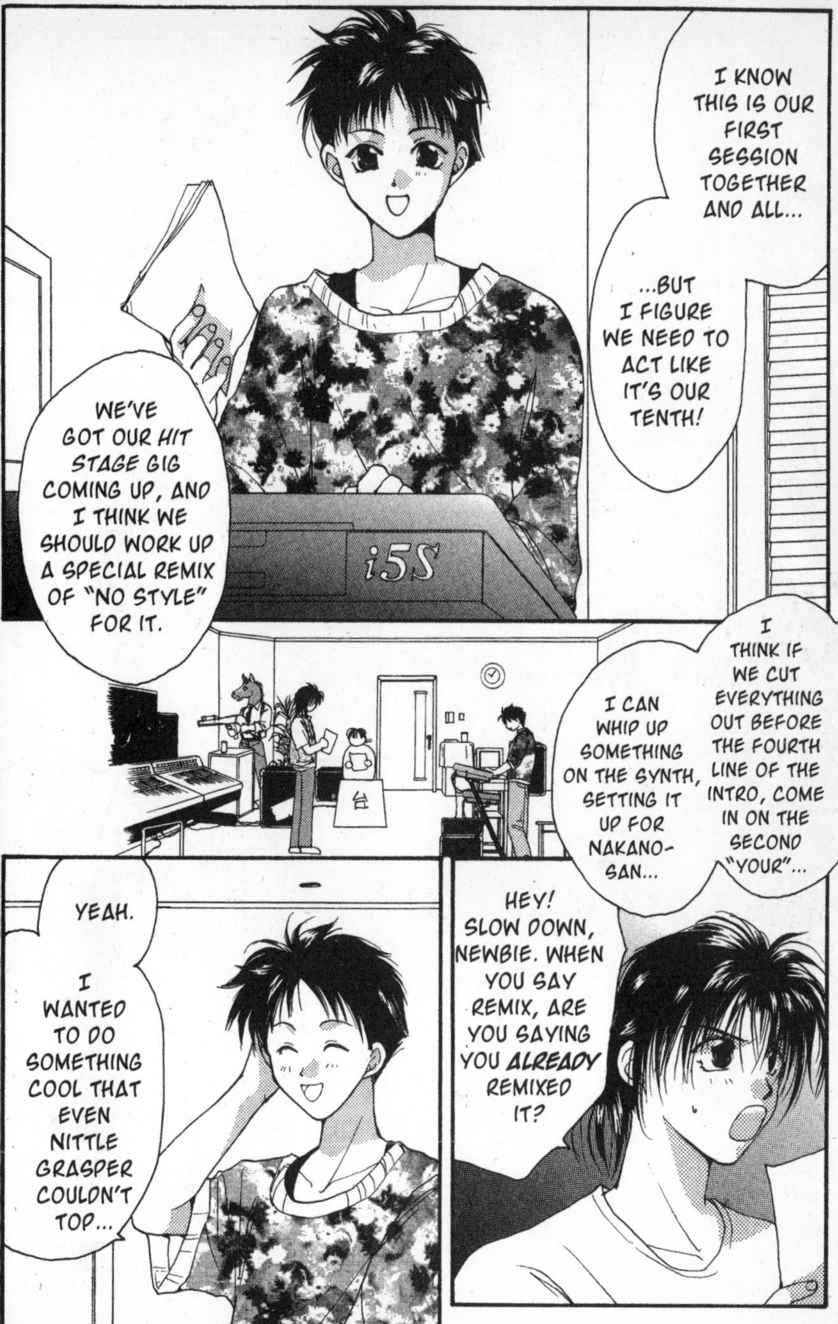
I KNOW THIS IS OUR FIRST SESSION TOGETHER AND ALL...
...BUT I FIGURE WE NEED TO ACT LIKE IT'S OUR TENTH!
WE'VE GOT OUR HIT STAGE GIG COMING UP, AND I THINK WE SHOULD WORK UP A SPECIAL REMIX OF "NO STYLE" FOR IT.
i5S
I THINK IF WE CUT EVERYTHING OUT BEFORE THE FOURTH LINE OF THE INTRO, COME IN ON THE SECOND "YOUR"...
I CAN WHIP UP SOMETHING ON THE SYNTH, SETTING IT UP FOR NAKANO-SAN...
台
HEY! SLOW DOWN, NEWBIE. WHEN YOU SAY REMIX, ARE YOU SAYING YOU ALREADY REMIXED IT?
YEAH.
I WANTED TO DO SOMETHING COOL THAT EVEN NITTLE GRASPER COULDN'T TOP...

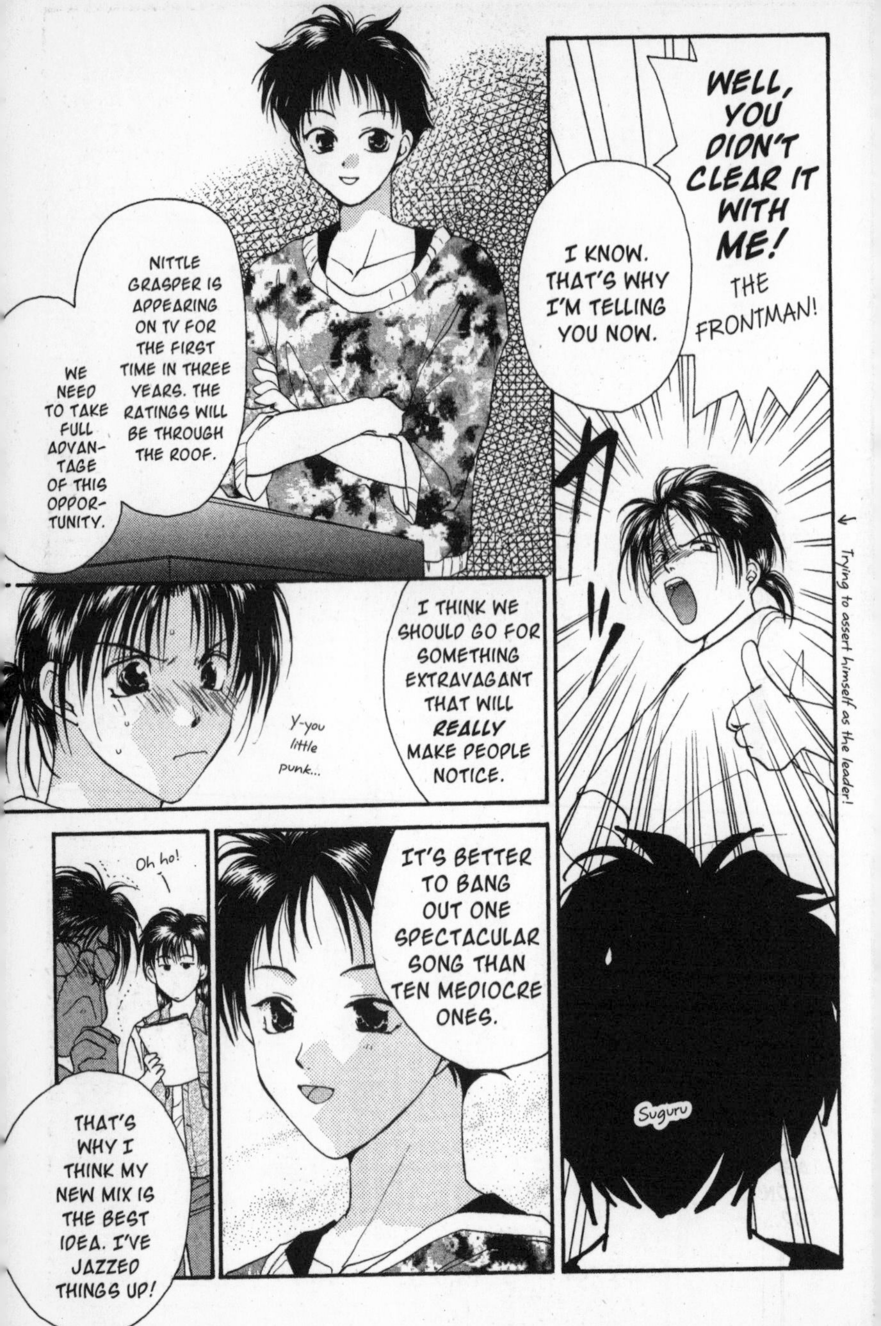
WELL, YOU DIDN'T CLEAR IT WITH ME! THE FRONTMAN!
I KNOW. THAT'S WHY I'M TELLING YOU NOW.
Trying to assert himself as the leader!
Suguru
NITTLE GRASPER IS APPEARING ON TV FOR THE FIRST TIME IN THREE YEARS. THE RATINGS WILL BE THROUGH THE ROOF. WE NEED TO TAKE FULL ADVANTAGE OF THIS OPPORTUNITY.
I THINK WE SHOULD GO FOR SOMETHING EXTRAVAGANT THAT WILL REALLY MAKE PEOPLE NOTICE.
Y-you little punk...
IT'S BETTER TO BANG OUT ONE SPECTACULAR SONG THAN TEN MEDIOCRE ONES.
Oh ho!
THAT'S WHY I THINK MY NEW MIX IS THE BEST IDEA. I'VE JAZZED THINGS UP!

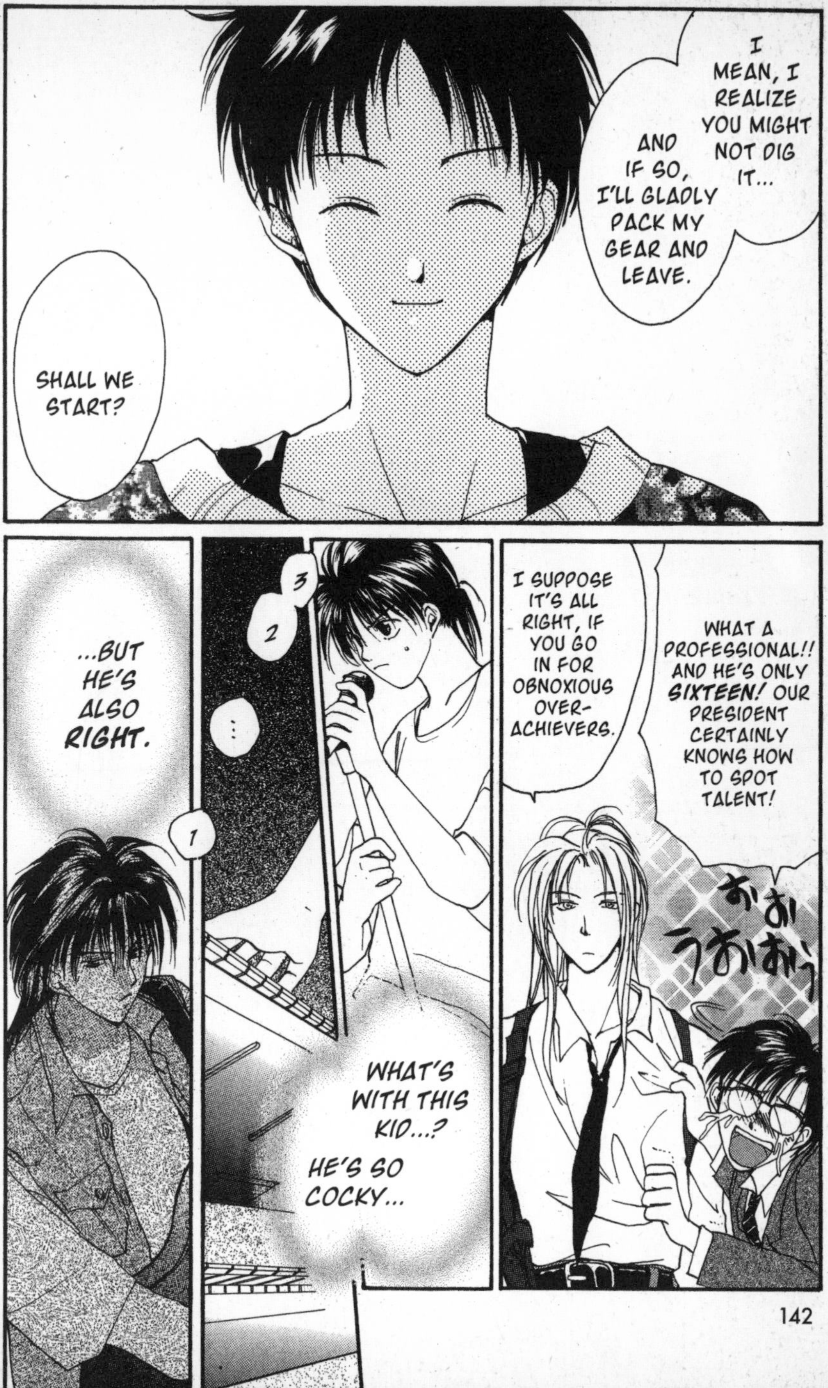

I MEAN, I REALIZE YOU MIGHT NOT DIG IT...
AND IF SO, I'LL GLADLY PACK MY GEAR AND LEAVE.
SHALL WE START?
WHAT A PROFESSIONAL!! AND HE'S ONLY **SIXTEEN!** OUR PRESIDENT CERTAINLY KNOWS HOW TO SPOT TALENT!
おおうおおう
I SUPPOSE IT'S ALL RIGHT, IF YOU GO IN FOR OBNOXIOUS OVER-ACHIEVERS.
3
2
...
WHAT'S WITH THIS KID...?
HE'S SO COCKY...
...BUT HE'S ALSO **RIGHT.**
1

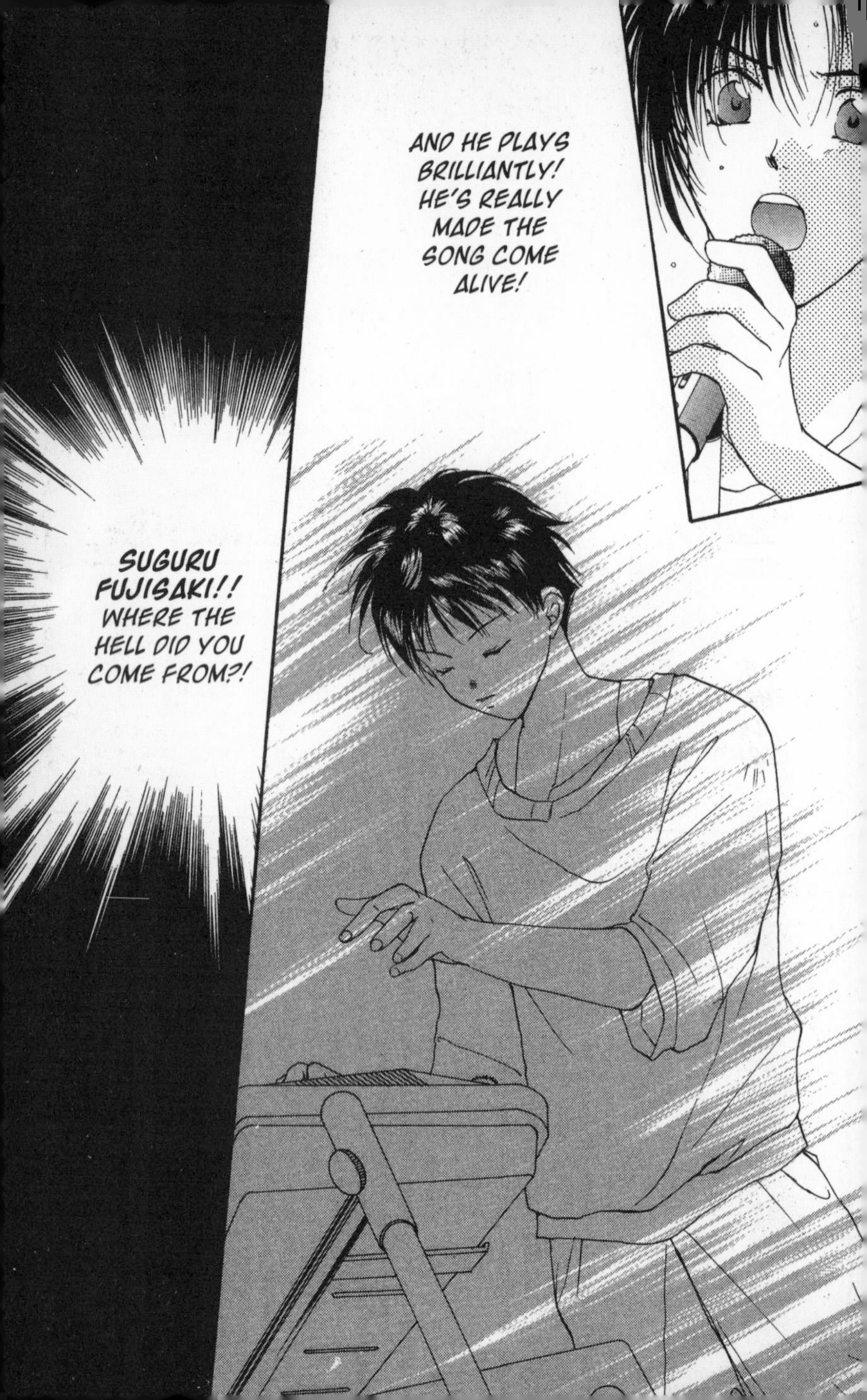
AND HE PLAYS BRILLIANTLY! HE'S REALLY MADE THE SONG COME ALIVE!
SUGURU FUJISAKI!! WHERE THE HELL DID YOU COME FROM?!

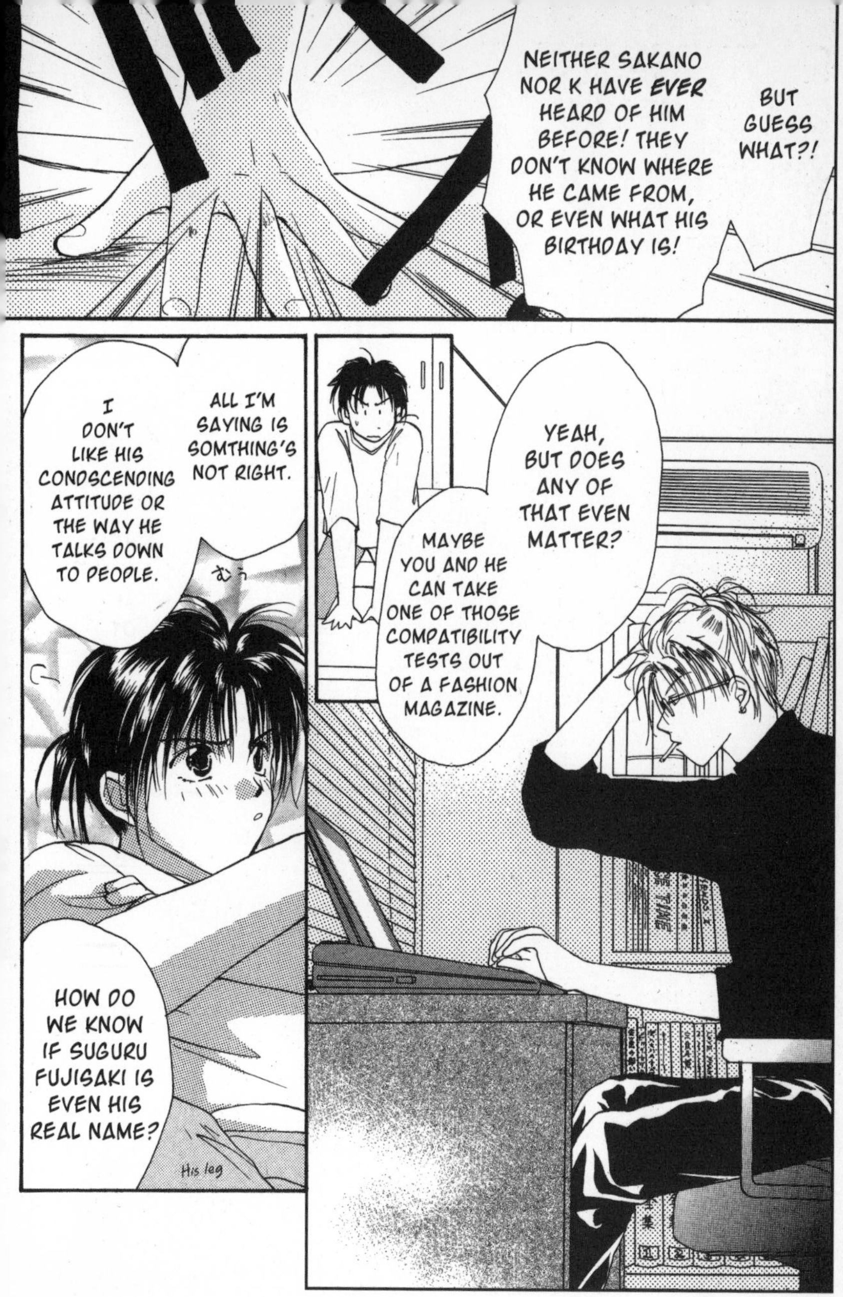
BUT GUESS WHAT?!
NEITHER SAKANO NOR K HAVE *EVER* HEARD OF HIM BEFORE! THEY DON'T KNOW WHERE HE CAME FROM, OR EVEN WHAT HIS BIRTHDAY IS!
YEAH, BUT DOES ANY OF THAT EVEN MATTER?
MAYBE YOU AND HE CAN TAKE ONE OF THOSE COMPATIBILITY TESTS OUT OF A FASHION MAGAZINE.
ALL I'M SAYING IS SOMTHING'S NOT RIGHT.
I DON'T LIKE HIS CONDSCENDING ATTITUDE OR THE WAY HE TALKS DOWN TO PEOPLE.
むぅ
HOW DO WE KNOW IF SUGURU FUJISAKI IS EVEN HIS REAL NAME?
His leg

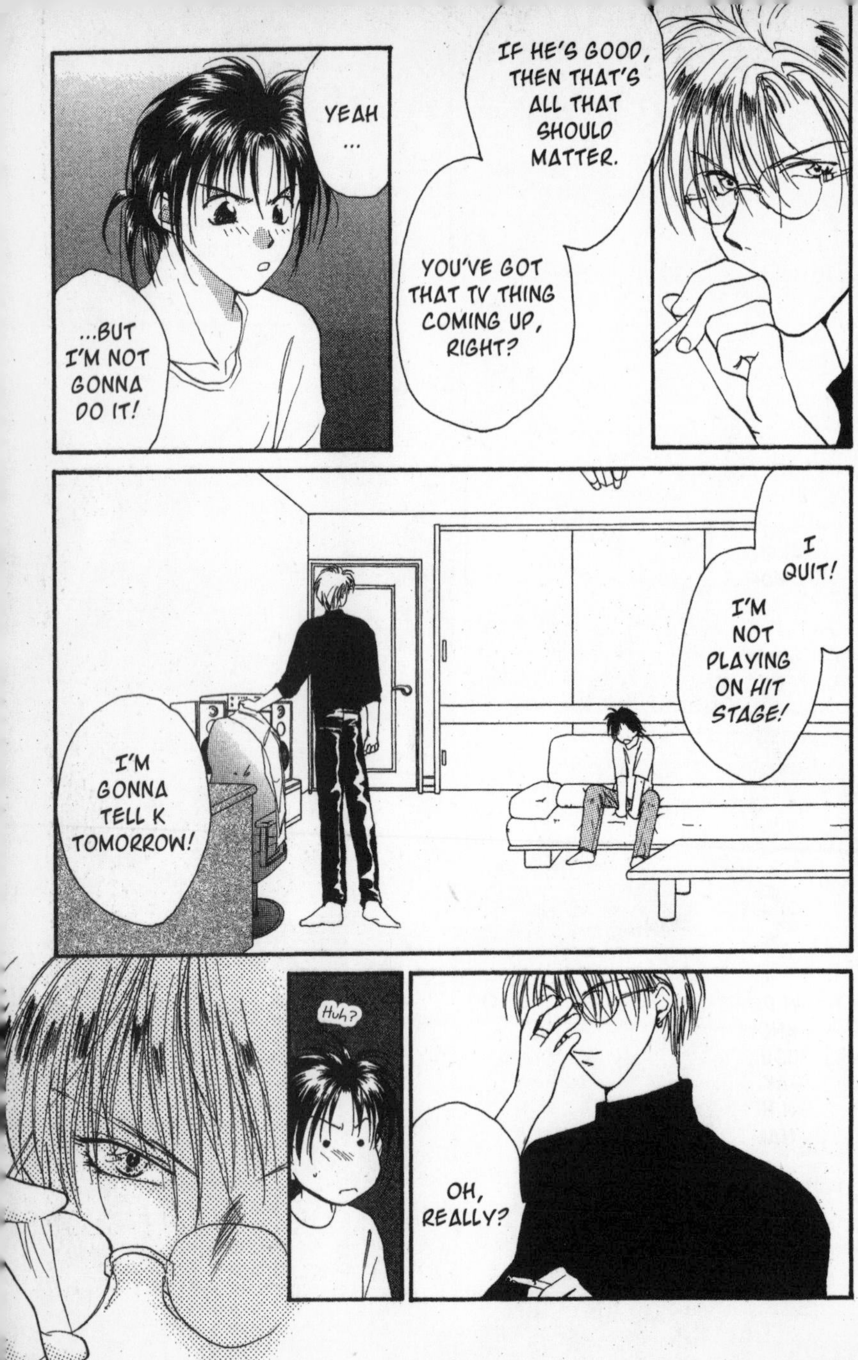
IF HE'S GOOD, THEN THAT'S ALL THAT SHOULD MATTER.
YOU'VE GOT THAT TV THING COMING UP, RIGHT?
YEAH ...
...BUT I'M NOT GONNA DO IT!
I QUIT!
I'M NOT PLAYING ON HIT STAGE!
I'M GONNA TELL K TOMORROW!
OH, REALLY?
Huh?

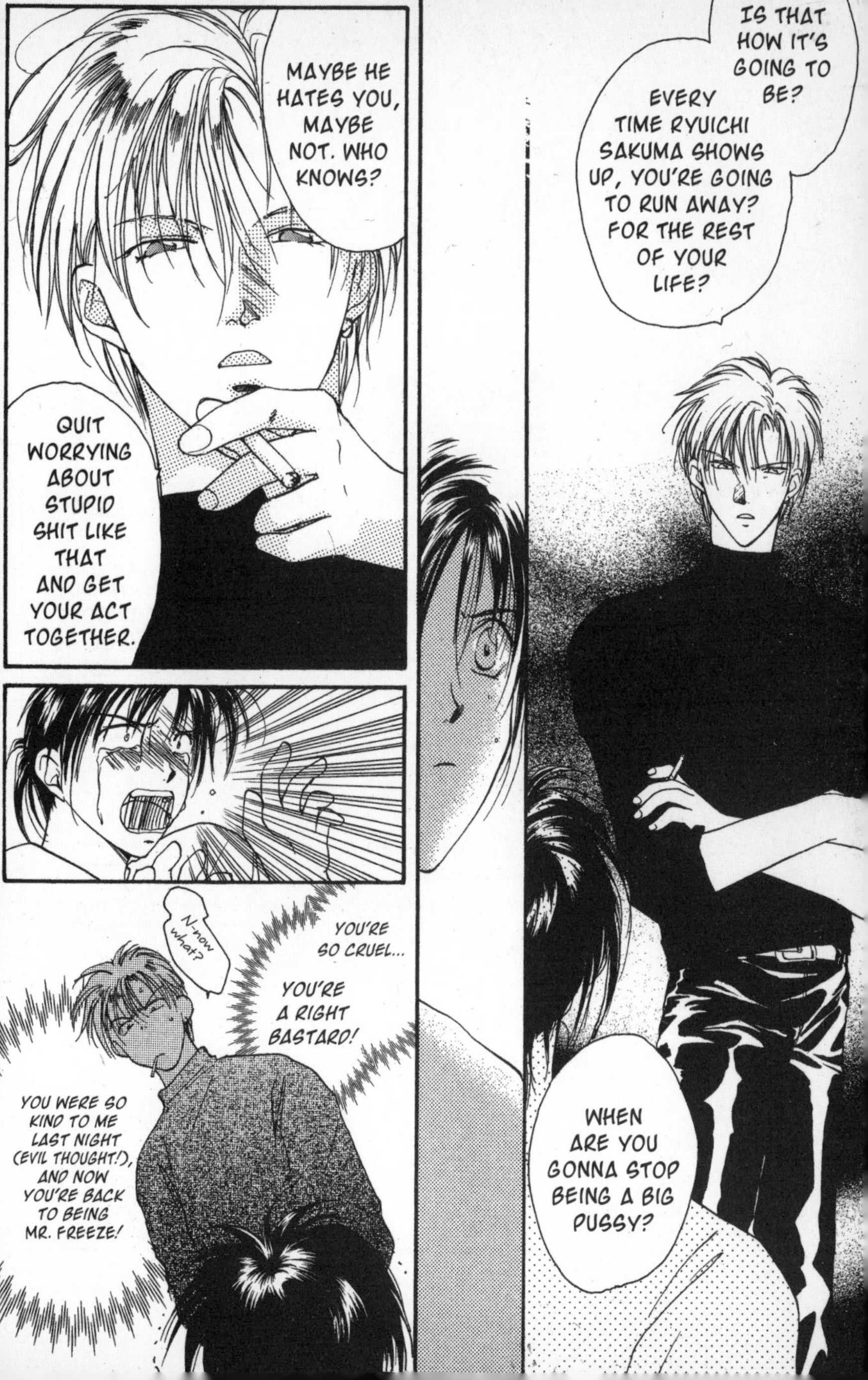
IS THAT HOW IT'S GOING TO BE?
EVERY TIME RYUICHI SAKUMA SHOWS UP, YOU'RE GOING TO RUN AWAY? FOR THE REST OF YOUR LIFE?
WHEN ARE YOU GONNA STOP BEING A BIG PUSSY?
MAYBE HE HATES YOU, MAYBE NOT. WHO KNOWS?
QUIT WORRYING ABOUT STUPID SHIT LIKE THAT AND GET YOUR ACT TOGETHER.
YOU'RE SO CRUEL...
YOU'RE A RIGHT BASTARD!
N-now what?
YOU WERE SO KIND TO ME LAST NIGHT (EVIL THOUGHT!), AND NOW YOU'RE BACK TO BEING MR. FREEZE!

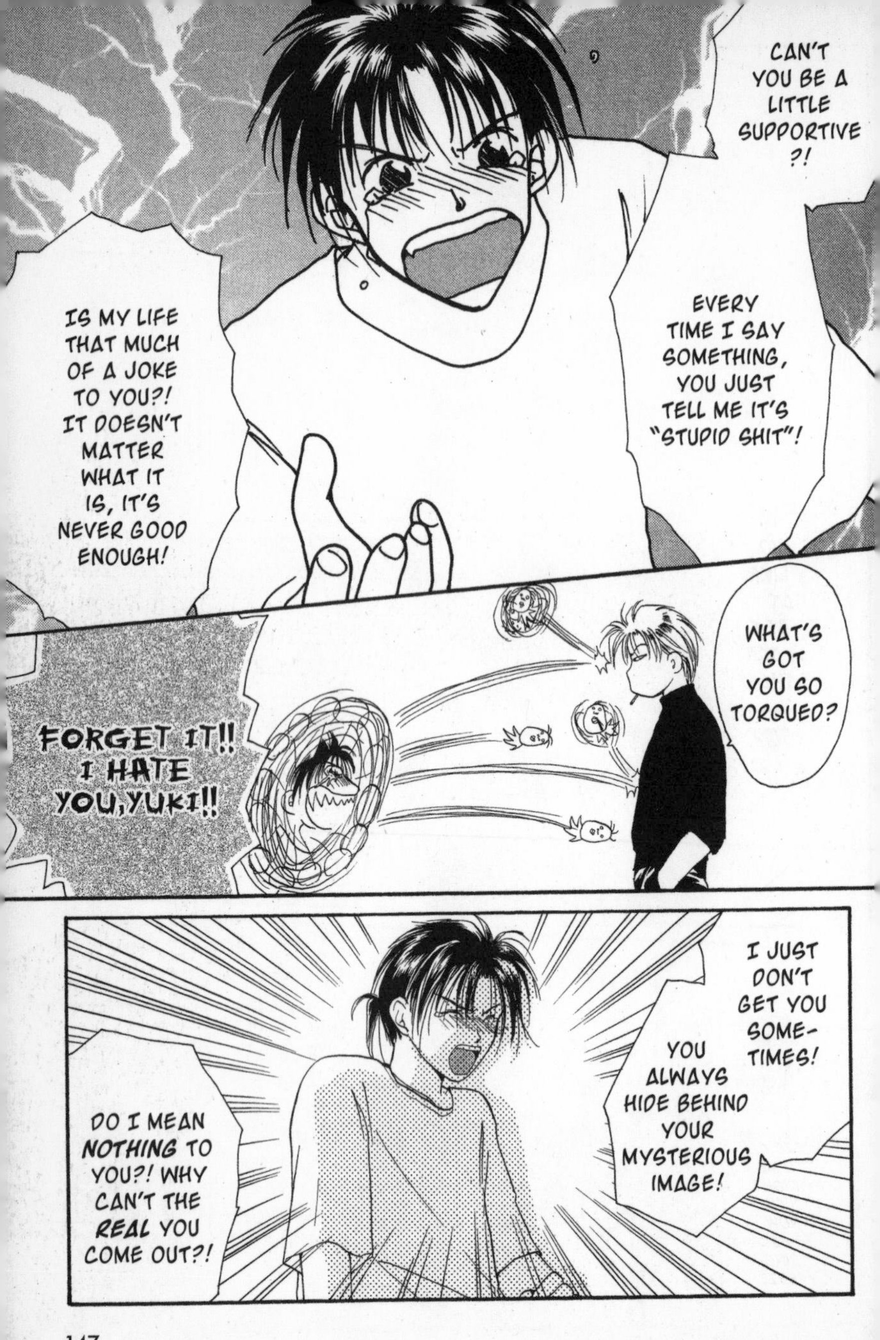
CAN'T YOU BE A LITTLE SUPPORTIVE?!
EVERY TIME I SAY SOMETHING, YOU JUST TELL ME IT'S "STUPID SHIT"!
IS MY LIFE THAT MUCH OF A JOKE TO YOU?! IT DOESN'T MATTER WHAT IT IS, IT'S NEVER GOOD ENOUGH!
WHAT'S GOT YOU SO TORQUED?
FORGET IT!! I HATE YOU, YUKI!!
I JUST DON'T GET YOU SOME-TIMES!
YOU ALWAYS HIDE BEHIND YOUR MYSTERIOUS IMAGE!
DO I MEAN *NOTHING* TO YOU?! WHY CAN'T THE *REAL* YOU COME OUT?!

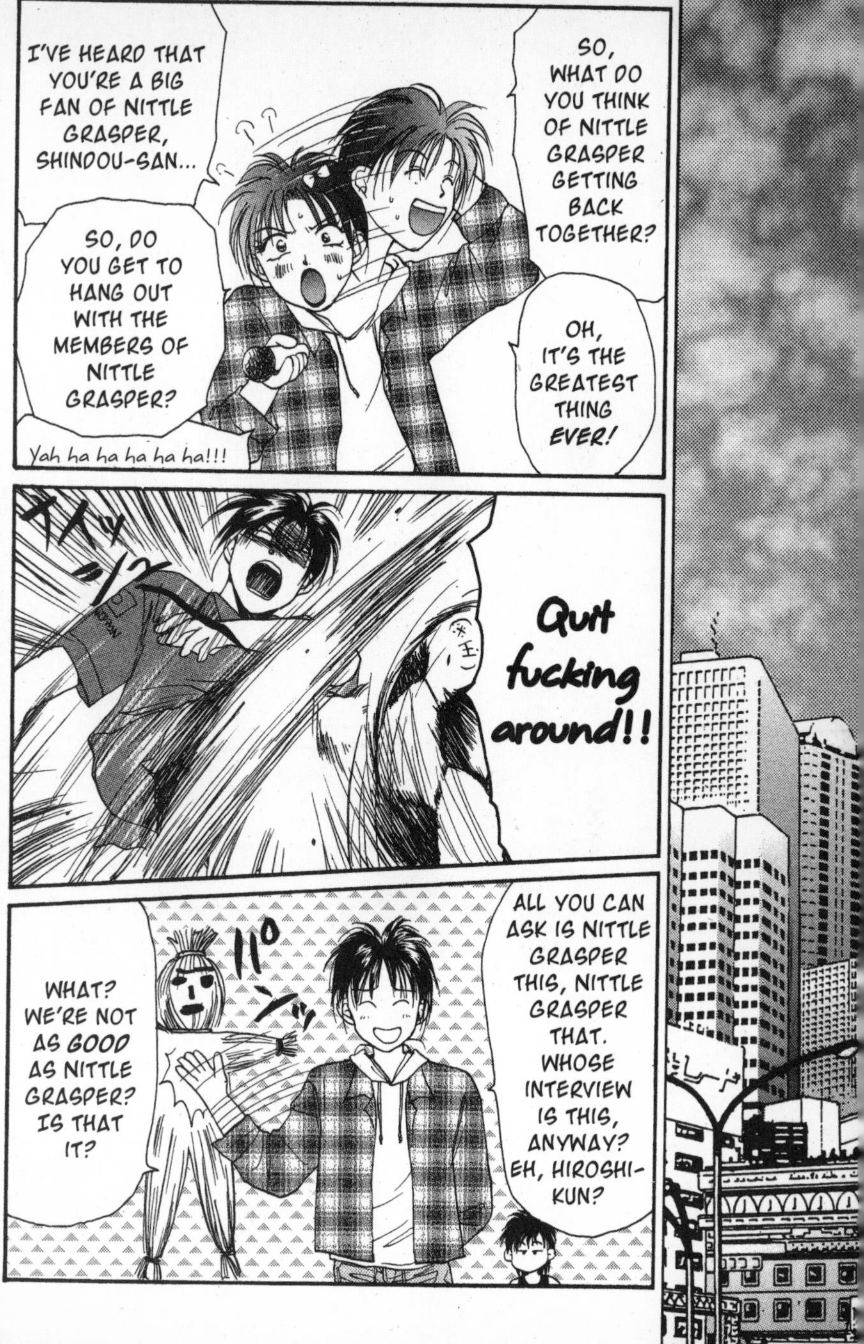
SO, WHAT DO YOU THINK OF NITTLE GRASPER GETTING BACK TOGETHER?
I'VE HEARD THAT YOU'RE A BIG FAN OF NITTLE GRASPER, SHINDOU-SAN...
OH, IT'S THE GREATEST THING *EVER!*
SO, DO YOU GET TO HANG OUT WITH THE MEMBERS OF NITTLE GRASPER?
Yah ha ha ha ha ha!!!
Quit fucking around!!
ALL YOU CAN ASK IS NITTLE GRASPER THIS, NITTLE GRASPER THAT. WHOSE INTERVIEW IS THIS, ANYWAY? EH, HIROSHI-KUN?
WHAT? WE'RE NOT AS *GOOD* AS NITTLE GRASPER? IS THAT IT?

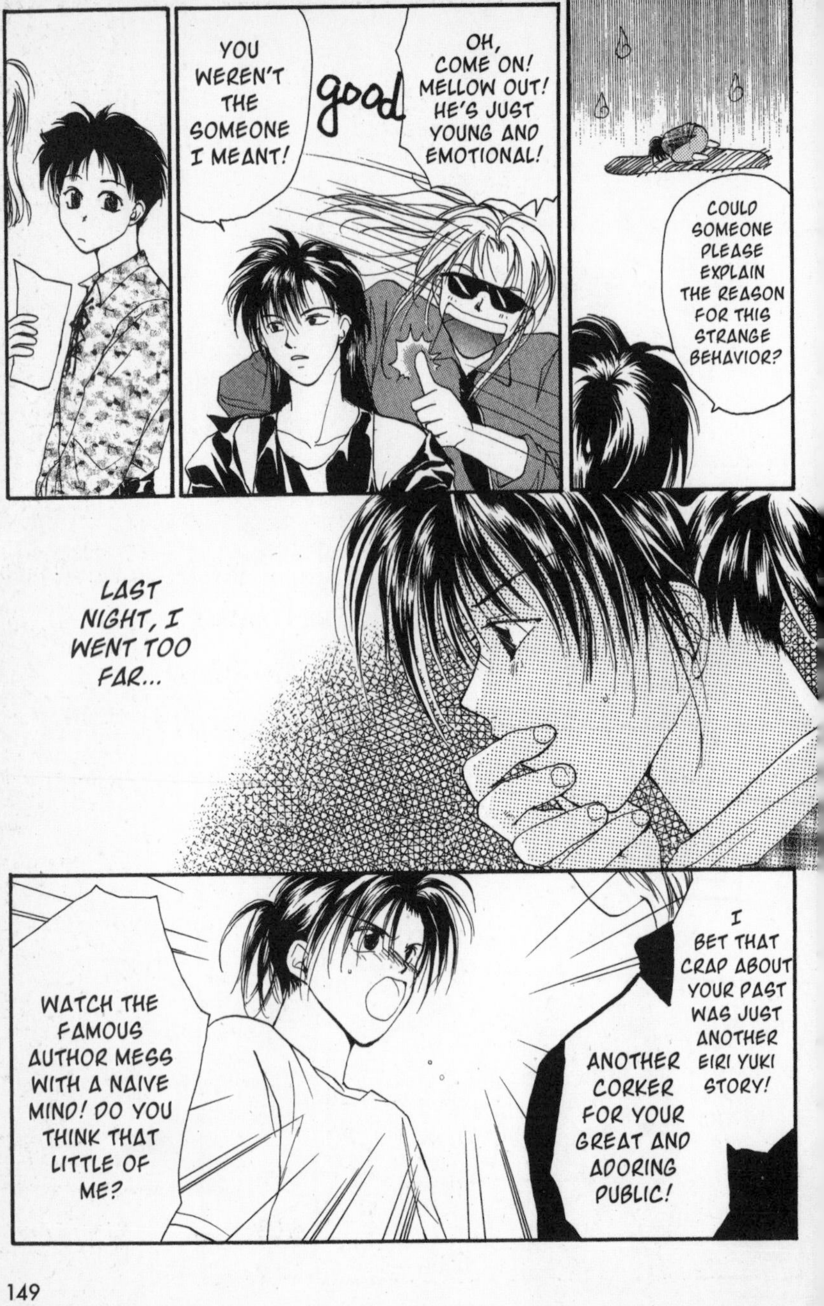
COULD SOMEONE PLEASE EXPLAIN THE REASON FOR THIS STRANGE BEHAVIOR?
OH, COME ON! MELLOW OUT! HE'S JUST YOUNG AND EMOTIONAL!
good
YOU WEREN'T THE SOMEONE I MEANT!
LAST NIGHT, I WENT TOO FAR...
I BET THAT CRAP ABOUT YOUR PAST WAS JUST ANOTHER EIRI YUKI STORY!
ANOTHER CORKER FOR YOUR GREAT AND ADORING PUBLIC!
WATCH THE FAMOUS AUTHOR MESS WITH A NAIVE MIND! DO YOU THINK THAT LITTLE OF ME?

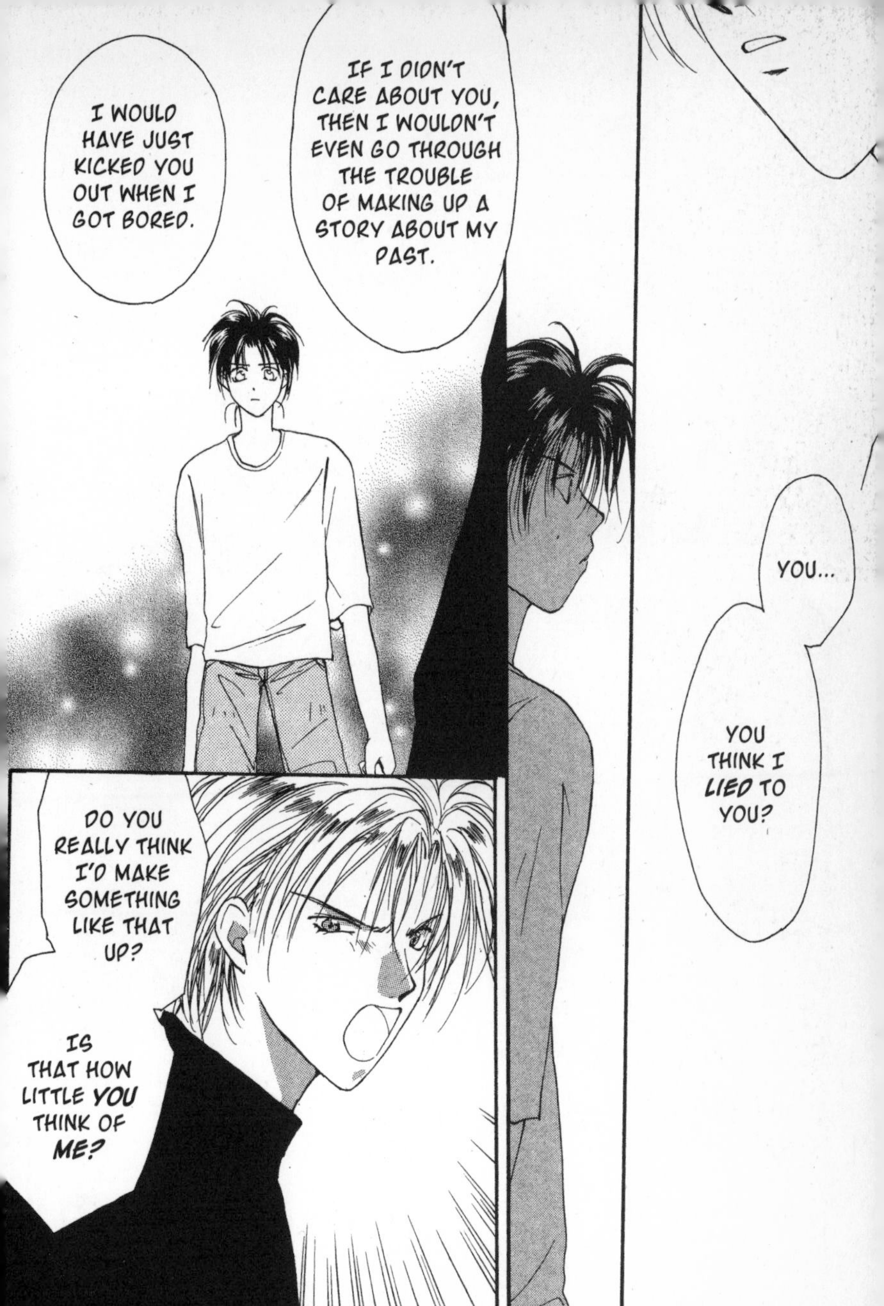
YOU...
YOU THINK I *LIED* TO YOU?
IF I DIDN'T CARE ABOUT YOU, THEN I WOULDN'T EVEN GO THROUGH THE TROUBLE OF MAKING UP A STORY ABOUT MY PAST.
I WOULD HAVE JUST KICKED YOU OUT WHEN I GOT BORED.
DO YOU REALLY THINK I'D MAKE SOMETHING LIKE THAT UP?
IS THAT HOW LITTLE *YOU* THINK OF *ME?*

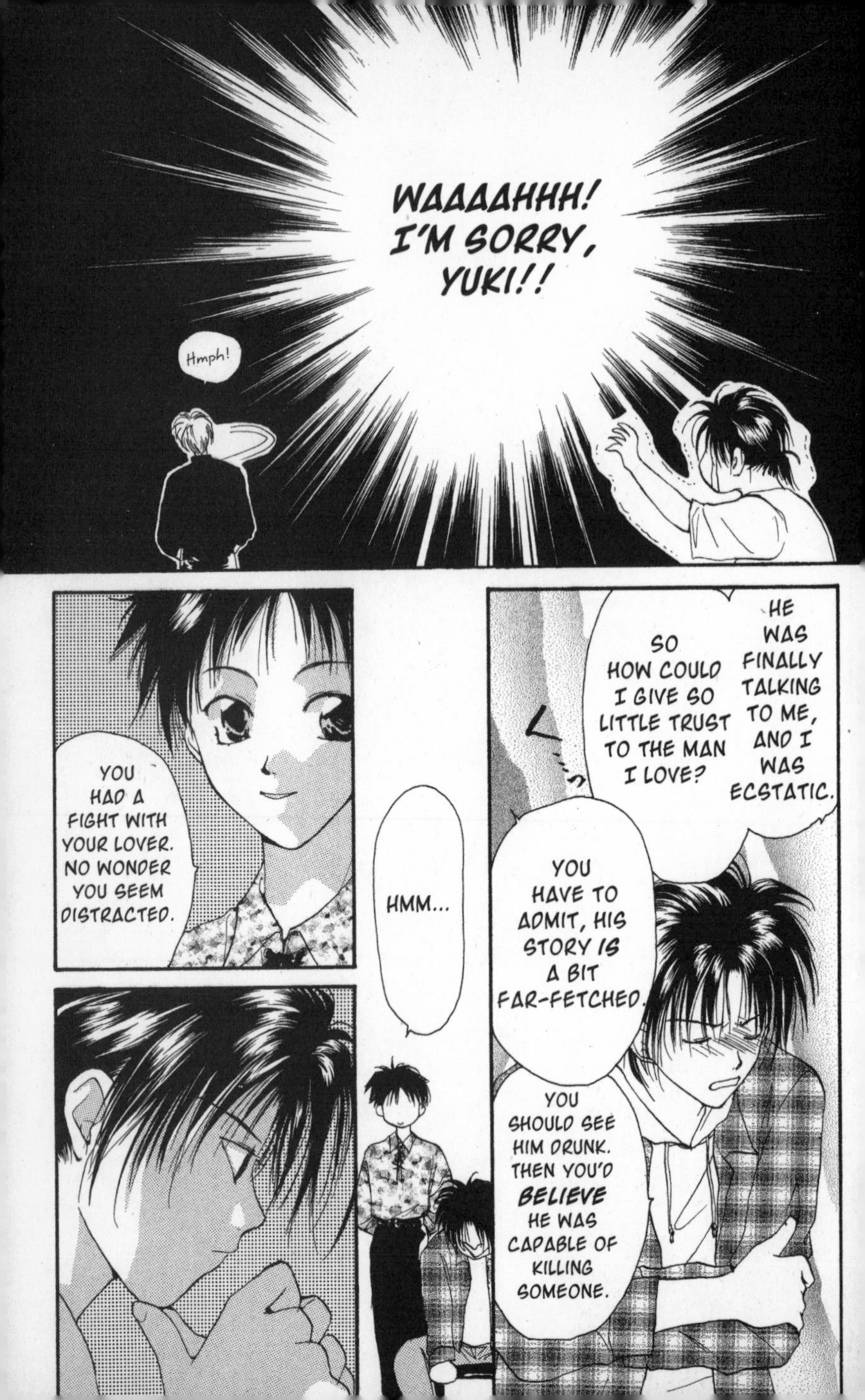

WAAAAHHH! I'M SORRY, YUKI!!
Hmph!
HE WAS FINALLY TALKING TO ME, AND I WAS ECSTATIC.
SO HOW COULD I GIVE SO LITTLE TRUST TO THE MAN I LOVE?
YOU HAVE TO ADMIT, HIS STORY *IS* A BIT FAR-FETCHED.
YOU SHOULD SEE HIM DRUNK. THEN YOU'D ***BELIEVE*** HE WAS CAPABLE OF KILLING SOMEONE.
YOU HAD A FIGHT WITH YOUR LOVER. NO WONDER YOU SEEM DISTRACTED.
HMM...

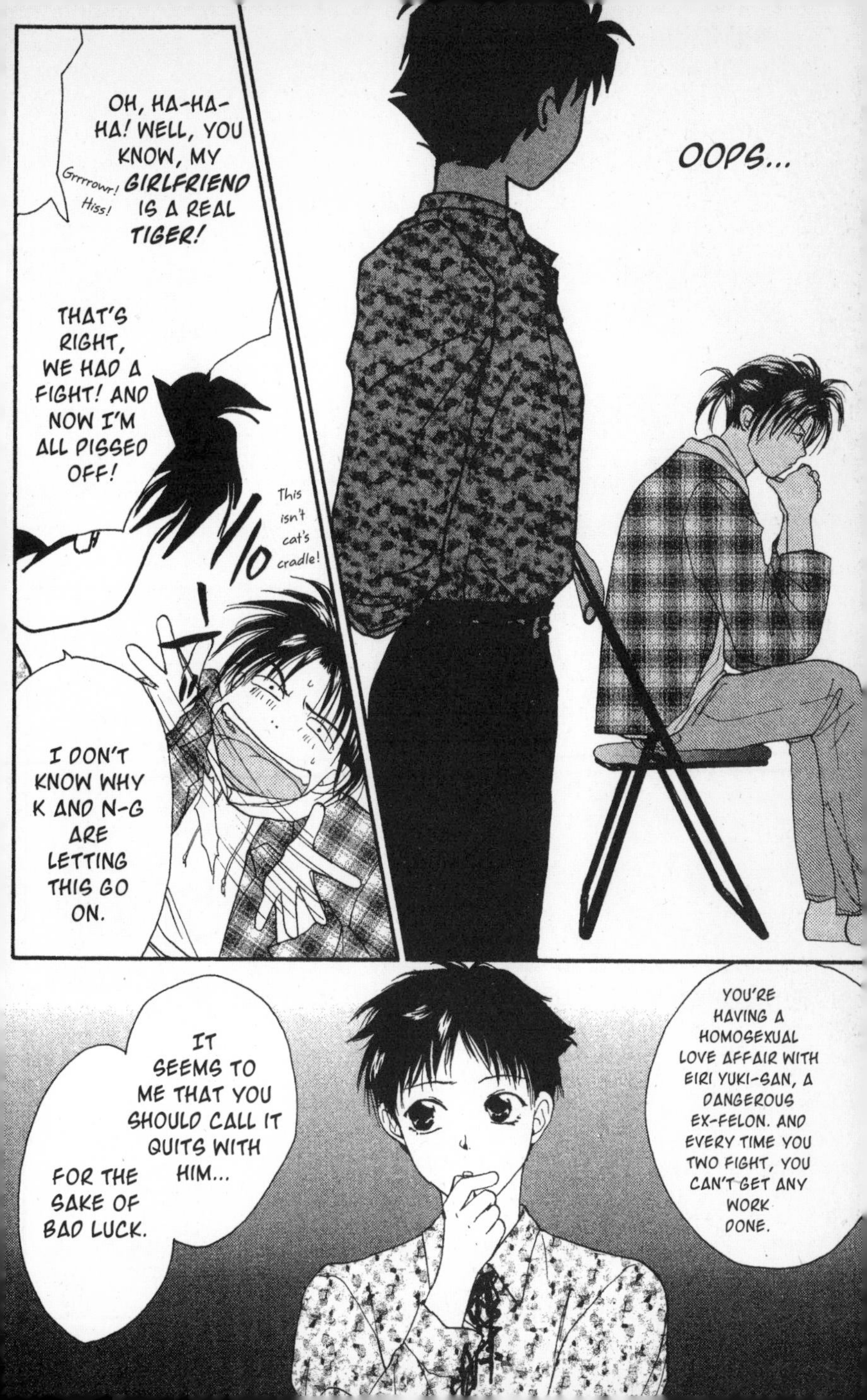
OOPS...
OH, HA-HA-HA! WELL, YOU KNOW, MY GIRLFRIEND IS A REAL TIGER!
Grrrrowr! Hiss!
THAT'S RIGHT, WE HAD A FIGHT! AND NOW I'M ALL PISSED OFF!
This isn't cat's cradle!
I DON'T KNOW WHY K AND N-G ARE LETTING THIS GO ON.
YOU'RE HAVING A HOMOSEXUAL LOVE AFFAIR WITH EIRI YUKI-SAN, A DANGEROUS EX-FELON. AND EVERY TIME YOU TWO FIGHT, YOU CAN'T GET ANY WORK DONE.
IT SEEMS TO ME THAT YOU SHOULD CALL IT QUITS WITH HIM...
FOR THE SAKE OF BAD LUCK.

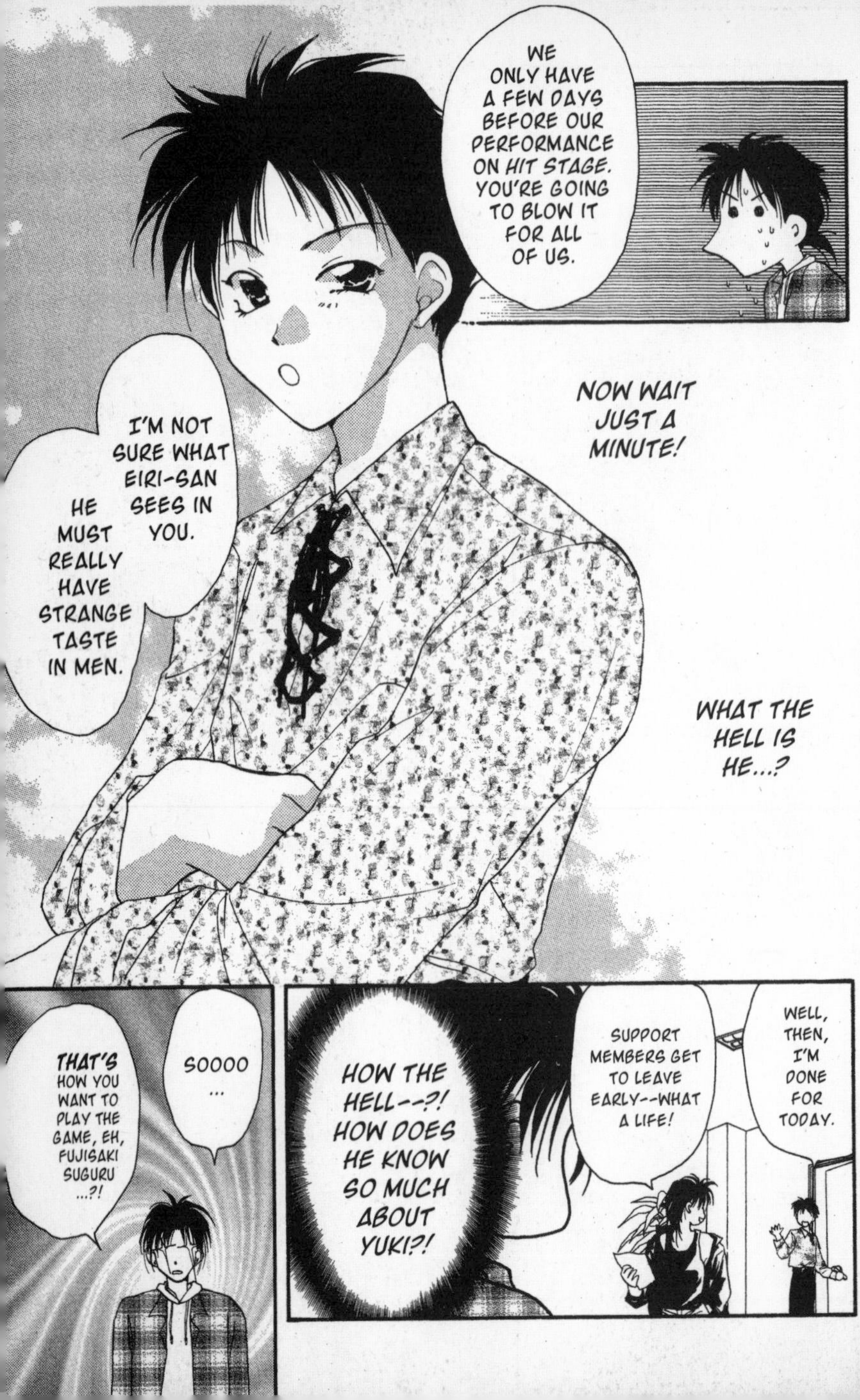
WE ONLY HAVE A FEW DAYS BEFORE OUR PERFORMANCE ON HIT STAGE. YOU'RE GOING TO BLOW IT FOR ALL OF US.
NOW WAIT JUST A MINUTE!
I'M NOT SURE WHAT EIRI-SAN SEES IN YOU.
HE MUST REALLY HAVE STRANGE TASTE IN MEN.
WHAT THE HELL IS HE...?
WELL, THEN, I'M DONE FOR TODAY.
SUPPORT MEMBERS GET TO LEAVE EARLY--WHAT A LIFE!
HOW THE HELL--?! HOW DOES HE KNOW SO MUCH ABOUT YUKI?!
SOOOO ...
THAT'S HOW YOU WANT TO PLAY THE GAME, EH, FUJISAKI SUGURU ...?!

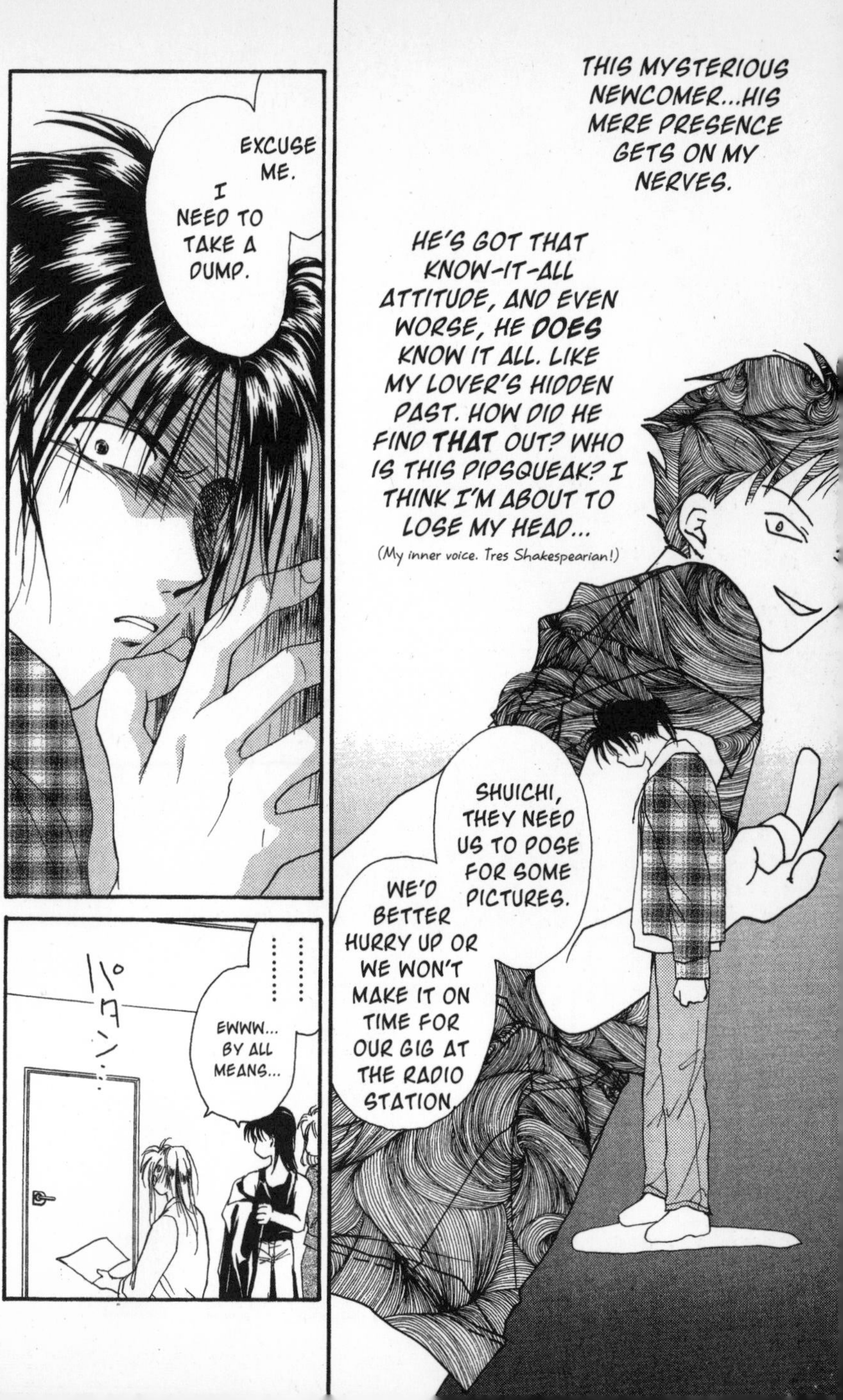
THIS MYSTERIOUS NEWCOMER...HIS MERE PRESENCE GETS ON MY NERVES.
HE'S GOT THAT KNOW-IT-ALL ATTITUDE, AND EVEN WORSE, HE DOES KNOW IT ALL. LIKE MY LOVER'S HIDDEN PAST. HOW DID HE FIND THAT OUT? WHO IS THIS PIPSQUEAK? I THINK I'M ABOUT TO LOSE MY HEAD...
(My inner voice. Tres Shakespearian!)
SHUICHI, THEY NEED US TO POSE FOR SOME PICTURES.
WE'D BETTER HURRY UP OR WE WON'T MAKE IT ON TIME FOR OUR GIG AT THE RADIO STATION.
EXCUSE ME. I NEED TO TAKE A DUMP.
......
EWWW... BY ALL MEANS...
パタン…

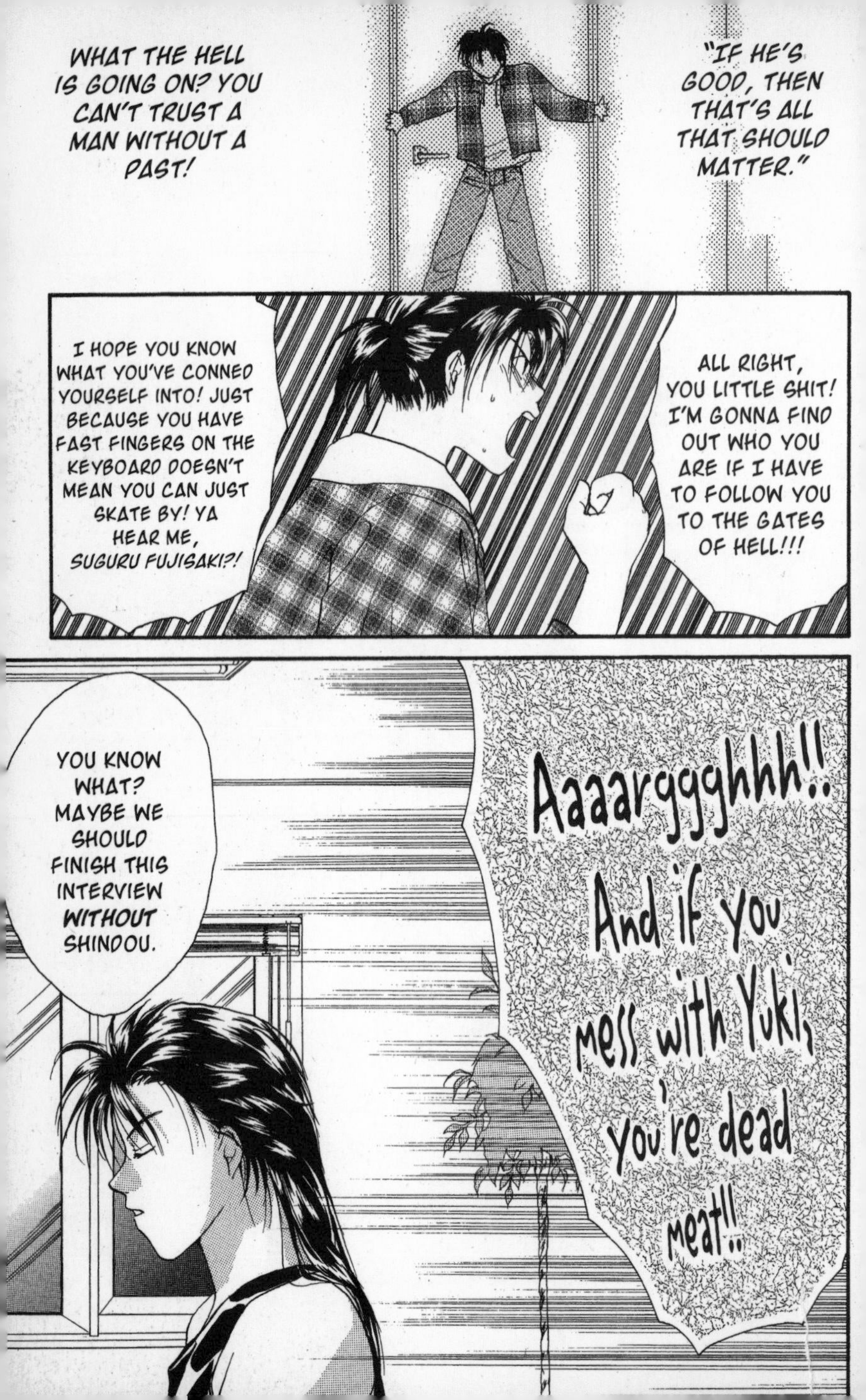
"IF HE'S GOOD, THEN THAT'S ALL THAT SHOULD MATTER."
WHAT THE HELL IS GOING ON? YOU CAN'T TRUST A MAN WITHOUT A PAST!
ALL RIGHT, YOU LITTLE SHIT! I'M GONNA FIND OUT WHO YOU ARE IF I HAVE TO FOLLOW YOU TO THE GATES OF HELL!!!
I HOPE YOU KNOW WHAT YOU'VE CONNED YOURSELF INTO! JUST BECAUSE YOU HAVE FAST FINGERS ON THE KEYBOARD DOESN'T MEAN YOU CAN JUST SKATE BY! YA HEAR ME, SUGURU FUJISAKI?!
Aaaargggghhh!.. And if you mess with Yuki, you're dead meat!..
YOU KNOW WHAT? MAYBE WE SHOULD FINISH THIS INTERVIEW WITHOUT SHINDOU.

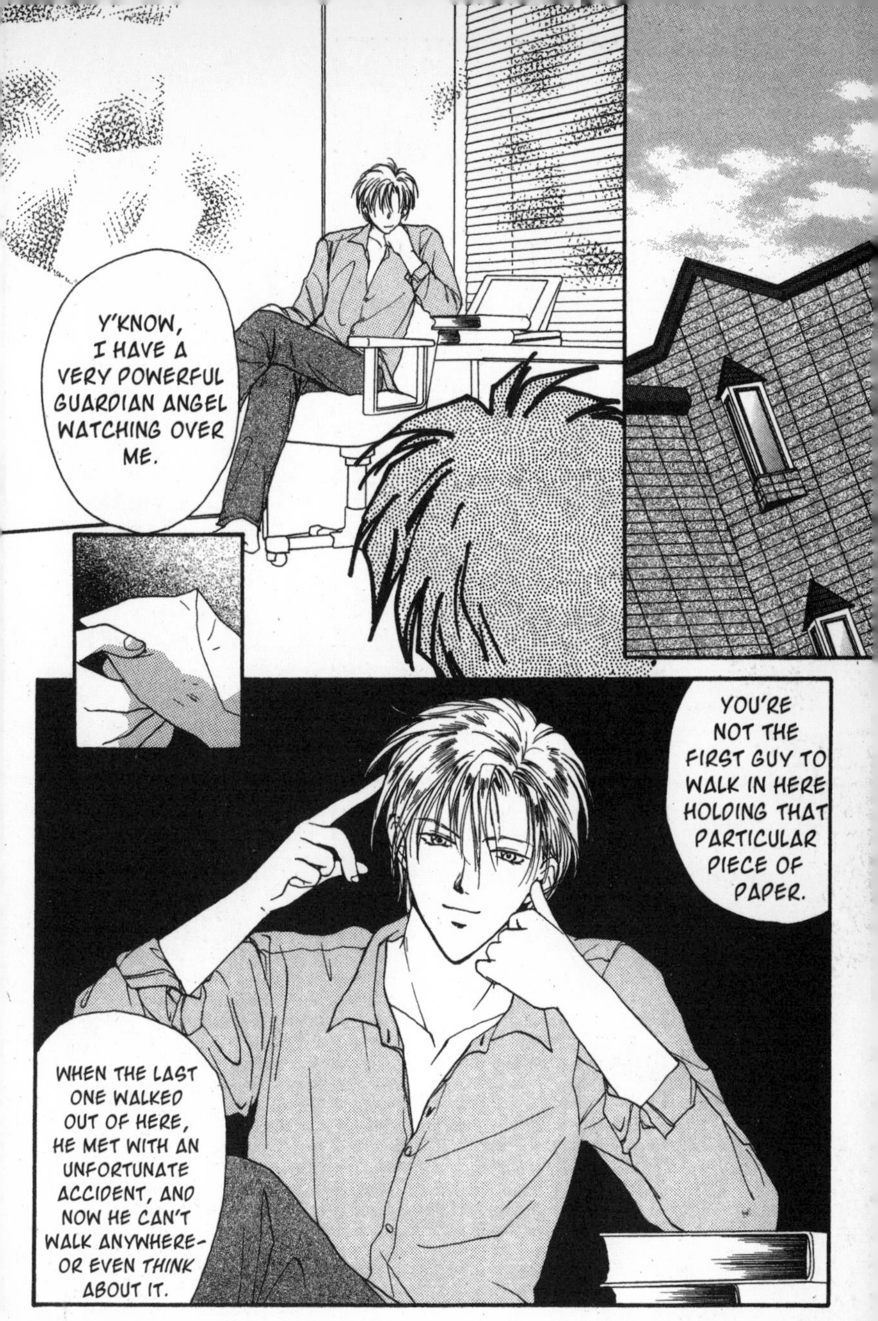
Y'KNOW, I HAVE A VERY POWERFUL GUARDIAN ANGEL WATCHING OVER ME.
YOU'RE NOT THE FIRST GUY TO WALK IN HERE HOLDING THAT PARTICULAR PIECE OF PAPER.
WHEN THE LAST ONE WALKED OUT OF HERE, HE MET WITH AN UNFORTUNATE ACCIDENT, AND NOW HE CAN'T WALK ANYWHERE- OR EVEN *THINK* ABOUT IT.

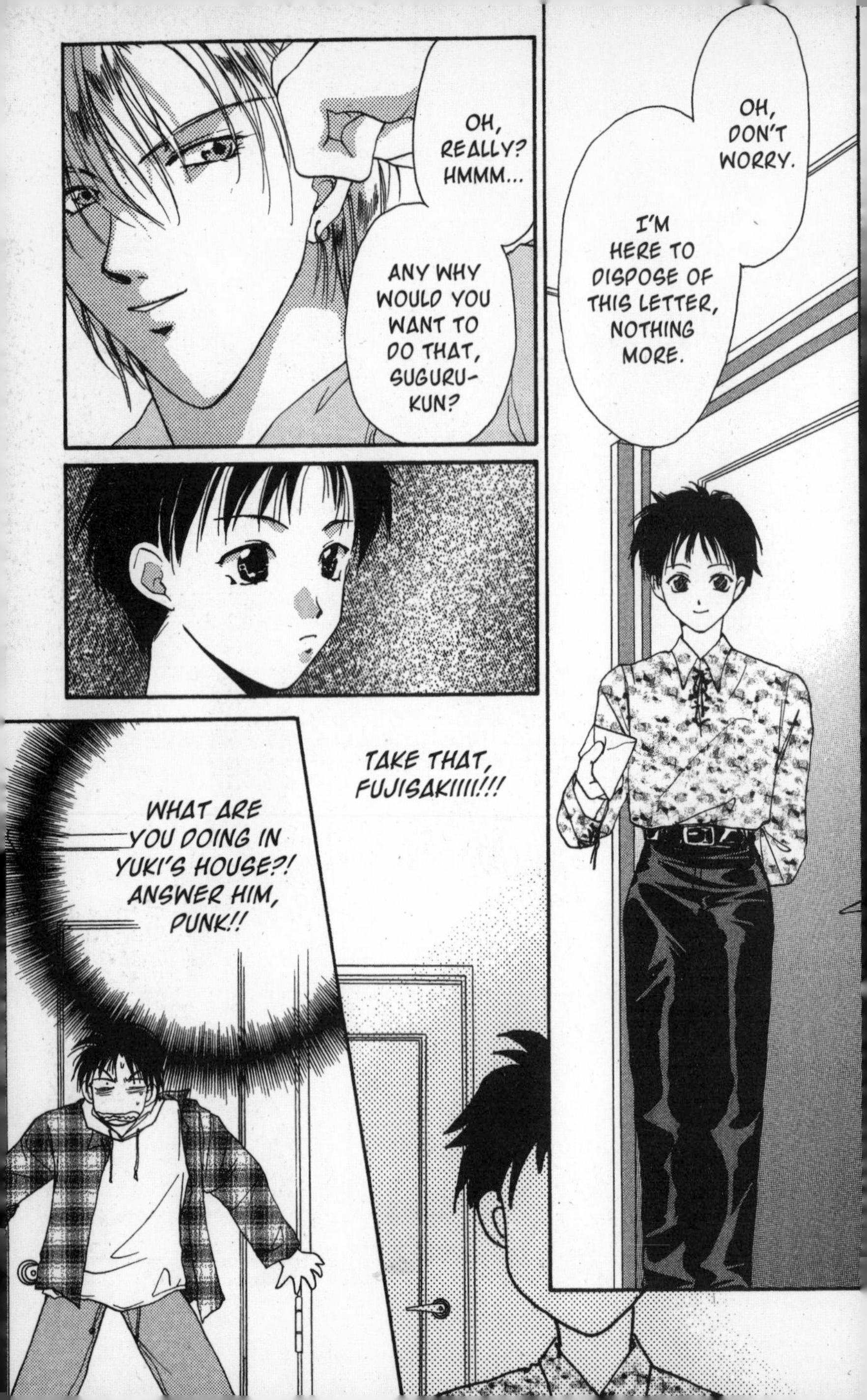
OH, DON'T WORRY.
I'M HERE TO DISPOSE OF THIS LETTER, NOTHING MORE.
OH, REALLY? HMMM...
ANY WHY WOULD YOU WANT TO DO THAT, SUGURU-KUN?
TAKE THAT, FUJISAKIIIII!!!
WHAT ARE YOU DOING IN YUKI'S HOUSE?! ANSWER HIM, PUNK!!

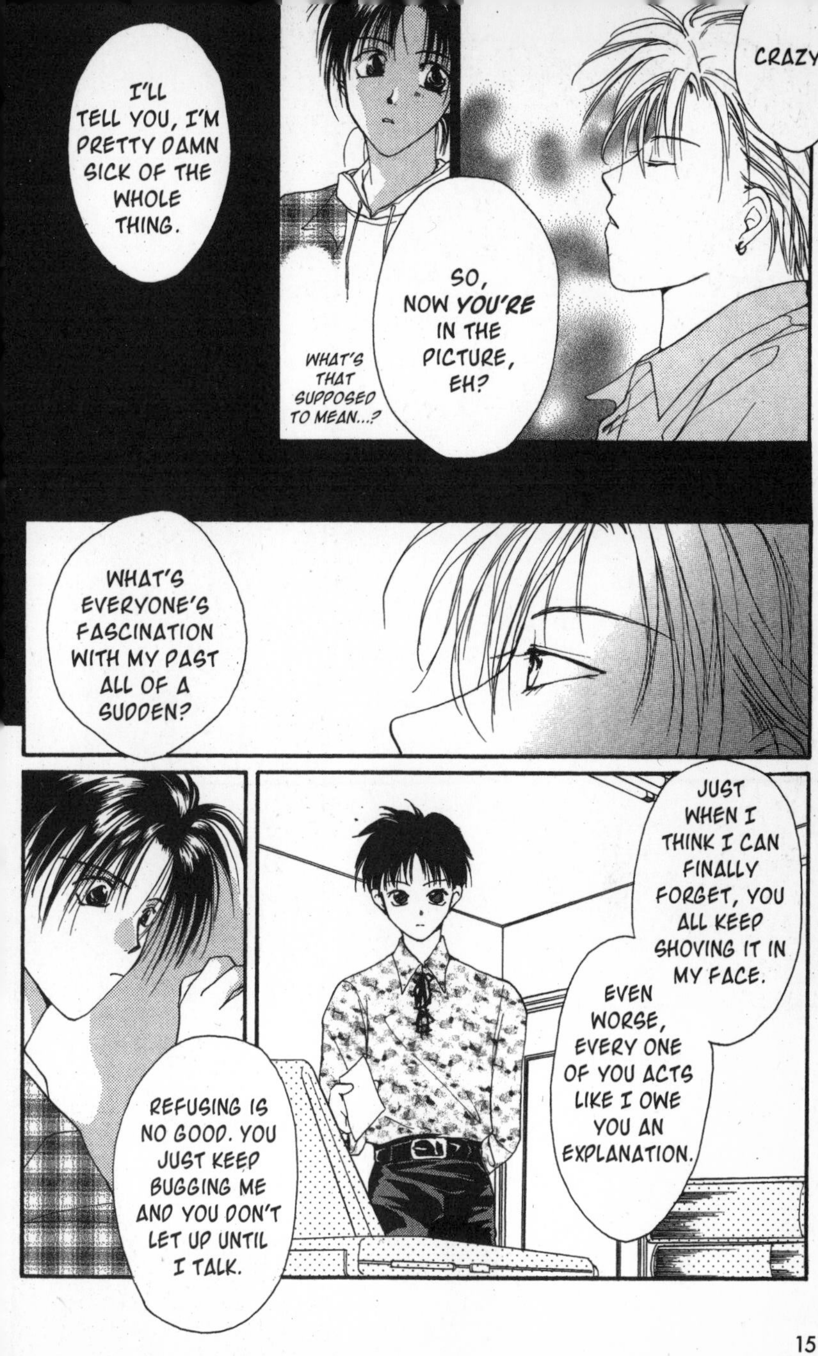
CRAZY...
SO, NOW *YOU'RE* IN THE PICTURE, EH?
WHAT'S THAT SUPPOSED TO MEAN...?
I'LL TELL YOU, I'M PRETTY DAMN SICK OF THE WHOLE THING.
WHAT'S EVERYONE'S FASCINATION WITH MY PAST ALL OF A SUDDEN?
JUST WHEN I THINK I CAN FINALLY FORGET, YOU ALL KEEP SHOVING IT IN MY FACE.
EVEN WORSE, EVERY ONE OF YOU ACTS LIKE I OWE YOU AN EXPLANATION.
REFUSING IS NO GOOD. YOU JUST KEEP BUGGING ME AND YOU DON'T LET UP UNTIL I TALK.

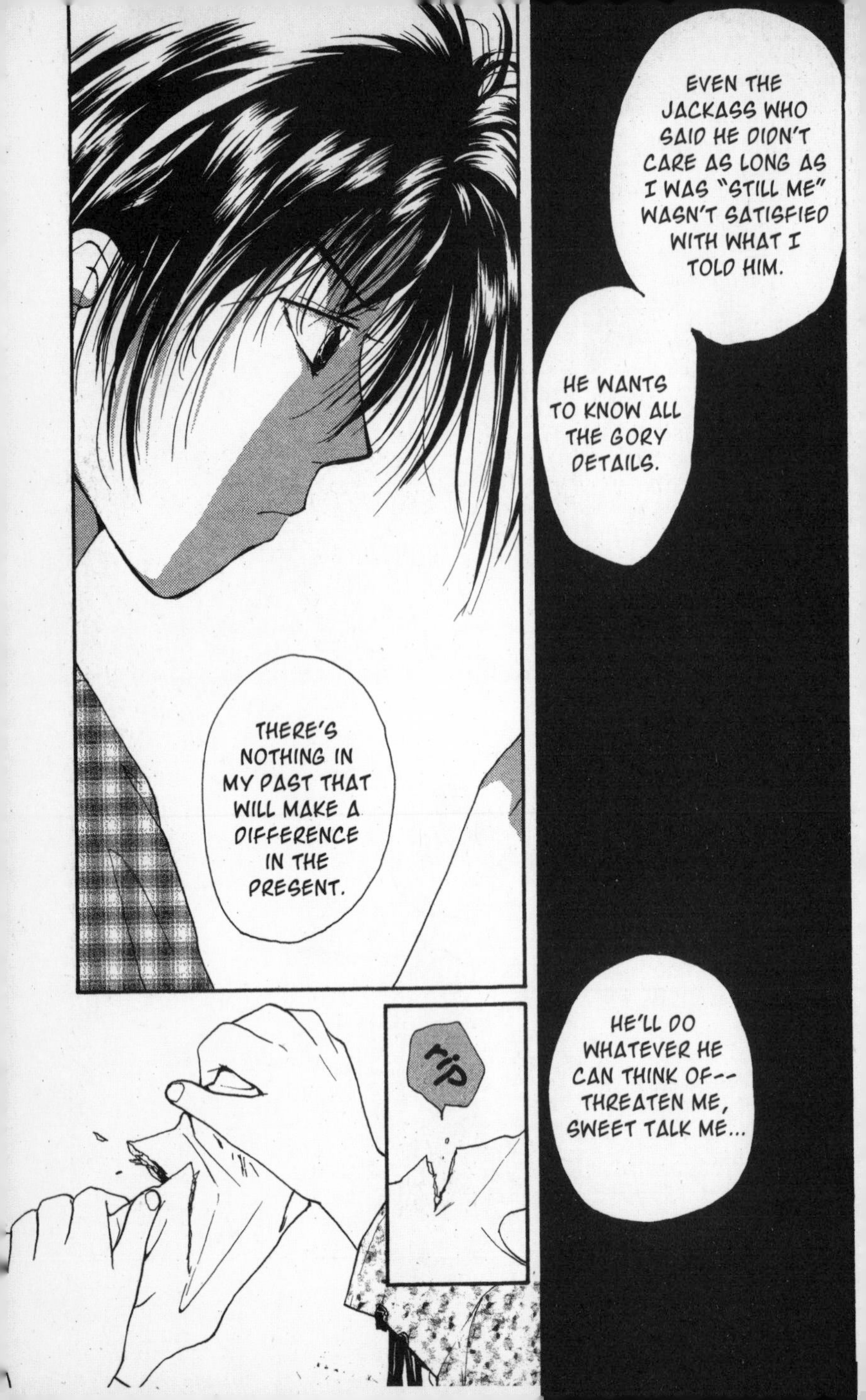
EVEN THE JACKASS WHO SAID HE DIDN'T CARE AS LONG AS I WAS "STILL ME" WASN'T SATISFIED WITH WHAT I TOLD HIM.
HE WANTS TO KNOW ALL THE GORY DETAILS.
HE'LL DO WHATEVER HE CAN THINK OF--THREATEN ME, SWEET TALK ME...
THERE'S NOTHING IN MY PAST THAT WILL MAKE A DIFFERENCE IN THE PRESENT.
rip

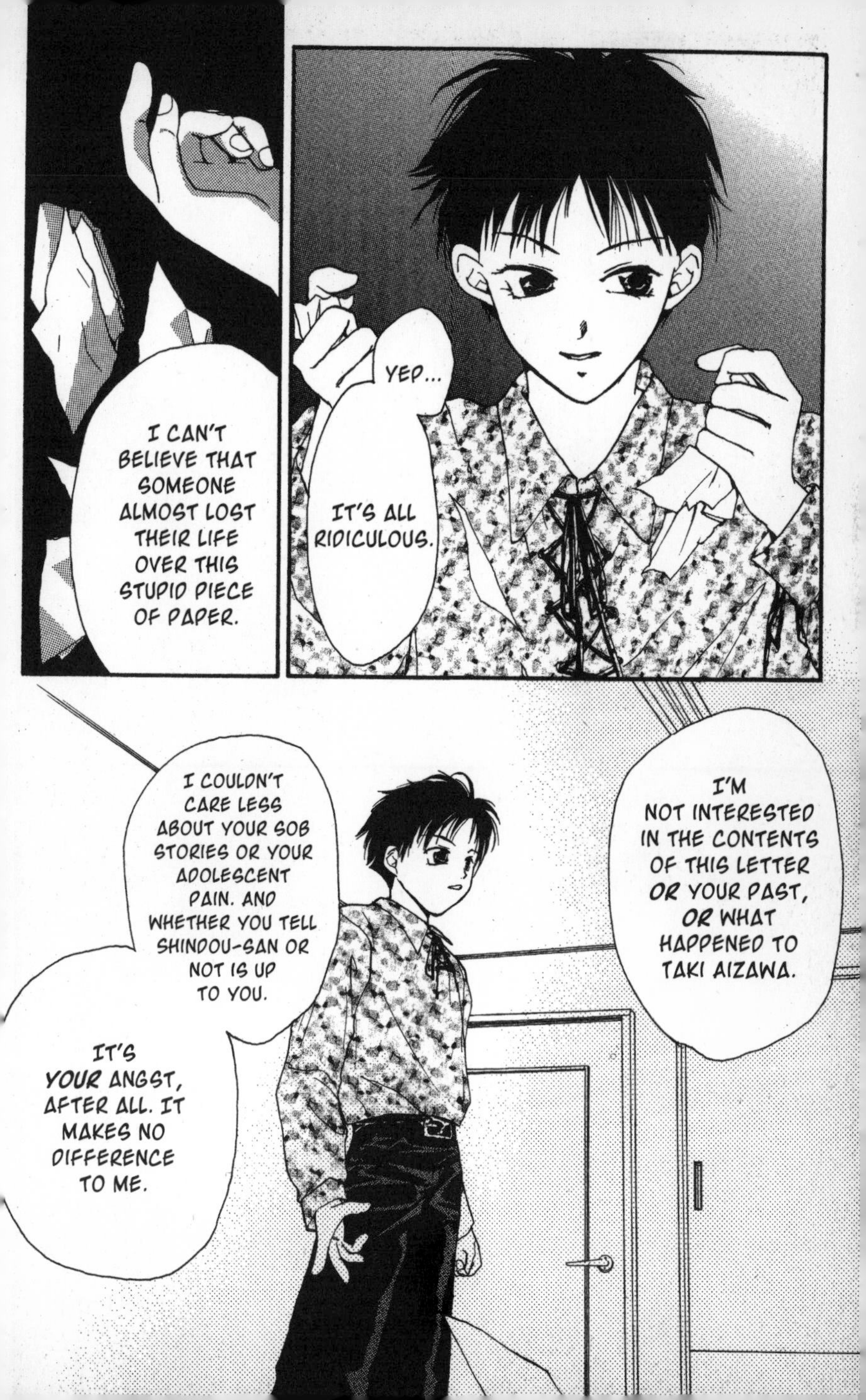
YEP...
IT'S ALL RIDICULOUS.
I CAN'T BELIEVE THAT SOMEONE ALMOST LOST THEIR LIFE OVER THIS STUPID PIECE OF PAPER.
I'M NOT INTERESTED IN THE CONTENTS OF THIS LETTER *OR* YOUR PAST, *OR* WHAT HAPPENED TO TAKI AIZAWA.
I COULDN'T CARE LESS ABOUT YOUR SOB STORIES OR YOUR ADOLESCENT PAIN. AND WHETHER YOU TELL SHINDOU-SAN OR NOT IS UP TO YOU.
IT'S *YOUR* ANGST, AFTER ALL. IT MAKES NO DIFFERENCE TO ME.

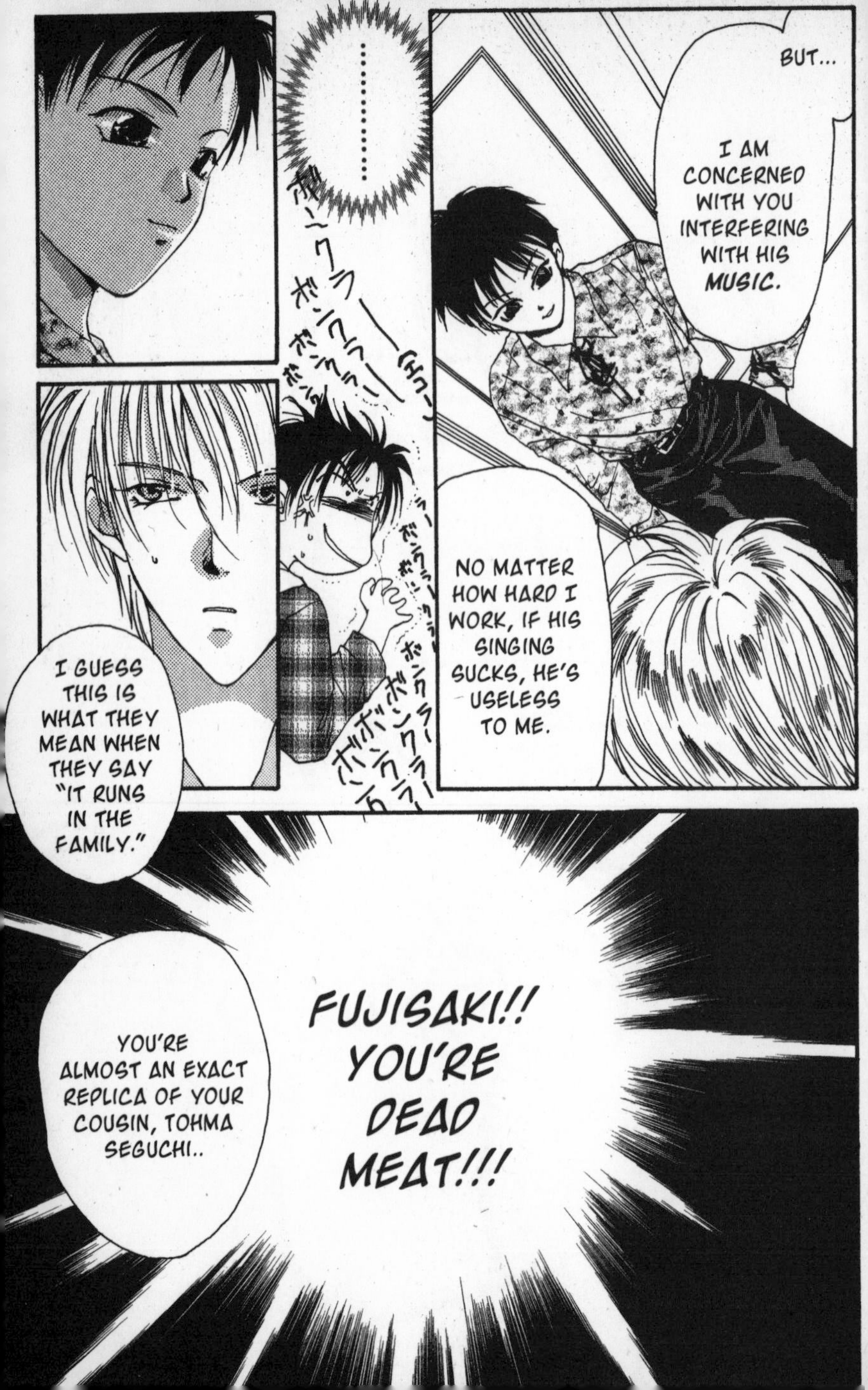
BUT...
I AM CONCERNED WITH YOU INTERFERING WITH HIS MUSIC.
NO MATTER HOW HARD I WORK, IF HIS SINGING SUCKS, HE'S USELESS TO ME.
......
I GUESS THIS IS WHAT THEY MEAN WHEN THEY SAY "IT RUNS IN THE FAMILY."
YOU'RE ALMOST AN EXACT REPLICA OF YOUR COUSIN, TOHMA SEGUCHI..
FUJISAKI!! YOU'RE DEAD MEAT!!!

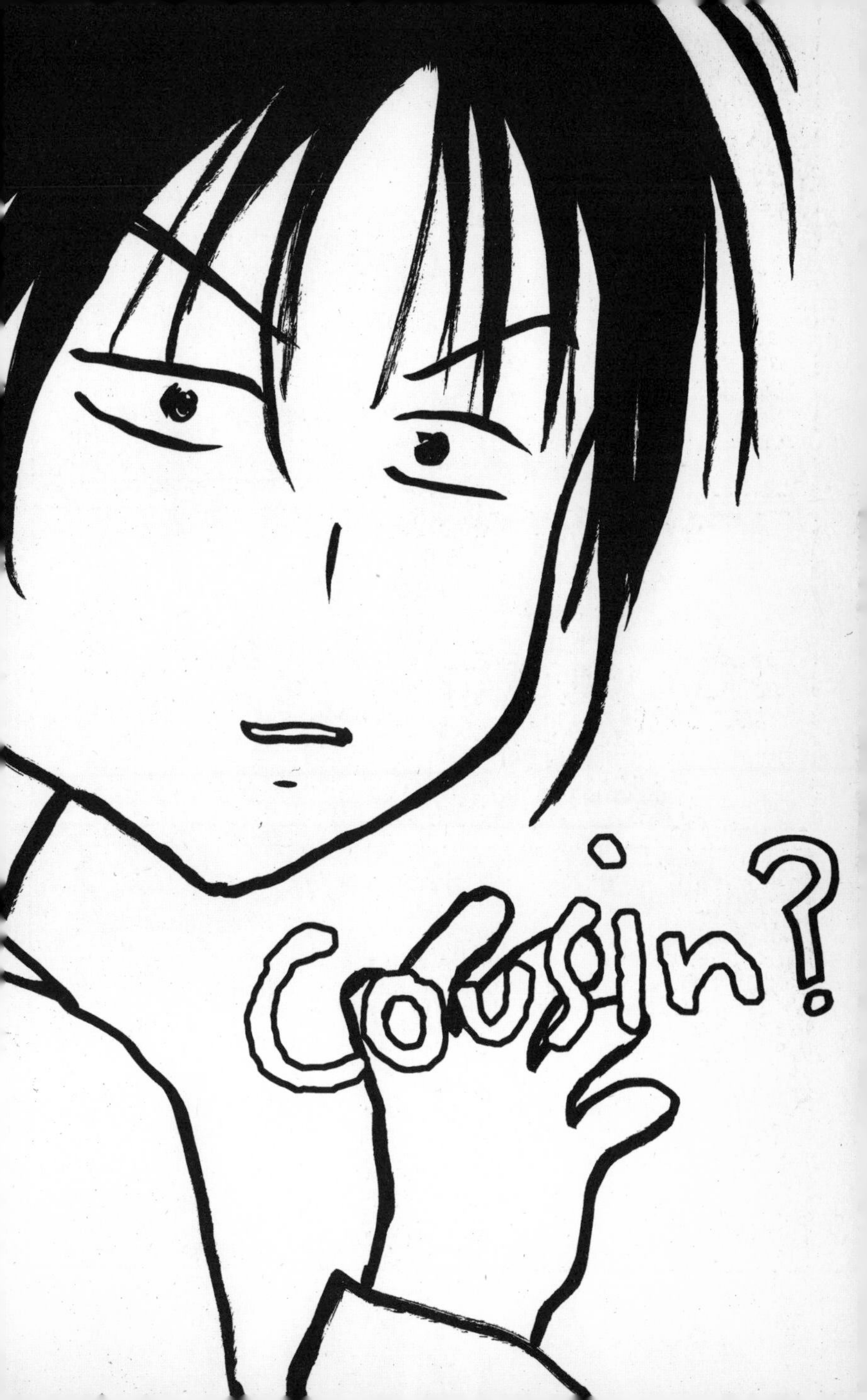
Cousin?

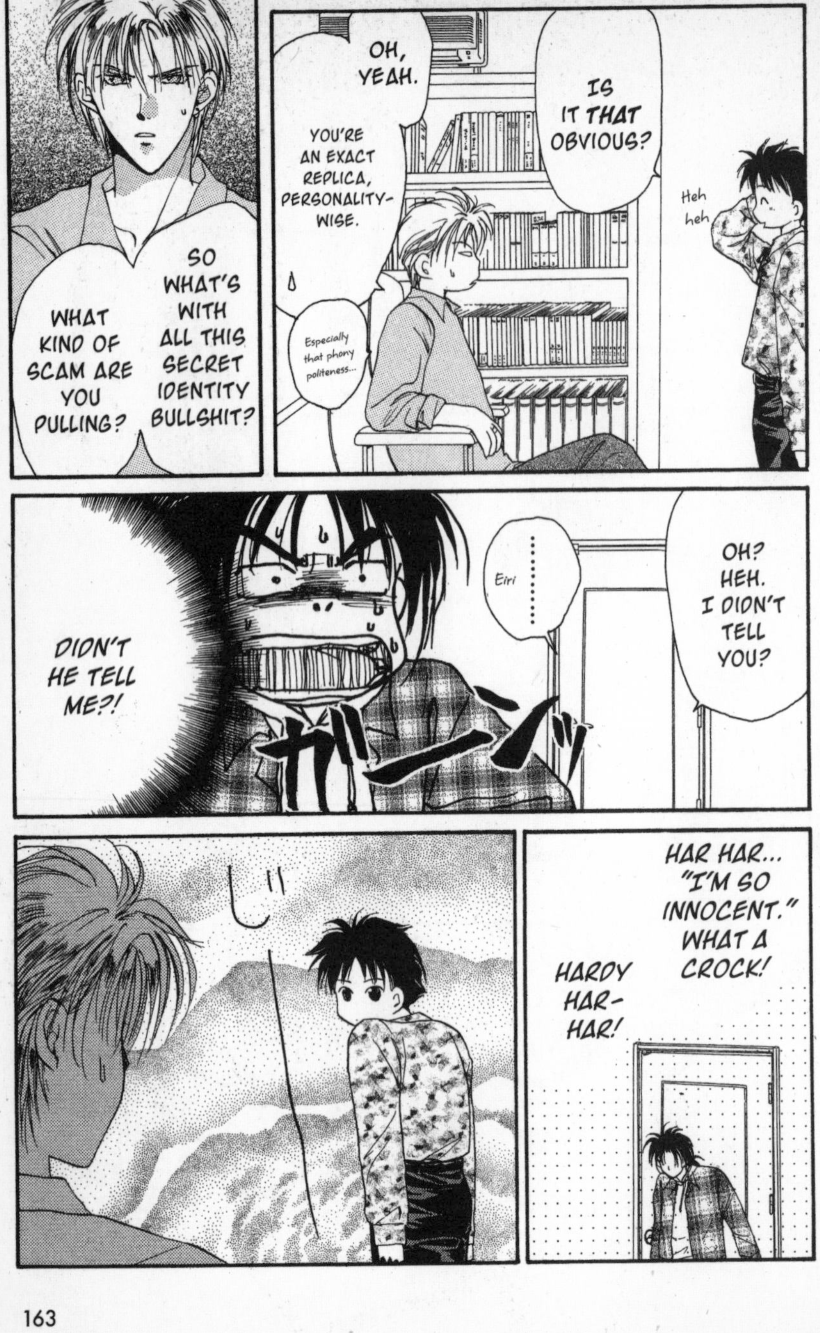
IS IT THAT OBVIOUS?
Heh heh
OH, YEAH.
YOU'RE AN EXACT REPLICA, PERSONALITY-WISE.
Especially that phony politeness...
SO WHAT'S WITH ALL THIS SECRET IDENTITY BULLSHIT?
WHAT KIND OF SCAM ARE YOU PULLING?
OH? HEH. I DIDN'T TELL YOU?
Eiri ......
DIDN'T HE TELL ME?!
HAR HAR... "I'M SO INNOCENT." WHAT A CROCK!
HARDY HAR-HAR!

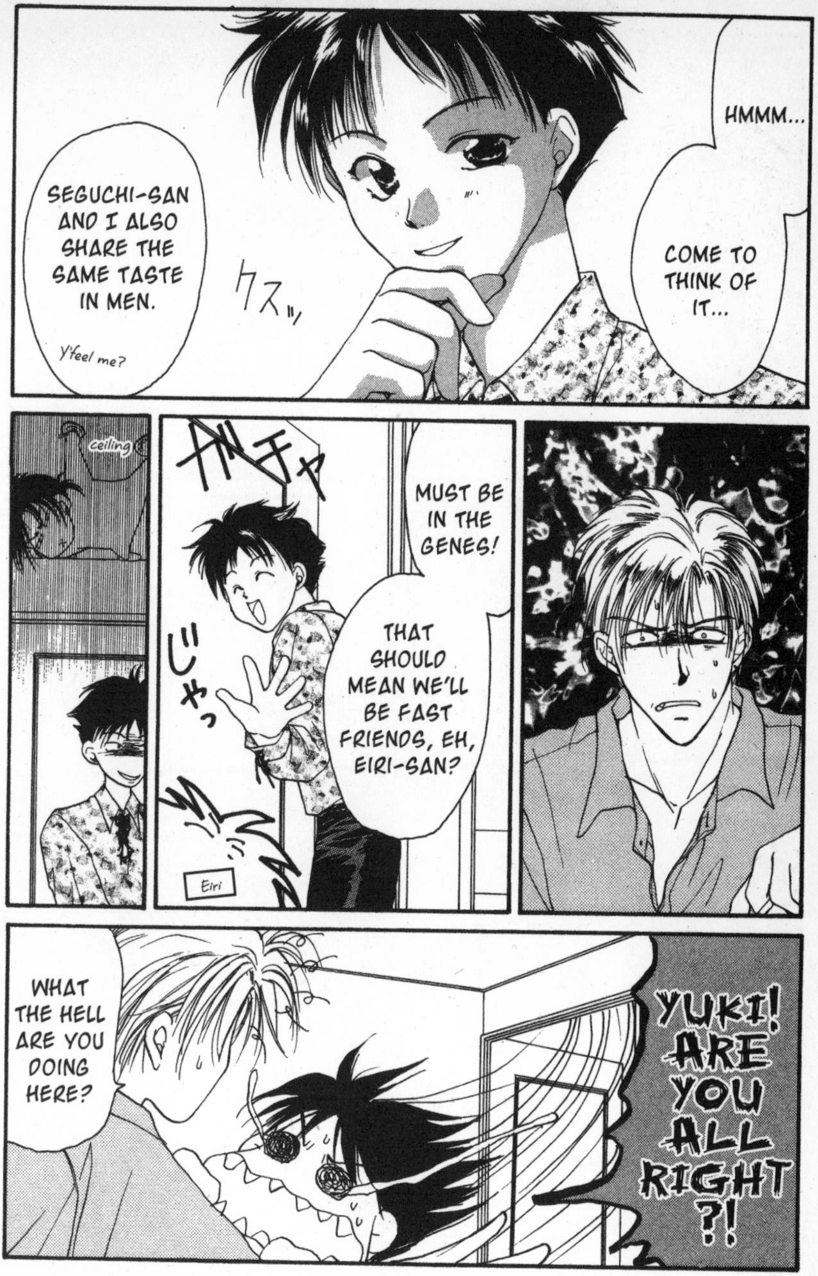
HMMM...
COME TO THINK OF IT...
クスッ
SEGUCHI-SAN AND I ALSO SHARE THE SAME TASTE IN MEN.
Y'feel me?
ガチャ
MUST BE IN THE GENES!
THAT SHOULD MEAN WE'LL BE FAST FRIENDS, EH, EIRI-SAN?
じゃっ
Eiri
ceiling
YUKI! ARE YOU ALL RIGHT?!
WHAT THE HELL ARE YOU DOING HERE?

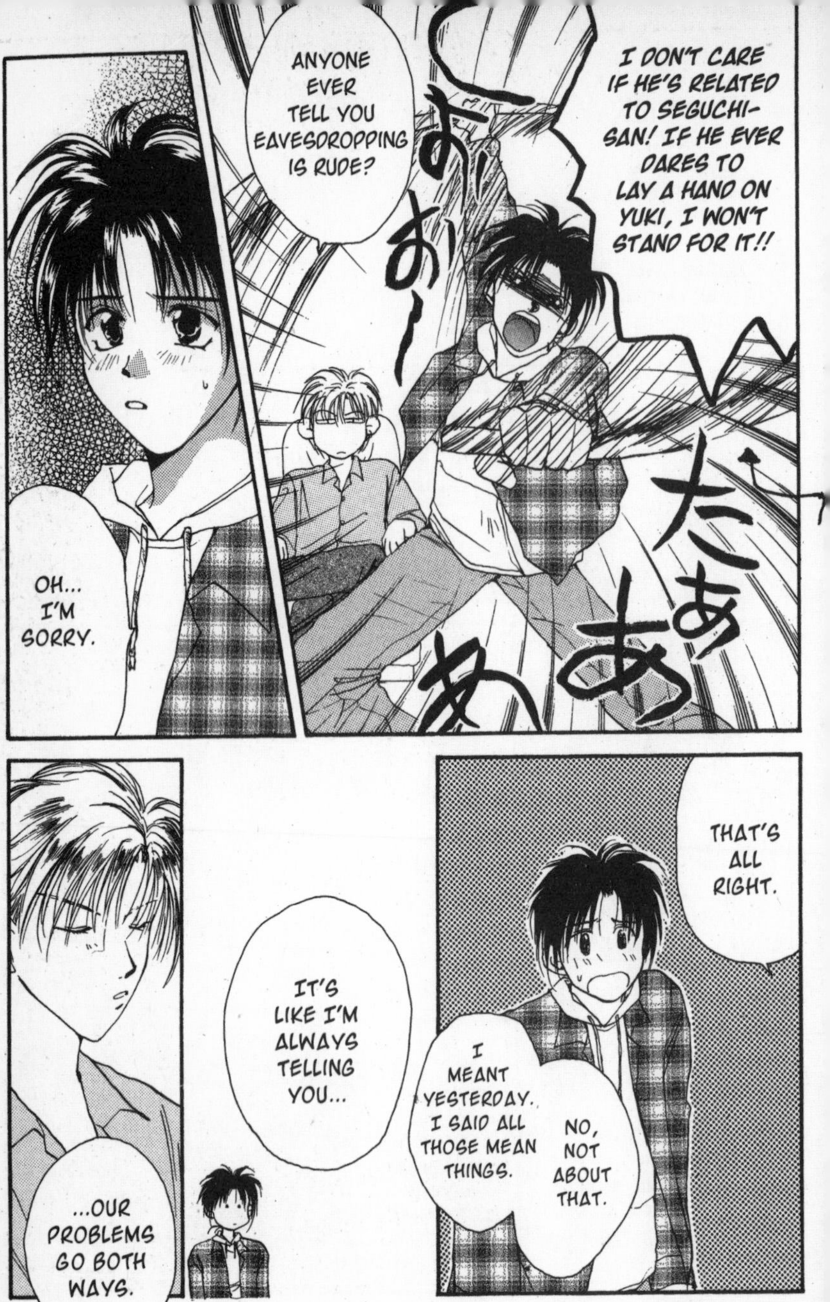
I DON'T CARE IF HE'S RELATED TO SEGUCHI-SAN! IF HE EVER DARES TO LAY A HAND ON YUKI, I WON'T STAND FOR IT!!
たあああ
ANYONE EVER TELL YOU EAVESDROPPING IS RUDE?
OH... I'M SORRY.
THAT'S ALL RIGHT.
NO, NOT ABOUT THAT.
I MEANT YESTERDAY. I SAID ALL THOSE MEAN THINGS.
IT'S LIKE I'M ALWAYS TELLING YOU...
...OUR PROBLEMS GO BOTH WAYS.

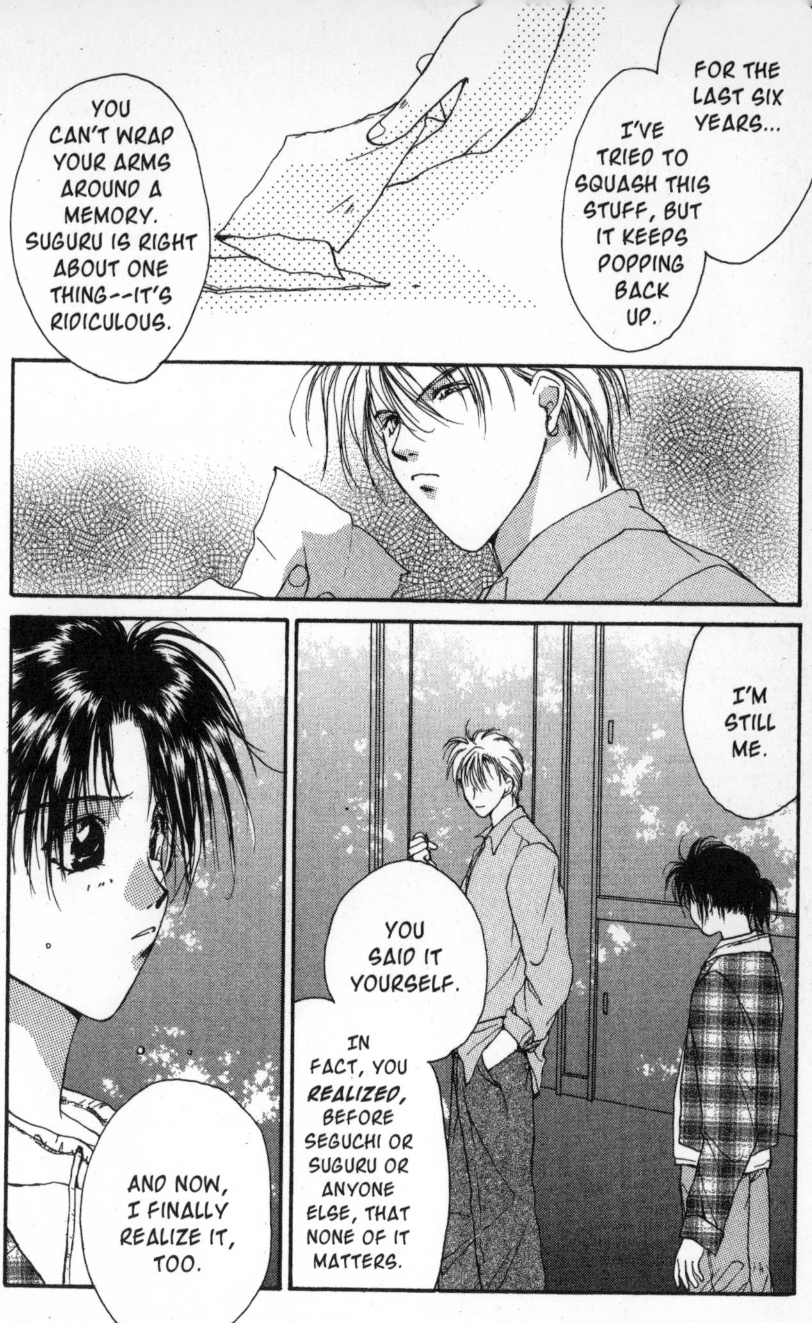
FOR THE LAST SIX YEARS... I'VE TRIED TO SQUASH THIS STUFF, BUT IT KEEPS POPPING BACK UP.
YOU CAN'T WRAP YOUR ARMS AROUND A MEMORY. SUGURU IS RIGHT ABOUT ONE THING--IT'S RIDICULOUS.
I'M STILL ME.
YOU SAID IT YOURSELF.
IN FACT, YOU *REALIZED*, BEFORE SEGUCHI OR SUGURU OR ANYONE ELSE, THAT NONE OF IT MATTERS.
AND NOW, I FINALLY REALIZE IT, TOO.

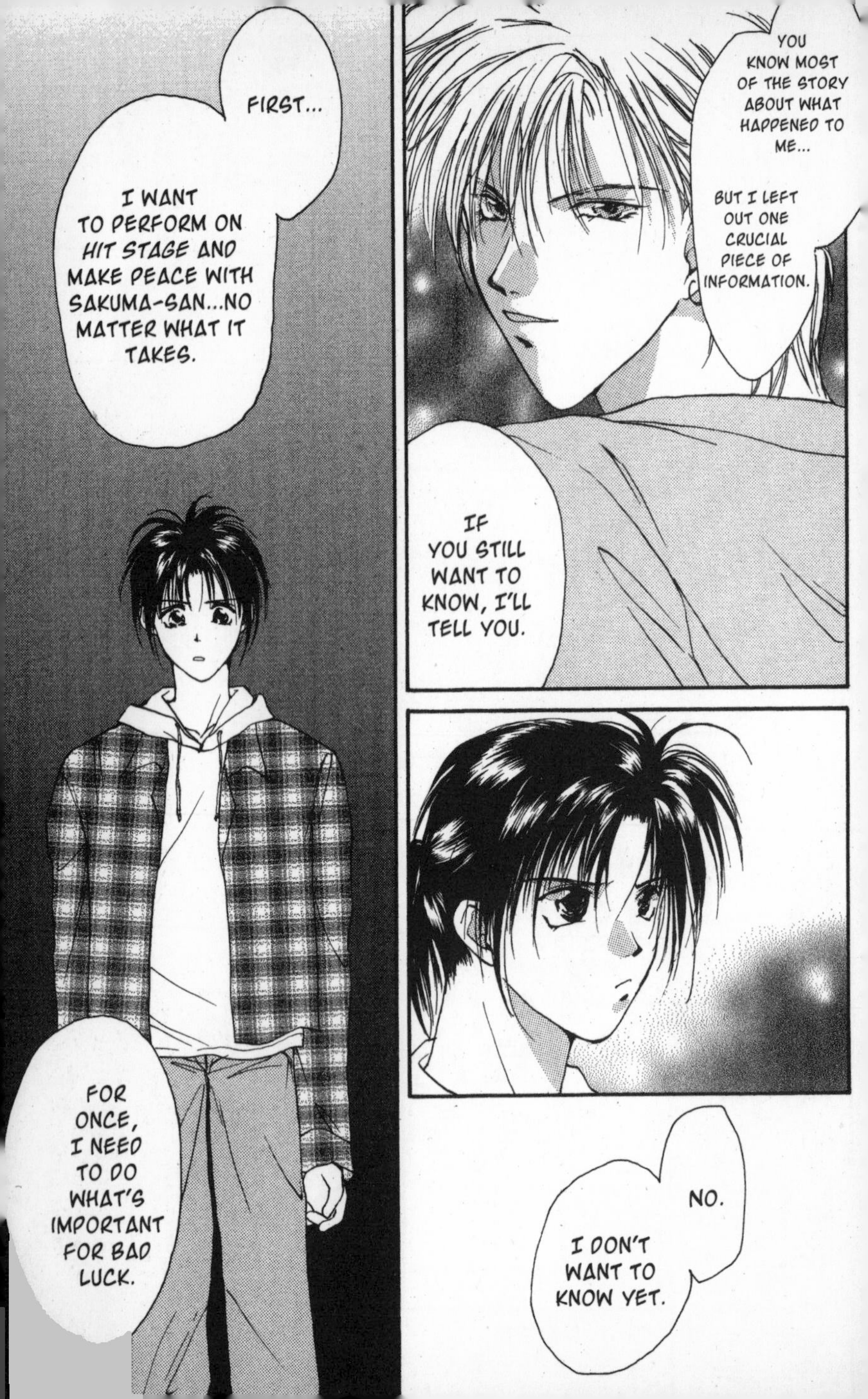
YOU KNOW MOST OF THE STORY ABOUT WHAT HAPPENED TO ME...
BUT I LEFT OUT ONE CRUCIAL PIECE OF INFORMATION.
IF YOU STILL WANT TO KNOW, I'LL TELL YOU.
NO.
I DON'T WANT TO KNOW YET.
FIRST...
I WANT TO PERFORM ON HIT STAGE AND MAKE PEACE WITH SAKUMA-SAN...NO MATTER WHAT IT TAKES.
FOR ONCE, I NEED TO DO WHAT'S IMPORTANT FOR BAD LUCK.

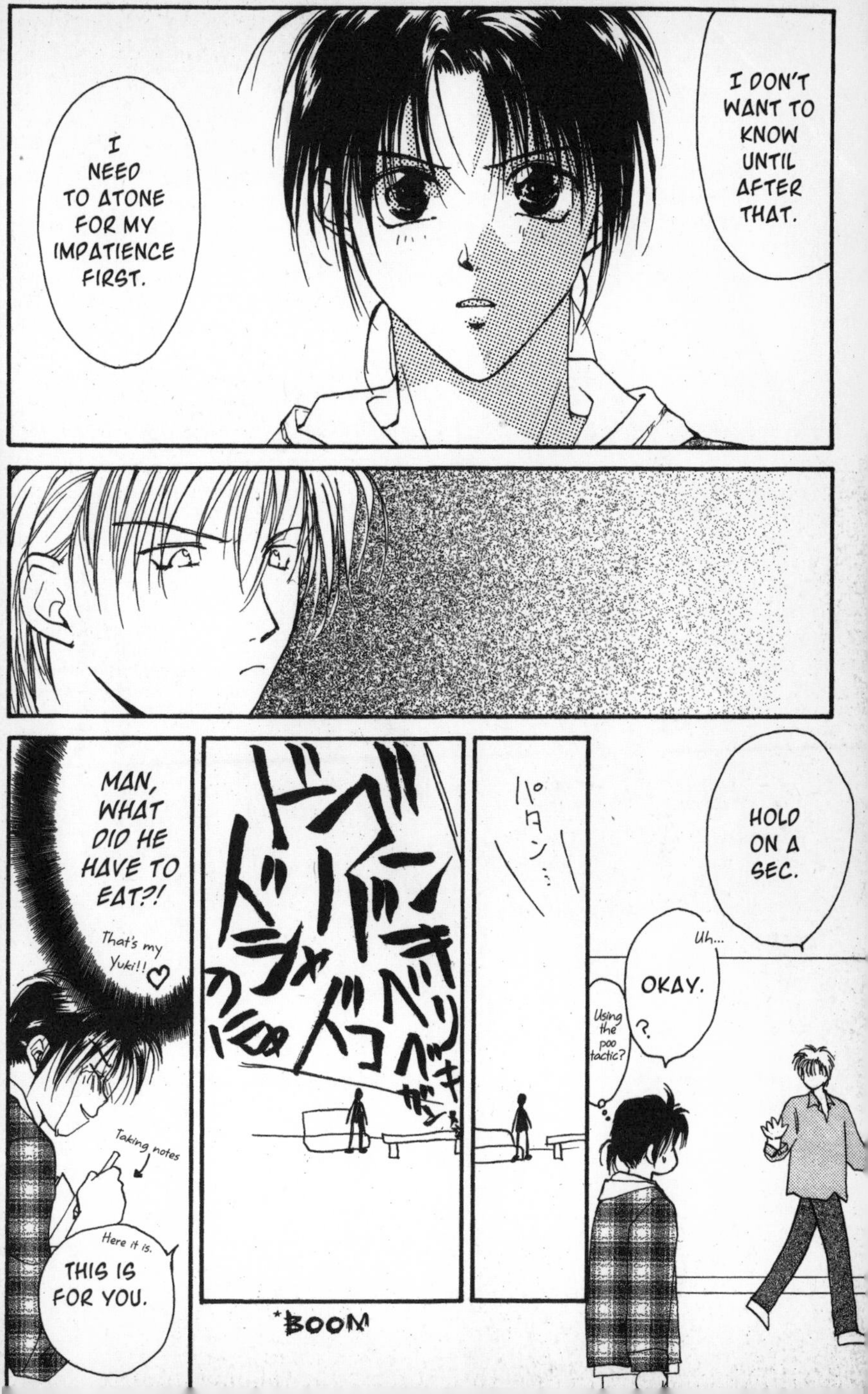
I DON'T WANT TO KNOW UNTIL AFTER THAT.
I NEED TO ATONE FOR MY IMPATIENCE FIRST.
HOLD ON A SEC.
Uh...
OKAY.
?
Using the poo tactic?
パタン…
*BOOM
MAN, WHAT DID HE HAVE TO EAT?!
That's my Yuki!! ♡
Taking notes
Here it is.
THIS IS FOR YOU.

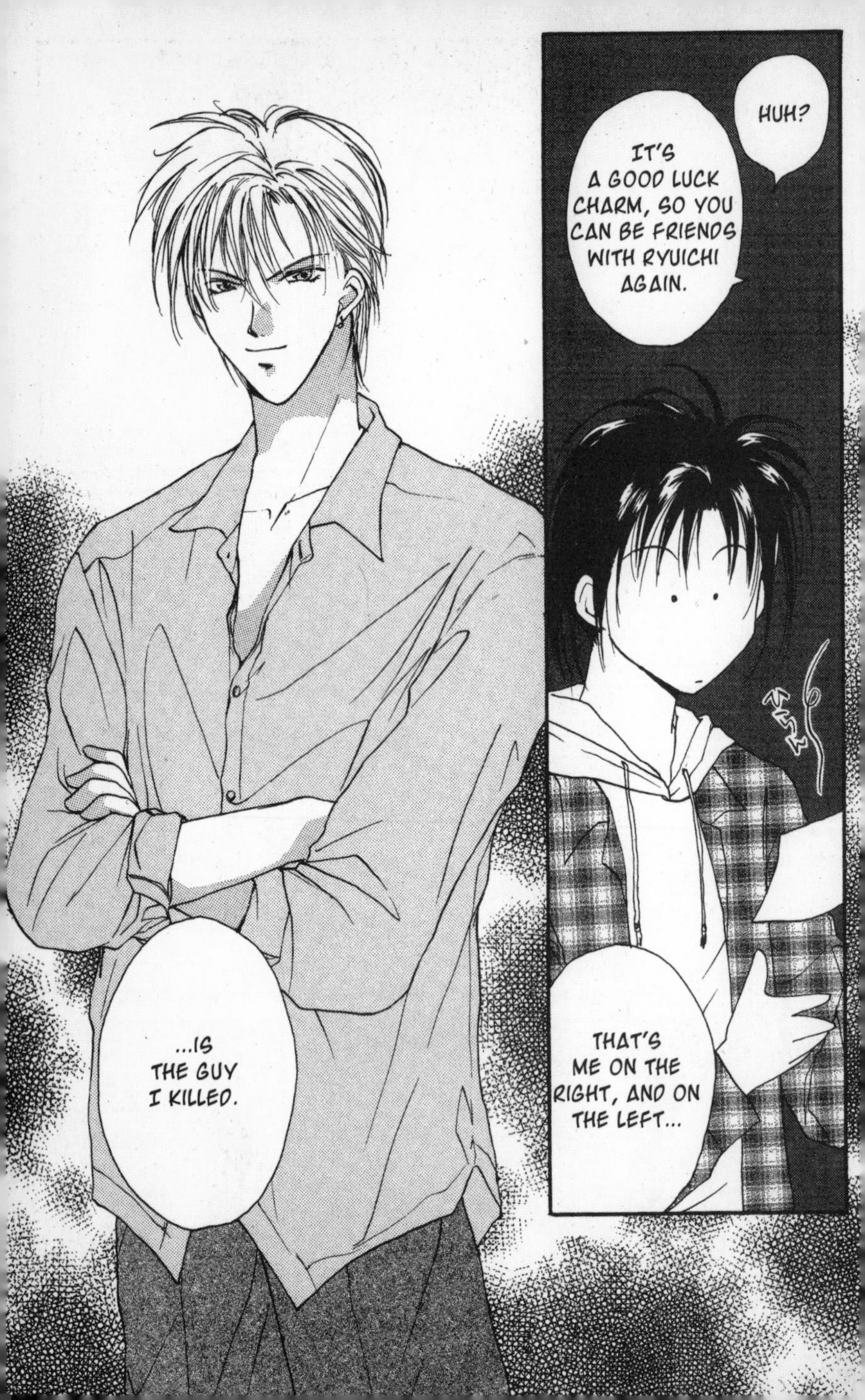
HUH?
IT'S A GOOD LUCK CHARM, SO YOU CAN BE FRIENDS WITH RYUICHI AGAIN.
THAT'S ME ON THE RIGHT, AND ON THE LEFT...
...IS THE GUY I KILLED.

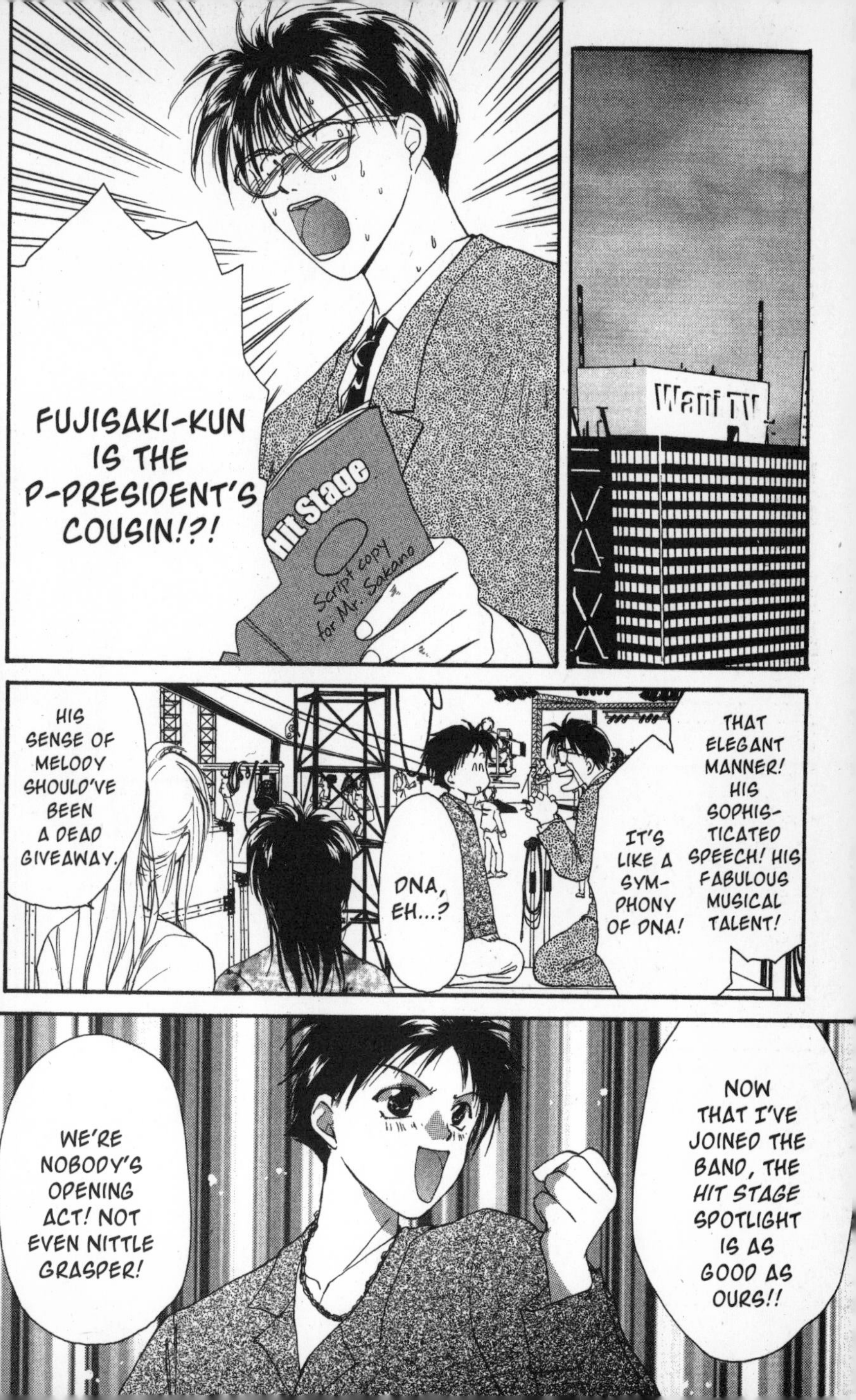
Wani TV
FUJISAKI-KUN IS THE P-PRESIDENT'S COUSIN!?!
Hit Stage
Script copy for Mr. Sakano
THAT ELEGANT MANNER! HIS SOPHISTICATED SPEECH! HIS FABULOUS MUSICAL TALENT!
IT'S LIKE A SYMPHONY OF DNA!
DNA, EH...?
HIS SENSE OF MELODY SHOULD'VE BEEN A DEAD GIVEAWAY.
NOW THAT I'VE JOINED THE BAND, THE HIT STAGE SPOTLIGHT IS AS GOOD AS OURS!!
WE'RE NOBODY'S OPENING ACT! NOT EVEN NITTLE GRASPER!

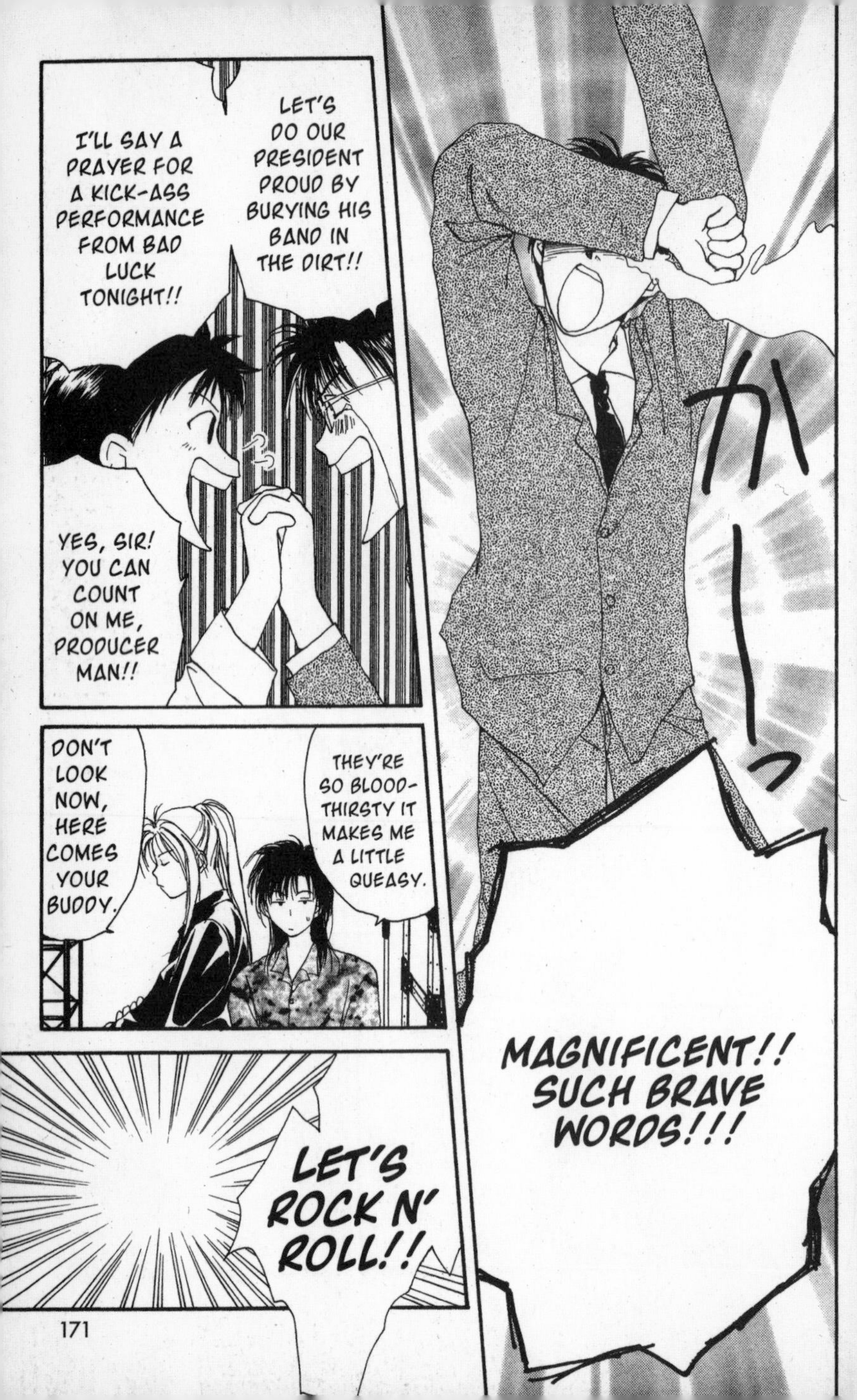
かーっ
MAGNIFICENT!! SUCH BRAVE WORDS!!!
LET'S DO OUR PRESIDENT PROUD BY BURYING HIS BAND IN THE DIRT!!
I'LL SAY A PRAYER FOR A KICK-ASS PERFORMANCE FROM BAD LUCK TONIGHT!!
YES, SIR! YOU CAN COUNT ON ME, PRODUCER MAN!!
THEY'RE SO BLOOD-THIRSTY IT MAKES ME A LITTLE QUEASY.
DON'T LOOK NOW, HERE COMES YOUR BUDDY.
LET'S ROCK N' ROLL!!

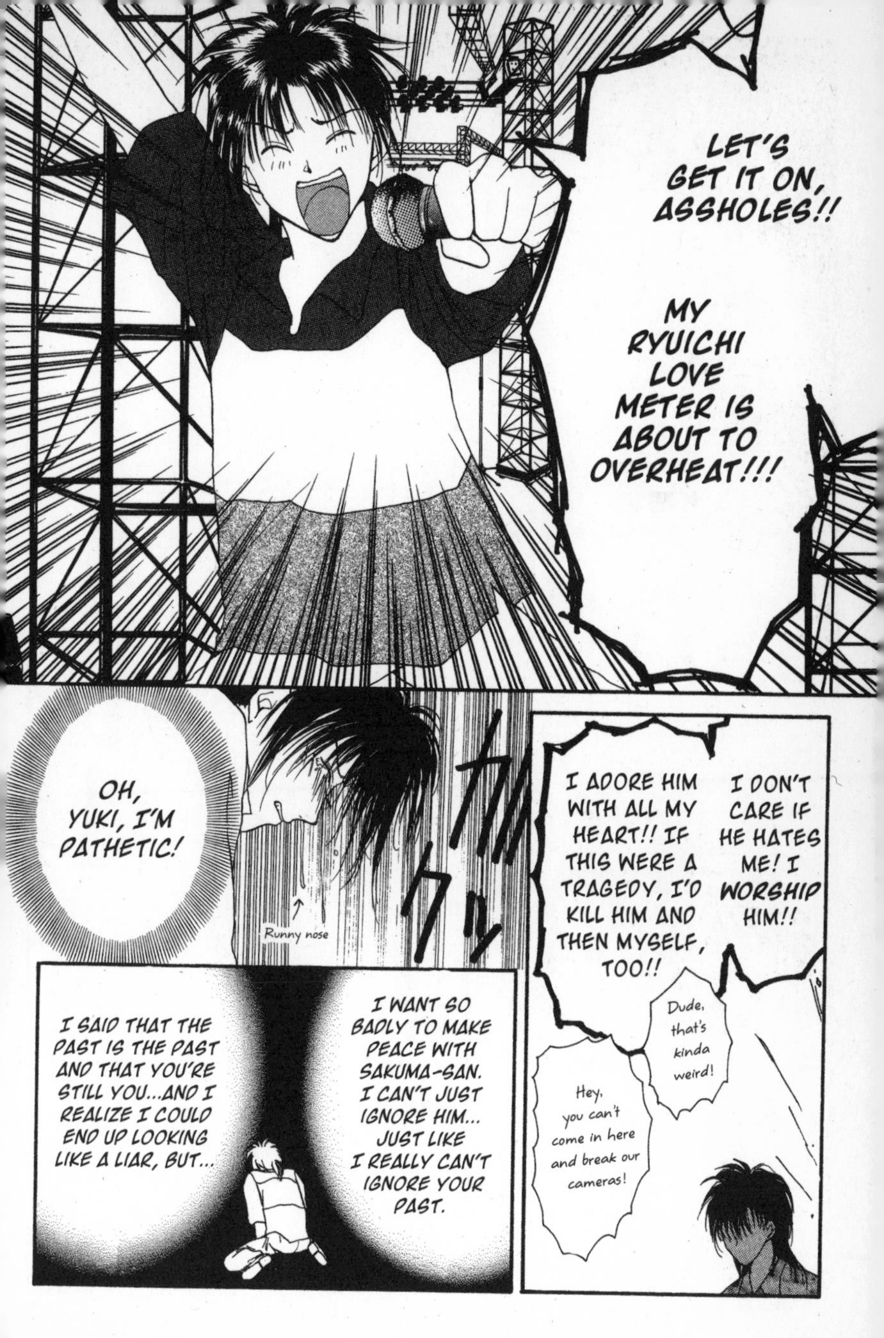
LET'S GET IT ON, ASSHOLES!!
MY RYUICHI LOVE METER IS ABOUT TO OVERHEAT!!!
I DON'T CARE IF HE HATES ME! I WORSHIP HIM!!
I ADORE HIM WITH ALL MY HEART!! IF THIS WERE A TRAGEDY, I'D KILL HIM AND THEN MYSELF, TOO!!
Dude, that's kinda weird!
Hey, you can't come in here and break our cameras!
カッ
OH, YUKI, I'M PATHETIC!
Runny nose
I SAID THAT THE PAST IS THE PAST AND THAT YOU'RE STILL YOU...AND I REALIZE I COULD END UP LOOKING LIKE A LIAR, BUT...
I WANT SO BADLY TO MAKE PEACE WITH SAKUMA-SAN. I CAN'T JUST IGNORE HIM... JUST LIKE I REALLY CAN'T IGNORE YOUR PAST.

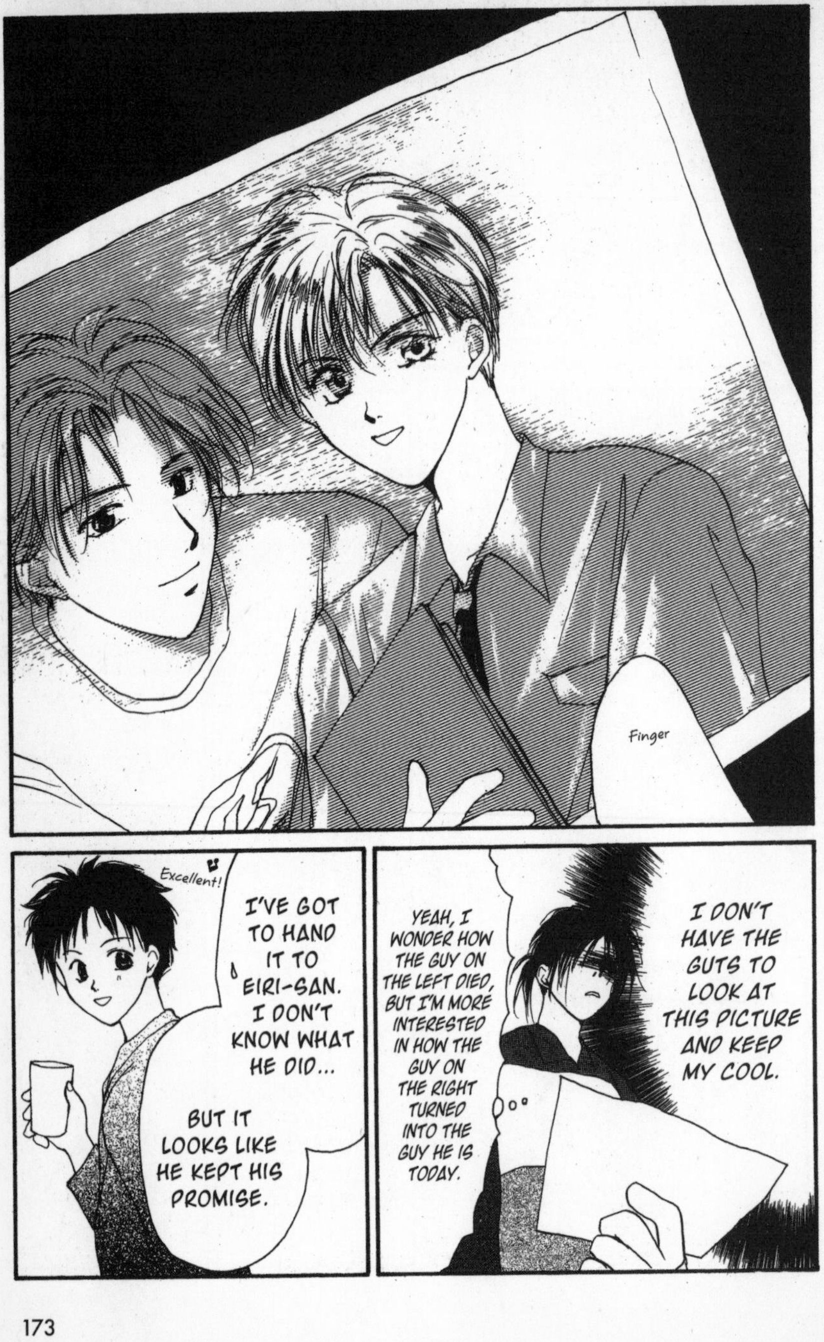
Finger
I DON'T HAVE THE GUTS TO LOOK AT THIS PICTURE AND KEEP MY COOL.
YEAH, I WONDER HOW THE GUY ON THE LEFT DIED, BUT I'M MORE INTERESTED IN HOW THE GUY ON THE RIGHT TURNED INTO THE GUY HE IS TODAY.
Excellent!
I'VE GOT TO HAND IT TO EIRI-SAN. I DON'T KNOW WHAT HE DID...
BUT IT LOOKS LIKE HE KEPT HIS PROMISE.

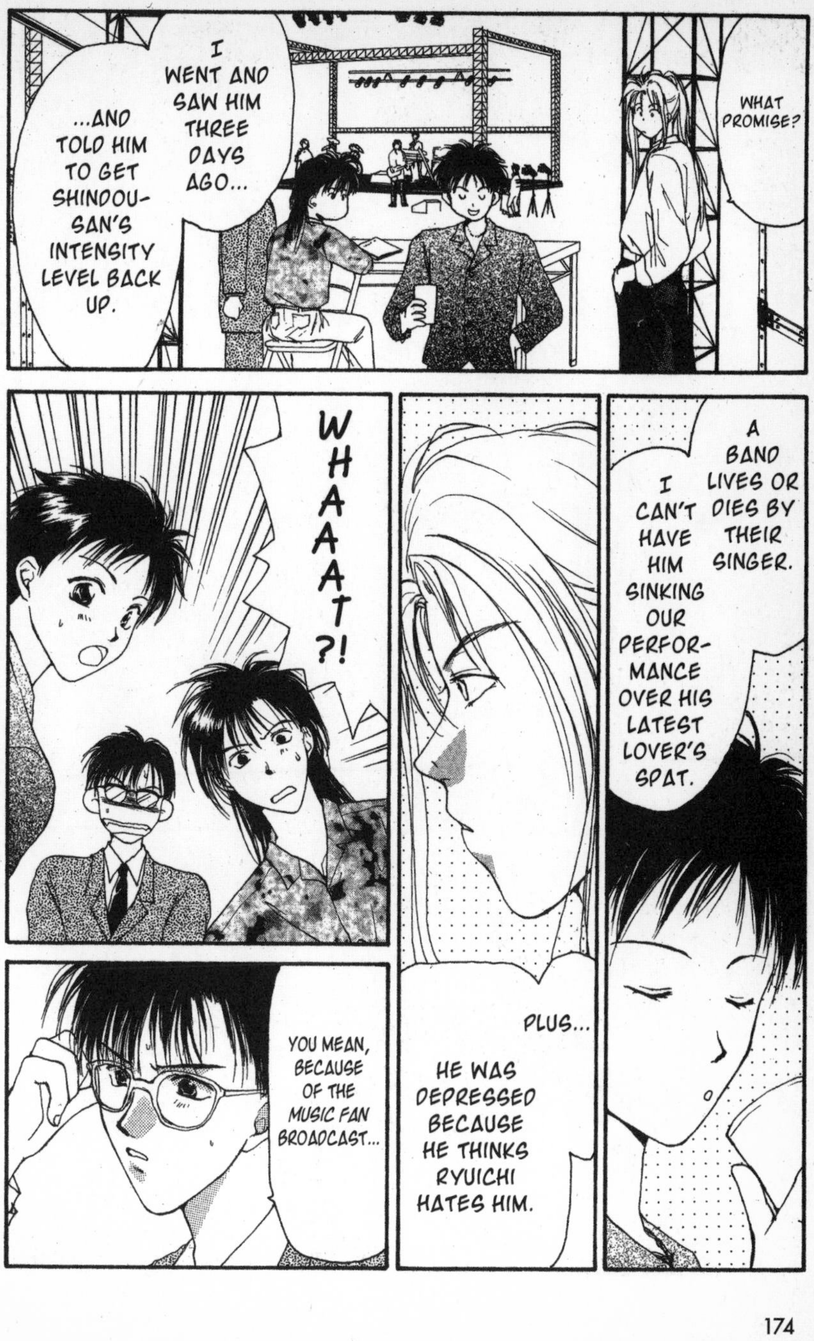
WHAT PROMISE?
I WENT AND SAW HIM THREE DAYS AGO...
...AND TOLD HIM TO GET SHINDOU-SAN'S INTENSITY LEVEL BACK UP.
A BAND LIVES OR DIES BY THEIR SINGER.
I CAN'T HAVE HIM SINKING OUR PERFORMANCE OVER HIS LATEST LOVER'S SPAT.
PLUS...
HE WAS DEPRESSED BECAUSE HE THINKS RYUICHI HATES HIM.
WHAAAAT?!
YOU MEAN, BECAUSE OF THE MUSIC FAN BROADCAST...

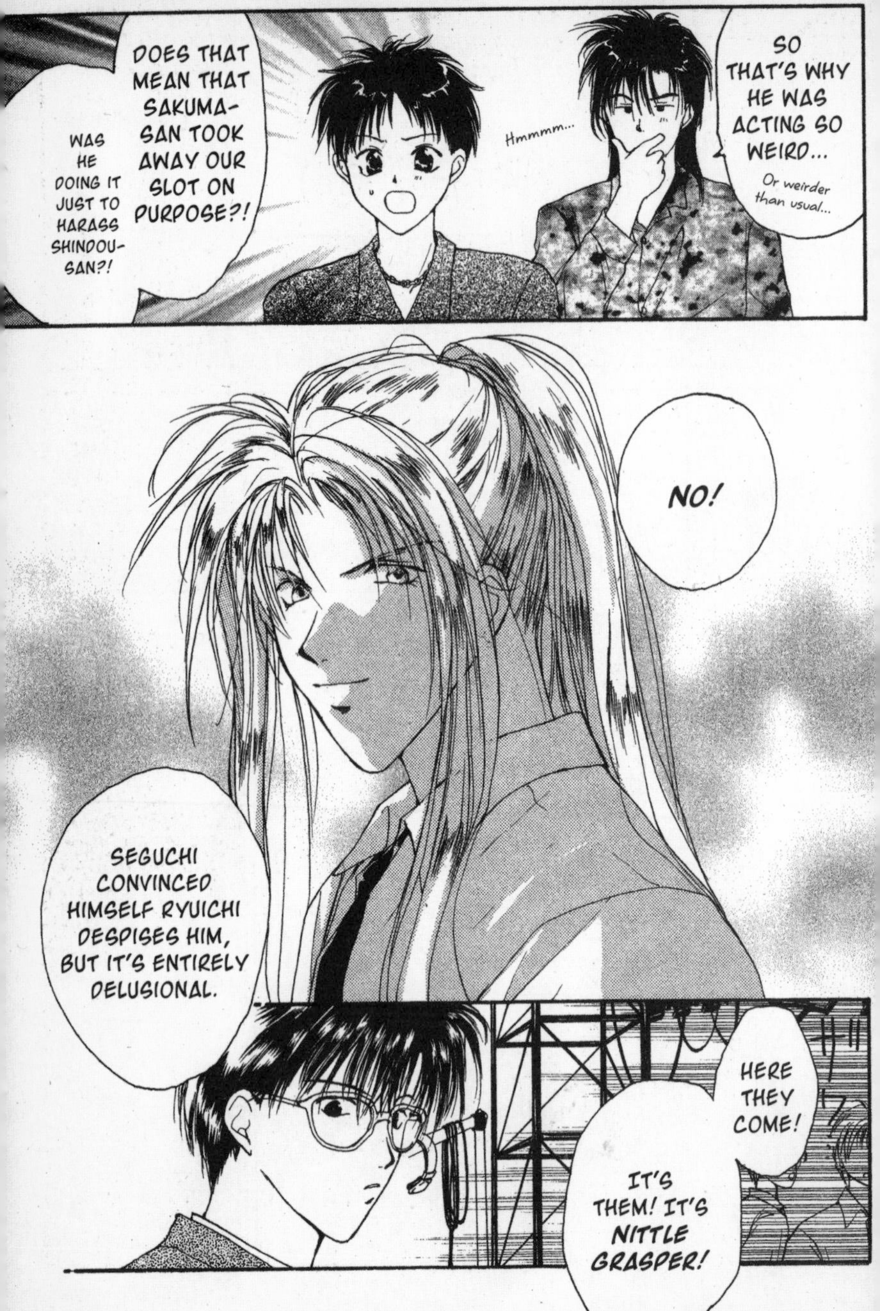
SO THAT'S WHY HE WAS ACTING SO WEIRD...
Or weirder than usual...
Hmmmm...
DOES THAT MEAN THAT SAKUMA-SAN TOOK AWAY OUR SLOT ON PURPOSE?!
WAS HE DOING IT JUST TO HARASS SHINDOU-SAN?!
NO!
SEGUCHI CONVINCED HIMSELF RYUICHI DESPISES HIM, BUT IT'S ENTIRELY DELUSIONAL.
HERE THEY COME!
IT'S THEM! IT'S NITTLE GRASPER!

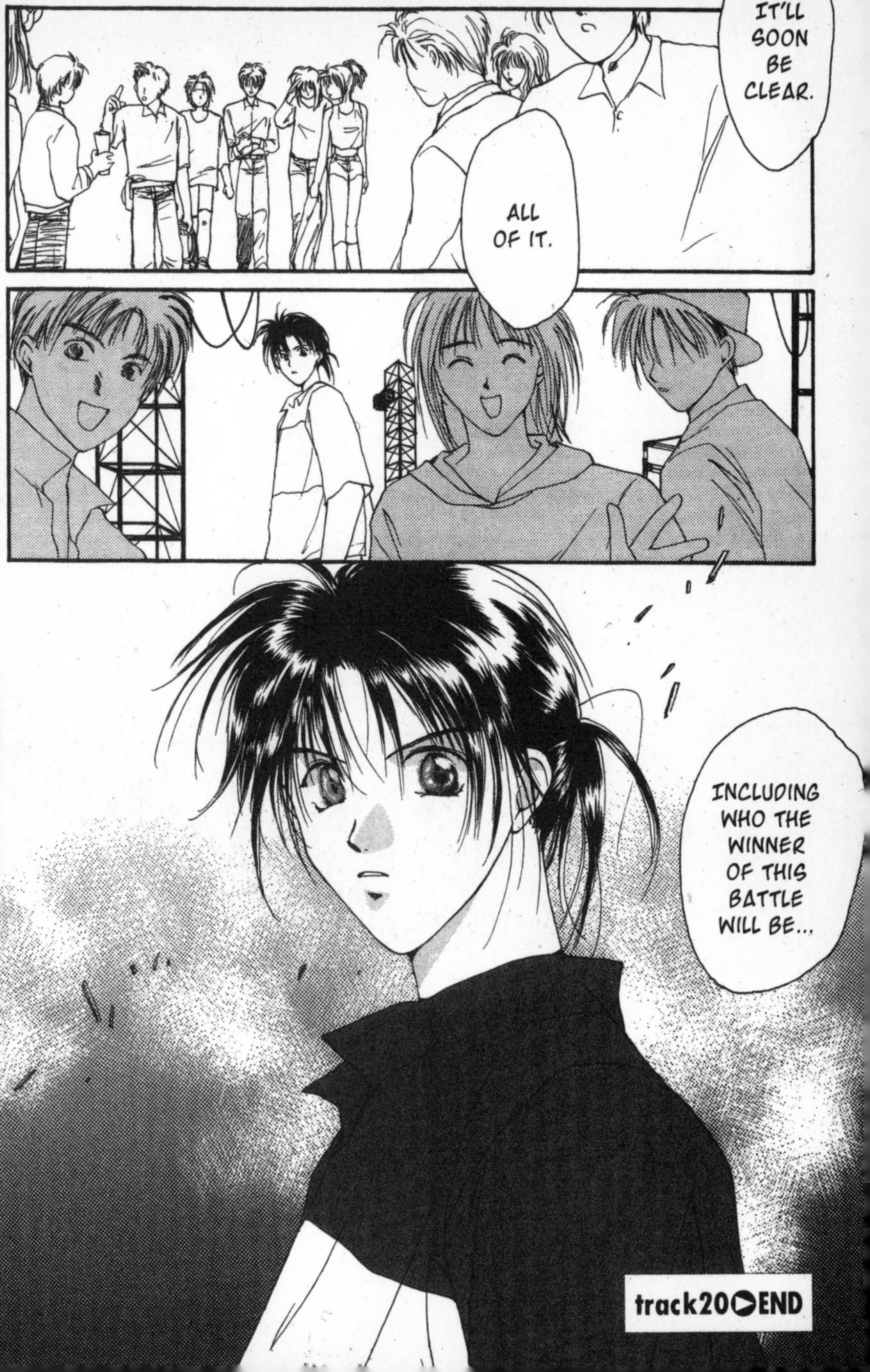
IT'LL SOON BE CLEAR.
ALL OF IT.
INCLUDING WHO THE WINNER OF THIS BATTLE WILL BE...
track20▶END

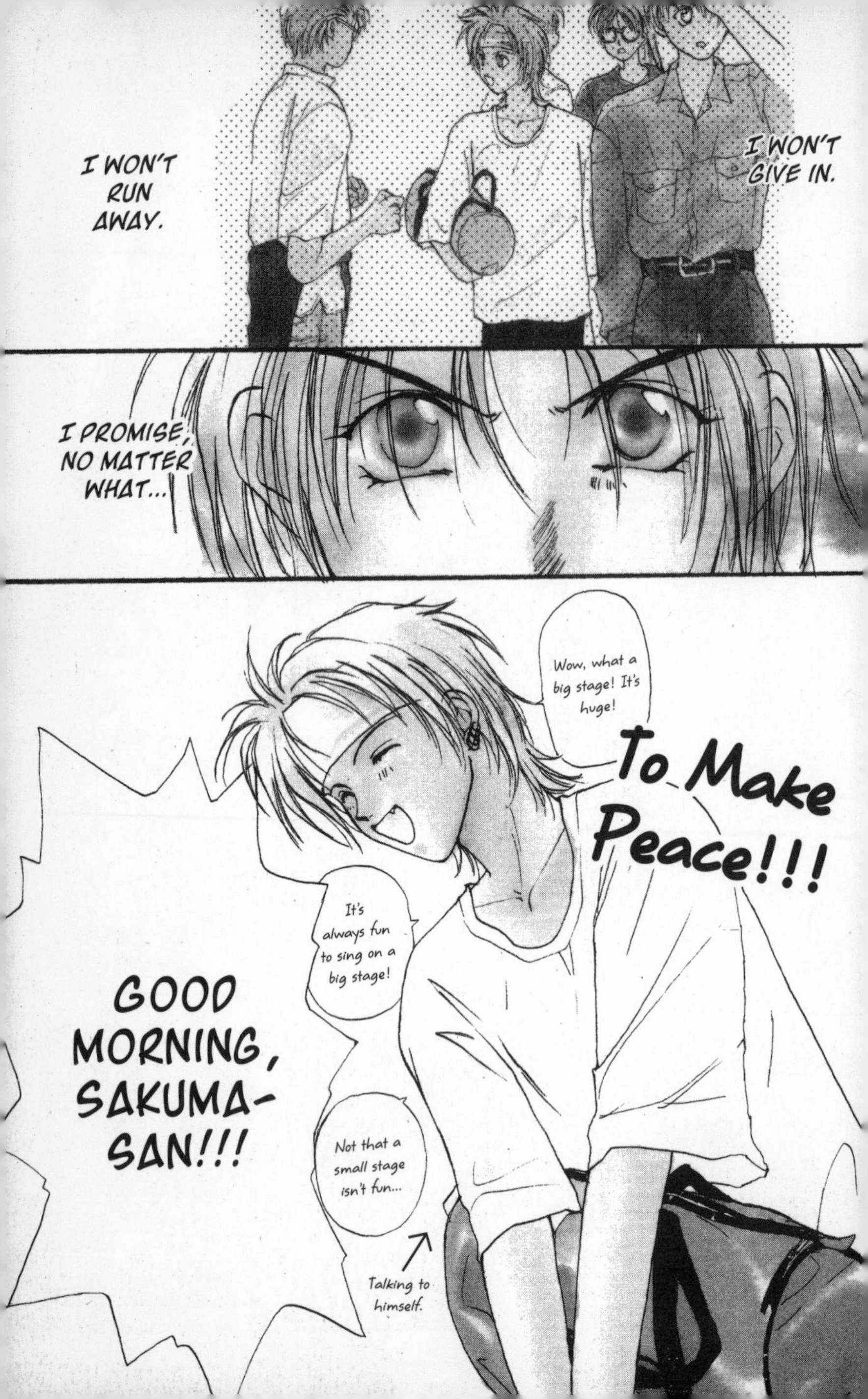
I WON'T GIVE IN.
I WON'T RUN AWAY.
I PROMISE, NO MATTER WHAT...
Wow, what a big stage! It's huge!
To Make Peace!!!
It's always fun to sing on a big stage!
GOOD MORNING, SAKUMA-SAN!!!
Not that a small stage isn't fun...
Talking to himself.

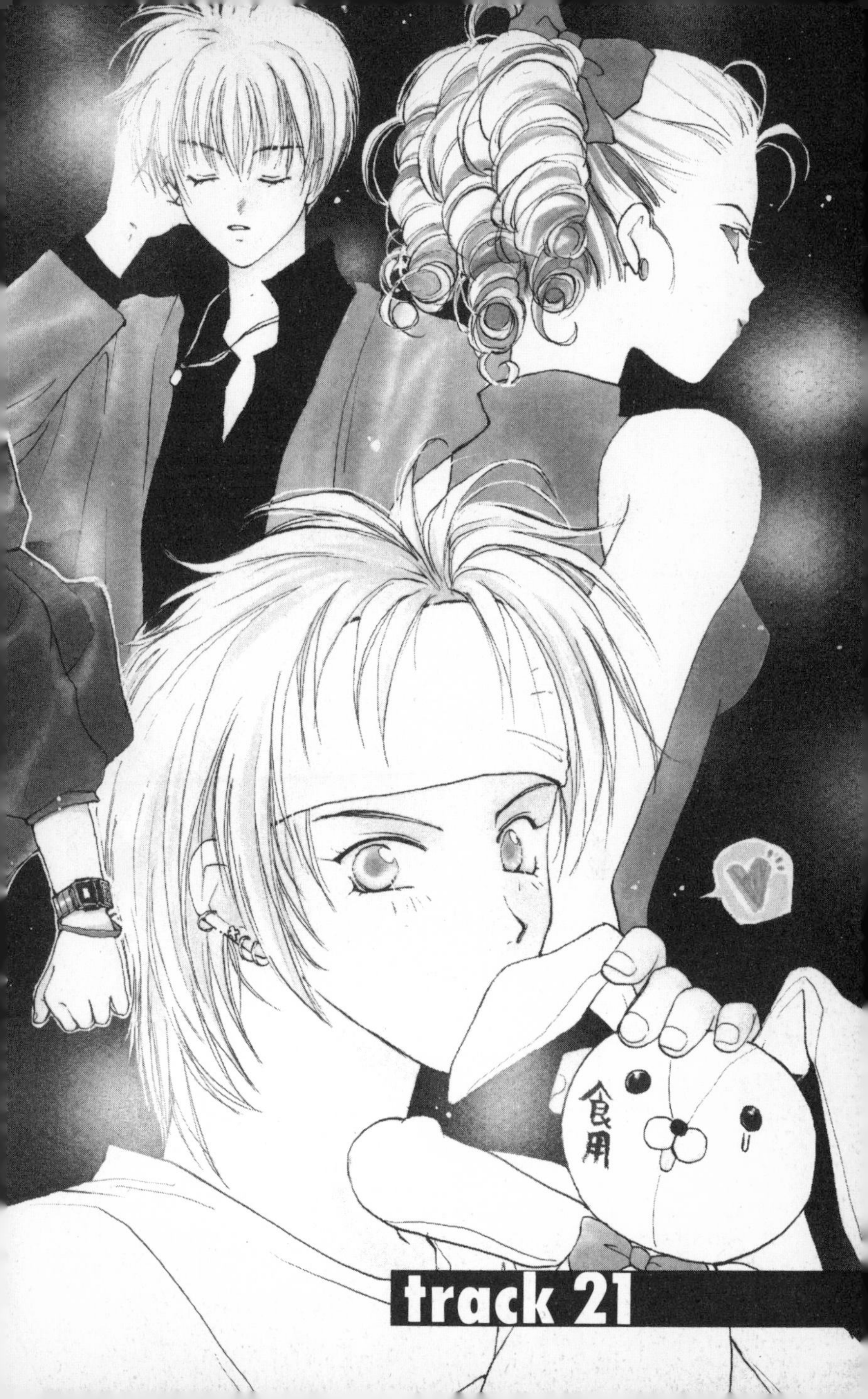
食用

track 21

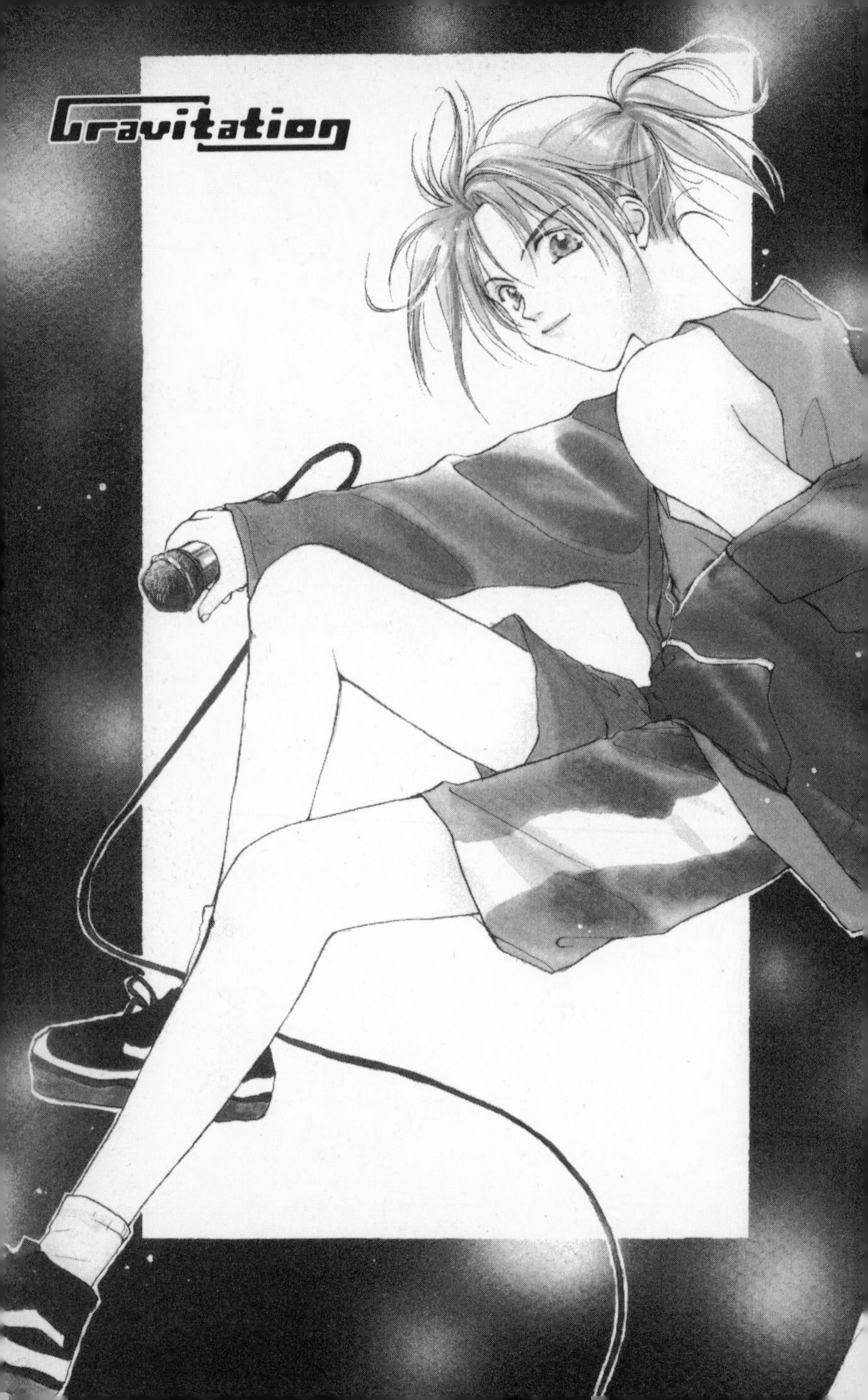
Gravitation

Complete!

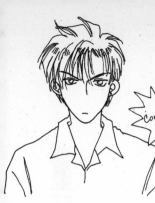

Book 5 Bonus
EIRI YUKI DATA FILE

Occupation: Novelist
Accessories: Glasses, Earring, Cigarettes
Born: February 23 Blood Type: AB
Height: 186 cm Weight: 74 kg (Yes, for real!)

HP
SENSITIVITY
AGGRESSIVENESS
DEFENSE
OFFENSE
RECEPTIVENESS
MAGIC
MP

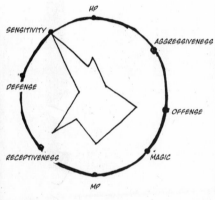

If you'll take a look at the chart on the left, I'm sure you'll be surprised to see how his current status shapes up. Most peculiar is his low score in Aggressiveness, and his high score in Receptiveness. We'll get to the reasons for that as the story progresses. Yes, pay particular attention to the extremely high score in Sensitivity. Most people assume him to be frigid, but that is not the case. If you want proof, try tickling the soles of his feet. This normally calm and collected guy will show you a shockingly different side to his personality. HP, Defense, and Physical Strength are, due to the nature of his occupation, low. In other words, he is very delicate.

MAGIC ATTACK Although he's a big guy, Eiri's HP is quite low. A magic attack from behind is the recommended offense. However, if you get him angry, his levels rise 2 billion points, so don't take him lightly.	"....."	He resorts to this tactic quite often, especially when his levels are low. As the story develops, his personality will continue to evolve, and he'll use this method of silence less frequently—so unleash this weapon early if you want to see your enemies go down!
	"SHUT UP!"	When used against Shuichi, this weapon is quite effective. However, against Tohma, it is usually countered by the fearsome unfathomable smile.
	"SO YOU WANT TO KNOW MY SECRET?"	His most powerful magic weapon. However, to use it first requires the possession of an item: photo from the past. When used against Shuichi in battle, his offensive levels drop 900,008,526 points.

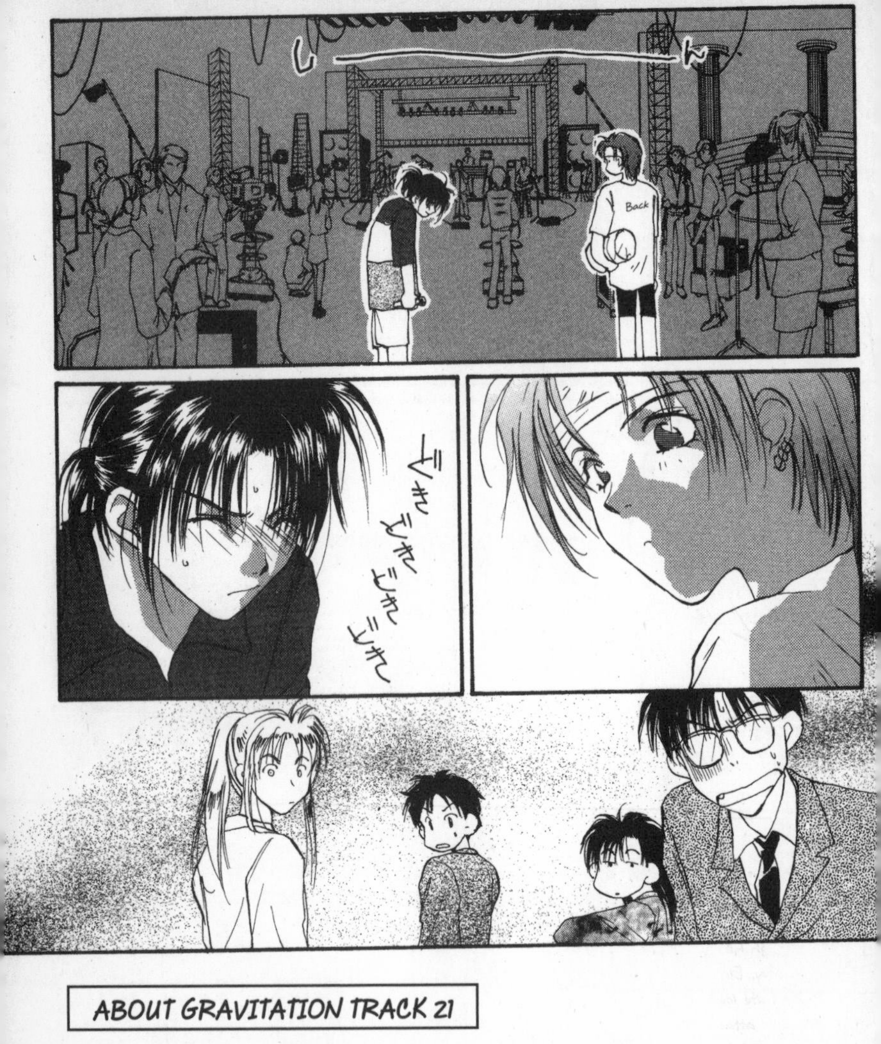
し————ん
どき どき どき どき

ABOUT GRAVITATION TRACK 21

The day has finally come. Nittle Grasper vs. Bad Luck.
To those of you who thought this might be the final chapter—not so fast.
There's no way a manga as complicated as this could tie up all the loose ends that quickly. Depending on how I feel, I could either just cut it short, or have it go on and on forever. How magnificent! I'm on the verge of being in the go "on and on forever" mode. In that case, somebody has to die. I don't want to resort to the "it was all a dream" plot twist. I thought about doing a "Eiri turns out to be a woman" revelation. That could have been fun.

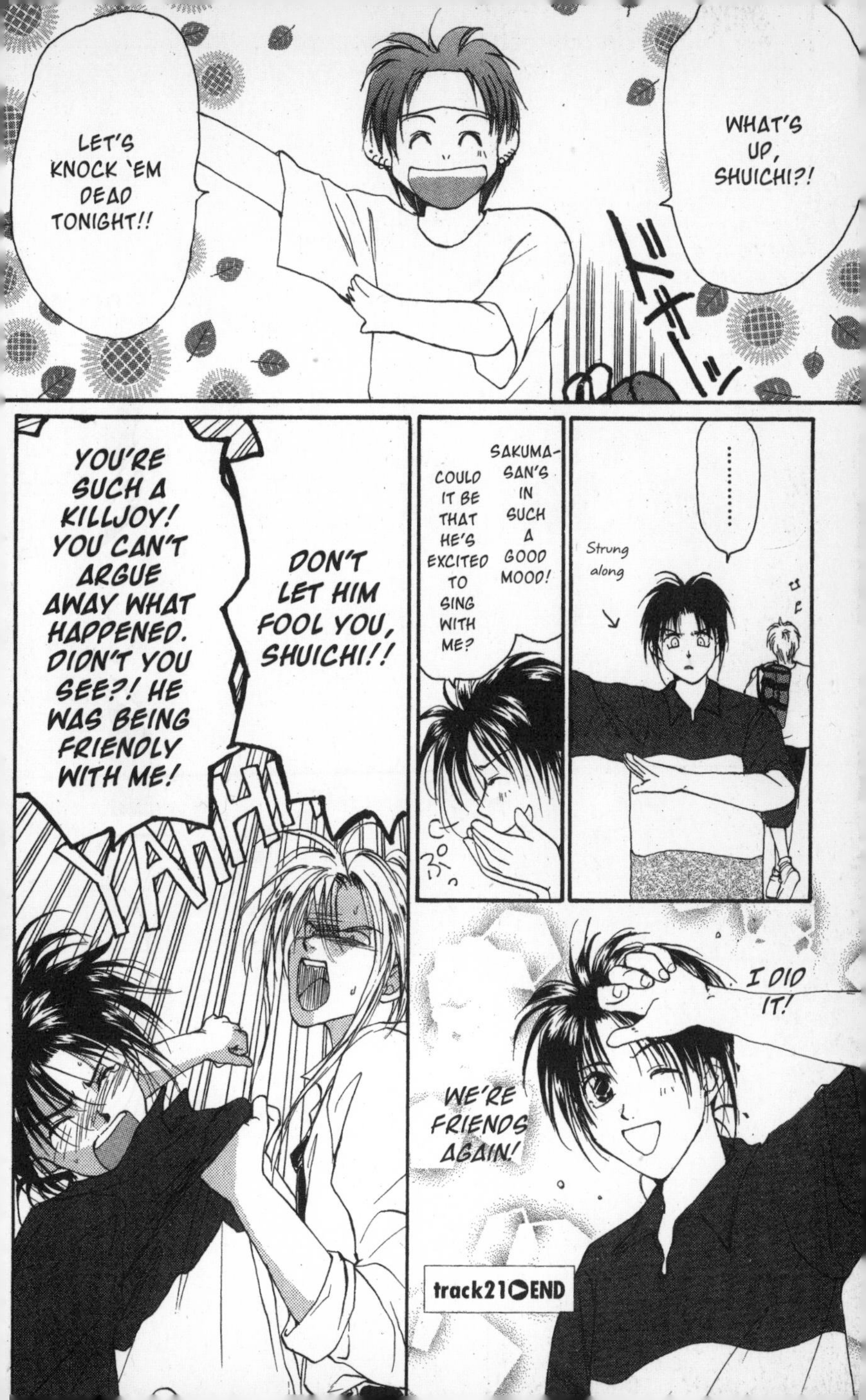
WHAT'S UP, SHUICHI?!
LET'S KNOCK 'EM DEAD TONIGHT!!
......
Strung along
SAKUMA-SAN'S IN SUCH A GOOD MOOD!
COULD IT BE THAT HE'S EXCITED TO SING WITH ME?
I DID IT!
WE'RE FRIENDS AGAIN!
track21▶END
DON'T LET HIM FOOL YOU, SHUICHI!!
YOU'RE SUCH A KILLJOY! YOU CAN'T ARGUE AWAY WHAT HAPPENED. DIDN'T YOU SEE?! HE WAS BEING FRIENDLY WITH ME!
YAHH!

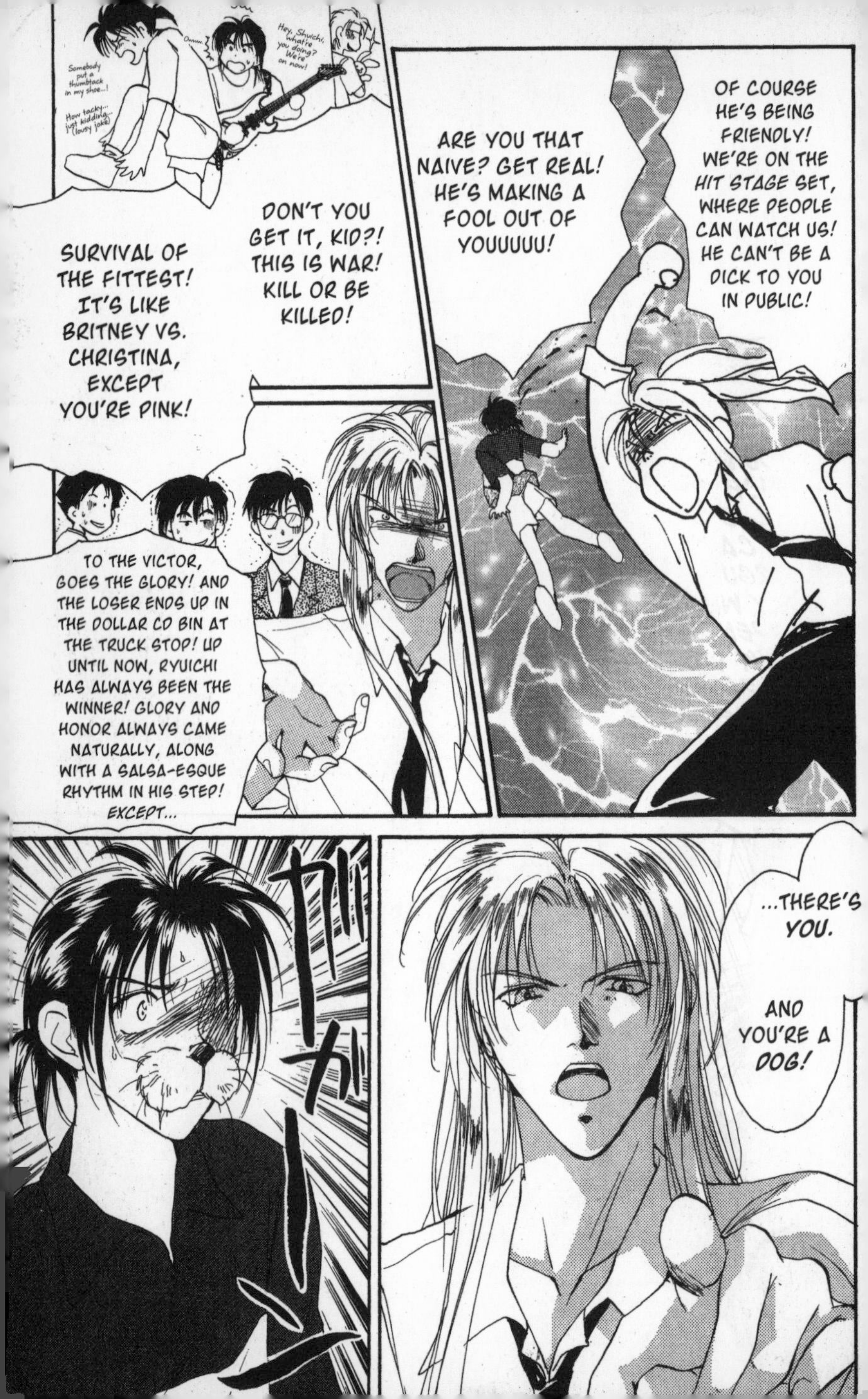
OF COURSE HE'S BEING FRIENDLY! WE'RE ON THE HIT STAGE SET, WHERE PEOPLE CAN WATCH US! HE CAN'T BE A DICK TO YOU IN PUBLIC!
ARE YOU THAT NAIVE? GET REAL! HE'S MAKING A FOOL OUT OF YOUUUUU!
Hey, Shuichi, what're you doing? We're on now!
Owww
Somebody put a thumbtack in my shoe...!
How tacky... just kidding... (lousy joke)
DON'T YOU GET IT, KID?! THIS IS WAR! KILL OR BE KILLED!
SURVIVAL OF THE FITTEST! IT'S LIKE BRITNEY VS. CHRISTINA, EXCEPT YOU'RE PINK!
TO THE VICTOR, GOES THE GLORY! AND THE LOSER ENDS UP IN THE DOLLAR CD BIN AT THE TRUCK STOP! UP UNTIL NOW, RYUICHI HAS ALWAYS BEEN THE WINNER! GLORY AND HONOR ALWAYS CAME NATURALLY, ALONG WITH A SALSA-ESQUE RHYTHM IN HIS STEP! EXCEPT...
...THERE'S YOU.
AND YOU'RE A DOG!

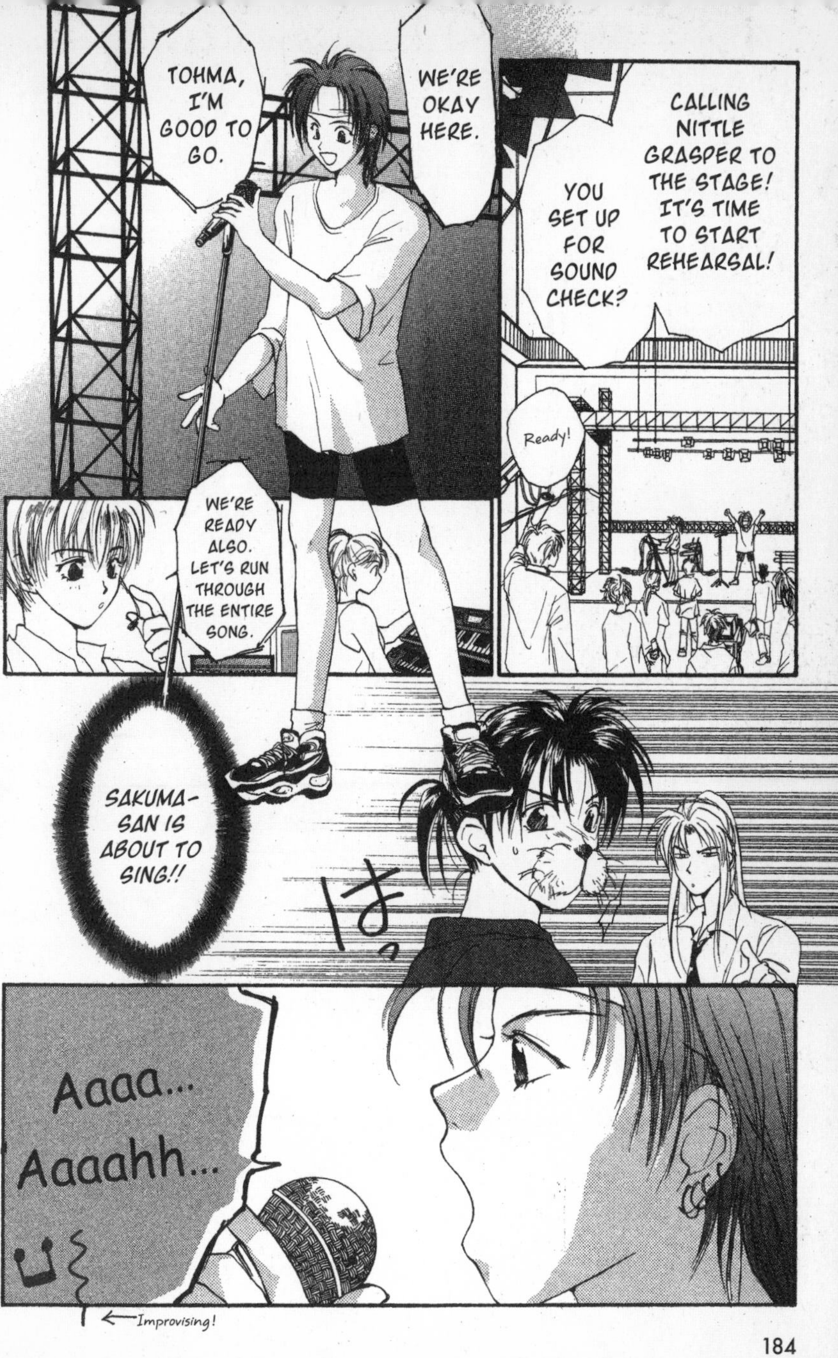
CALLING NITTLE GRASPER TO THE STAGE! IT'S TIME TO START REHEARSAL!
YOU SET UP FOR SOUND CHECK?
Ready!
WE'RE OKAY HERE.
TOHMA, I'M GOOD TO GO.
WE'RE READY ALSO. LET'S RUN THROUGH THE ENTIRE SONG.
SAKUMA-SAN IS ABOUT TO SING!!
はっ
Aaaa... Aaaahh...
Improvising!

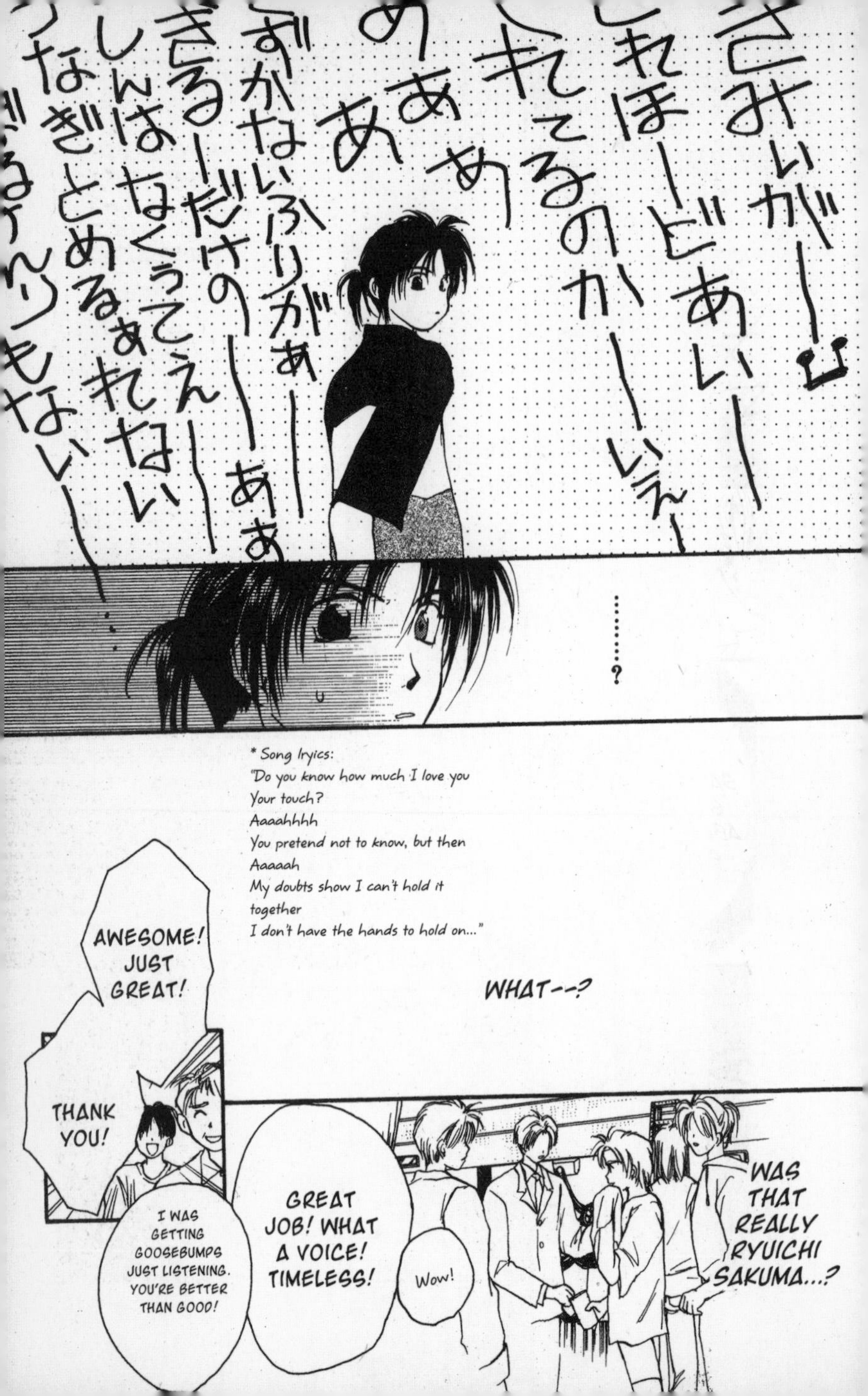
さみぃがーー♪
しれほーどあいーー
入れてめるのかーーいえ〜
めああ
ずかないふりがぁーー ああ
きるーだけのーーえ
しんはーなくうてえーー
なぎとめるきれない
ざみれりもないーー
…
……?
* Song lryics:
"Do you know how much I love you
Your touch?
Aaaahhhh
You pretend not to know, but then
Aaaaah
My doubts show I can't hold it together
I don't have the hands to hold on..."
WHAT--?
WAS THAT REALLY RYUICHI SAKUMA...?
Wow!
GREAT JOB! WHAT A VOICE! TIMELESS!
I WAS GETTING GOOSEBUMPS JUST LISTENING. YOU'RE BETTER THAN GOOD!
AWESOME! JUST GREAT!
THANK YOU!

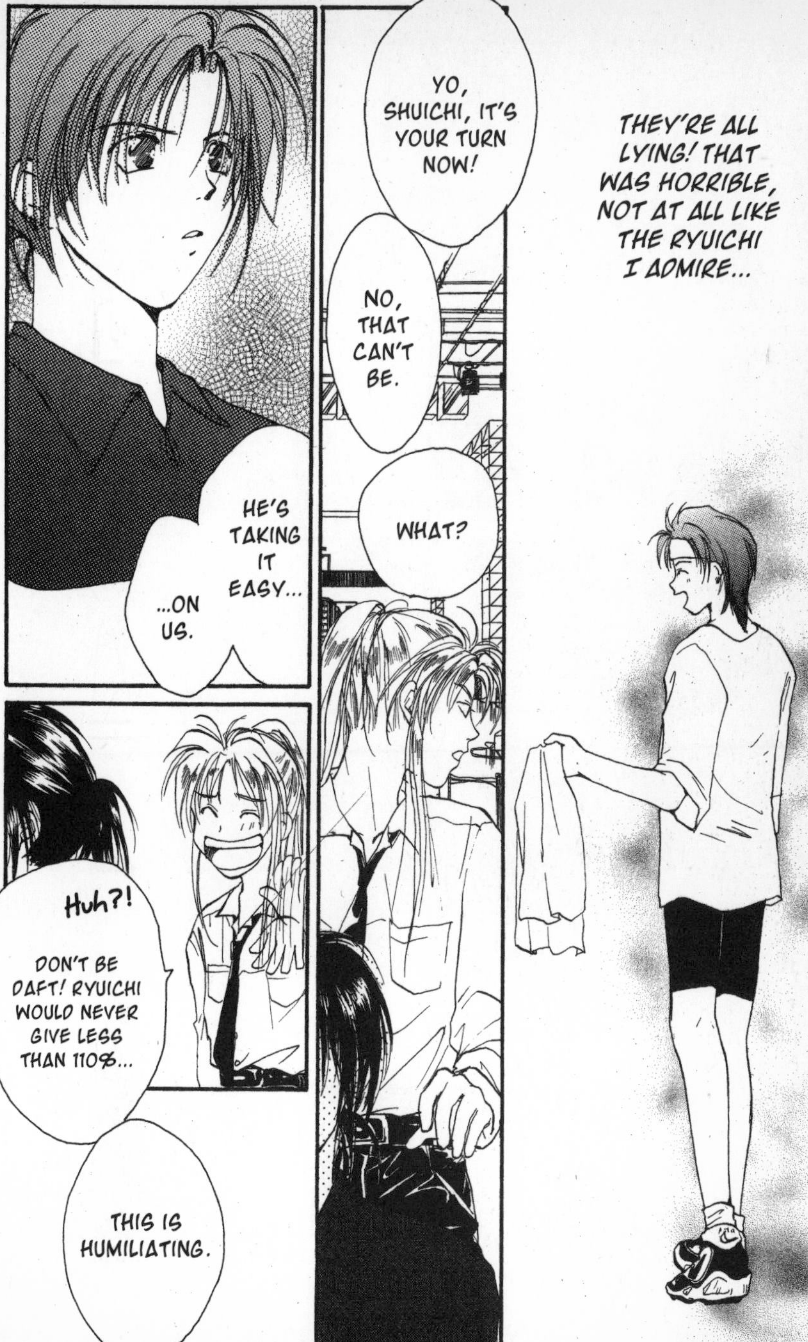
THEY'RE ALL LYING! THAT WAS HORRIBLE, NOT AT ALL LIKE THE RYUICHI I ADMIRE...
YO, SHUICHI, IT'S YOUR TURN NOW!
NO, THAT CAN'T BE.
WHAT?
HE'S TAKING IT EASY...
...ON US.
Huh?!
DON'T BE DAFT! RYUICHI WOULD NEVER GIVE LESS THAN 110%...
THIS IS HUMILIATING.

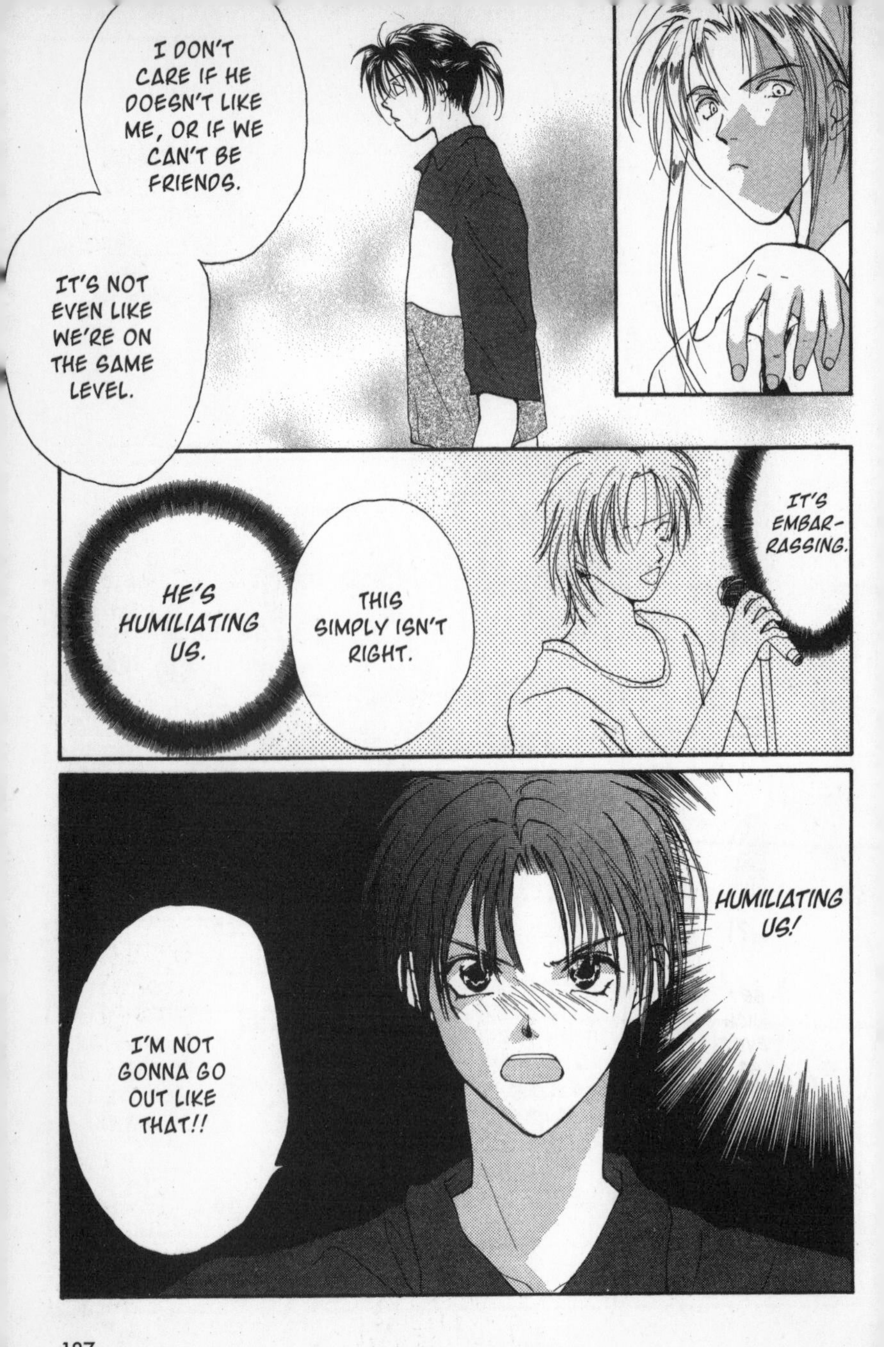
I DON'T CARE IF HE DOESN'T LIKE ME, OR IF WE CAN'T BE FRIENDS.
IT'S NOT EVEN LIKE WE'RE ON THE SAME LEVEL.
IT'S EMBARRASSING.
THIS SIMPLY ISN'T RIGHT.
HE'S HUMILIATING US.
HUMILIATING US!
I'M NOT GONNA GO OUT LIKE THAT!!

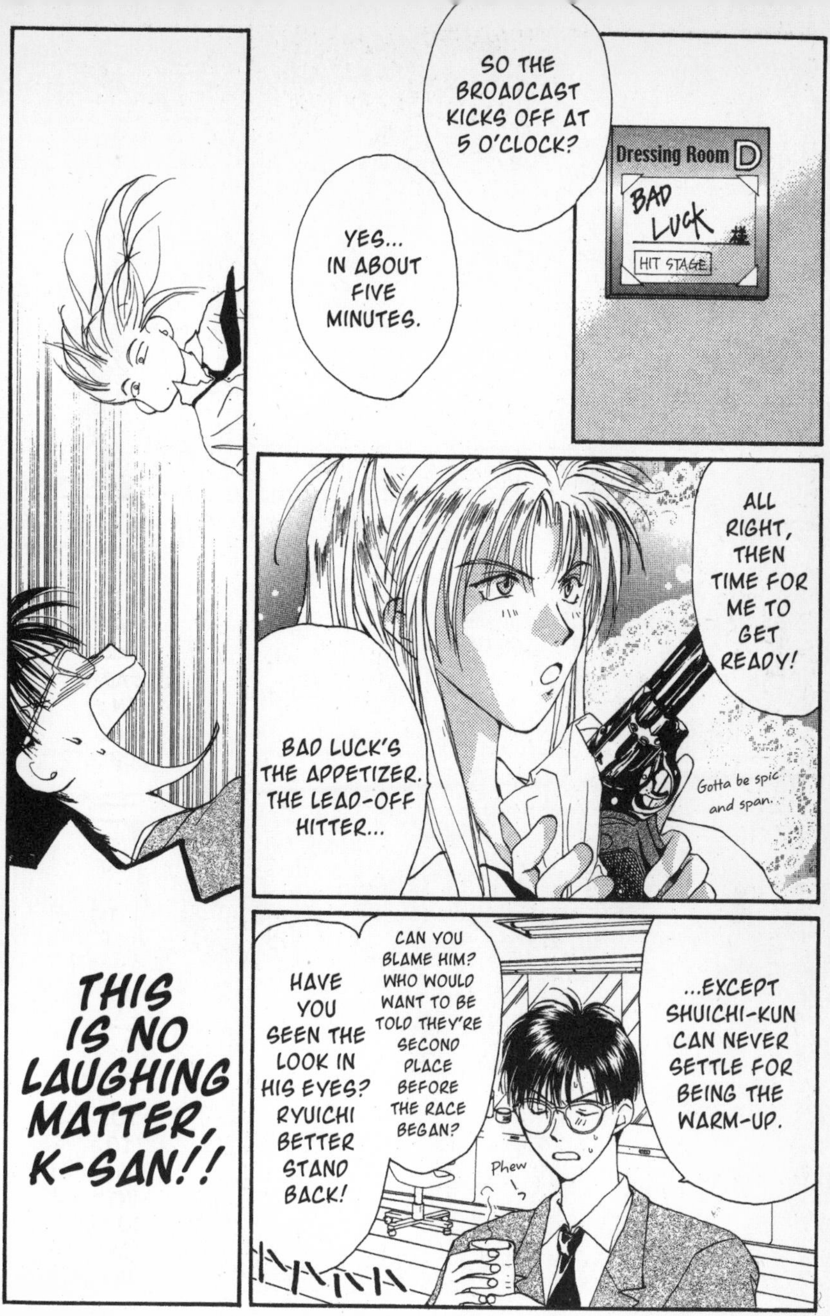
Dressing Room D
BAD LUCK
HIT STAGE
SO THE BROADCAST KICKS OFF AT 5 O'CLOCK?
YES... IN ABOUT FIVE MINUTES.
ALL RIGHT, THEN TIME FOR ME TO GET READY!
Gotta be spic and span.
BAD LUCK'S THE APPETIZER. THE LEAD-OFF HITTER...
...EXCEPT SHUICHI-KUN CAN NEVER SETTLE FOR BEING THE WARM-UP.
Phew
CAN YOU BLAME HIM? WHO WOULD WANT TO BE TOLD THEY'RE SECOND PLACE BEFORE THE RACE BEGAN?
HAVE YOU SEEN THE LOOK IN HIS EYES? RYUICHI BETTER STAND BACK!
THIS IS NO LAUGHING MATTER, K-SAN!!

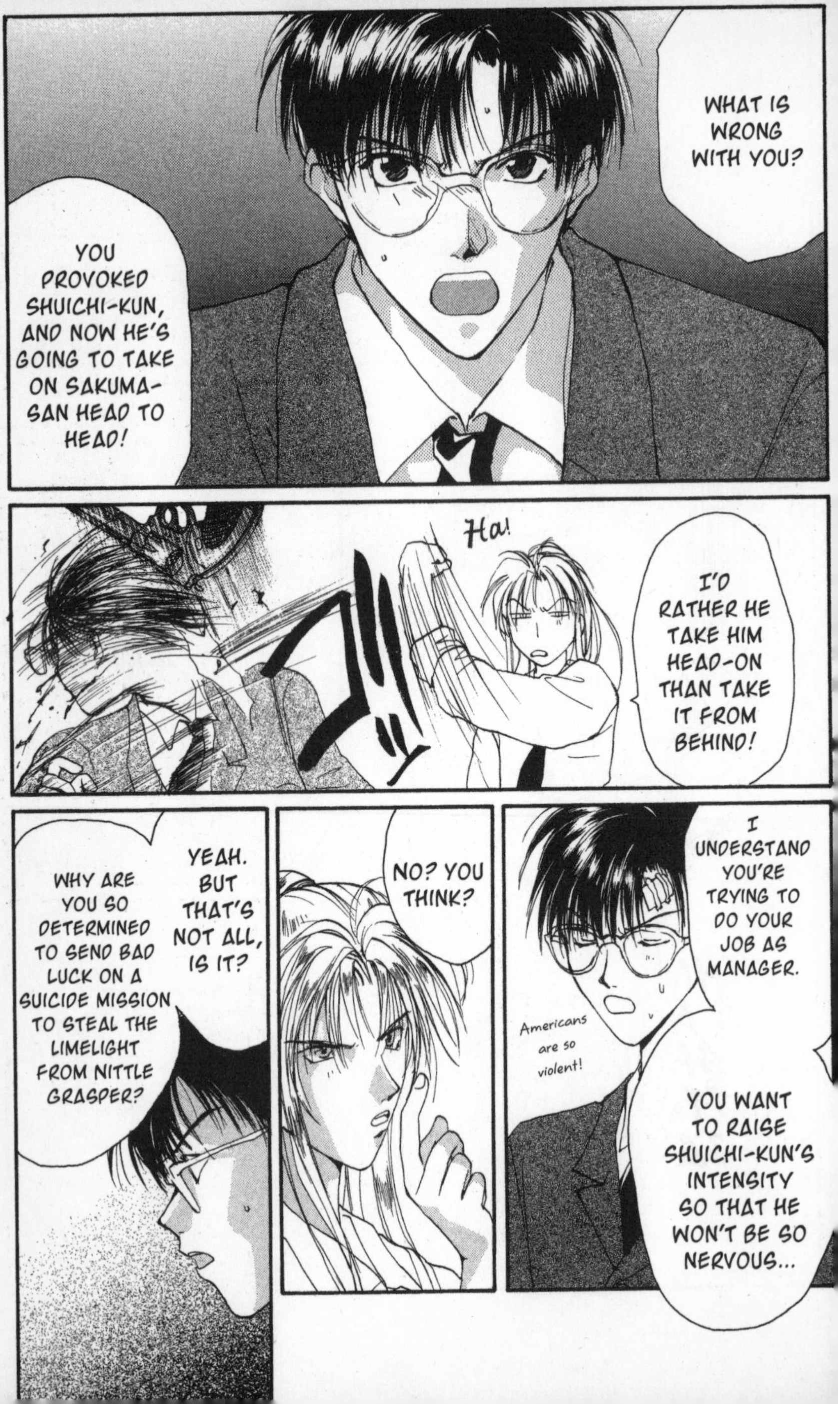
WHAT IS WRONG WITH YOU?
YOU PROVOKED SHUICHI-KUN, AND NOW HE'S GOING TO TAKE ON SAKUMA-SAN HEAD TO HEAD!
Ha!
I'D RATHER HE TAKE HIM HEAD-ON THAN TAKE IT FROM BEHIND!
I UNDERSTAND YOU'RE TRYING TO DO YOUR JOB AS MANAGER.
YOU WANT TO RAISE SHUICHI-KUN'S INTENSITY SO THAT HE WON'T BE SO NERVOUS...
Americans are so violent!
NO? YOU THINK?
YEAH. BUT THAT'S NOT ALL, IS IT?
WHY ARE YOU SO DETERMINED TO SEND BAD LUCK ON A SUICIDE MISSION TO STEAL THE LIMELIGHT FROM NITTLE GRASPER?

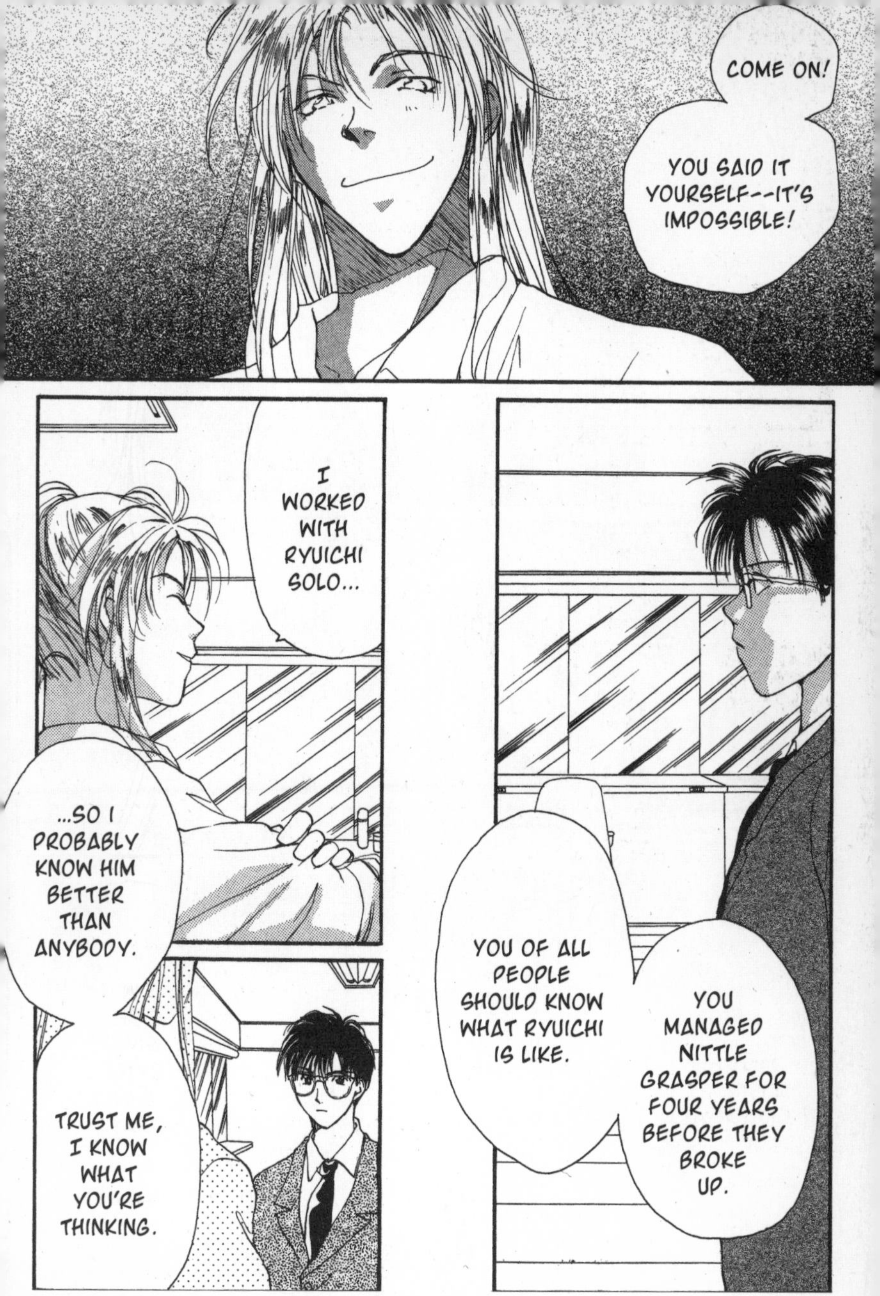
COME ON!
YOU SAID IT YOURSELF--IT'S IMPOSSIBLE!
YOU MANAGED NITTLE GRASPER FOR FOUR YEARS BEFORE THEY BROKE UP.
YOU OF ALL PEOPLE SHOULD KNOW WHAT RYUICHI IS LIKE.
I WORKED WITH RYUICHI SOLO...
...SO I PROBABLY KNOW HIM BETTER THAN ANYBODY.
TRUST ME, I KNOW WHAT YOU'RE THINKING.

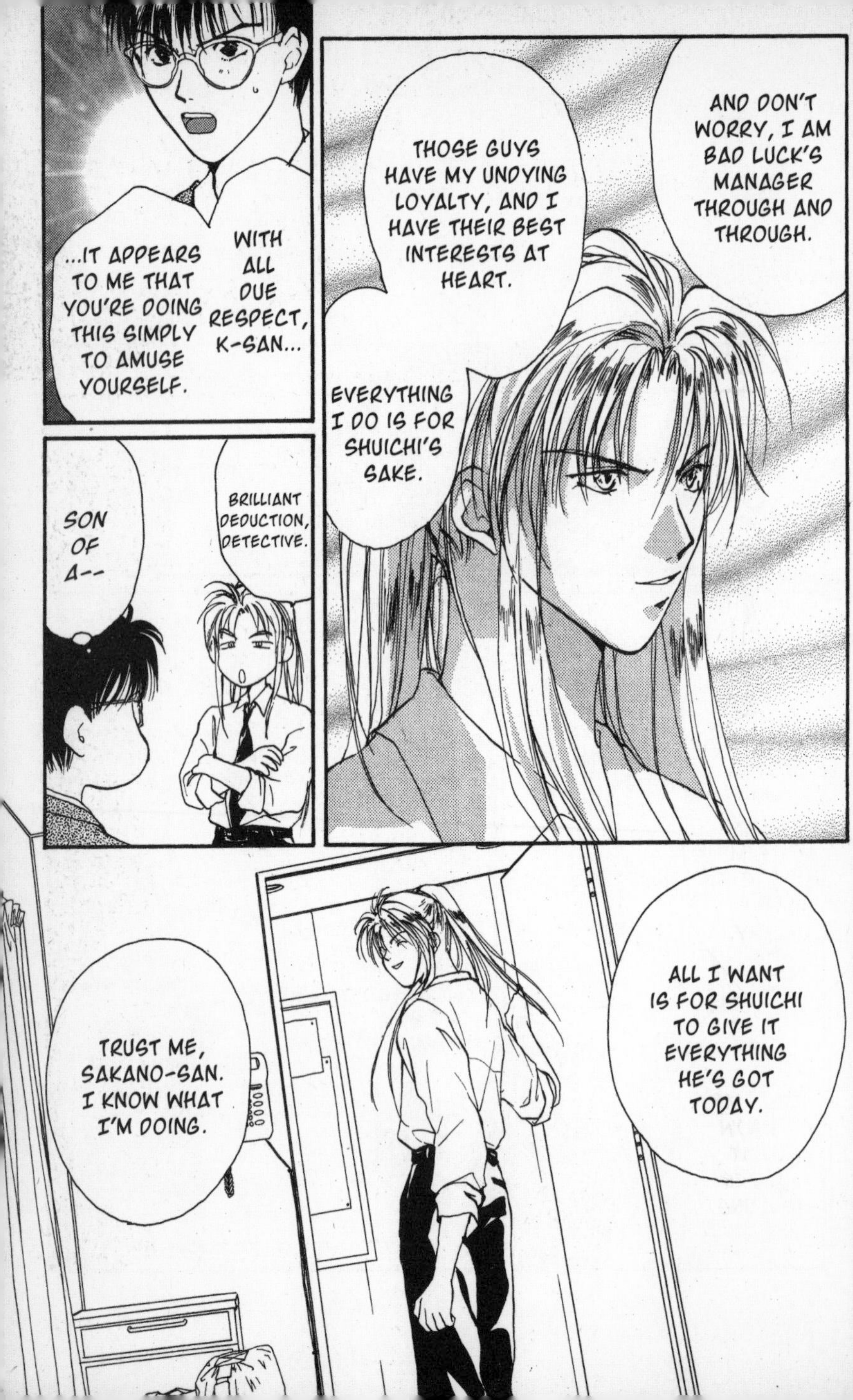
AND DON'T WORRY, I AM BAD LUCK'S MANAGER THROUGH AND THROUGH.
THOSE GUYS HAVE MY UNDYING LOYALTY, AND I HAVE THEIR BEST INTERESTS AT HEART.
EVERYTHING I DO IS FOR SHUICHI'S SAKE.
WITH ALL DUE RESPECT, K-SAN...
...IT APPEARS TO ME THAT YOU'RE DOING THIS SIMPLY TO AMUSE YOURSELF.
BRILLIANT DEDUCTION, DETECTIVE.
SON OF A--
ALL I WANT IS FOR SHUICHI TO GIVE IT EVERYTHING HE'S GOT TODAY.
TRUST ME, SAKANO-SAN. I KNOW WHAT I'M DOING.

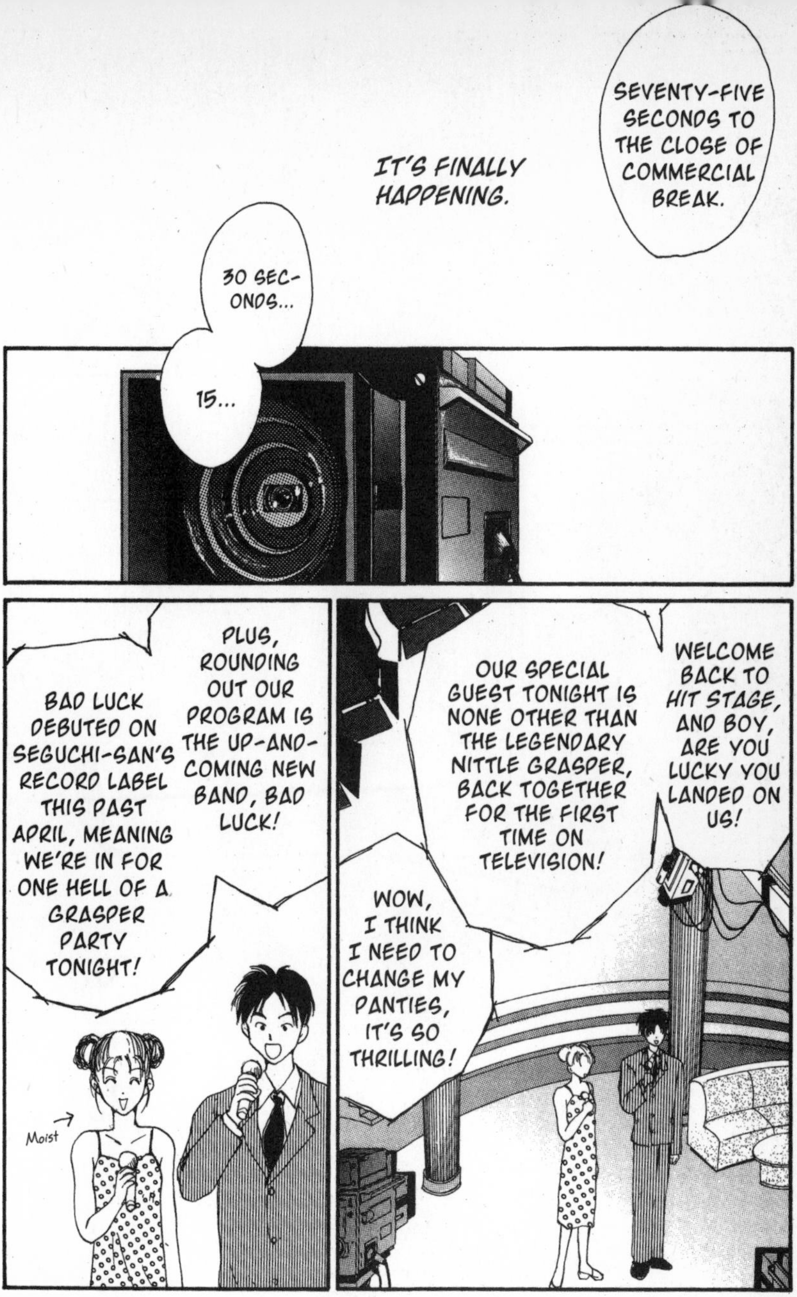
SEVENTY-FIVE SECONDS TO THE CLOSE OF COMMERCIAL BREAK.
IT'S FINALLY HAPPENING.
30 SEC-ONDS...
15...
WELCOME BACK TO HIT STAGE, AND BOY, ARE YOU LUCKY YOU LANDED ON US!
OUR SPECIAL GUEST TONIGHT IS NONE OTHER THAN THE LEGENDARY NITTLE GRASPER, BACK TOGETHER FOR THE FIRST TIME ON TELEVISION!
WOW, I THINK I NEED TO CHANGE MY PANTIES, IT'S SO THRILLING!
PLUS, ROUNDING OUT OUR PROGRAM IS THE UP-AND-COMING NEW BAND, BAD LUCK!
BAD LUCK DEBUTED ON SEGUCHI-SAN'S RECORD LABEL THIS PAST APRIL, MEANING WE'RE IN FOR ONE HELL OF A GRASPER PARTY TONIGHT!
Moist

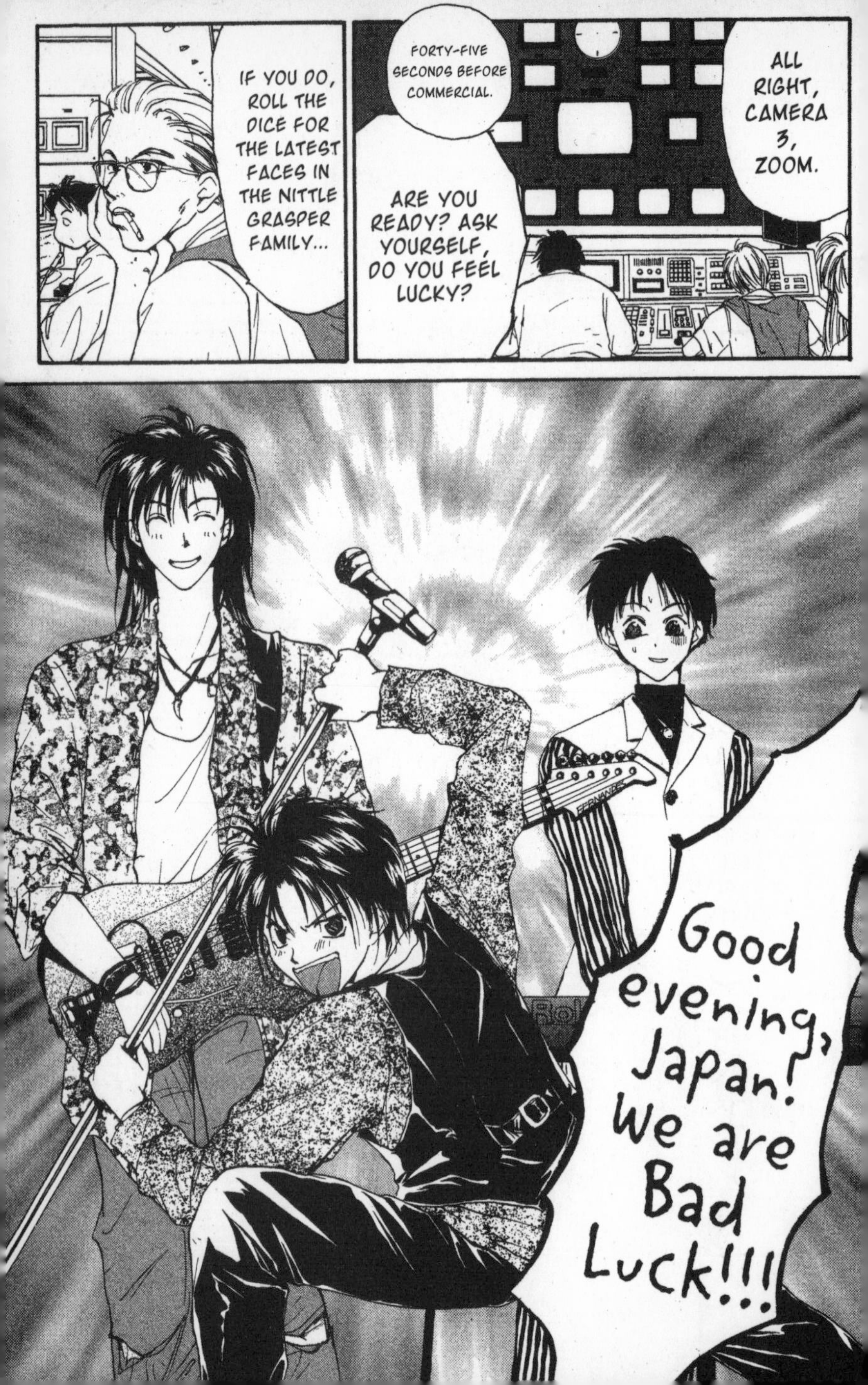
ALL RIGHT, CAMERA 3, ZOOM.
FORTY-FIVE SECONDS BEFORE COMMERCIAL.
ARE YOU READY? ASK YOURSELF, DO YOU FEEL LUCKY?
IF YOU DO, ROLL THE DICE FOR THE LATEST FACES IN THE NITTLE GRASPER FAMILY...
Good evening, Japan! We are Bad Luck!!!

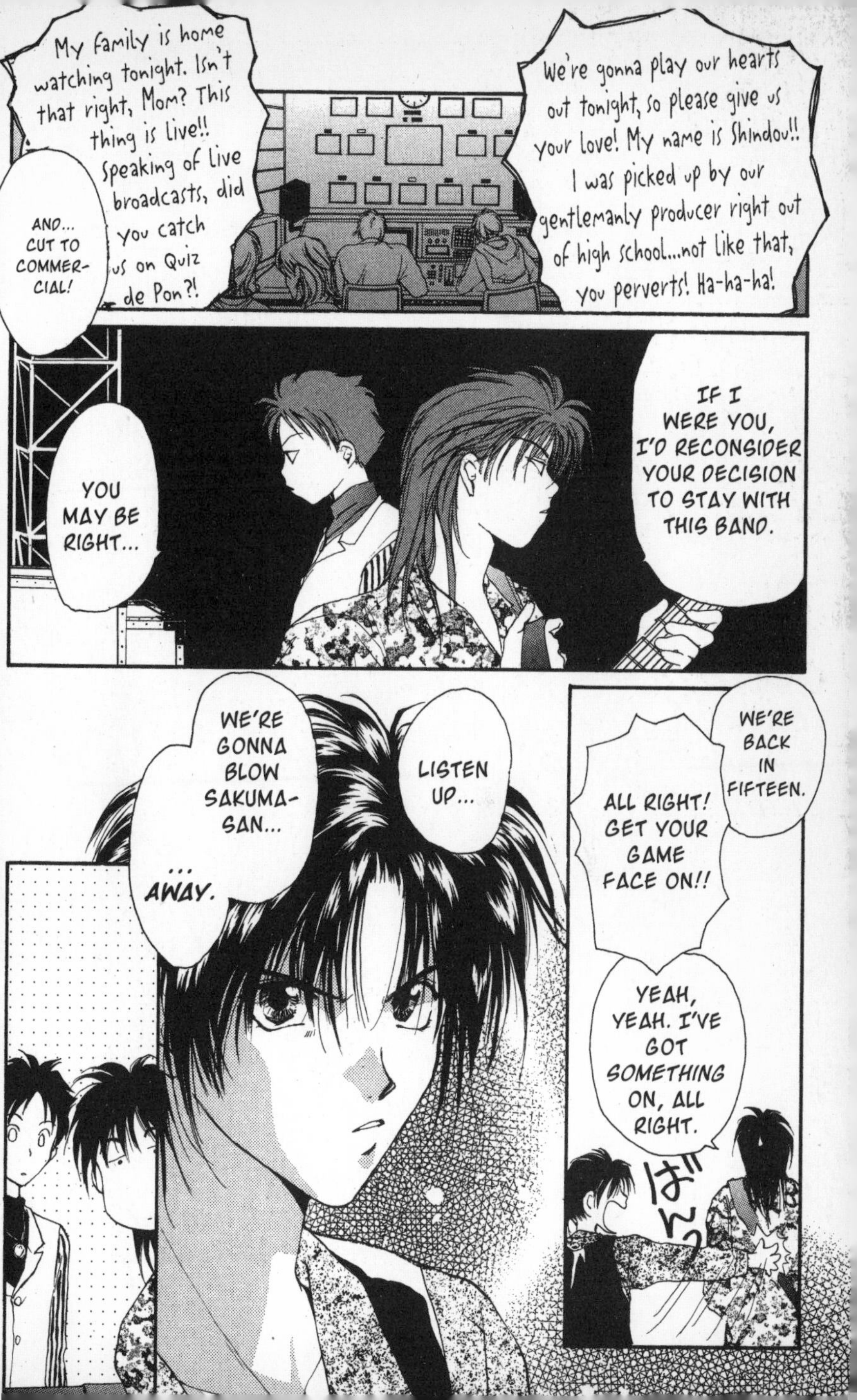
We're gonna play our hearts out tonight, so please give us your love! My name is Shindou!! I was picked up by our gentlemanly producer right out of high school...not like that, you perverts! Ha-ha-ha!
My family is home watching tonight. Isn't that right, Mom? This thing is live!! Speaking of live broadcasts, did you catch us on Quiz de Pon?!
AND... CUT TO COMMERCIAL!
IF I WERE YOU, I'D RECONSIDER YOUR DECISION TO STAY WITH THIS BAND.
YOU MAY BE RIGHT...
WE'RE BACK IN FIFTEEN.
ALL RIGHT! GET YOUR GAME FACE ON!!
YEAH, YEAH. I'VE GOT SOMETHING ON, ALL RIGHT.
ばんっ
LISTEN UP...
WE'RE GONNA BLOW SAKUMA-SAN...
... AWAY.

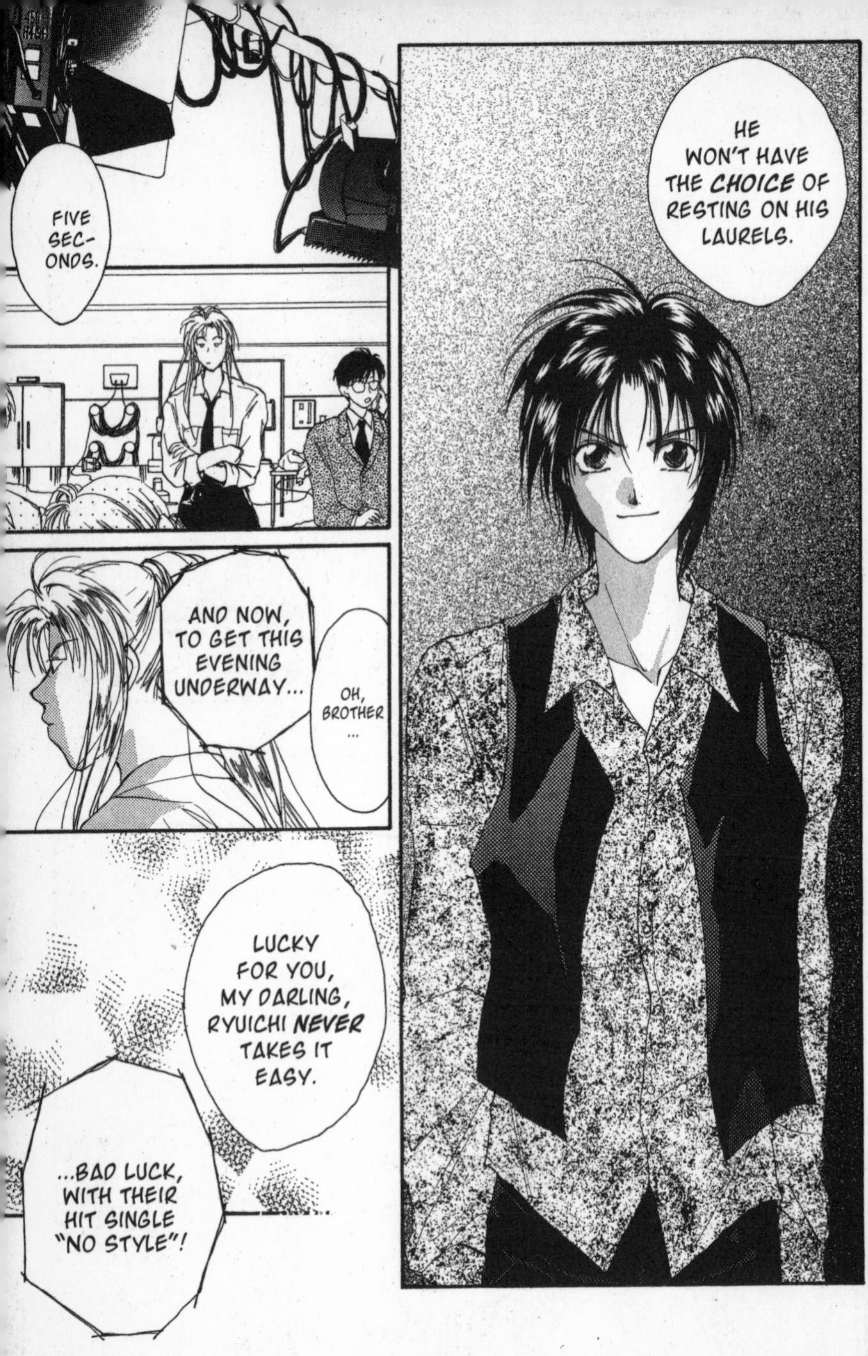
HE WON'T HAVE THE *CHOICE* OF RESTING ON HIS LAURELS.
FIVE SEC-ONDS.
AND NOW, TO GET THIS EVENING UNDERWAY...
OH, BROTHER ...
LUCKY FOR YOU, MY DARLING, RYUICHI *NEVER* TAKES IT EASY.
...BAD LUCK, WITH THEIR HIT SINGLE "NO STYLE"!

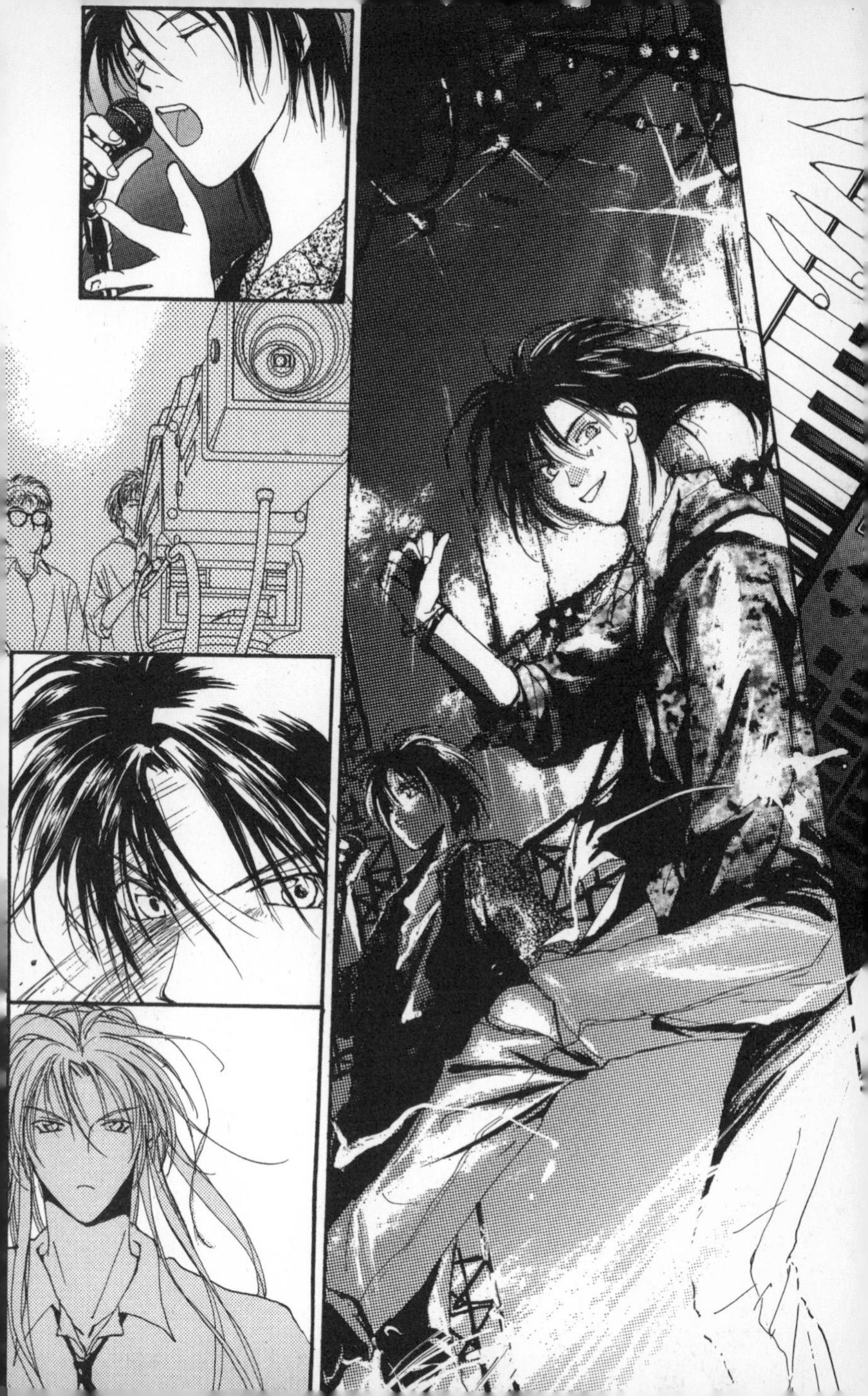

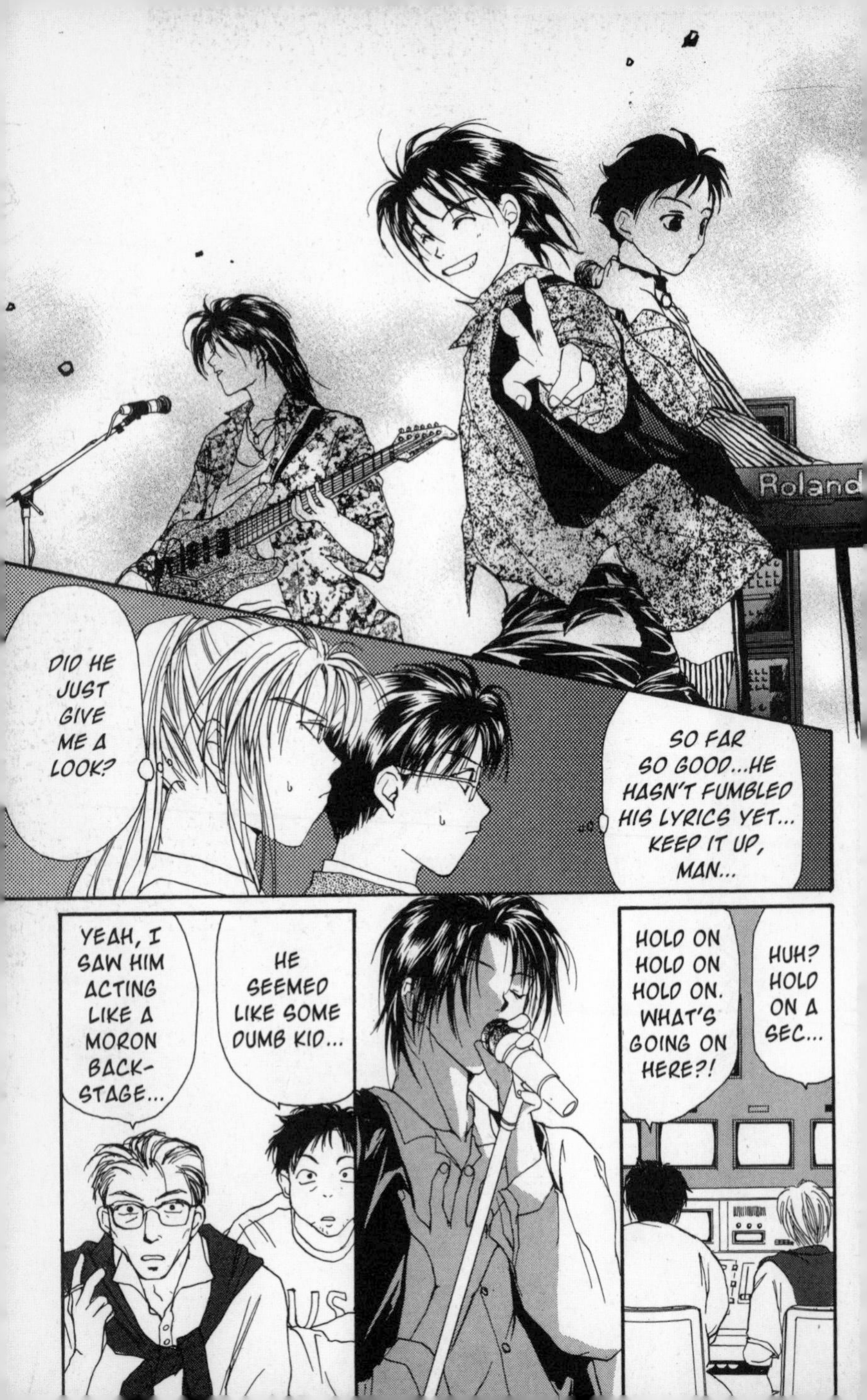
Roland
SO FAR SO GOOD...HE HASN'T FUMBLED HIS LYRICS YET... KEEP IT UP, MAN...
DID HE JUST GIVE ME A LOOK?
HUH? HOLD ON A SEC...
HOLD ON HOLD ON HOLD ON. WHAT'S GOING ON HERE?!
HE SEEMED LIKE SOME DUMB KID...
YEAH, I SAW HIM ACTING LIKE A MORON BACK-STAGE...

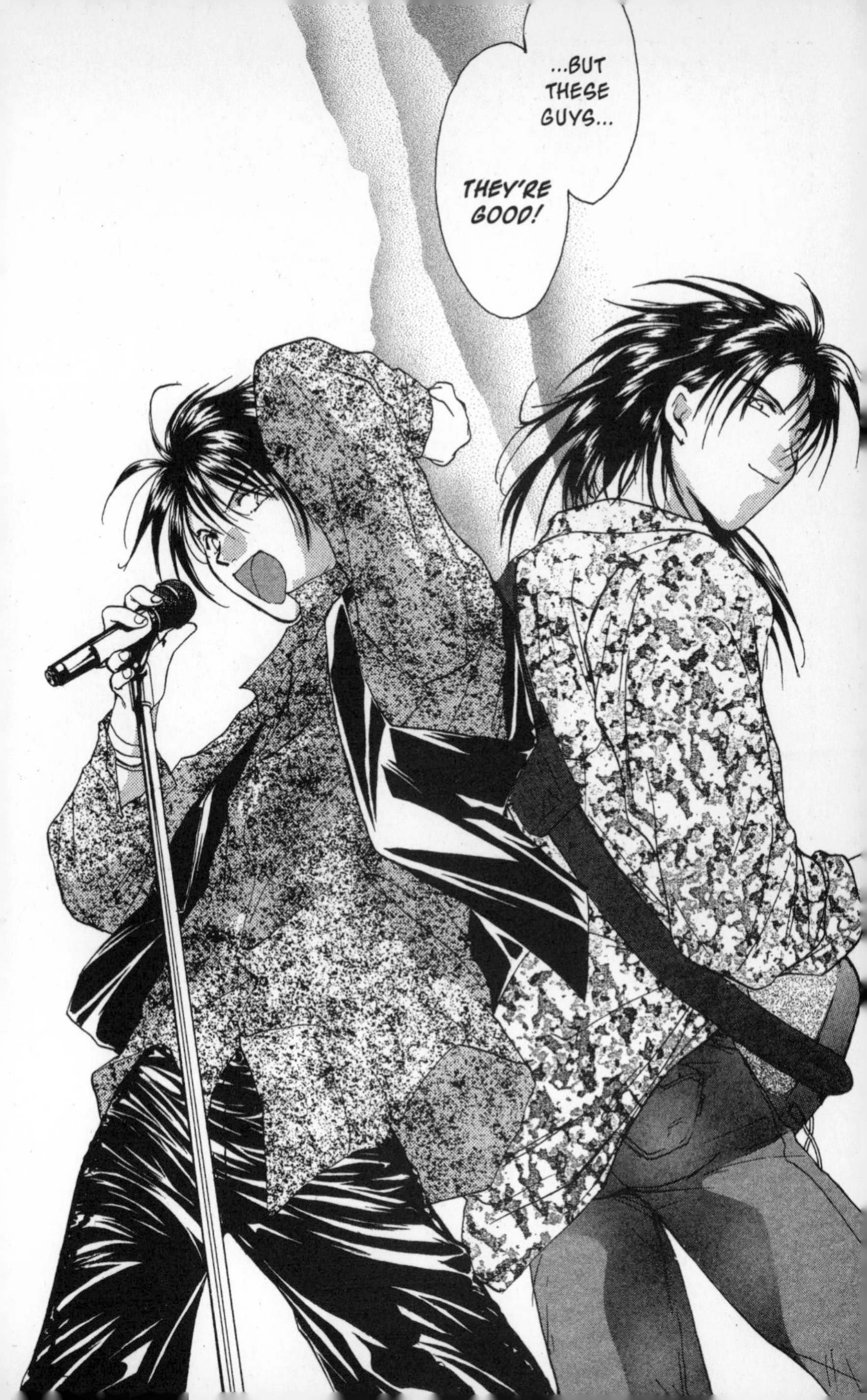
...BUT THESE GUYS...
THEY'RE GOOD!

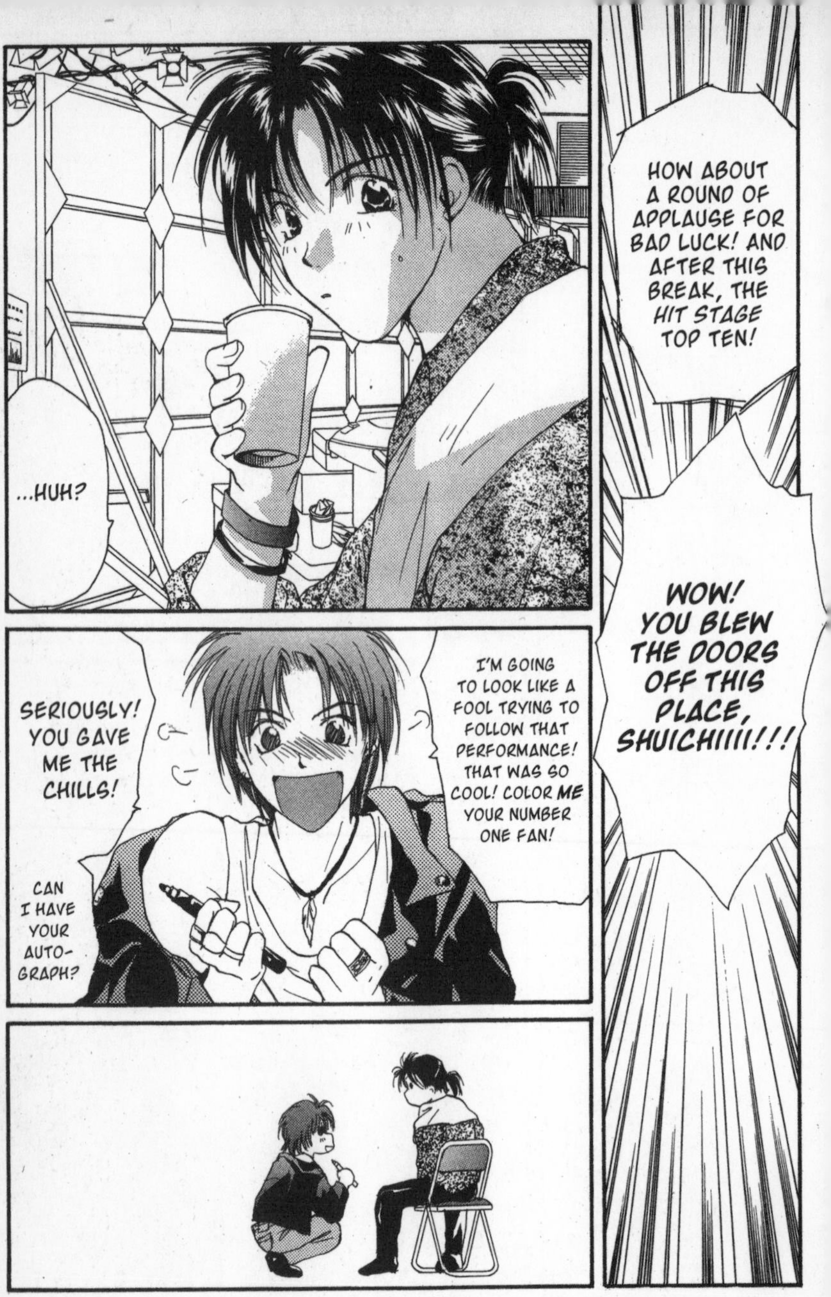
HOW ABOUT A ROUND OF APPLAUSE FOR BAD LUCK! AND AFTER THIS BREAK, THE HIT STAGE TOP TEN!
WOW! YOU BLEW THE DOORS OFF THIS PLACE, SHUICHIIIII!!!
...HUH?
I'M GOING TO LOOK LIKE A FOOL TRYING TO FOLLOW THAT PERFORMANCE! THAT WAS SO COOL! COLOR ME YOUR NUMBER ONE FAN!
SERIOUSLY! YOU GAVE ME THE CHILLS!
CAN I HAVE YOUR AUTO-GRAPH?

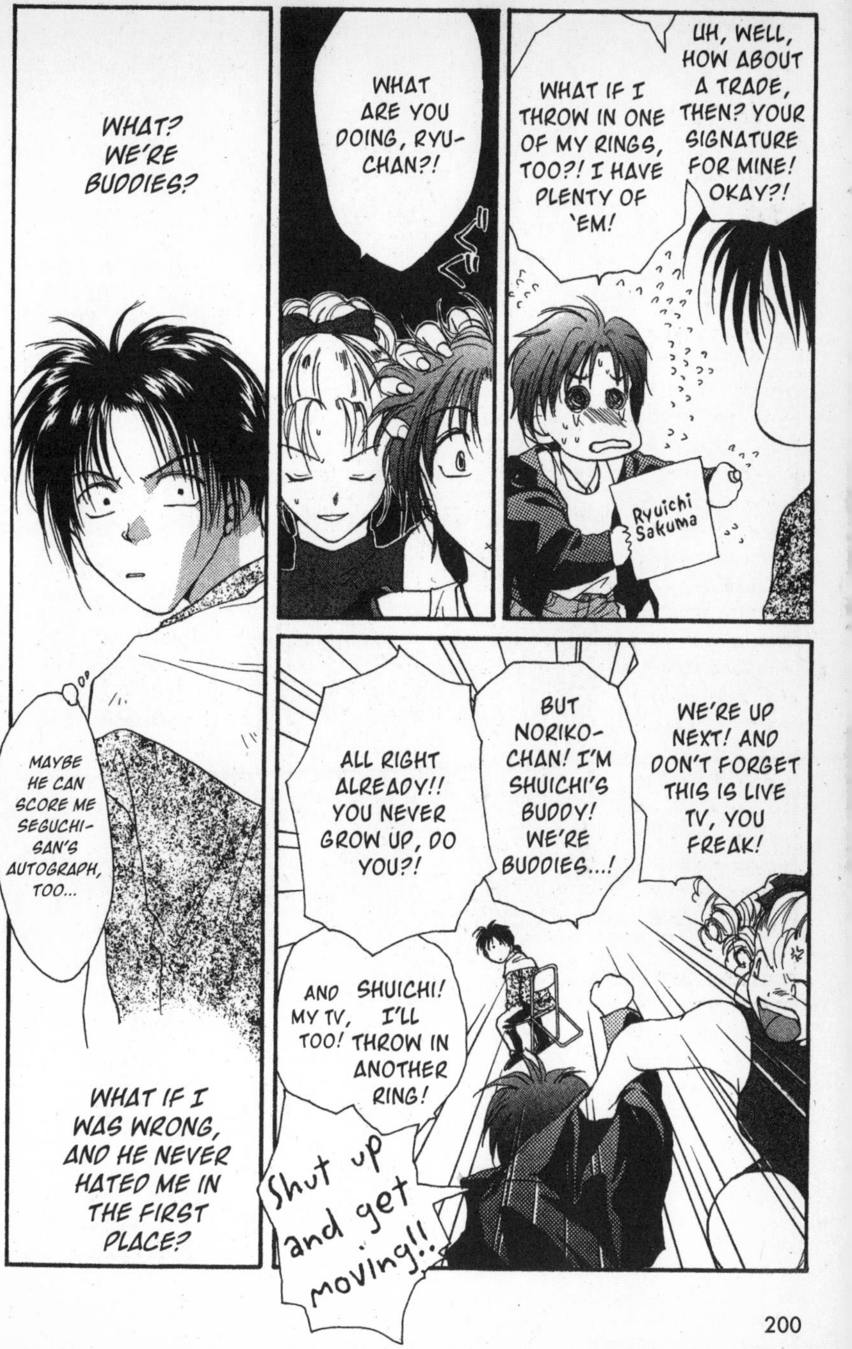
UH, WELL, HOW ABOUT A TRADE, THEN? YOUR SIGNATURE FOR MINE! OKAY?!
WHAT IF I THROW IN ONE OF MY RINGS, TOO?! I HAVE PLENTY OF 'EM!
Ryuichi Sakuma
WHAT ARE YOU DOING, RYU-CHAN?!
WE'RE UP NEXT! AND DON'T FORGET THIS IS LIVE TV, YOU FREAK!
BUT NORIKO-CHAN! I'M SHUICHI'S BUDDY! WE'RE BUDDIES...!
ALL RIGHT ALREADY!! YOU NEVER GROW UP, DO YOU?!
SHUICHI! I'LL THROW IN ANOTHER RING!
AND MY TV, TOO!
Shut up and get moving!!
WHAT? WE'RE BUDDIES?
MAYBE HE CAN SCORE ME SEGUCHI-SAN'S AUTOGRAPH, TOO...
WHAT IF I WAS WRONG, AND HE NEVER HATED ME IN THE FIRST PLACE?

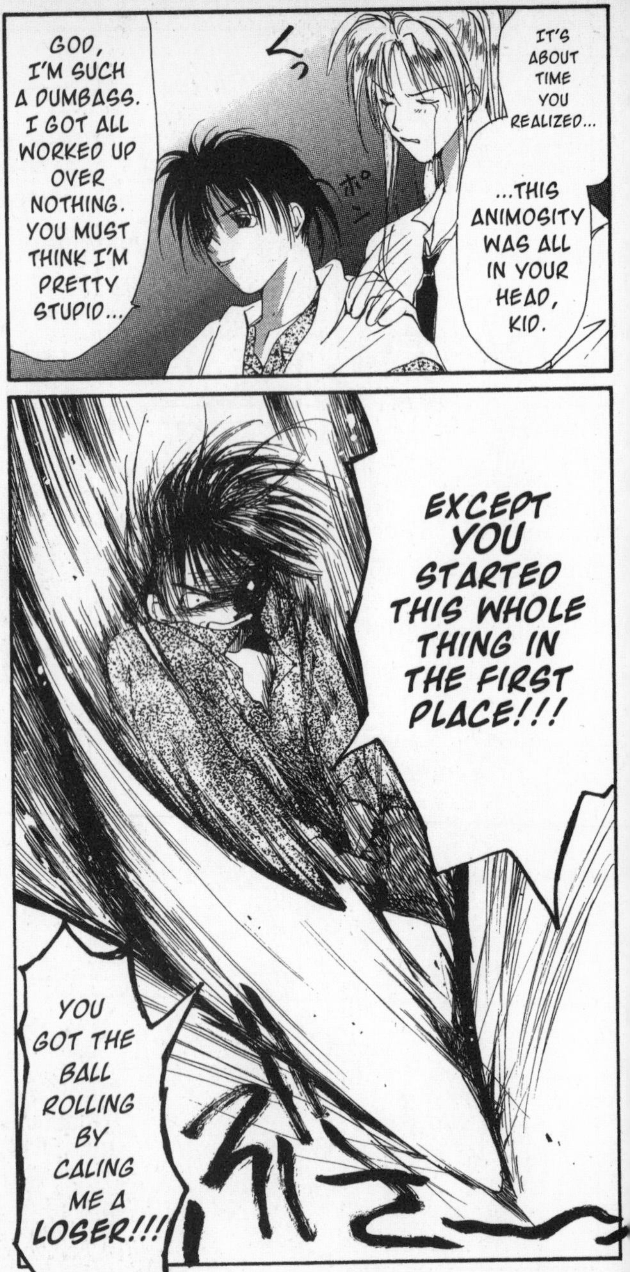
IT'S ABOUT TIME YOU REALIZED...
...THIS ANIMOSITY WAS ALL IN YOUR HEAD, KID.
GOD, I'M SUCH A DUMBASS. I GOT ALL WORKED UP OVER NOTHING. YOU MUST THINK I'M PRETTY STUPID...
EXCEPT YOU STARTED THIS WHOLE THING IN THE FIRST PLACE!!!
YOU GOT THE BALL ROLLING BY CALING ME A LOSER!!!

MORE ABOUT TRACK 21

Speaking of which, what's left to show in this story? I went all the way to Tokyo to do research. It was a rough trip! Somehow, I ended up at a taping of a program called "Go Ahead and Laugh," and all sorts of wild things happened. I got a lot of great souvenirs, and it was extremely tiring, but I had such a great time. Sorry, I'm writing like this is some field trip report. As to what kind of research I did, I wanted to see the inside of a TV studio. And don't you dare say stuff like, "Well, it doesn't show in the finished product!"

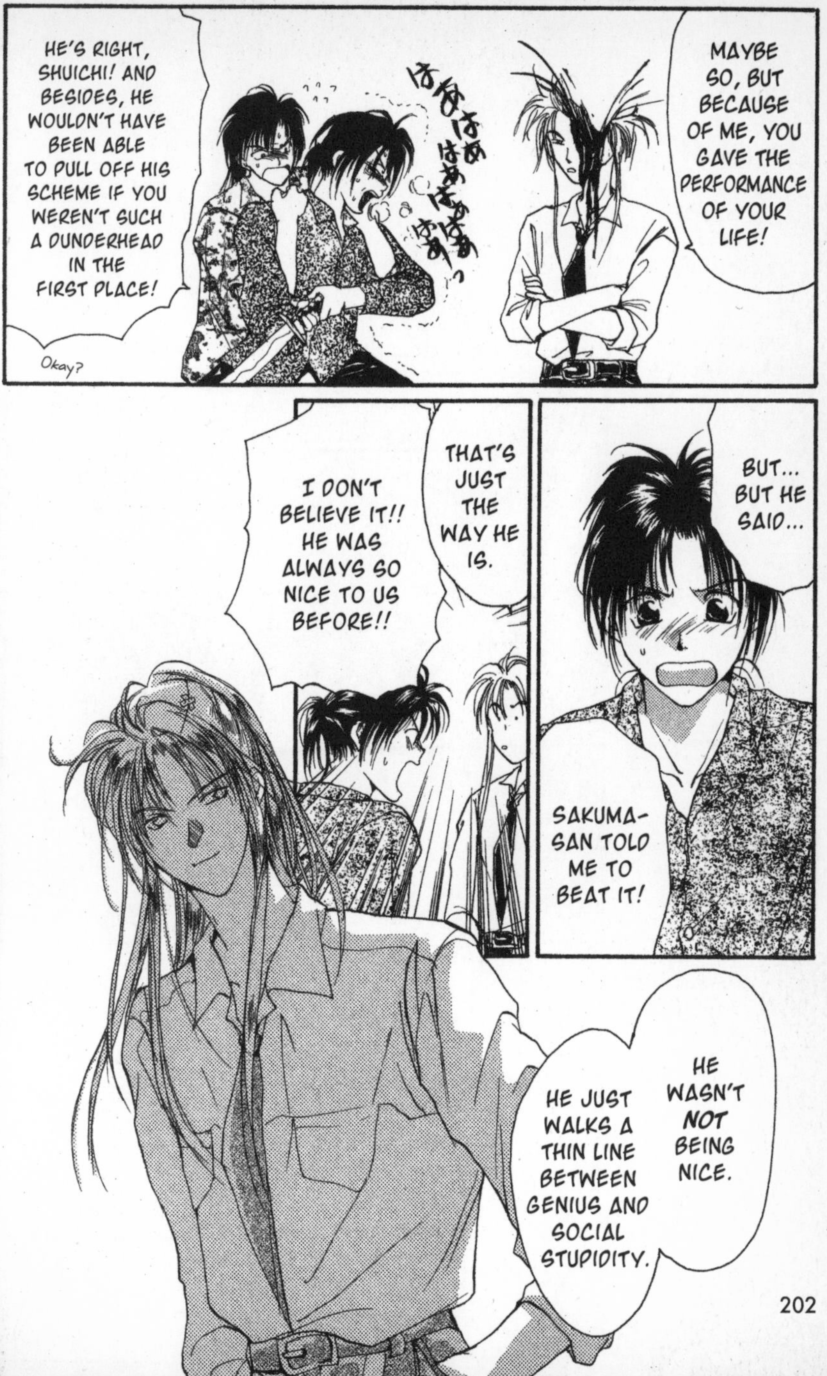
MAYBE SO, BUT BECAUSE OF ME, YOU GAVE THE PERFORMANCE OF YOUR LIFE!
HE'S RIGHT, SHUICHI! AND BESIDES, HE WOULDN'T HAVE BEEN ABLE TO PULL OFF HIS SCHEME IF YOU WEREN'T SUCH A DUNDERHEAD IN THE FIRST PLACE!
Okay?
BUT... BUT HE SAID...
SAKUMA-SAN TOLD ME TO BEAT IT!
THAT'S JUST THE WAY HE IS.
I DON'T BELIEVE IT!! HE WAS ALWAYS SO NICE TO US BEFORE!!
HE WASN'T *NOT* BEING NICE.
HE JUST WALKS A THIN LINE BETWEEN GENIUS AND SOCIAL STUPIDITY.

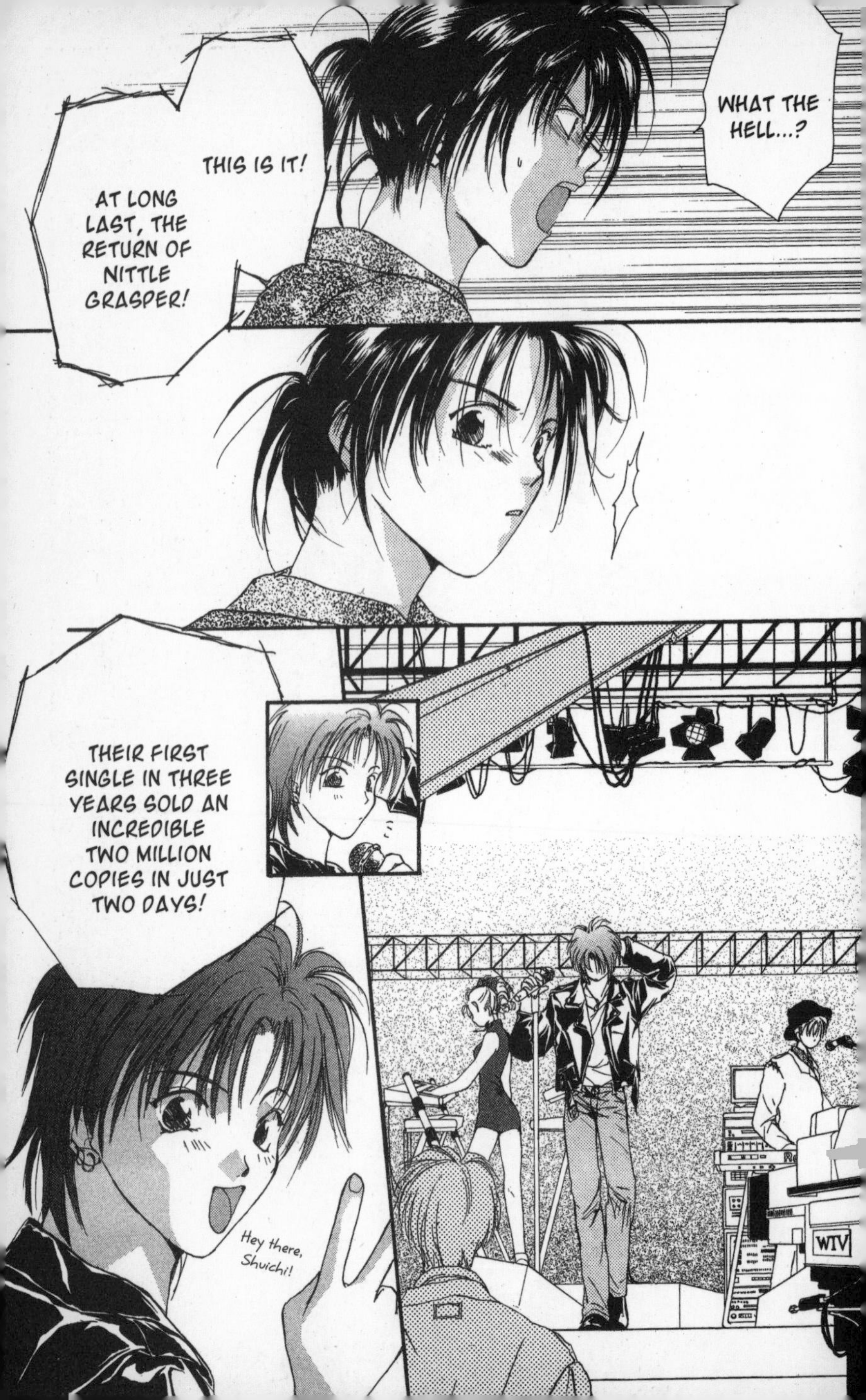
WHAT THE HELL...?
THIS IS IT!
AT LONG LAST, THE RETURN OF NITTLE GRASPER!
THEIR FIRST SINGLE IN THREE YEARS SOLD AN INCREDIBLE TWO MILLION COPIES IN JUST TWO DAYS!
Hey there, Shuichi!

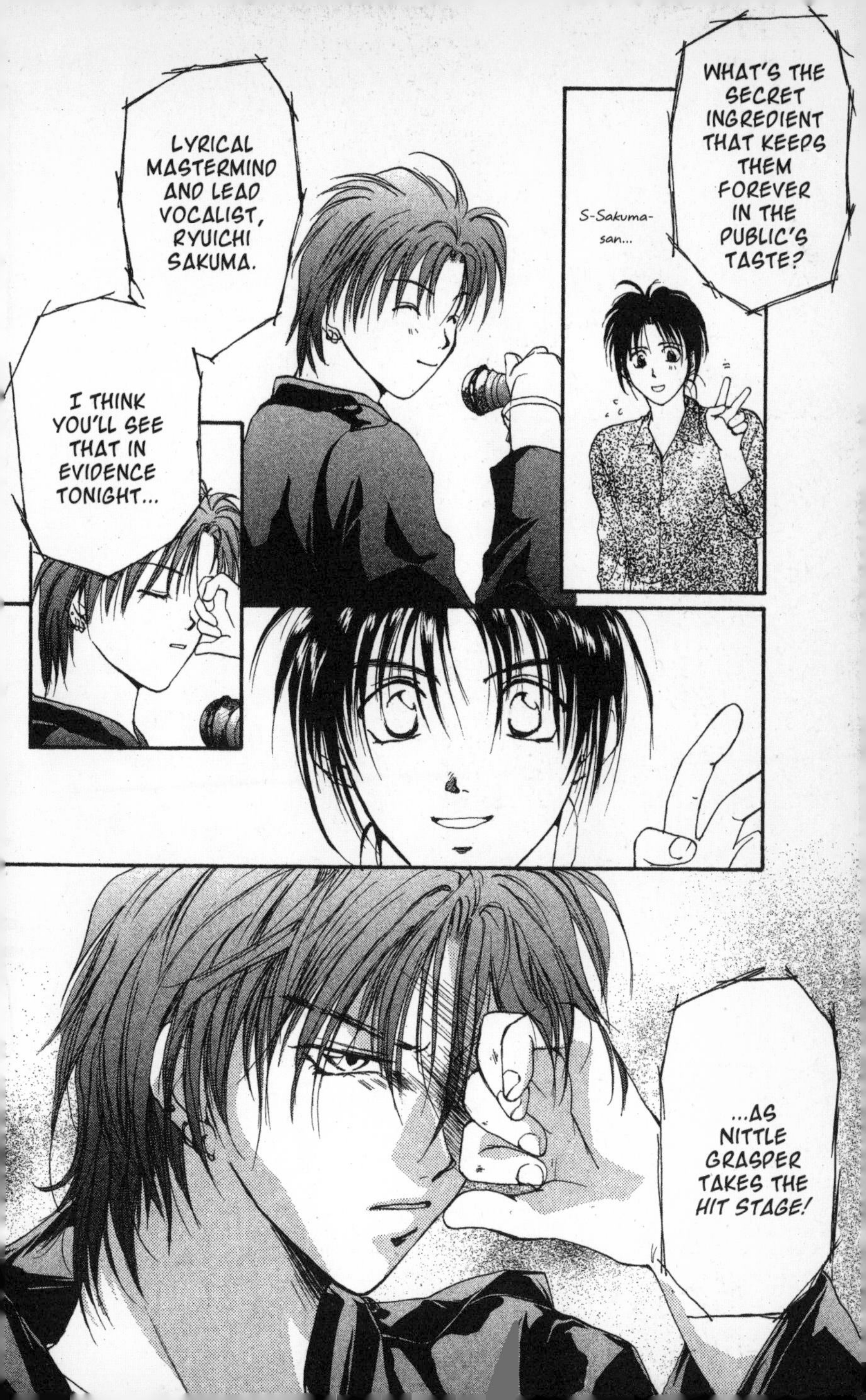
WHAT'S THE SECRET INGREDIENT THAT KEEPS THEM FOREVER IN THE PUBLIC'S TASTE?
S-Sakuma-san...
LYRICAL MASTERMIND AND LEAD VOCALIST, RYUICHI SAKUMA.
I THINK YOU'LL SEE THAT IN EVIDENCE TONIGHT...
...AS NITTLE GRASPER TAKES THE HIT STAGE!

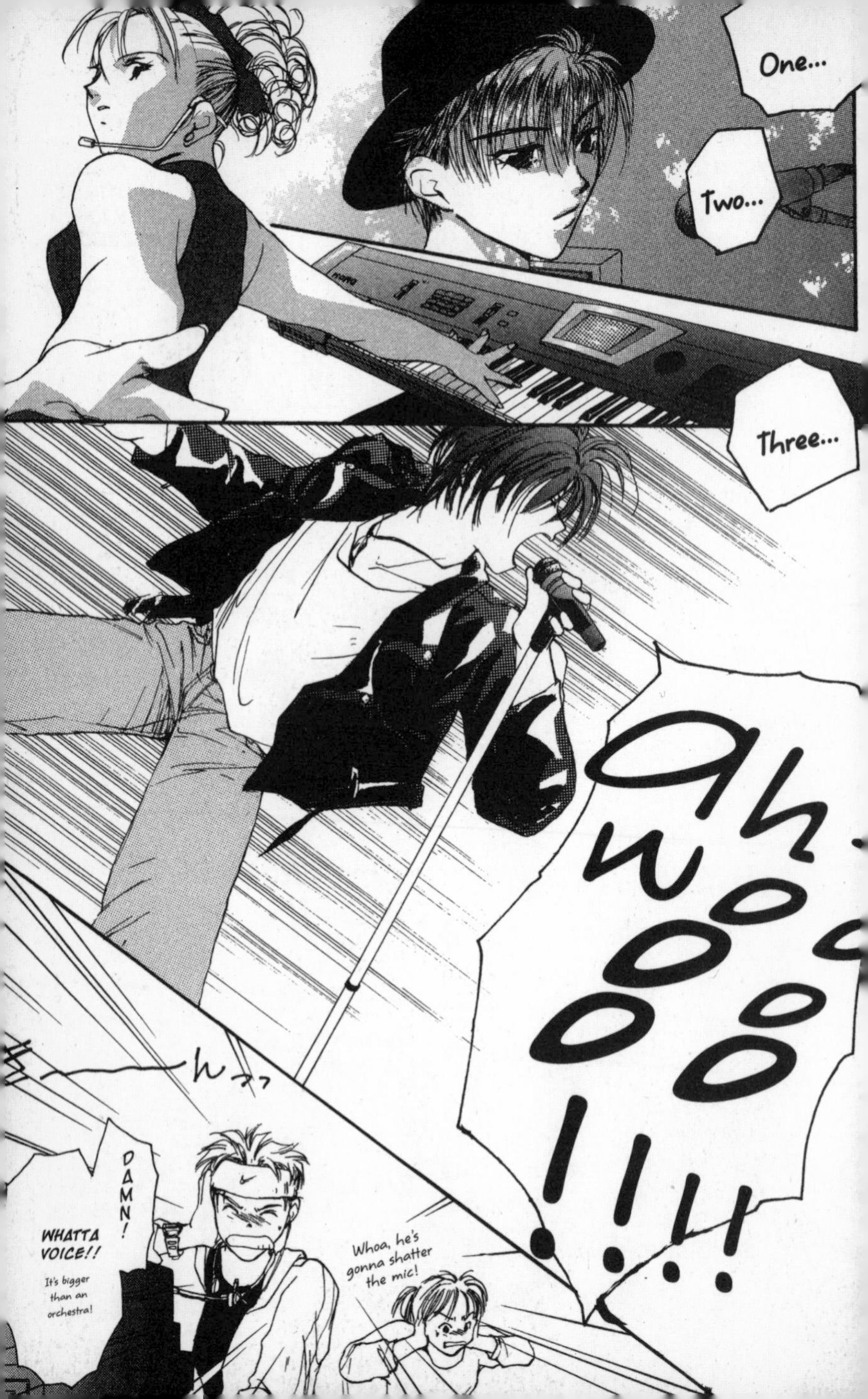
One...
Two...
Three...
Ahwoooooo!!!!
DAMN!
WHATTA VOICE!!
It's bigger than an orchestra!
Whoa, he's gonna shatter the mic!

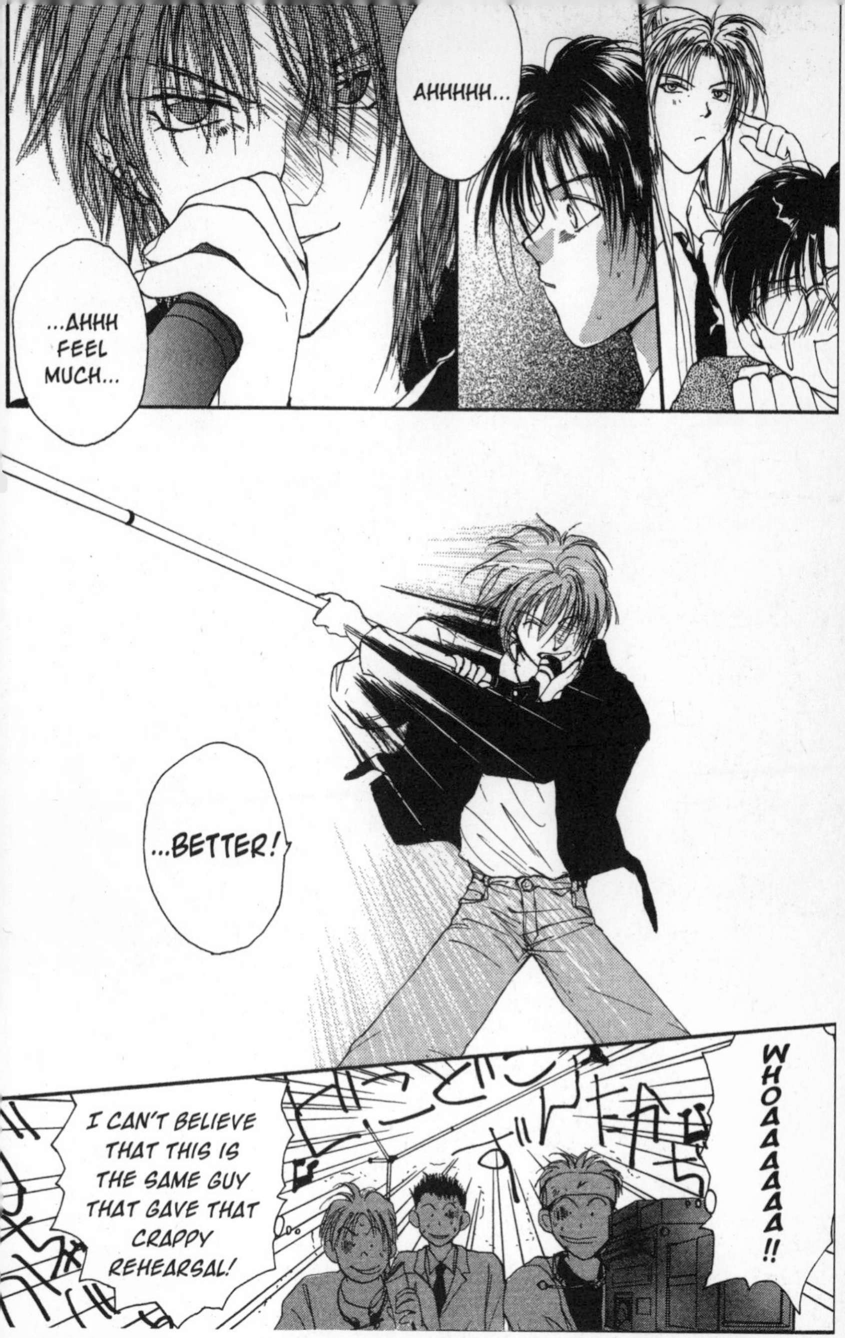
AHHHHH...
...AHHH FEEL MUCH...
...BETTER!
WHOAAAAAAA!!
I CAN'T BELIEVE THAT THIS IS THE SAME GUY THAT GAVE THAT CRAPPY REHEARSAL!

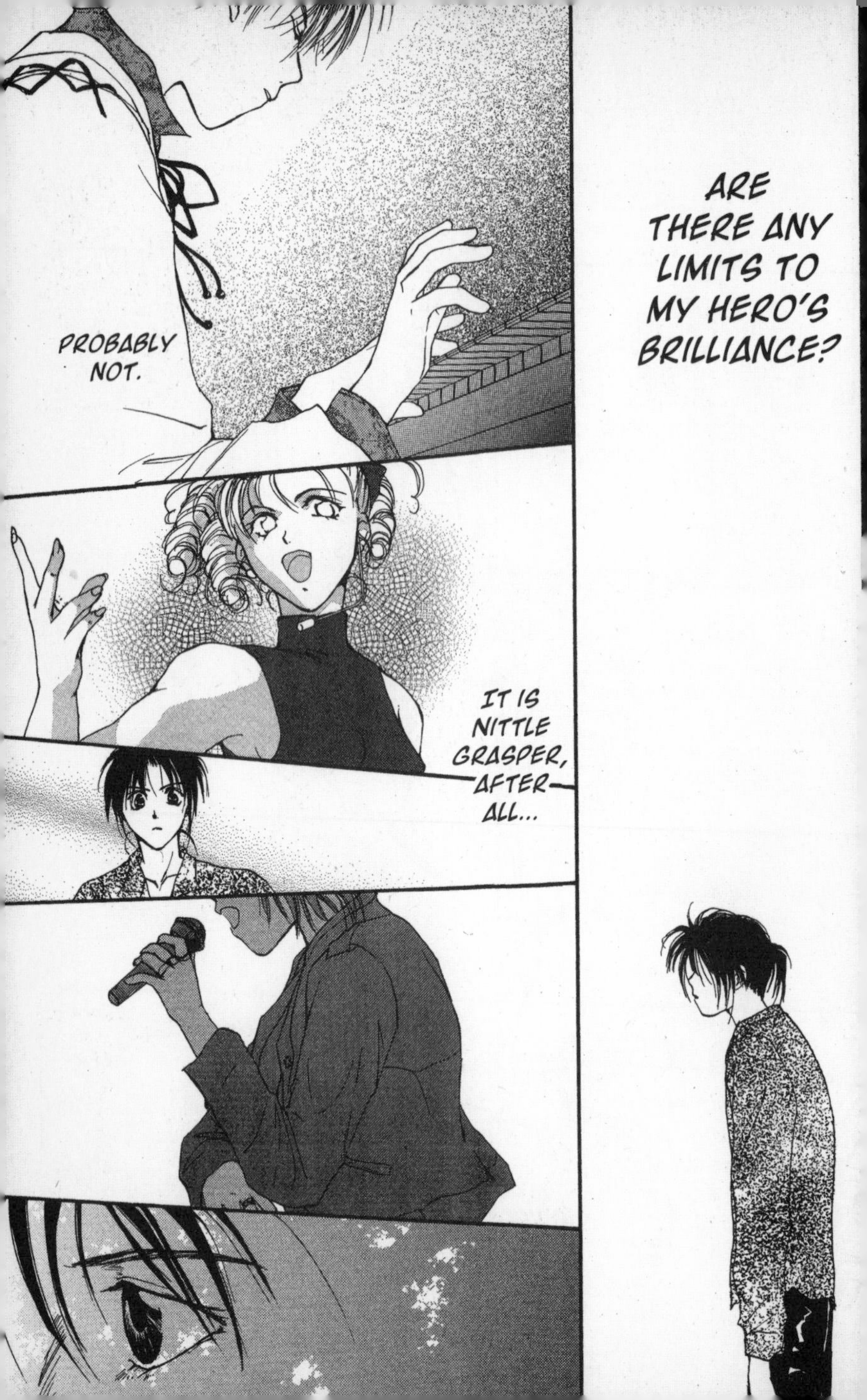
ARE THERE ANY LIMITS TO MY HERO'S BRILLIANCE?
PROBABLY NOT.
IT IS NITTLE GRASPER, AFTER ALL...

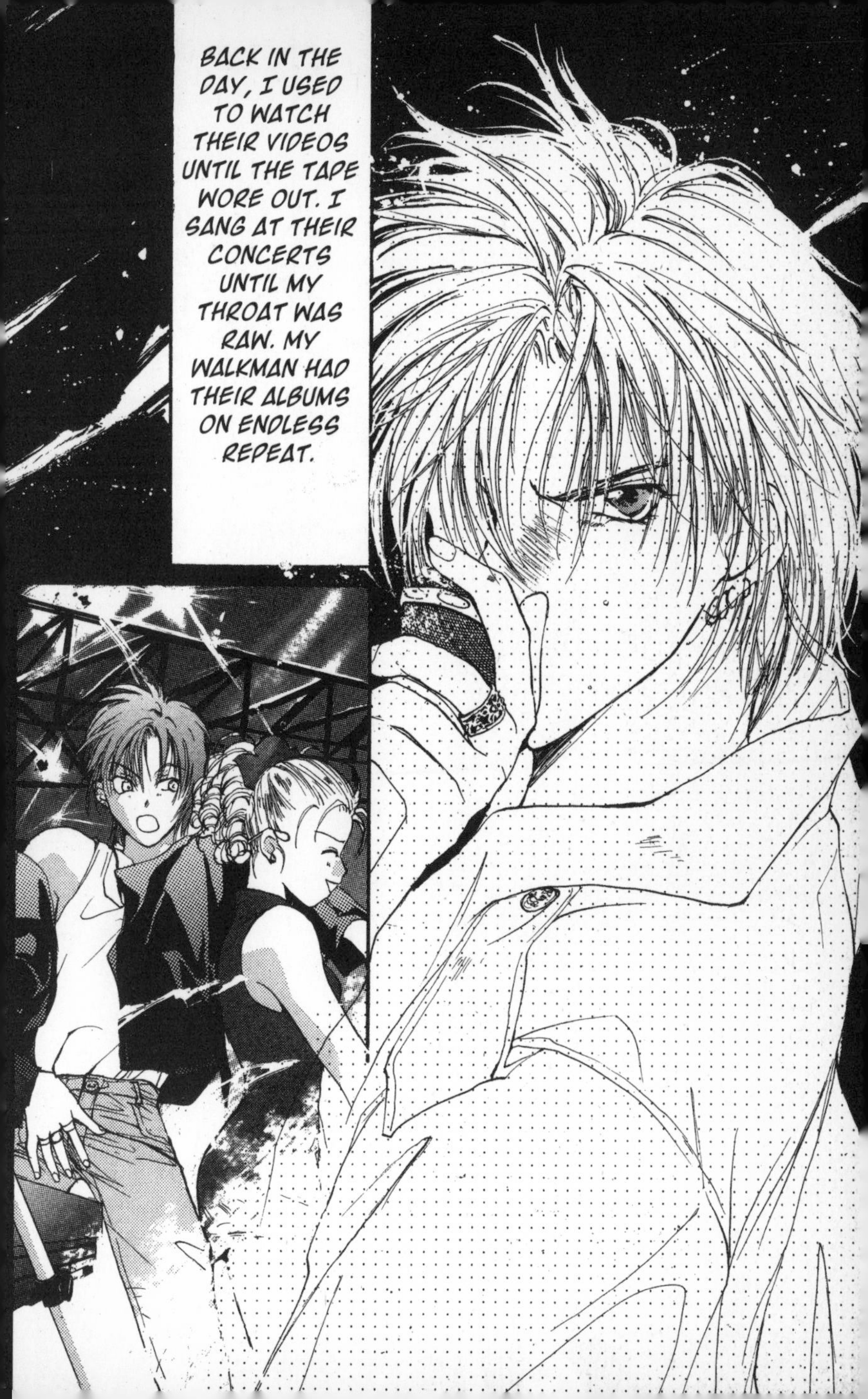
BACK IN THE DAY, I USED TO WATCH THEIR VIDEOS UNTIL THE TAPE WORE OUT. I SANG AT THEIR CONCERTS UNTIL MY THROAT WAS RAW. MY WALKMAN HAD THEIR ALBUMS ON ENDLESS REPEAT.

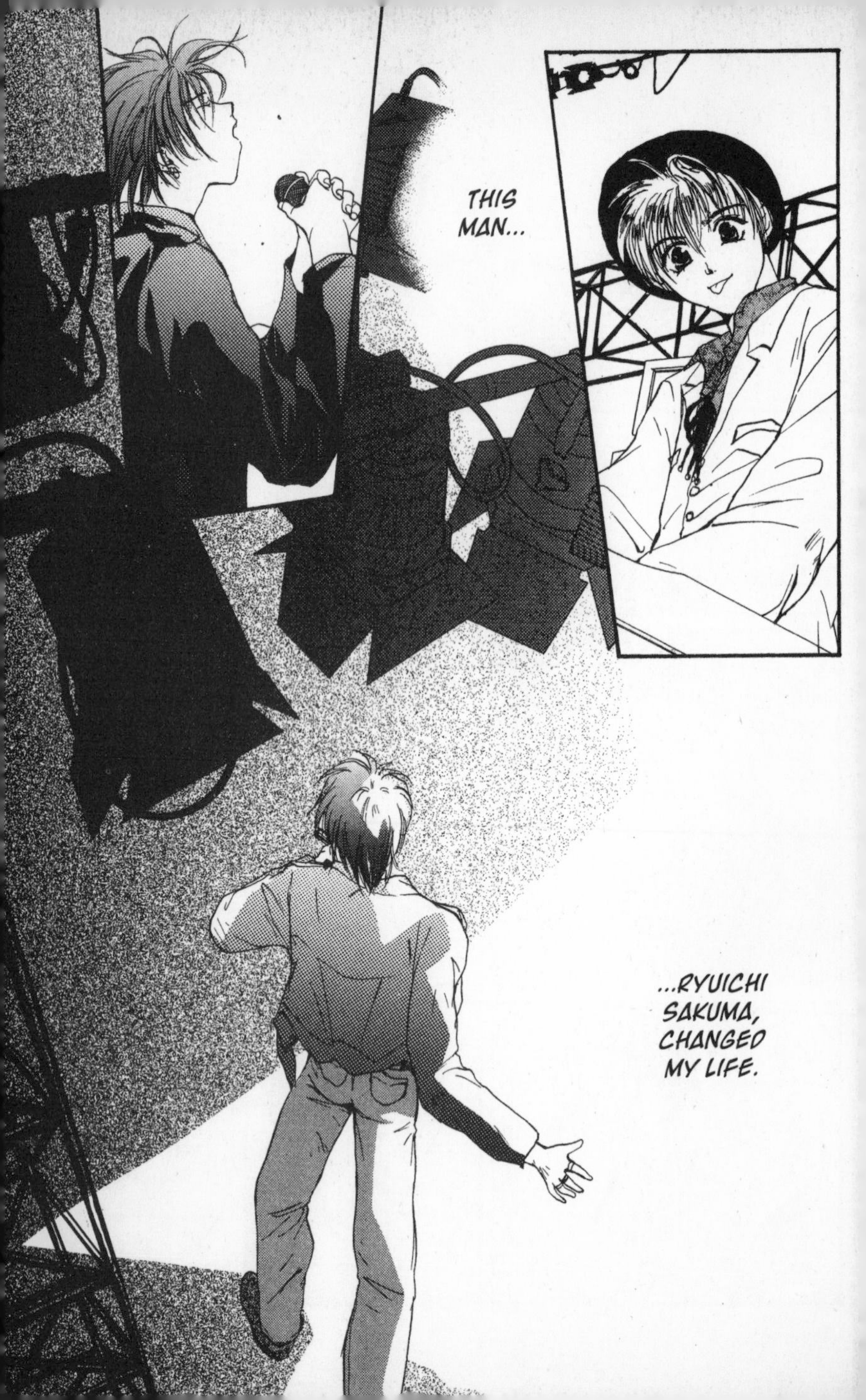
THIS MAN...
...RYUICHI SAKUMA, CHANGED MY LIFE.

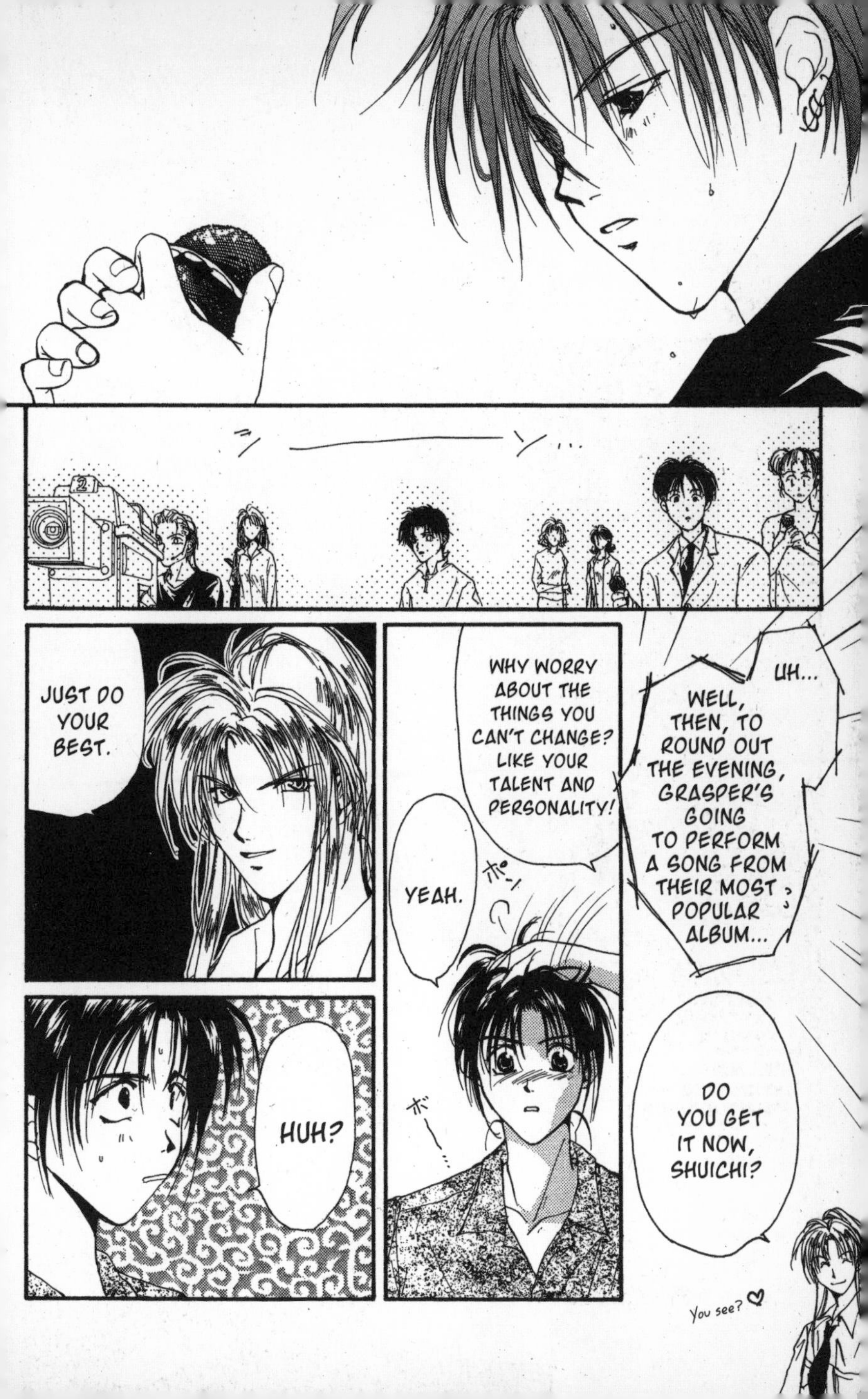
シ———ン…
UH... WELL, THEN, TO ROUND OUT THE EVENING, GRASPER'S GOING TO PERFORM A SONG FROM THEIR MOST POPULAR ALBUM...
WHY WORRY ABOUT THE THINGS YOU CAN'T CHANGE? LIKE YOUR TALENT AND PERSONALITY!
YEAH.
ポー
ボー…
JUST DO YOUR BEST.
HUH?
DO YOU GET IT NOW, SHUICHI?
You see?

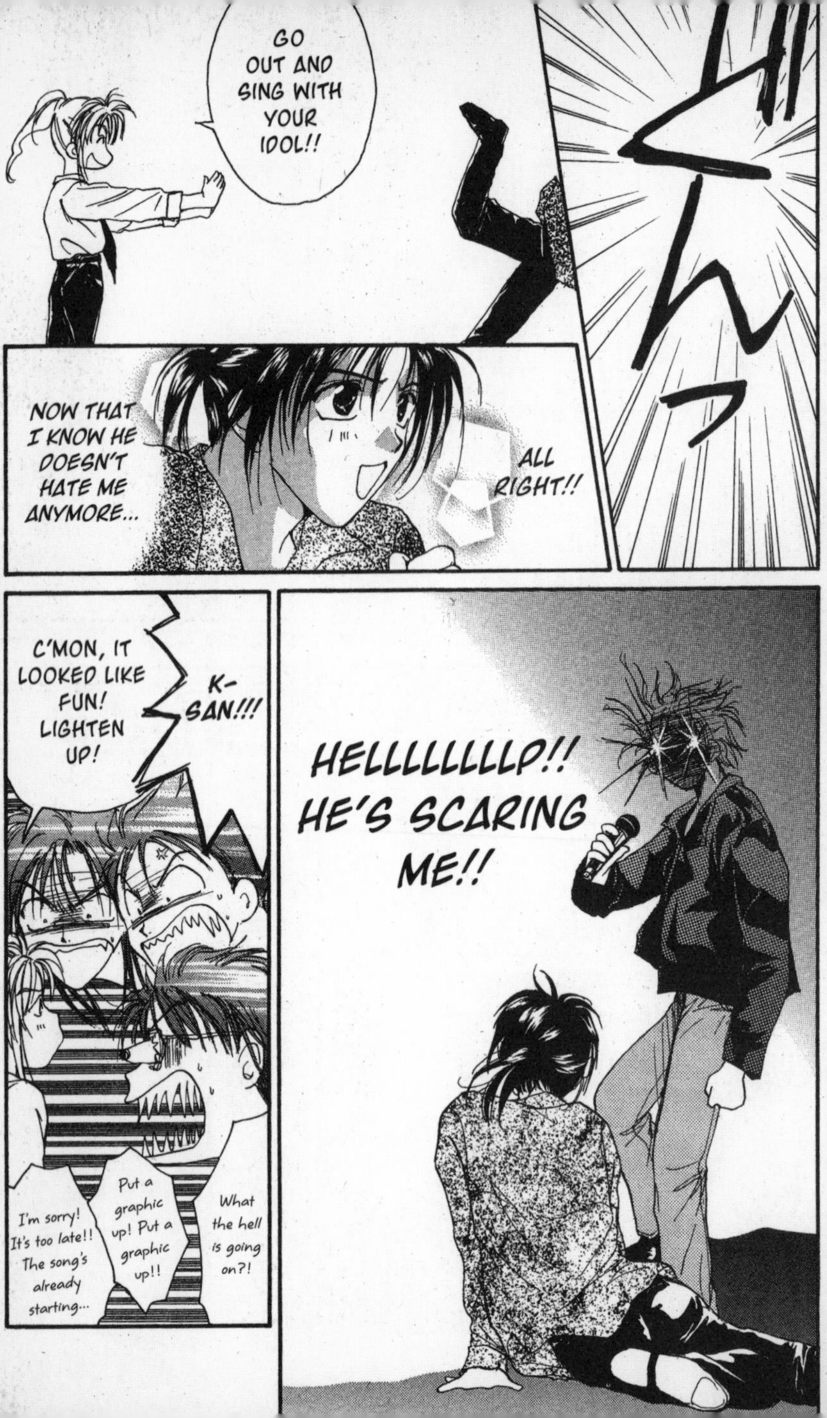
GO OUT AND SING WITH YOUR IDOL!!
NOW THAT I KNOW HE DOESN'T HATE ME ANYMORE...
ALL RIGHT!!
HELLLLLLLLP!! HE'S SCARING ME!!
K-SAN!!!
C'MON, IT LOOKED LIKE FUN! LIGHTEN UP!
What the hell is going on?!
Put a graphic up! Put a graphic up!!
I'm sorry! It's too late!! The song's already starting...

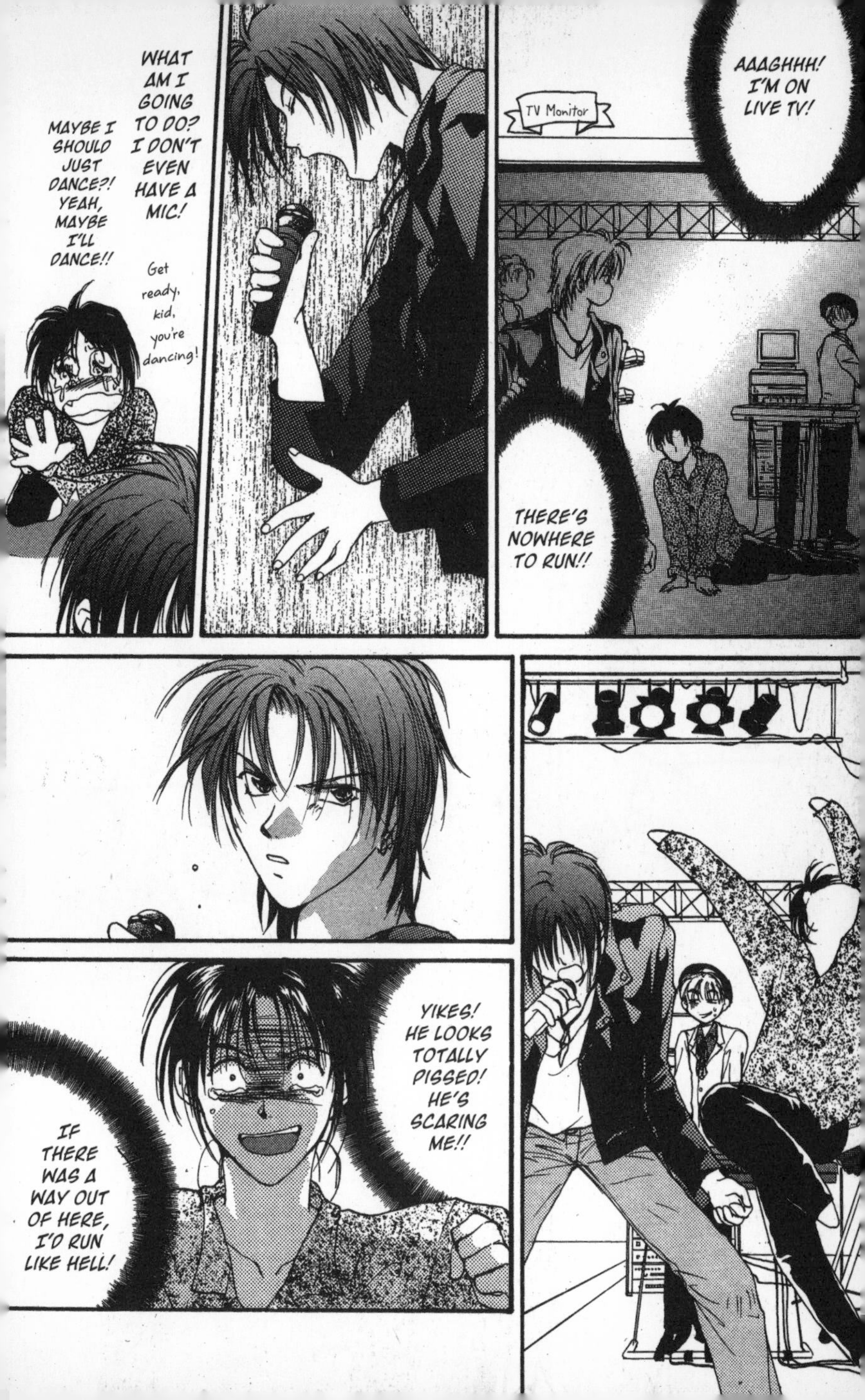
TV Monitor
AAAGHHH! I'M ON LIVE TV!
THERE'S NOWHERE TO RUN!!
WHAT AM I GOING TO DO? I DON'T EVEN HAVE A MIC!
MAYBE I SHOULD JUST DANCE?! YEAH, MAYBE I'LL DANCE!!
Get ready, kid, you're dancing!
YIKES! HE LOOKS TOTALLY PISSED! HE'S SCARING ME!!
IF THERE WAS A WAY OUT OF HERE, I'D RUN LIKE HELL!

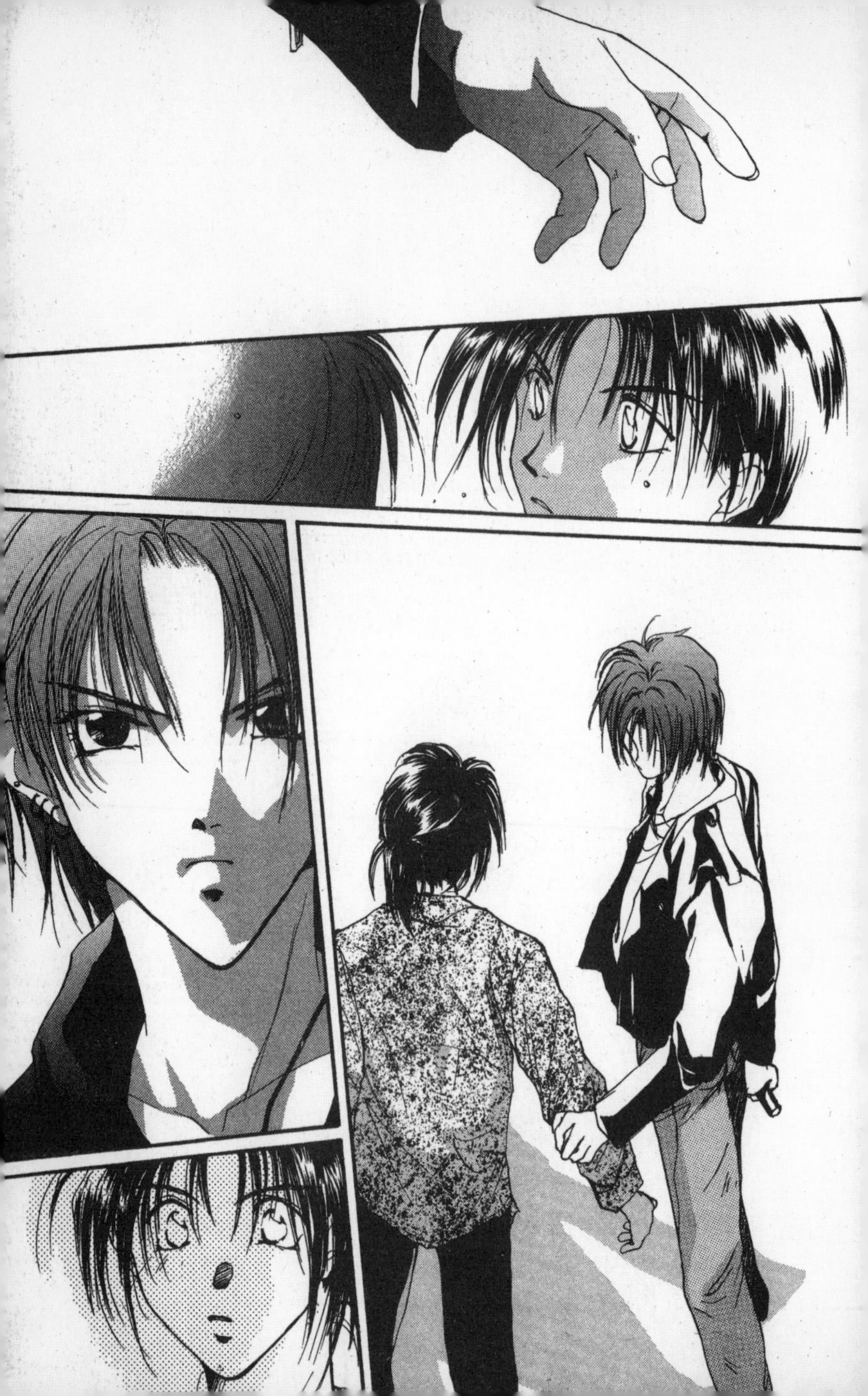

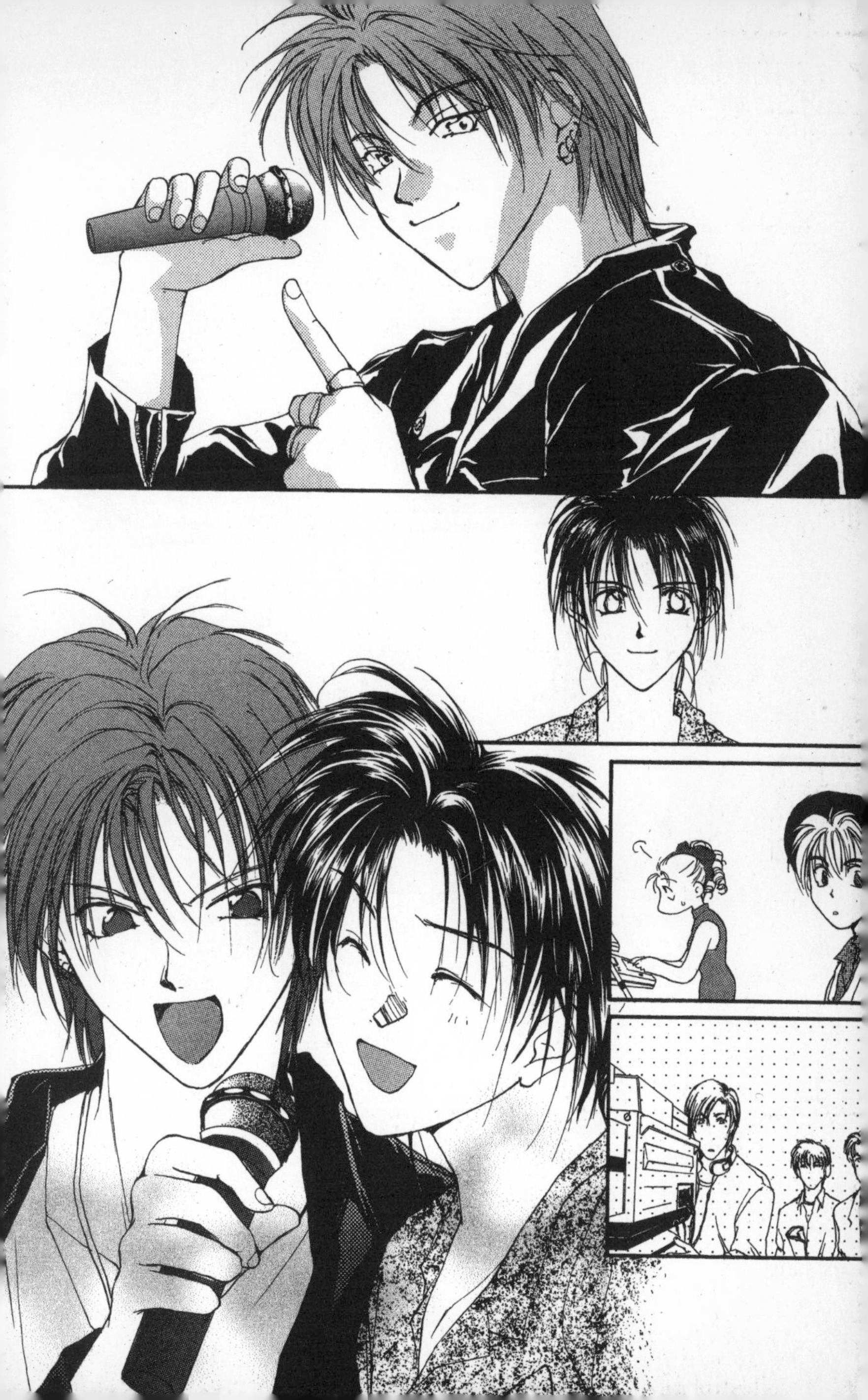

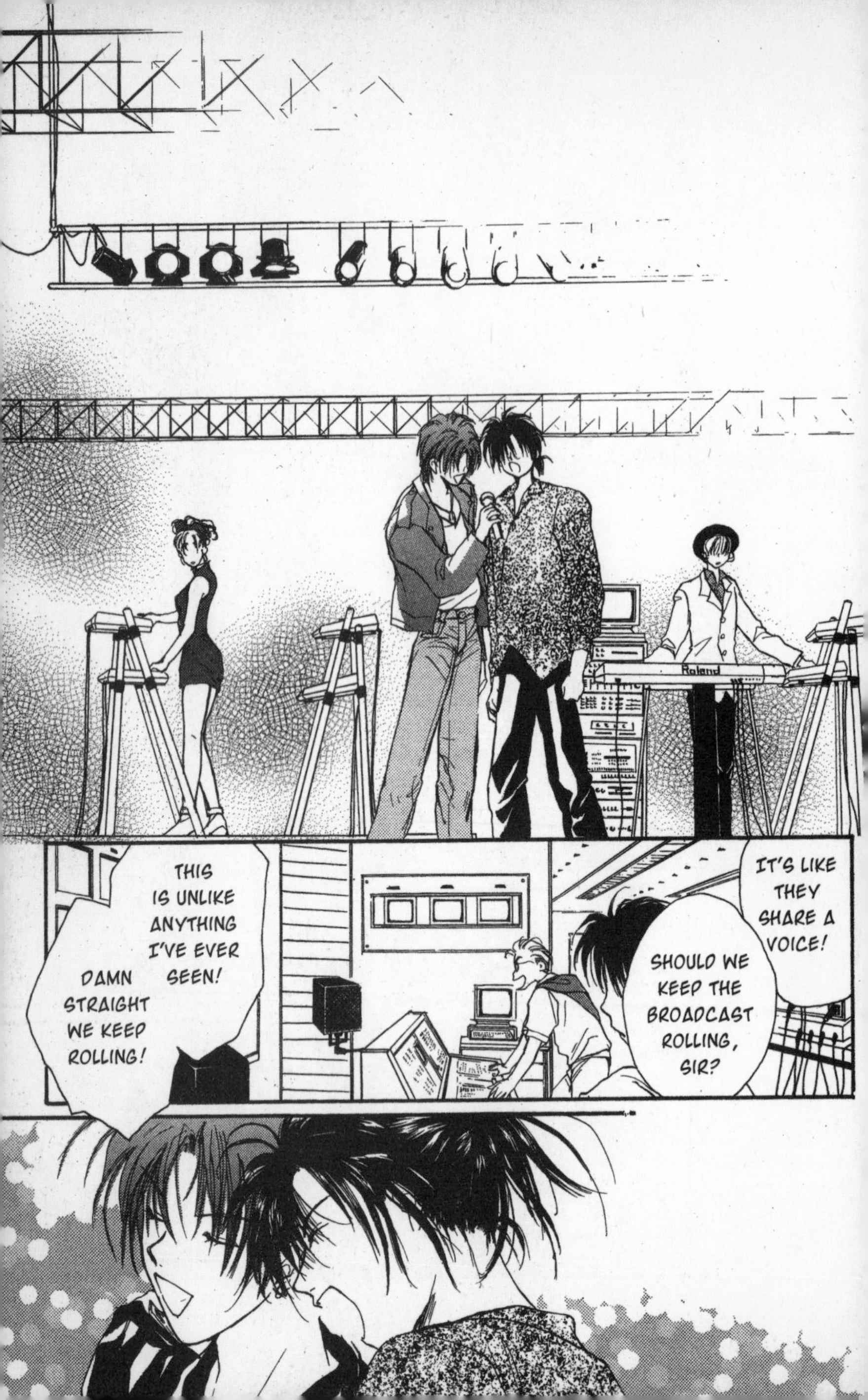
IT'S LIKE THEY SHARE A VOICE!
SHOULD WE KEEP THE BROADCAST ROLLING, SIR?
THIS IS UNLIKE ANYTHING I'VE EVER SEEN!
DAMN STRAIGHT WE KEEP ROLLING!

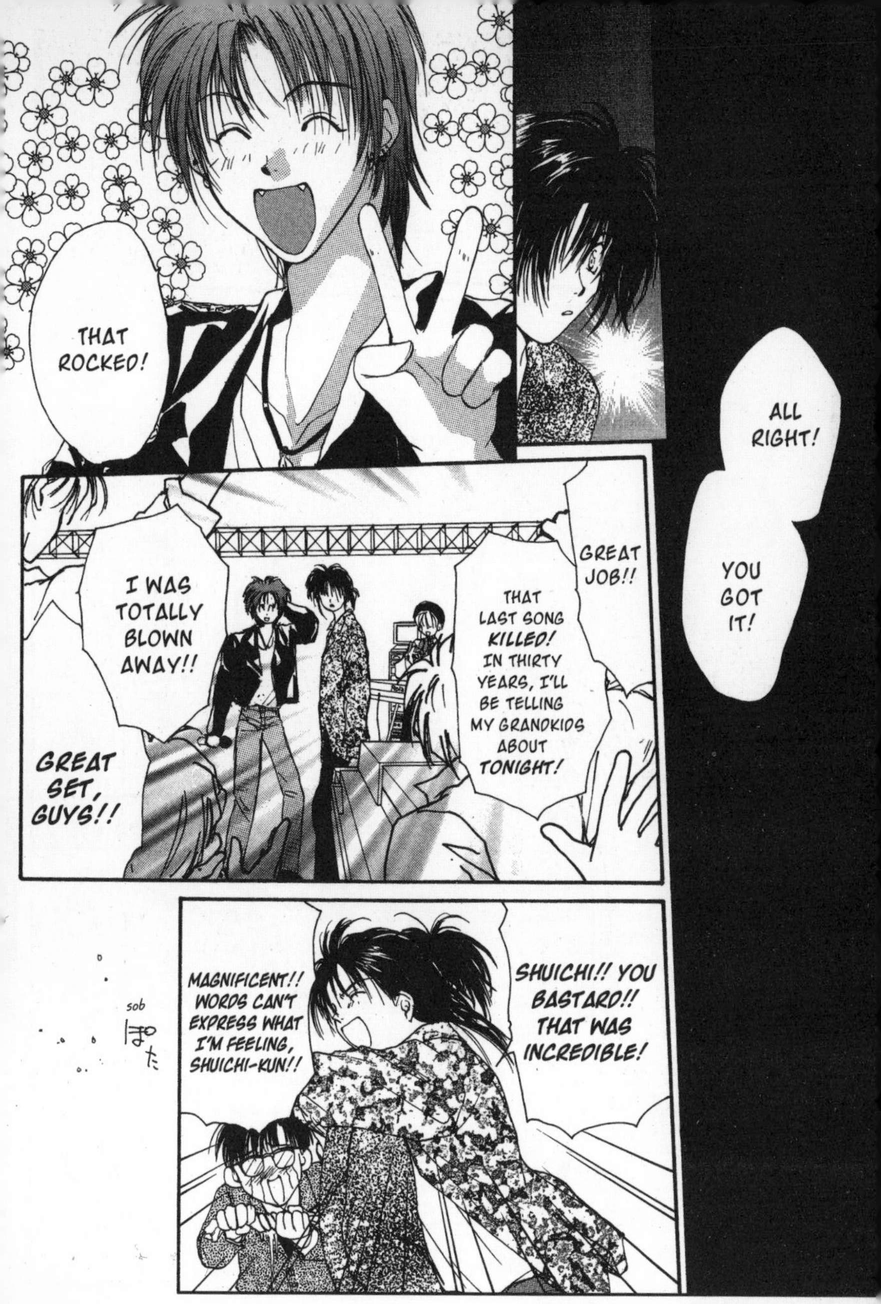
ALL RIGHT!
YOU GOT IT!
THAT ROCKED!
GREAT JOB!!
THAT LAST SONG KILLED! IN THIRTY YEARS, I'LL BE TELLING MY GRANDKIDS ABOUT TONIGHT!
I WAS TOTALLY BLOWN AWAY!!
GREAT SET, GUYS!!
SHUICHI!! YOU BASTARD!! THAT WAS INCREDIBLE!
MAGNIFICENT!! WORDS CAN'T EXPRESS WHAT I'M FEELING, SHUICHI-KUN!!
sob
ぽた

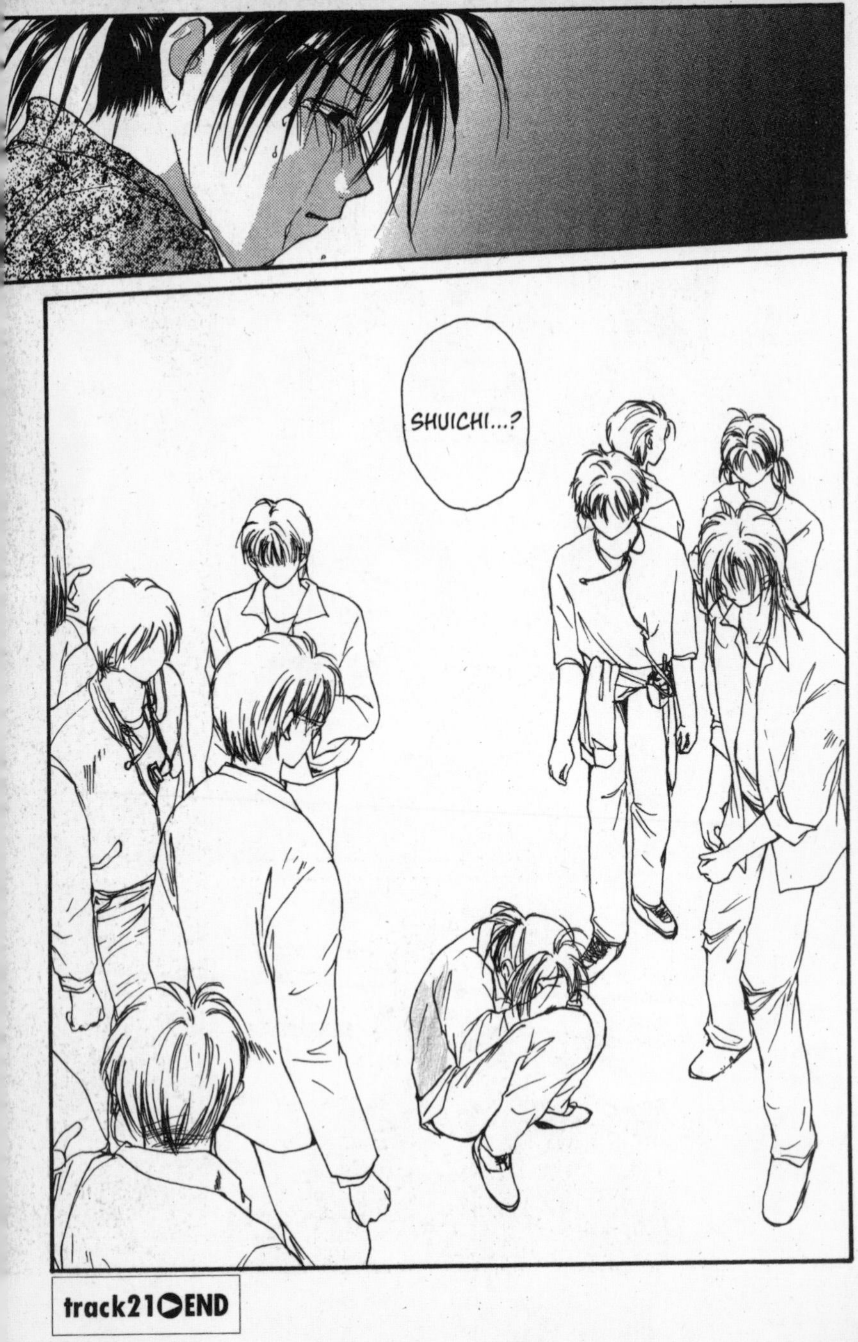
SHUICHI...?

track21 ▶ END

Gravitation

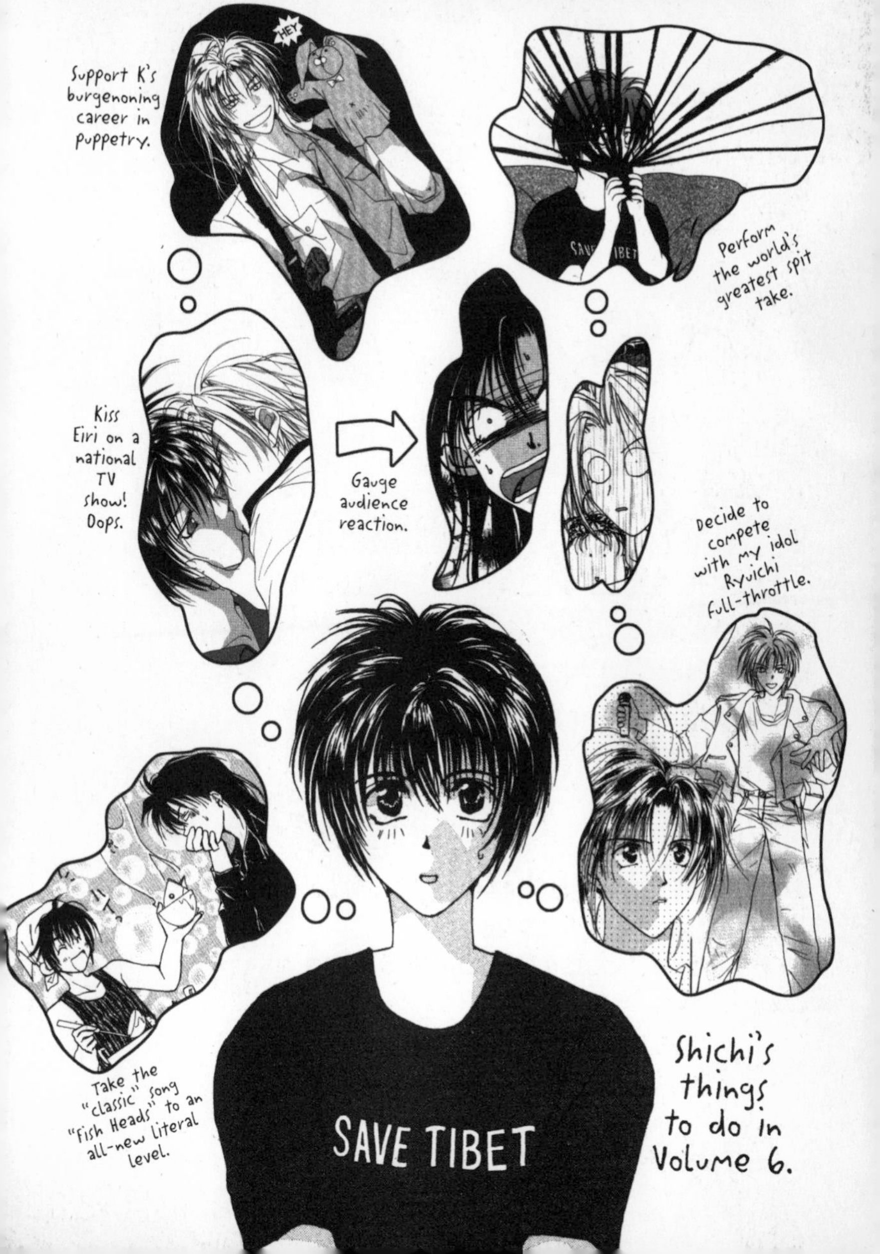
HEY
Perform the world's greatest spit take.
SAVE TIBET
Support K's burgenoning career in puppetry.
Decide to compete with my idol Ryuichi full-throttle.
Gauge audience reaction.
Kiss Eiri on a national TV show! Oops.
Shichi's things to do in Volume 6.
SAVE TIBET
Take the "classic" song "Fish Heads" to an all-new literal level.

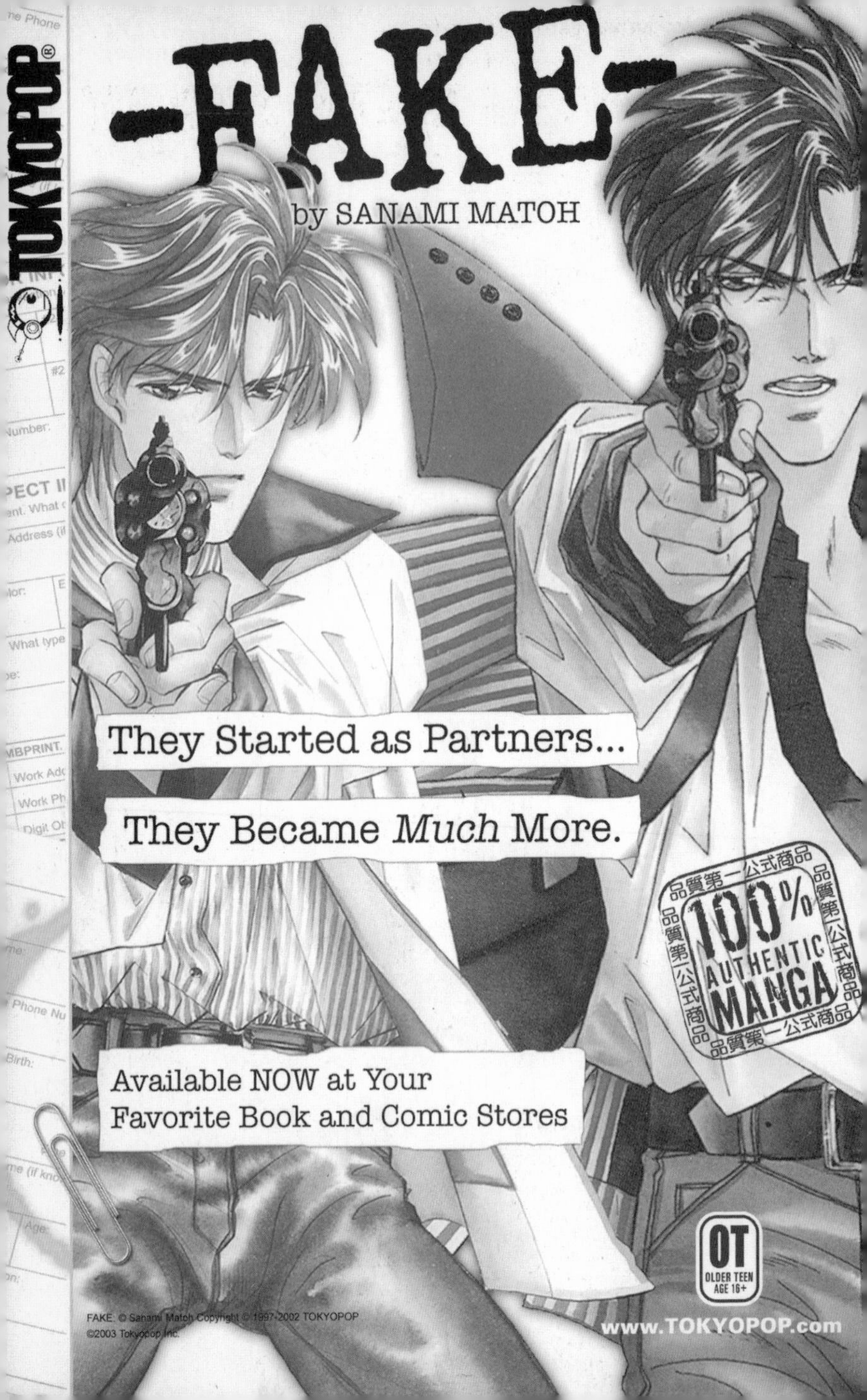
TOKYOPOP
-FAKE-
by SANAMI MATOH
They Started as Partners...
They Became *Much* More.
品質第一公式商品
100% AUTHENTIC MANGA
Available NOW at Your
Favorite Book and Comic Stores
OT
OLDER TEEN
AGE 16+
FAKE: © Sanami Matoh Copyright © 1997-2002 TOKYOPOP
©2003 Tokyopop Inc.
www.TOKYOPOP.com

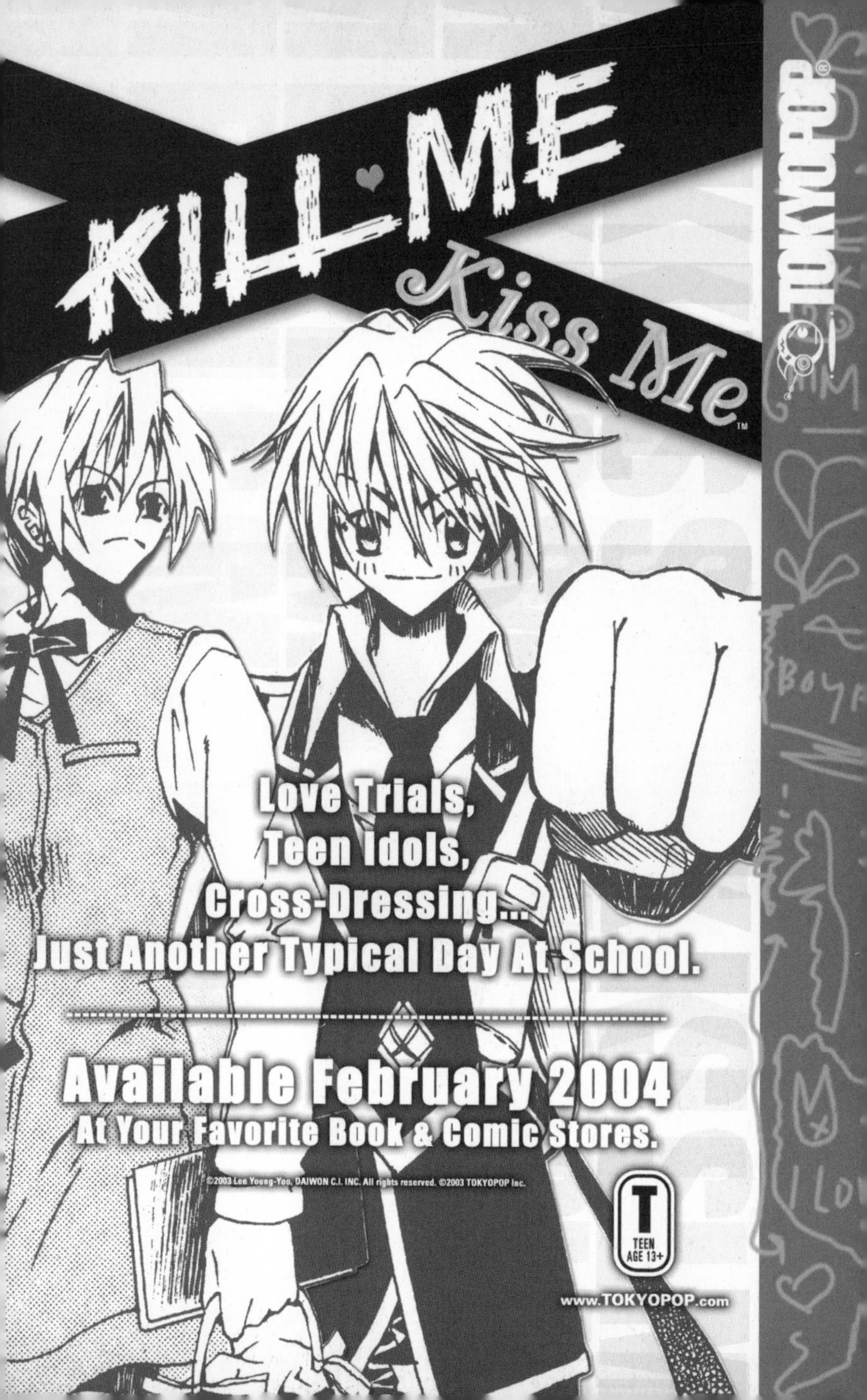
KILL♥ME
Kiss Me™
TOKYOPOP®
Love Trials,
Teen Idols,
Cross-Dressing...
Just Another Typical Day At School.
Available February 2004
At Your Favorite Book & Comic Stores.
©2003 Lee Young-Yoo, DAIWON C.I. INC. All rights reserved. ©2003 TOKYOPOP Inc.
T
TEEN
AGE 13+
www.TOKYOPOP.com

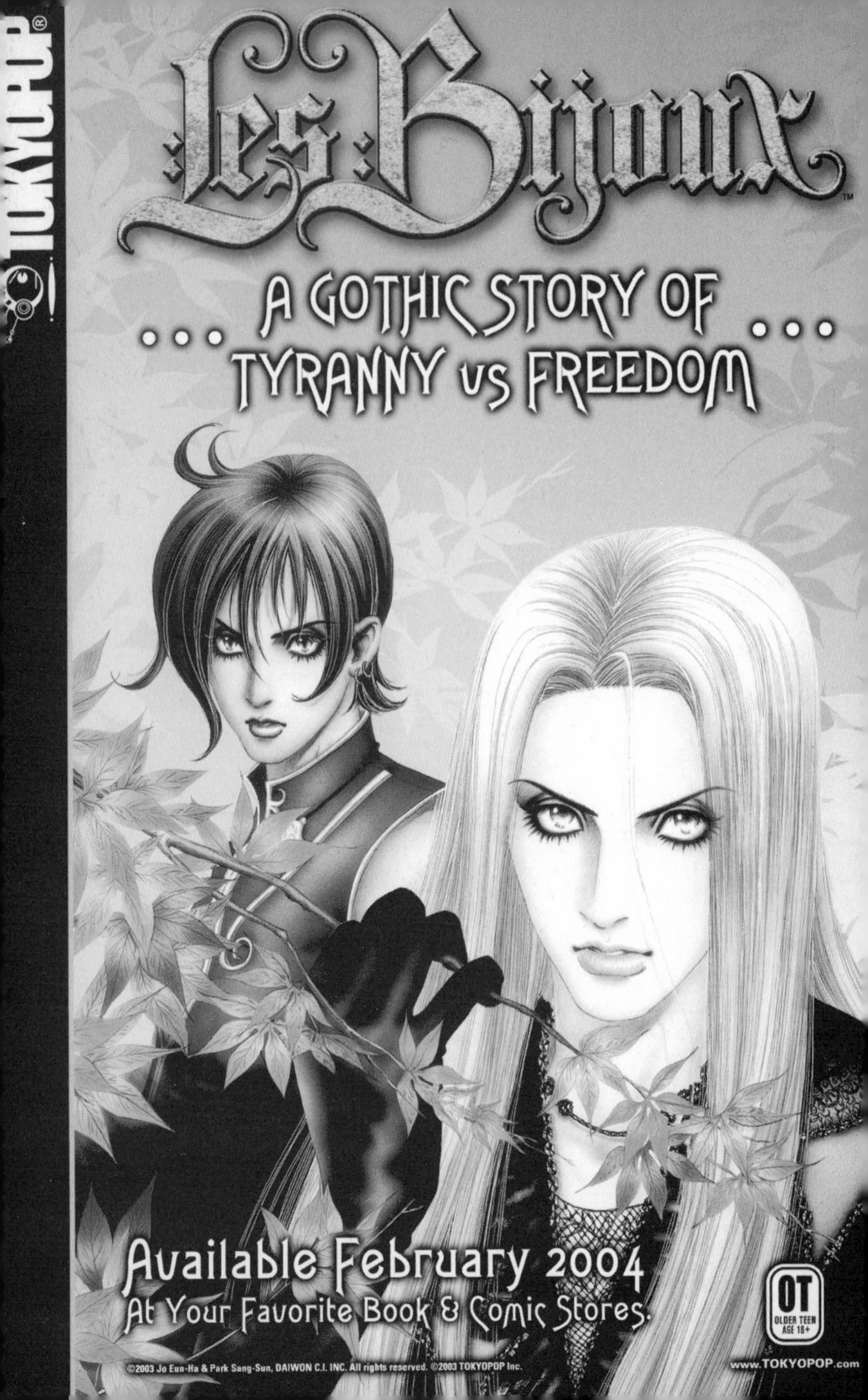
TOKYOPOP
Les Bijoux™
...A GOTHIC STORY OF TYRANNY vs FREEDOM...
Available February 2004
At Your Favorite Book & Comic Stores.
OT OLDER TEEN AGE 16+
©2003 Jo Eun-Ha & Park Sang-Sun, DAIWON C.I. INC. All rights reserved. ©2003 TOKYOPOP Inc.
www.TOKYOPOP.com

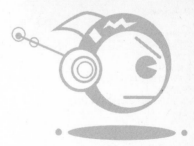

STOP!

This is the back of the book.
You wouldn't want to spoil a great ending!

This book is printed "manga-style," in the authentic Japanese right-to-left format. Since none of the artwork has been flipped or altered, readers get to experience the story just as the creator intended. You've been asking for it, so TOKYOPOP® delivered: authentic, hot-off-the-press, and far more fun!

DIRECTIONS

If this is your first time reading manga-style, here's a quick guide to help you understand how it works.

It's easy… just start in the top right panel and follow the numbers. Have fun, and look for more 100% authentic manga from TOKYOPOP®!

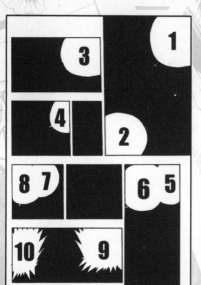